SAVAGE EARTH
ERADICATION

By
JK Franks

This book is a work of fiction. The characters, incidents, and dialogues are products of the author's imagination and are not to be construed as real. Any resemblance to actual events or persons, living or dead, is entirely coincidental.

JK FRANKS
MEDIA

eBook 978-1-7362153-8-8
Paperback 978-1-7362153-9-5
Hardback 979-8-9884788-0-5

Published by JK Franks Media LLC, 2023
Editor: Debra Riggle

Email the author at author@jkfranks.com
Friend him on Facebook at facebook.com/groups/JKFranks
Visit the author's website at www.jkfranks.com

First Edition

For Skye

Within you beats a warrior's heart and an unlimited capacity for awesomeness. Life is an adventure and it is yours to conquer

.

It's not over when you lose,
It's over when you quit...
— **Unknown**

PROLOGUE

Lance Corporal Hadroop slowly lowered the tactical binoculars and adjusted the controls for the correct IR band; he also increased the light amplification to compensate for the fast-approaching darkness. The day had been scorching, but once the white-hot sun dropped below the horizon, a thick blanket of clouds closed in.

His view was nearly perfect. The binoculars augmented and filtered the view to crystal clarity. Hadroop cursed under his breath and swept the optics from side to side. A grassy plain, broken only by patches of the strange violet-colored vines. In the fading light, he thought they looked more like the color of blood, but he kept that to himself.

The grass waved in the soft breeze, with it the scent of death, but nothing else seemed to move.

"Zero contacts, sir. I'm sorry, but I don't see it," the corporal said reluctantly.

"Well shit, Son, I saw it." Captain Jordan Hauk said.

He was in a position no commander ever wanted to be. Backed up with his back to the sea, unable to retreat farther but with an unknown enemy taking out chunks of his platoon seemingly at will.

"Something moved out there, and it wasn't those damn vines."

Jesus, the world had gone to shit in record time. The captain looked south with a smile that quickly turned into a grimace. He'd spent a couple of summers down here soon after basic. There had been a golf course he and his buddies would occasionally play over near Arkansas. Hit the ball and drink a beer. Now, there were fighting fucking monsters. Not literally monsters, at least he didn't think so. Truth was, no one had gotten even the slightest glimpse of these and lived. They had seen ...other things. Battled shit over at Lackland that was still giving him nightmares.

Red-7 was a recon team. They didn't have all the same fancy gadgets as the more prestigious battle groups. Basic heads-up displays, no cutting edge helmets with built-in sensor arrays. Shit, even the suit cams only recorded the last six hours. Command's thinking was if a battle went on for longer than that, you were incompetent or dead. Hauk looked down at the tiny device clipped to his chest armor plate. The green on-light had gone off probably the previous day. He unclipped it and threw it out into the marsh.

Something splashed water close by, leaving only a ripple of waves. He hoped it was just a gator, something he could at least understand.

"Corporal," he waited until the young officer made eye contact. "Thanks for volunteering. Grab Howell and go find out what it is." Hauk lowered his own binoculars and glanced at his tactical computer wrapped around his forearm. "Be back in half an hour. Maintain comms silence unless you see something—do not engage on your own. You got me?"

The dark-skinned younger man seemed ready to say something but thought better of it. Soldiers did not challenge orders from the captain, especially with the week they were all having. For the first couple of weeks since the outbreak of war, they had been on a French-flagged transport ship. The rumored target had been somewhere in central America. Then, they were suddenly recalled to this hell-hole on some humanitarian mission.

Hadroop didn't necessarily consider the Texas Gulf Coast a hell-hole... not before this at least. Now, that was exactly what it was. They had been fighting and losing every day since the landing craft dropped them off thirty miles away near Galveston. Those thirty miles had turned into hundreds, yet they were nearly back where it had all begun.

For the corporal, the fact they were fighting and losing was less terrifying than what they had been fighting; at least here in the wetland marsh, the damn mechanical monsters couldn't get them. Well...at least they hadn't managed to yet. He passed by the sentry and motioned to one of the men watching from the front line to follow. Howell fell out and hurried over. Hadroop gave him the crib notes version of the plan. He watched as the young man's face fell. There was no easy way to tell someone they were about to put their life at risk just to appease their commander's curiosity. Still, he trusted his captain. Hauk had led them through countless battles, and Red-7 was already an elite squad with the victories to help boost all their confidence.

Hadroop led them out into the marsh. Dark, blood-warm water swirled around his legs. The battle suit kept the water away from his skin, but his light duty helmet didn't block out the musty smell of decay. He heard movement off to the right and swung up his tactical rifle. Captain Hauk's calm voice was immediately in his ear.

"Nothing to worry about, Corporal, just some of the local wildlife. Howell is covering your six."

The man's calm reassurance did little to calm the corporal, but Hadroop was a solid soldier. The last week shook him, like all the men. All but the captain. Hauk himself had seemed unfazed by everything that had gone down since the day the missiles fell. That was just the kind of man he was, though, hard, implacable. Some said he was made of stone, but Hadroop knew better. He felt a light tap on his left shoulder and glanced back to see what the other man had seen. There to the right, fifty yards offshore, a body floated. He sighted in to make sure it was human. They had seen things, shadows or glimpses of things that looked human from a distance but clearly weren't.

"We have a body, Captain."

He got no response. Something bumped his leg, and he stepped back quickly, pointing the rifle down into the water. Another body was slowly rising but still totally submerged in the shallow water, It stared lifelessly back up at him. It had been a young woman, just a girl. Her long black hair waved in the light current he'd made walking past. The lower part of her face was gone, as was her right shoulder. One breast showed putrid white flesh. Even in the failing light, he could tell the girl had once been beautiful. Now she was just damage and ruin and food for the beast that inhabited this swampy piece of real estate.

"There's another one," Howell said, his New England accent clipping the words off.

Hadroop hadn't made up his mind on Howell yet. This was a test. The boy seemed competent but always looking to get out of assignments.

The lieutenant moved a leg and felt another fleshy object. He reluctantly changed the optics settings to one that filtered the visible objects by density. Dialing it in, the bodies all emerged in his vision like ghosts from the fog.

"More bodies, lots of bodies, Cap."

Jordan Hauk watched his men through the binoculars. They were solid soldiers, but lack of sleep and constant battles had them all on edge. Bodies in the water weren't a surprise, but he let his men deal with their fears in their own way. Somewhere in this expanse of grass and water was supposed to be a landing craft. The last 'fuck you' from the Alliance naval ship Arago. When the ANS Arago pulled out four days before the rendezvous, the encrypted message still enraged the Army captain. Vague coordinates followed by, 'Your extraction vessel is here, good luck and au revoir.'

"Bastards!" Hauk spit out into the mud.

He swept the glass once more to the left. He'd seen movement. Of that, he was sure. Just a flash of motion that flared a primal response in the more ancient parts of his brain. Would they be prey or predator? If this mission had shown him anything, it was that his unit could be both. Maybe it was just one of the multitude of native animals they'd already encountered. A deer or coyote, maybe a fast cow? *Were cows ever fast?* It could have been an animal; shit...it could have been nearly anything.

Jordan Hauk was not what anyone would call a victim, yet even he was aware of the mind-numbing lack of hope this mission had. Not just for likely failing to meet their objective; he had little chance of even getting the rest of his men out alive. He let out a breath and spat. No, he would not be prey today. If there was something out there, he was going to kill it.

CHAPTER ONE

Lieutenant Deborah Riggs stared at the holodisplay. Earth, home, was quickly becoming a hostile environment. She was out of her league up here on this massive ship. She understood only a few of the onboard systems and none of the capabilities. Deb was a drop trooper. As the saying went, 'It took a special kind of stupid to get fired out of a ship like a bullet, hoping you hit your target and survive long enough to fight.'

She smiled. Those were Kovach's words—now his body was back in the med bay being prepared by the medbots for his final mission. Soon, his body would be dropped into deep space. She shoved that thought aside. It had to wait. There was too much going on. She'd taken command once they boarded. The ship, one of the older monolith space carriers, had been in retrofit orbit. A team of Marine engineers were aboard. Not the incredibly useful combat engineers, but actual engineers, technicians, and mechanics. Not one ounce of fighting ability in the entire crew, but they could make the ship fly. That was better than Bayou or any of her team could manage.

"Packer, take the helm," she ordered. Captain Packer, the pilot of the TriCraft, reluctantly sat at the helm as one of the technicians went over the control interface...again. Packer was good, but the smaller, stealth dropship he normally piloted was a fraction of the size and complexity of the Stone Mountain.

The ship was fully stocked but light on armaments. It had been scheduled to fly to moon base Gateway once the new crew came aboard. There, they would have dropped off the engineers and picked up a new quartermaster who oversaw the loading of munitions and armaments.

She tapped a name on her datapad. Specialist Otero's face came on the screen. She was pretty and frightened. Bayou had tagged her as the de facto leader of the maintenance crew. "Otero, update on engines."

"Yes, ma'am," the woman said. "The maneuvering thrusters will take some time to calibrate, but primary boosters are available now."

Bayou had been on other Space Force craft most of her career, so she understood much of what was involved. Still, her place was down there in the fight, not up here above it all. After listening to G-Force's debrief and viewing his data feed, she had no illusions about the carnage that was being unleashed hundreds of miles below them.

"Thank you, Otero. Can you orient us for trans-lunar course?"

"Yes, we can do that with the main gimbals." She looked offscreen uneasily. "May I ask why the moon?"

Most of the Marine engineers had been stationed out here on various ships. They previously had their own habitat in high orbit and cycled down to the planet frequently. No one enjoyed the ride out to the moon for a rotation shift. Lunar duty was dull and joyless, and the base commander there had a bit of a reputation.

"We need ordinance, we need a combat pilot and senior officers. Something I don't think we will get from Earth anytime soon."

Otero looked concerned but kept those thoughts to herself. "Aye, we will have the safeties unlocked within the hour and nav control transferred to the bridge. Ma'am, can I ask? What's it like down there?"

Bayou bit the inside of her cheek as she considered the question. "Where are you from?"

"Phoenix Metroplex, sir... I mean, ma'am."

Bayou nodded, glancing at the map on the holodisplay before glancing back to the datapad. "Much of the Southwest is in good shape so far, but don't get your hopes up. The devastation is widespread, and we still aren't sure what all we are up against. If you have family there, they're probably safer than anywhere else right now."

Bayou could see the woman's eyes welling with tears, but she nodded and tapped to close out the video.

"You heard that right," Bayou yelled over to her newly minted carrier pilot. "Get us underway to Gateway base, best possible speed. We are sitting ducks up here for whomever is shooting carriers out of orbit."

Going to the moon was really just to buy them time. Deborah knew she was no leader, hell, she was barely a lieutenant. Joe had always been the leader, even when he reported to Captain Rollo Hinge. Master Sergeant Kovach had been up and down the rank ladder, sometimes at his own choosing. He was senior to everyone but rejected all signs of authority except when it really mattered. In her mind, there had been no one better at making command decisions. And no one less enthusiastic about doing it.

She heard excited voices from farther down the main corridor.

"LT, we have an incoming distress signal."

"Shit," Bayou groaned as she looked over at Halo, who was manning the comms station.

Carol Reynolds burst through the hatch to the bridge, her face a mask of... something. Fright, joy? Bayou wasn't quite sure. "Come right away, they need you."

Carol was the civilian who had been with the master sergeant on his ill-fated trip into Tennessee. She and her son had been brought aboard. Riggs liked the woman and her boy, Lux. Both had quickly made themselves useful additions to the small crew.

Bayou put up a finger to silence the woman. "What do you have, Halo?"

"We have an Alliance Recon Team in trouble on the Texas Gulf Coast."

Bayou's heart sank; she knew before she even asked the next question, "Who is it?"

"Red-7, ma'am."

"Fuck!" Her stoic face masked much of the pain that statement caused.

She looked at Carol shaking her head. "Sorry, I am not meant for this."

"Halo, is Captain Hauk still in command of that unit?" She had a long history with the leader of the famed Red-7 assault force. That had been her original unit; she still treasured the battle patch that now adorned her duty bag.

"He is, but the naval ship has abandoned them, they have what he deemed a high value asset, taking heavy casualties and requesting an extract."

"Enemy combatants?" Bayou asked.

Halo knew what she meant, human or well... all the other shit. "Non-human, ma'am. Had them live briefly, now they are on time delay as we have moved out of direct comms range."

Shit, she kept forgetting about the comms delay. With the repeaters and quantum comms units down, they were basically back to line-of-sight communications. Carol was now frantically pulling on her right arm.

"You have to come, Deborah."

"Packer, get me some mission option on using the dropship to go get that squad. Tell Otero to hold on Luna transition for now."

Bayou patted her sidearm and headed for the hatch, then turned to her other Banshee team member.

"Halo, see if you can get details on Hauk's mission and who that high-value asset is." She trusted Red-7 could likely save themselves, and she wasn't risking her ship or her team for some politico bigwig.

She followed Carol down the maze of metal corridors ducking through hatches. The woman was talking at a fever pitch, but for a change, didn't seem frightened by whatever she had found.

They turned the corner to the medical bay, and Bayou suddenly found her feet refusing to move forward. She didn't want to go back in there. She couldn't face seeing her friend, her mentor, lying on that cold table.

Carol stopped walking, feeling the sudden resistance from Riggs. She smiled and patted her hand. "It's good, Bayou. Trust me, you will want to see."

CHAPTER TWO

"Goddamn, Cap, the damn things are everywhere."

Hauk got a good look at the closest one as it grabbed the side of the overturned launch.

"Goddamn ugly bastards, ain't they?"

"Senior, you ain't wrong," Captain Hauk yelled over his shoulder to Senior Chief Grayson.

"Head back for shore," Hauk said reluctantly. The water route wasn't going to work. He had known they could swim but quickly realized they were even more capable, more lethal in the water than on dry land.

Several of the semi-inflatable launches got the surf line ahead of them, beaching hard on the packed sand. Hauk's boat along with at least one other had been flipped, and now they were swimming for shore. With all the gear, it was more like creative drowning. The weight would pull them down to the bottom where they would run for several yards before kicking off to the surface top and catch a quick breath before doing it again.

Then, just as he neared shore, one of the reptilian beasts was in front of him. The damn thing's proportions were just all wrong. Its arms were too long; its bony fingers looked almost delicate with fine webbing between each. The main appendage, though, was the curved razor-sharp claw. On one hand, the claw met with a smaller version on an opposing digit, allowing it to shear off anything it could grasp. Hauk had already seen the result of that in some of his unit's casualties.

The thing's head was about twice the size of a human. Its body was covered in a layer of small, iridescent scales broken up by tufts of fine, pale hair. The color reflected seemed usually to be an emerald green, maybe a teal, but he'd seen some of them that blended in perfectly with their surroundings. Perfectly camouflaged, like a chameleon or octopus.

The mouth seemed almost like an afterthought. It was rudimentary with thick, rubbery lips, and when it opened, you could see rows of quavering tentacles and concentric circles of needle-like fangs that looked like they belonged to an eel or maybe something ancient and reptilian. Jordan shuddered at the sight.

This one seemed to have been stunned, Hauk saw a bloody gash along the side of its head. One of his men had gotten a lucky shot, the thing was down but not out. Jordan pushed past it and struggled up onto the beach. The Senior Chief and several others helped him back to his feet.

The wounded creature flopped out of the next wave almost at their feet. As he stared at one of the monsters that had been trying to kill his team, the first thing Hauk thought was that he regretted that he had ever taken this assignment. Removing a glove, he ran a hand over the creature's scaly surface. He should go get the scientist; he needed an opinion from someone smarter than himself. Unfortunately, she was a computer genius, not a biologist.

Realistically, all he needed to know about the thing was how to kill it. Feeling the neck for any signs of life, he realized they already knew how. They'd already brought down dozens of the things, but the bastards were hard to kill... too damn hard. This was the first one they'd been able to examine up close. He slid his tactical knife out of its sheath.

Jordan Hauk brought the knife down sharply, but the blade skittered off the thing's scaly hide. Without warning, another of the things leapt from the water over the boat and was on top of the Army captain in seconds, pinning the knife hand to the ground.

"What in the fuck?"

The thing's jaws opened, and that mouth full of needle-sharp teeth and tentacles lunged toward his neck. Hauk released the knife and just got his arm under the thing's head, keeping the beast's deadly mouth away from his by just inches. The thing was so close that Hauk could smell its foul breath. An odor of death, blood, and rot. This was not anything natural. It was clearly not of this world, unless he'd slipped from that beach into a hidden doorway to hell.

It was unbelievably strong. Hauk was a finely tuned, elite soldier, yet he felt like a toddler trying to fight off a raging bull. He assumed some of his men would be fighting it as well. Surely, someone had put a few rounds into it by now, but Jordan Hauk's entire world had shrunk down to these few feet of Texas coastline and the monster at the end of his arm.

The creature flung him down like a rag doll, then jumped on him again in an attempt to crush the man. Hauk's light body armor prevented that, but the enormous weight of the beast hurt like hell just the same. Then, Jordan felt the thing pulling him into the water. In horror, he realized that, like a gator, it was going to hold its prey beneath the waves and drown him. That wasn't something the lightweight, Recon battle suit could protect him from.

The sounds of battle worked their way back into Hauk's consciousness. He was confident in Red-7's abilities, but they had lost so many men and picked up strays along the way, men he wasn't sure of yet. Now, like him, they were all fighting their own battles. He wanted to help, needed to help, but he had no capacity to think of anything but his own enemy. He needed to get to his weapons. The knife was gone... somewhere, and his rifle was pinned between his back and the ground. He felt the unnatural ridge crushing up against his spine.

He drove upward with a vicious knee strike, putting every ounce of his weight behind the blow, then drove a powerful fist right into the middle of the thing's gruesome face. The armor-assisted blows would have turned a normal man's insides to jelly, but it didn't even faze this fucking monster. It puffed out another foul breath and growled at Hauk. It came in as if to bite the captain, then jumped back slicing sideways with that damn deadly claw. Hauk felt the bladed appendage cutting through flesh and armor. The pain was a hot jolt to his system, one that probably saved his life. Looking down, he saw the opening to grab the gun still locked into his hip lock holster.

Jordan's bare hands were bloody, and the gun felt awkward in his grip. Something was wrong. But he didn't have time to think about it, just fire. The first two shots bounced off the creature's hide just like his knife had. Even from point-blank, the thing was fucking bullet proof. Jordan sagged to the ground in exhaustion or desperation, he wasn't sure which. The monster struck out with its other arm and connected against the man's chest sending him sprawling across the beach.

It hissed as it approached, and standing over the man, it drew back its oversized claw for the killing strike. Hauk fired in desperation at every part of the thing's body. His Silka pistol was on full auto. The ammo count displaying inside his face shield was dropping fast. None of the shots did anything. Nothing, until one stray round passed through the meaty part of its upper thigh. The creature's claw buried itself in the sand by Jordan's neck as the ugly thing dropped to all fours. It howled in pain and arched backward. Jordan put more rounds into the thing's thigh, then reached up and shoved the pistol into the gaping maw of a mouth and ran his magazine dry.

Holding the creature's massive head by a clump of hair, he kept on firing until the monster's head exploded in a shower of blood and gore. The rotten stench immediately multiplied tenfold. Hauk thought he was going to be sick, but snapping out of his rage, he let the thing slide off his arm and into the water. He turned to the closest sounds of battle and moved to help the next man.

Hauk's team had the numbers and slowly fought the damn things back. They didn't have all the fun toys like the RDTs or Seal Teams 12, but Red-7 got shit done. Most of the squad carried traditional 5.56 Silka 88 tactical assault rifles. Hell of a stopping power, and you could drop the damn thing in the mud for a week and still come up putting rounds on target from 150 yards. Try that with one of those fancy Glissons. Still, Jordan Hauk desperately wanted more guns, bigger guns, and he wanted that fucking French bastard who'd left them stranded here. Goddamn Alliance Navy...what a joke.

CHAPTER THREE

I watched the lines of incomprehensible code scrolling up. My brain was remarkably clear, yet the last memory I had was dying. I knew for certain I had died, and now I was what? Something else. My insides ached; my bones ached. The constant agony of...of, hell, I don't know. Growing pains maybe. But so much deeper and somehow worse. You don't hurt when you die...right? Shit, who could I ask? *No one, moron, you are the only one you know who has died and come back*. I was really fucked. My internal monologue was now mirroring the voice of my pops.

Upgrade complete, compiling new boot sequence.

I read the text window before closing. When I was wounded in battle over a year ago, I had allowed them to augment my body, and part of that had been installing a sophisticated battle AI chip in my head. Ada, the AI personality, had been my constant inner voice since that day, and in all this time, I had never seen her display code. In fact, I rarely even thought of her as a computer. I knew the chip and integrated systems ran mostly off my body's electrical energy, so when I died, she died. So, if that was true...what was going on with her now?

"Kovach!"

I heard the voice; it seemed to come from a great distance. I tried to open my eyes. I tried again... nothing. I then attempted to do a mental inventory, arms, legs, fingers. Yeah, that wasn't working either. So, maybe I am a computer now. Ada figured out how to back me up to a storage drive somewhere. Joe Kovach, the Luddite who preferred no tech, now was *all* tech. I almost laughed. That's when I realized the constant ache of the last few minutes was gone. I felt no pain, no sensation at all, just a feeling of fuzzy blankness. And yes, that is a terribly unhelpful description, but fuck it, I'm dead. Maybe... likely... but fuck... who knows?

Honestly, I have lived with pain most of my adult life. Some minor, like my old sports injury where I tweaked my left knee sliding into second base. Some much more persistent, like the part of my spine that metal alloy replaced after an enemy pulse rifle blew it out. Pain is one way you know you're human. I was clearly no longer human. Strangely, I was not alarmed by this, nor even surprised. The blank feeling also filled me with calm. I was okay being a computer.

Except...

"Oh, my God!"

That was another voice, one that evoked some very happy memories.

"Jesus!"

I couldn't tell if it was expressions of shock or admiration. Maybe something in the middle. Maybe I was simply stoned; was that better than being dead?

"Joseph, can you hear me?"

I knew that voice. "Yes, Ada. Are you dead, too?" I asked internally.

"We are not dead, Joe... not anymore."

"Someone, cover that up."

I also knew that voice; it was... it was, Bayou. *What is she covering up? Can I see? Nope, eyes still aren't working*. But I apparently was not dead. Unless Ada was fucking with me.

"I am not fucking with you, Joe."

So, she can read my thoughts now. She used to have some of that ability, I could subvocalize commands, but now she can do more, apparently.

"So, you were the one who was upgraded," I said.

Ada didn't respond immediately, which concerned me.

"I believe we both were," my AI eventually answered. "How do you feel?"

"I feel... I feel nothing. No sensation, well, except...."

Let's just skip over what I was feeling. It doesn't fit into the hero narrative I am desperately trying to build here. It would simply illustrate that 1. I am a guy, and 2. All guys are pigs with only one thing on their mind. Maybe heaven had sexy angels or something... I couldn't explain it. My body was happy to be alive and decided to have inappropriate reactions.

"Yeah, let's not discuss that one," Ada responded quickly. "Joe, I have several new subroutines. Don't ask me why, but they are here in my options menu. I can now adjust your sensitivity to your surroundings, like turning up the gain on a microphone."

"Okay," I said, the increasing levels of uncertainty clear in my voice. Well, the voice in my head at least.

"Touch first."

I felt a breeze, then cold, first across what might have been my chest, then my arms. I could feel the individual hairs moving in the micro-breeze. Suddenly, my brain began computing vectors and angles, and I had the rough dimensions of the room as well as the airflow from the overhead ducts. I was on a ship.

"Was that you?"

Ada answered slowly, "I believe it was 'us.' We calculated the room's dimensions from a slight air current on your arm hair. That was at the lowest sensitivity setting. Shall I try higher?"

"Absolutely!" I said. Then, I felt pressure on my back. Gravity, artificial, .72 Earth normal. A spaceship in high Earth orbit. In additional settings, I could sense the heat signatures of three bodies in the room. I learned I could speed up my heart rate or slow it to a stop apparently with no ill effects. My normal body temp now seemed to be about 102, but I could lower it at will to below eighty.

A hand rested on my leg and gave a light caress. I knew whose hand it was even though I still could not see or speak. My hearing and vision had been augmented in the initial treatments with Doctor Reichert, and now I suspected they were both significantly improved over even that. As Ada brought more of my systems back online, my eyes snapped open apparently surprising the two women and one man in the room. They were saying something, but even though I heard the words, my brain was struggling to process all the incoming data. The guy I knew, his name was Bishop, call sign Priest; he was on my squad. His face held a wry grin, and his eyes flicked to my waist. That was where both women kept looming as well.

"Ada, do I have an erection?'

"Umm... yes, Joseph. Its unnaturally large, and I don't seem to be able to do anything to cancel it. So, yes...we are still ignoring it."

Okay, the comfortable blankness was evaporating fast. The two women were my second-in-command, Lieutenant Riggs, call sign Bayou, and Carol Reynolds. I come back to life, and the first thing they see is my boner. I made Ada give me enough muscle control to look down. The crisp white sheet was tent-poling. I'm not sure, but that seemed to have been enhanced as well. Before the thought fully formed, a series of equations and measurements filled out the space informing me that indeed it had and by exactly how much. Too much information.

What in the ever-loving fuck was going on? *Wake me up, Ada, enough of this shit.*

The remnants of foggy bliss were yanked away as an immediate onrush of all sensation rushed in to fill the void. I could hear myself screaming, then I was sitting up on a surgical bed, the robotic arms above my bed jerking back and forth unsure as to what to do.

"None of you goddamn say, 'Welcome to the Matrix.'"

"That's a wicked looking piece of manhood you got there, Kovach. Did you bring that back from the other side?"

"Fuck you, Priest."

"Yep, it's still him," the man said coming up and giving me an awkward hug. "Welcome back."

The two women fell on him, Carol's tears mixed with Bayou's relieved laughter.

"How is this possible?" Bayou asked, finally catching her breath.

"He's immortal," Priest offered. "Probably made a deal with Satan or some shit."

"But your organ rejection, that was real. You went into that damn place but never found the meds to stop it."

Ada had been busy trying to unravel the same mystery and now thought she had the answer.

I relayed it to the others.

"The meds were apparently not anti-rejection drugs."

They all looked confused, I totally got that.

"More likely they were suppressors. Ada feels like they were keeping my body below a threshold, one they could control. Beyond that, they weren't sure they could handle me, or maybe the good doctor didn't want someone to know my full capabilities."

"What does that mean, are you superhuman or something?" Bayou asked.

"No idea, but I'm different, and I'm healed."

Riggs drew blood into the scanner and reviewed the display. "Your blood chemistry has completely changed. It is full of respirosites and ummm... other nanoparticles, most of which the system can't even identify. Your blood O2 levels are off the chart, I'm not even sure you need your heart and lungs to function as the cells themselves seem capable of generating their own oxygen. Also, your body core temperature is several degrees higher than normal."

I had already known that. "Is that dangerous?"

Riggs looked over the data before shaking her head. "I don't think so. Probably a change in metabolism. I believe this is just your new normal."

"Kovach the Invincible!"

"Priest, shut the fuck up and help me off this table."

I swung my legs over the side and saw Sumo grinning back up at me from beneath the bed.

"He hasn't moved," Carol said.

"He also doesn't seem surprised," Priest said, giving me support as I tried to stand.

"Hey, big guy, miss me?"

The beautiful dog licked my hand and gave a gentle chuff, then lay back and rested his head on his paws.

"Why can't you guys be like that? I may be resurrected, but already old news to him."

"Prowler, please get some clothes on. You have to cover that thing up. We have work to do if you're mission capable," Riggs said.

"I'm good," I answered, taking the dark blue deck suit Carol was holding out. Then, seeing my um, issues, I opted for looser fitting pants and a pullover.

The other two left the med bay with instructions for me to meet them on the bridge. Carol helped me get dressed, which was welcome but unnecessary. She very much wanted to help me with my problem, but that had to wait. "How's your boy?"

"He's wonderful. Thank you again!" she said. The grin was genuine.

I nodded, knowing I had played little in his rescue.

"Your friend, Voss, shot me," I said.

"Damiana did that?" Carol seemed genuinely surprised.

I nodded, and together we headed down the hall. I didn't need the help, in fact, I felt fantastic, but I accepted it just the same. Carol wanted to be close, maybe she needed me to be here. I don't know, but it felt good.

"I hate to ask this, but how long was I…"

"Gone?"

I nodded.

"Three days."

"Jesus Christ," I said without thinking.

"Close, but no," she said squeezing my still raging cock. "We are going to have to handle that before it gets hung on something," she whispered in a devilish tone.

"It's already…"

"Oh, my God, will you two stow it."

"Sorry, Ada."

"That was your Combat AI?" Carol asked.

"Yeah, you heard her?" Normally Ada had to have a comms connection to speak with others.

"I did, but I'm not sure how. Her voice just seemed to be in my head, my ear."

"Ada got some upgrades, too," I said, entering the bridge wing.

"Holy shit, this is a monolith class carrier," I said easing up to Bayou. "Who's in command?"

Bayou looked at an imaginary watch on her wrist and said, "As of now—you."

CHAPTER FOUR

"You boosted a damn nice spaceship, Riggs."

The former ROK soldier, G-force, and Halo turned at the sound of my voice. The look of shock was clear on both.

"Jesus H. Christ! I thought you were dead, mate," Halo said, eyeing me like I just materialized out of the vacuum of space.

"Yeah, I was. I got better," I said in my best British accent.

Both men fist bumped me, then Halo hugged me tightly. "Really effing great to see you back, brother."

"Same. So, bring me up to speed."

It didn't take long; fifteen minutes later, I was scratching a patchy beard and probably wondering the same things Bayou had previously. Onboard the massive ship there were eight of us, including Carol and her son. The maintenance team included twenty-two engineers and several maintenance bots, two dogs, and apparently a cat who had stowed away from the last crew. Thirty people on a ship that was meant for thousands.

"The ship's internal systems have been resisting our authorization," the pilot said. "We don't have the right command codes to break orbit and lock in new courses."

Internally, I asked Ada to see what she could do. Like the ship's AI, they would both likely have similar levels of encryption, possibly both based on the same military crypto-architecture.

"Other than that, we have control?"

"Yes, sir!" Packer said. "The engineers have helped, but almost everything you need to know about ship systems are on the flats."

Flats were essentially video postcards that you could place on any surface, and they would play tutorials on how to use what was beneath it. They were flat video, not holographic, but made a simple task very easy to familiarize yourself with. I'd gotten used to them over the many ships I'd been aboard. There were just too many things to learn for people to teach you, from how to take a shower in low gravity to what to avoid when firing live rounds in the onboard range room. Ship systems got updated frequently, so new flats showed up all over on a near daily basis.

"Roger that!" I responded.

"So, let's focus on Hauk's men first. Seems like that is the priority. I know we can't take every group in distress aboard, but I wouldn't mind having more trained shooters."

"Halo, did you get a name on the asset?" Bayou asked.

"Negative contact with Red-7 so far."

"Packer, ready the dropship for extract," I ordered.

"Sorry, sir, the carrier has the TriCraft locked in its docking cradle. Maintenance logs say it's time for her repulsers to be cycled out."

"Fuck!" The damn repulsers were a mystery all on their own. They provided all the lift and propulsion for the odd little spaceship. Even the mechanics who did the replacements for them didn't seem to understand how they worked. Every twenty-four thousand flight hours, each of the glowing cylinders had to be removed, placed inside a special containment case and shipped to a ground side base for maintenance and recycling. The entire process was a closely guarded secret, including an elite group of heavily armed sentries that stood guard over each step of the swap.

The TriCraft and its unique drive system was one of the Alliance's biggest secrets, and they took no chance of it falling into enemy hands. "So, the dropship is essentially dead weight to us now, is that what I am hearing, Captain Packer? 'Cause I don't think we're going to be getting refreshed units anytime soon."

Packer had a smirk on his face that intrigued me.

"Go on, Packer, speak your mind."

He looked down, brushing some invisible thing from his shirt, seemingly uncertain if he should even say what he was thinking. Finally, he apparently won his mental wrestling match and confirmed what I'd been thinking for years.

"It's a hoax." He paused for effect. "Swapping the drives out, I mean. We don't need to. As far as we can tell, the repulser engines never degrade."

The other members of Banshee looked at him like he had just blasphemed the Lord's name. The entire process was so highly classified that few people even knew enough to question its legitimacy. My dad, the legendary colonel, was one that had. He'd claimed that no one even knew how the damn things worked. No one alive at least.

"Any proof to back that up?" I asked.

"Well, yes. First off, the performance never drops, and I have run ships well over the mysterious twenty-four-K cycle's mark several times. But also... well, sir, we routinely marked our units."

"You marked them?" Bayou asked.

Packer nodded. "We did, yes... with micro etching in ways that you would have to know what you were looking for to even spot."

"And they showed back up on other TriCraft," I offered.

"Yep," the pilot answered. "Sometimes the same day, occasionally on the same ship. The techs would just move them around. They come out really easily if you have the right tool."

"Good enough for me. Ada, try to cancel out that maintenance hold. We need that ship. In the meantime, what else can we do for that squad?"

"Ballistic entry, we can give them more firepower."

I grimaced. Priest was right, but that just put more men at risk. I knew Hauk by reputation mainly. Liked him, but was it worth taking that chance? "Packer, can you move us in close enough for launch?"

"Yes, sir, sort of. We have little orbital maneuvering, but we will pass over the target area on several upcoming passes. And we have launch capabilities. It won't be an LEO drop, though."

They all knew what that meant. LEO, or low Earth orbit, drops in the flying coffins were bad, but only experienced a few minutes of the intense reentry effect, the bone jarring and highly dangerous atmospheric burn. High altitude drops increased that time and risk exponentially. The Space Force had specially designed drop pods for HAO jumps, very expensive pods that even I had never been allowed to look at. Unlike the standard atmos pods, these were X-class and supplied directly by Hammer Industries. "We have X-class pods?"

Packer nodded. "The new ones with the retrieval system to bring them back aboard after use."

"Okay, Banshee, prep for launch on next pass. Pilot, get us in position."

Bayou placed her hand on my arm. "You can't go, Master Sergeant. We must have you up here."

I chewed on the inside of my cheek while I mulled over which of my responses to hurl at the lieutenant.

"Joe, we're playing for survival here. Not just our survival, but as a species. This won't be the only time we're needed. You can plan ahead, try and figure out what comes next. You've been through a lot. We can go get those guys. We need you to be in command."

I didn't like it, but I saw her logic. Then Ada decided for me.

"The system still has you listed as dead, Kovach, so the only launch you would be authorized for is a funeral pod."

"Fuck... again. Get me back on the payroll, Ada. Do whatever to unfuck my life, okay?"

Carol asked me to come meet her son in the meantime. She glanced down again as she came over. "Maybe we should stop somewhere along the way first just to get you tidied up a bit."

I couldn't hide my grin. "Lead the way."

CHAPTER FIVE

The gunfire was drawing closer, but that wasn't what she was focusing on. She had built her entire career by getting information no one else could. Calling her a hacker was like calling Da Vinci a doodler. All modern systems used Qubit matrix storage, a tremendous advantage over the clunky binary code of the past. Xero could predict, manipulate, and know where data was leading before anyone else.

Now, she had intercepted a data feed that simply could not be true. She looked out at the sunlight reflecting off the water. Ripples shimmered as something large moved beneath the surface. If this was true, then a single entity may have orchestrated the entire plan for Eradication Day. She reran the analysis again; it seemed inconceivable that one person brought down the world's major powers and unleased a near biblical horde of horrors on the survivors. Who on Earth hated humanity to that degree?

That was what she was chasing down now; she could piece together much of the how. Shell companies, off the books deals, some significant government black budgets. They all pointed in one direction, but so far, no identity to attach to all these dirty deals. It was a puzzle, and she was good at solving puzzles. Still, a master had put together this one.

The P-cell in her portable server was running low. The internal quantum processors sucked up energy like a drug addict snorting coke.

She looked for a power tap she could recharge on, then remembered where she was. The gunfire was closer, followed by occasional screams of pain. Maybe there was an outlet on the far side of camp, surely the command tent needed power.

Not that Xero was unconcerned with the carnage that was playing out around her. Well... not only that. Years ago, they would have said she was on the spectrum. Now it was back to just being antisocial. Everything about her was purposeful and designed to keep people at bay. Her fierce looks, the tattoos and piercings, the clothes, voice, the entire package told everyone to fuck off. Most weren't even sure she was a she. She liked androgyny, she could be anybody, or more often, nobody. Thankfully, superficial things like gender had become much less divisive since the turn of the century.

Despite her default state of disdain from her fellow humans, not even she would have wished this on them. She ran slender fingers through her short black hair. It was an unconscious gesture that helped her focus that razor sharp mind on solving this puzzle. The sudden hand on her shoulder was intrusive and insulting, and seconds later, the young private found himself disarmed on his back looking up into her steel-grey eyes.

"The... the captain, he send for you. Me to bring you."

She placed his broken English and pronounced accent to Basque country of Spain, close to the border with France, but not so close. The mental games continued even when her mind was at rest. Everything was a puzzle. She helped the soldier back to his feet and wordlessly followed.

~

"You find anything else?"

The captain wasted no time; he had a sharp mind that Xero found surprising and appealing. She would like to fuck him... but not now, now she had other priorities.

"I'm not cleared to reveal anything to you, Captain Hauk."

He knew that, and truthfully, he didn't give a shit what this wisp of a woman knew. Unless it was actionable intel that might help his unit unfuck themselves from this situation.

"Xero, Command gave me the mission to pick you up. I don't know why, but so far, that order has cost me nearly two dozen lives. That number will go higher before the day is over." He retreated to a bunk and opened up a hard case withdrawing a flask and two cups. He poured two fingers into each and handed one to the hacker.

Xero took it thankfully with a small bow. Good scotch from a Japanese distillery was what she smelled. She could detect the grains used and even a whiff of the salty seaweed that had been added to the smoldering fires used to dry the grain before distilling. She sipped it, savoring the flavor.

"Hakushu, Oban style from Nagano," she stated. "Thank you."

The girl, or guy, knew its stuff, Hauk thought. Could she help him, though? He was burning through the troops at an alarming rate, no exfil and no reinforcements. He needed options.

"Xero," he began. He hated using the hacker name, but that seemed to be the only identity anyone had on her. "We're deep in the shit. I'm going to level with you, I don't know if we can get out of this goddamn marsh alive."

"I understand, Captain. You are one of the best, we will be fine, but my analysis will survive whether I do or..." All of her work was saved into the cloud and would be distributed to key parties if she were unresponsive for any period for more than forty-eight hours.

"So, you know the TWC bastard who attacked us?"

At least he didn't think it was the Russians or the Chinese like media had first reported, Xero thought. "It was not anyone from the Third World Coalition, Captain. Not directly at least. I don't have a name, I have a profile, a very specific pattern."

"How does that help us?" Hauk asked, his frustration increasing with every passing minute.

Xero threw back the rest of the whiskey and lowered the cup delicately to her lap. "All we are is patterns, patterns of information. No two people have the same pattern. When you wake up, what you eat for breakfast, what newsfeed you watch, when you start work, and who you connect with during the day. It is as individual as a genetic sequence. I have this person's pattern locked in, now all we have to do is find the person who matches it."

Jordan Hauk was not an intelligence officer; he left the heavy mental lifting to others. He was a warrior, a fixer, but even he saw the obvious problem with Xero's analysis. "Ma'am, sir. Shit, do you have a preferred way of being addressed?"

"I am third sex, you may refer to me in whichever way you wish. My gender identity is not what defines me."

He nodded. Three-S, or third sex, had been a growing segment for the last half century. "Ok, ma'am. The problem is we have no idea who is even still alive. Last intel I got was upwards of 100 million dead in the U.S. alone. Many other countries are far worse, plus comms are down, most Internet bands are compromised. Where will you be looking?"

"The datasets are still out there; I can design recursive search algorithms to parse old data for pattern matches." She considered her datapad. "I could use a fresh P-cell or power supply, though."

He downed the last of his scotch and nodded, that made sense. It was embarrassing how much the military relied on computer analysis these days, but the data was just as important as the ammunition, even more so sometimes.

They heard excited voices from outside the tent. Their eyes met briefly before the captain pushed the flap aside and walked out. Three soldiers stood over the limp body of a creature that had to be over eight feet tall.

"This is another one of those things coming at us from the north," a sergeant said, toeing a boot into the scaly flesh at the base of the thing's neck. "You were right, thigh shots work great, Cap."

This 0one seemed slightly different but Hauk still thought they were the most disgusting thing he'd ever seen, but Xero bent down and examined it with an almost loving tenderness. She fanned out the tiny winglike fins that flowed from the head toward the broad shoulders. They snapped back and retracted into gill slits. She took a penlight from a pocket and examined the eyes, the mouth, and what may have been a nose, or ears. The analogy to humanoid was inaccurate beyond that.

Gunfire resumed behind them, and Hauk dismissed the men. He made Xero stand back while he removed his sidearm and double-tapped the greenish grey skull. He then donned his pulse rifle and tactical helmet from nearby. "What else should I know, Xero?" He pointed down at the thing. Xero pursed her lips in a way he found unusually erotic, especially for a Three-S.

"Not my area of knowledge, Captain Hauk, but best guess, they are hunters, they are designed to kill. I am guessing they have a genetic level of control at best. Natural instinct, not some elaborate plan. Captain, I think these were experiments that got loose, not some intentional mutant combatant."

He nodded, "Thanks. Use the Command tent, the power should be more stable. But leave me some whiskey."

Jordan Hauk had many reasons to seek the truth, but the one that burned the brightest was worry about his younger brother, Logan. Their parents had died suddenly his first year in the Army. They were overseas when a high-speed train was derailed by a terrorist attack. It had shaped his resolve and forced him and his brother even closer as Jordan took over the parental role. That hadn't lasted long, as Logan proved to be just as capable as his brother but in remarkably different ways. "Where are you, kid?" Jordan whispered into a night as dark as sackcloth.

CHAPTER SIX

"Wake me up before you go-go."

I slapped at my ear knowing that was a stupid thing to do. Carol was still asleep, and my internal clock said I'd been out only a couple of hours. I slipped on some workout pants and moved into the corridor.

"Pops, that you?" The ancient song was still blasting, and I couldn't think of who had sung it but knew it was one of his faves. The volume reduced incrementally, and my old man's voice came through, although a bit tinny.

"Hey, shithead, how did you enjoy the Nightmare Factory?"

I really hated telling him he was right and that I shouldn't have gone.

"It was fine," I lied.

"Liar. Nearly fucking killed you, didn't it?"

"No." Technically, that was correct, it had in fact killed me. My natural body functions had ceased. *So now what was I?* I still wasn't sure if my dad, the retired colonel, had secret access into my internal AI or just an excellent sense of intuition. Either way, he'd always known when I was lying, and apparently, his ability to expect enemy actions had made him a legend and an absolute horrible father. Well... horrible if you measured success by what you could slip past your parents.

"Okay, well now, if you are over your little vacation, you need to get back to work," he stated, while still humming away with the tune in the background.

"Vacation?" I asked dumbfounded. "How are things there?"

"I don't know, you know, I don't get out much."

The man was infuriating. In fact, he had turned being an asshole into an absolute art form. "You are in Florida, they attacked it, EMP blackout, and biological monstrosities are turning the coast into wastelands."

"Sounds like a Tuesday," my old man said.

I snort-laughed despite the absurdity.

"Have you seen Orlando when the snowbirds come down each year? Can't be worse than that."

"Okay, Dad, so what's on your mind?" Truthfully, he did call a lot just to check on me. By 'check on me,' I mean he delivered heaping loads of verbal abuse. But as strange as that seemed, it was his way of letting me know he loved me. Our banter was almost ritualistic now with each one trying to outdo the other... he always won.

"So, where you at, when you going to drop by?"

Dad was baiting me; I knew by now he knew exactly where I was. "Next time I get leave, Pops." It was a familiar lie; we both knew it.

"You don't need to go to Gateway, you need to stay in orbit."

The jarring shift in the conversation threw me mentally. "Why's that?"

"If you go to Luna, you will lose command of the starship. One of those old, idiotic, desk jockeys they have at Gateway base will assume command and start giving orders like they know what the hell is going on. You and Banshee need to stay fiercely independent."

The Luna bases were indeed thought of as a retirement home for old Space Force officers, that was true. I was less sure why we needed to be calling our own shots. "But we..."

He cut me off. "Hush, boy, grown-ups are speaking."

"Assholes are squeaking," I said under my breath.

"This war," he continued unabated, "will not be decided up there. The battle for our species will be right down here on terra-firma, and you fucking know it."

"Colonel, we have the high ground."

"At the moment, Master Sergeant." Okay, now we were moving into the tactical part of the conversation.

"You need trigger-pullers. Good ones, not the Alliance irregulars."

It was slightly offensive, but I knew he was talking about the regular Army of the Alliance nations. We'd been at peace too long, and the regular Army was practically useless against normal combatants much less the mutated monsters and robot hordes loose down there now.

"You were never much of a spacer, Pops. Not every war is decided by ground-pounders like you. If your only tool is a hammer, then every problem looks like a nail."

I heard the disgust in his reply.

"You read that off a sign in your therapist office? Look, kid, the fact is, life sucks. Sometimes you're the hammer, sometimes you're the nail. I am telling you it's time to be the goddamn hammer. You read me?"

I nodded despite myself. "I read you, sir."

"Good, look, I gotta go, Ms. Henderson next door wants to play pickleball, if you know what I mean."

Pickleball, I knew what he meant, and the mental image made me cringe. "One thing, Dad."

"Yeah, hurry up, kid, my 'only tool' is starting to look like that damn hammer you mentioned."

Carol was slipping out of the bunkroom. She gave me a quick silent peck on the lips before heading in the washroom's direction. "Something happened to me."

"Aghh... got it," he said. "It's called puberty, Son, and we knew it would happen one day. It's perfectly natural. You will start getting hair in pla..."

"Dad!"

"Yes?"

"Be serious. Doctor Reichert lied to me, didn't he? He did more enhancements than he was supposed to."

"Everybody lies, Son. The late doctor had a lot of secrets. Now you do, too. I would try to keep them to yourself for now. You don't need a bigger target on your back."

How did he know the doctor was dead? I wondered. "I get it, so you don't know why it happened."

"It happened because someone wanted it to happen, just like always." The music was getting louder, and I knew he was signaling the conversation was over. I felt the mental disconnect as the connection ended, and the music faded away.

"I have a set of coordinates presumably from your father," Ada said.

"Great." Where was he suggesting we go instead of the moon? "Florida, South America. Where?"

She displayed the coordinates directly onto my optical nerve.

"Those coordinates aren't terrestrial." Too many digits, and my newly upgraded brain had a good idea where it was before Ada confirmed it. "Do you have maneuvering worked out with the ship's AI yet?"

"I do."

Grabbing my shirt from the cabin, I headed back to the bridge. "Bayou."

"Yes," she answered immediately.

I gave her the coordinates with instructions to scan it and lay in a course at best speed.

CHAPTER SEVEN

Red-7 was still holding it mostly together, but the captain knew that wouldn't last forever. The sounds of gunfire were almost continuous now. It echoed across the beach like thunder as two crewed K8 Disruptors unleashed full auto hell on the beasts. Those rounds inflicted sufficient damage to bring the things down. Huge chunks of scaly flesh were torn away in gouts of purplish blood. The things dropped where they were hit in the sand or in the surf, but Jesus...more of them just kept on coming.

Jordan Hauk was proud of his men but knew this was not a winnable fight. The enemy had the numbers and no need of ammo, which was a very finite resource for his assaulters. He fired at one creature clambering up onto shore, shifted to the next, only to see it dive beneath the waves. There were just so many, he couldn't be sure what shots had found their mark. After the last encounter, he'd passed the word to aim for the thighs, but that was easier said than done. As the things emerged from the ocean, the legs appeared nearly the same color of murky green as the gulf waters.

Hauk gave the command to pull back. He hated giving up the beach, but they were minutes away from being overrun. The two men were kneeling and shooting at something a few yards behind him. He had no time to think about it as he dove for the scant concealment of the saw grass-covered dune. He rolled back up and was firing again in one fluid motion as the two men who covered him now moved past in a precise dance of life or death. The leapfrogging only worked if you could make kill shots on the approaching force. Even Hauk admitted most of his weren't.

Something caught the captain's eye. He shifted the scope deeper into the surf line, then froze. There, at the rear, was another creature... something different. Something more menacing even than the monsters. *Shit.* It also looked to be directing the fight, he saw limbs that looked more like tentacles and a flattened head. A slap on his shoulder let him know his men were now behind him. In that second, he'd lost sight of the new threat, but his racing heart hadn't forgotten the panic it had inspired.

Breathe, Hauk. Assess, think, act! It had been his mantra since basic, and it had always served him well. Instead of getting up and falling back, he stopped behind a fallen log and got down on a knee, then opened up again as several of the strange, reptilian shapes raced toward him. One went down as a Disruptor round tore away its left leg. The body cartwheeled across the sand like a rag doll.

The others never slowed, never looked at their fallen comrade. These ugly things might be the ultimate fighting force. Good tactics, effective armor and weapons, and... no genuine sense of self-preservation or fear.

One of the largest ones Hauk had seen was shoving its way through scrub trees, leaping forward on its strange backward-looking legs. The thing bellowed, blowing a mist out of its gaping mouth. It wanted them dead, and that signal seemed to rally the others around it. If the other thing in the water was the commander, this had to be the first sergeant. Hauk shot it in the face. It wasn't where he should have shot it, but the thing's lower half was hidden in the tangle of mangroves and sawgrass.

His shot was more luck than skill, but the thing gave a satisfying lurch as it crashed face-first to the ground.

Day after day of this had taken its toll on all of them. Again, Hauk forced himself to calm and keep picking up threats and putting them down. That sense of panic never went away, and at one point, when he realized one of his targets was stopping to feed on a fallen soldier, it threatened to consume him totally. He squeezed the trigger blocking out the details, the horror even of the agonizing screams of pain from his own men. Fear would end this battle in seconds and probably just get them all eaten. They had already fought too hard for that. *Make these lives mean something.*

Hauk signaled another retreat as he again told himself this was just another battle. *Assess, think, act!*

But while he kept repeating his mantra over and over, the more primitive part of his brain was screaming at him to get the fuck out of there.

"Sir!"

Hauk reluctantly shifted his focus from the targeting reticle to his senior chief.

"Talk, Grayson."

"We're losing them, sir. Our men...I mean. They were okay for a while, but you know... seeing what those things are doing to the bodies and all..."

Shit. Yeah, Captain Hauk understood fully. Battles were won or lost in the head long before they were decided on the ground. Seeing their friends and squad mates not just being killed but partially consumed by the enemy was too much. Many of these guys were just kids, and they were beyond the breaking point already. That was the only reason a hard ass like the senior chief would speak up for them now. He knew they were minutes away from total defeat. Hauk wanted to ask about the HVI, her and the other civilians they'd *acquired* but—fuck 'em. They were not his priority right now. In fact, the high value asset was why there were all here. Here fighting—and dying.

Hauk nodded, "Okay, Senior, strategic full retreat. Send two men back to find us some cover, something defensible. Leave your best trigger-pullers on the line as long as you can."

Grayson nodded, relaying the signal to his troops via comms and hand signals. "Sir, you need to go, too."

Hauk looked at the man with fury in his eyes. He couldn't retreat, he was not that kind of commander. He led from the front.

"Not all of us are going to make it off this beach, sir," the senior chief said. "For us to have a chance, one of them must be you."

The next monster popped up, surprising them both. Hauk stitched a line of shots across its midsection, and Grayson leveled his rifle directly into the thing's oversized eyes. It was pissed but didn't go down. Both men had to hammer five more rounds into the thing before one round clipped the thigh sending it backward, where it fell heavily and writhed like a fish out of water. *Some of these are much tougher than the others, why?* Hauk wondered.

The firing line pulled back a few dozen yards, the stationary men in back shooting over the heads of the front line, who would fire, scuttle back, and fire again. As the two lines merged, alternating soldiers would rise and move farther back in a mostly synchronized movement that kept rounds going downrange in a near-constant barrage. The men couldn't take it for long, hell, the rifles and ammo wouldn't take it. They needed time to cool down, go through a mandatory maintenance cycle every thousand rounds. That usually took less than a minute, but those were minutes none of them had right now.

Hauk moved up beside Howell, who was using the body of another soldier for cover. The kid had been one of the late additions from San Antonio, and Hauk wasn't sure about him yet. He popped up, seemed to shoot without aiming, then ducked back down. Clearly, he was using the 'spray and pray' battlefield technique. Still, one of the reptilian things spun sideways crashing into a tree and taking out a section of fencing in the process. There were just so many targets. He tapped the kid on the shoulder and motioned him to follow.

Hauk turned and began an awkward, stumbling run; he realized just how ragged the line was. It was a miracle they hadn't been overrun. It was incomplete, staggered, and nearly useless as anything defensible. Like him, his men were bone-tired, scared, and beginning to run low on ammo. As the captain watched, he saw their right flank begin to dissolve under the brutally relentless enemy attack.

They managed to reform another ragged skirmish line, then retreated through the scant trees, thinning out the line even more but staying ahead of the monstrous horde. Hauk estimated several hundred of the things were actively hunting his men. They'd already had running skirmishes with the things for several days, and he'd foolishly thought the water would slow them down. Of course, he'd also assumed his fucking extraction boat would be here. Now he knew the damn things were even better equipped for marine fighting than on land. Hell, everything about them looked aquatic, now that he thought about it.

He and the lieutenant were stopping and firing every few yards. They used a technique they called talking rifles to alternate fire, so both were never changing a magazine pack at the same time. Unfortunately, it wasn't slowing the monsters down. It seemed to the captain that each time they stopped to lay down covering fire, the things just got closer.

The senior chief soon figured this out as well. "Cease fire, men. Conserve ammo. Just fucking *run*!"

Hauk had a brief second of irritation at the man's order, but Grayson was right. They were accomplishing nothing here except delaying a bloody end to Red-7. Turning back inland, Hauk quickly spotted the advance team, the ones he was supposed to be with, huddled between the CML transport bots heading toward a group of squat buildings with solid polycrete block walls. Just then, the last of the K8s fell silent.

"Hadroop?"

"He's up there!" Grayson paused just long enough to yell the words back to the captain.

With one more glance at the monsters quickly closing in, Hauk turned and ran for his life.

~

Each man shrugged out of their heavy packs and slumped to the floor. Senior had them call out ammo and status. Hauk could see they'd somehow made it to the shelter with more than half of his unit intact. The readout on his sleeve gave him the running KIA and MIA counts. The situation was grim, they all understood that. Some were still just getting past the denial stage. This was the first face-to-face encounter with large numbers of the creatures. The hit-and-run tactics the things had used crossing the east Texas hellscape had only offered them glimpses and usually in the dark of night through the NVGs. Now they had all seen them fully, up close and very personal. It forced each man to confront the grotesque strangeness of this new world and the brutality it required to survive.

"Fire Squad Leaders!" Senior Chief Grayson was yelling.

Hauk knew he would get a perimeter guard rotation up and running. "Everyone else grab some calories, check mags, and two hours of sleep."

That wouldn't be enough, not by a long shot, they couldn't keep going like this. Hauk couldn't keep going. Already he felt the adrenaline leaving his body like a junkie coming off a high. It would leave them all desperate for sleep within minutes.

"Are we good here, Senior?" Hauk whispered, his parched voice sounding like sandpaper.

"From those things? Shit, Captain, I have no idea. Buildings good, have the civies near the rear, no exit back there. Got camels out doing recovery, hopefully they can get us a K8. Those damn Decimator rounds are the only thing that saved us out there."

Hauk nodded, "Lock it down and get some shut eye yourself. We have more fighting before this day is over."

"Where's McNeil?"

No response; they all knew what that meant. Corporal McNeil was the platoon's radioman. At roll call tomorrow his name would be called three times. *If there was a tomorrow.* Hauk had to think about who his backup was. "Kid, I need you to get comms up, like yesterday?" Hauk's voice was close to breaking now. He didn't want to sound panicked, but he was struggling to keep it from coming through. Gomez was already pulling the spare comms unit out of its case. "We need emergency extract *now*. Any available force, any means available."

"Sir, yes, sir!" Pfc. Joseph Gomez said as confidently as he could manage. Normally, he was a spotter for one of the snipers. He liked those assignments, away from the front lines. But then, his technical skills had gotten the attention of the old man, and now it was his job to get them out of this fucking beach trip from hell. Like the rest, Gomez was clueless on how this simple escort op had gone so fucking pear-shaped. Land on friendly soil, roll over to Lackland Space Base and pick up a friendly, then hustle back to the extract point. He read the display, and his voice sounded close to panic. "Unable to establish Satlink!"

CHAPTER EIGHT

TWO MONTHS AGO - TEMPORARY U.S. CAPITAL

She threw up her hands in exasperation. She hated... no detested, dealing with most people. They were all stupid, and this insipid bureaucrat was more so than most. She adopted a tone of a teacher talking to a kindergartener. Okay, maybe a drunk teacher. "Look, fuckwad, here's a thought, why don't you sit and listen to the facts before attempting to tell me what your opinion of my report is." The undersecretary of whatever bullshit department looked at her like she was something he might scrape off the bottom of his shoe. He was not so inclined as to hear her out and proceeded to tell her so very loudly.

Xero left the conference room, looking for the man's boss, the one who had set up this meeting. The government, like the rest of the country, was in shambles. Still, the bureaucratic machine tried its best to rise once again and find someone else to blame.

On Last Day, or Eradication Day, the term that was now gaining popularity with the survivors, the missiles, the micro EMPs, hell, even some of the more bizarre things that happened like the biogenetic sapphire detonations, were merely cover. She'd been ass-deep in tracking down a series of blockchain proxy server violations that had been leaking funds away from one of her client's accounts. Then she started seeing unusual patterns in cyberspace, major routers going dark and legitimate websites on the red or blue web replaced by black web mirror sites. Deep fakes designed to alarm and upset the normal routines. It was a coordinated cyberwar attack, and it had been masterfully done.

All of the major stock exchanges had been hit, not crippling blows, but alterations to the automated trading AIs. Alterations that cost major investors billions of dollars in lost income. The pre-programmed stop-loss commands that executed automatically in case of erratic trading did something else. Instead of shifting allocations to more conservative accounts, it doubled-downed the portfolios on even riskier stocks. Hundreds of billionaires and tens of thousands of millionaires were effectively broke by the end of that day, many of whom had no clue as they trusted the automated trading bots completely.

The stock market failures had been compounded by text alerts also from black web, fake sites showing individual banks were also failing, payroll checks were bouncing, and credit cards were being cancelled because of nonpayment. Even though many of these were obvious scams, the effect was just as real. Xero knew a lot about social engineering. People had a tendency to believe falsehoods over facts, especially if they were dramatic and personal.

She'd thought... maybe hoped, that was the worst of it. God, how wrong she had been. The power grid quickly became unreliable. Food became scarce after the government confiscated the larger synthesizers and most of the raw organic material the smaller ones could have used. Then, with little warning, she'd been roused from sleep by black-suited feds, hustled onto a military hyperjet, and flown down to Texas. They called it a rescue, but her word for it was rendition. *Rescue from what?*

Now she knew. The Space Force base south of San Antonio had lasted nineteen days. Nineteen days while all hell fell apart around them. Xero shuddered to think about it now, but no way in hell she would have remained there much longer. Then, on day twenty-three, Jordan Hauk rode in with orders to take her to another safe zone. Someone up the chain had apparently read one of her reports and wanted to know more. Why did she think most of the attacks of Last Day were just cover?

Then came the fucking creatures. The evil horde had pursued them relentlessly, turning a day trip back to the coast into a weeklong nightmare. A nightmare that was still unfolding. Still, her analytical brain couldn't get all the pieces to fit. Why the hacks on the financial markets, deep fakes, and attempts to take down several bands of the internet at once? Why cause such chaos and confusion if you are just going to kill everyone on Last Day anyway? Possibly to slow any reaction or make sure people were distracted by other issues. Every magician knows the best illusions keep the audience focused on what they think is going on instead of what is really happening.

Maybe aliens had decided to invade and saw the unprecedented level of social disorder as the perfect opportunity. *Nah,* Xero liked to think she believed in aliens but not the brainless killing monsters that the soldiers outside were fighting. Those things didn't appear smart at all, they just kept attacking and dying. More likely, she figured, it was more than one force that had pulled off the global attacks. One who handled the parts she was familiar with, the computer hacks that caused the financial meltdown, paired with enough media misinformation to dismantle all public trust. Then, the other group, the ones who had the military might to pull off synchronized attacks on all those countries.

Different factions with opposing strategies but a coordinated attack? The pieces just weren't fitting together.

So...which side made the monsters? she asked herself. *Or were those just released in response to the attack? If so—why?* Few people knew that a computer algorithm largely handled the nation's overall security and defensive strategy. After the massive security and intelligence missteps in the early part of the century, leaders had finally come to grips with the issue. No agency, nor hundreds of separate agencies, could adequately monitor ongoing threats much less have countermeasures in place in time to do any good. Over the course of a decade, the little fiefdoms of intelligence D.C. had created were exposed as being incompetent or downright contributing to the nation's issues. One by one, they were quietly stripped of authority, budgets, and manpower.

Due to her former role and her ongoing consulting with the federal government, Xero was intimately familiar with both the U.S. and the Alliance algorithmic structure. Both were very good and had proven themselves countless times thwarting would-be attackers from doing any significant harm. Still, the sheer randomness of the Last Day attacks had such a chaotic level of unpredictability that to her, it suggested they were all designed by a computer program. One designed to keep everyone off-balance. If that was the case, it was one with a devastating and very cold outcome as the goal. None of this made sense to her. Who stood to gain in the overall equation? It was a puzzle, and clearly one she needed to figure out.

Now she sat in this Army tent, drinking a stranger's liquor, listening to the unrelenting gunfire and almost as frequent nearby screams. She bowed her head considering the cost of failure. Her research so far had produced little that was actionable and revealed entire gulfs of data she was unaware of. With her skills and her background, neither seemed plausible. Through it all, she'd always had one person she could count on when times got tough. One person who's mind was almost as sharp, but more, a person even she respected. Right now, though, he was out of touch, and she did not know if her friend was even still alive. "Where are you, Orric?"

CHAPTER NINE

"These coordinates are for an area of empty space." Bayou looked at me hard. The lack of understanding matched my own.

"I get that, Riggs, but we need to check it out just the same."

My second in command and I had been together long enough for her trust to overrule her logic, especially when I said something stupid. But because of my recent departure from the living, she might give me some additional scrutiny. Her face was a mask of exhaustion and something else...

"What about the drop?" she asked, clearly annoyed.

"Hopefully, this detour doesn't delay us much, but I think it's important."

She turned to the crew and ordered Packer and the ship's AI to plot the course. Up here, time was a better measure than distance. The Stone Mountain was traveling at tens of thousands of miles per hour. Any decrease in speed automatically decreased altitude, which we had been doing for several hours. Now I was asking for a course change to a fixed point in space. No way to stop an orbital mass weighing close to 30,000 metric tons. Chances are, anything out there we would fly by too fast to even spot.

"It's doable," Packer said. He threw the course corrections up on the large holoscreen. I had the calculations in my head before the AI even finished updating the grid.

"Nominal effect on the Red-7 mission, make it happen." I turned to go talk to the rest of the team. Bayou's hand reached out, then pulled back slightly. My bare feet slid to a stop on the deck plating.

"Joe."

I heard the uncertainty in my friend's voice. "Spit it out, Riggs, what's on your mind?"

She uncharacteristically looked away before answering. "Are you..."

"Am I okay?" I answered. "Am I still me?" I think what she really needed to know was could she trust me. With all that had happened and the strangeness of my resurrection and 'new' upgrades, I probably had the same concerns. Her head nodded once.

"I'm me, Deb. But hang onto your concerns just in case. We're in uncharted territory here."

"Really glad you're back, Kovach."

We bumped fists just like the good old days.

"Me too, me too."

I hadn't been on a Monolith class carrier in years and made several wrong turns before Ada updated the layout in my head for me and gave me a visual line to follow. I knew where the ready room should be, but the green glowing line took a hard right a hundred feet before the aft hatch. I followed it into a break area where Sumo and a smaller dog were playing tug-o-war with an old stuffed animal. Their growls and barks were sounds of delight.

Carol was there, as well as a smaller male version of her that had to be her son. I knelt down, patting both of the dogs. And looking at the child, he didn't look like a survivor, but I knew he was. He was all Carol had talked about. "You must be Lux," I said, holding out a hand.

The boy ignored my outstretched hand and instead moved in and hugged me. My hand fell naturally on his back, and I felt his body shaking slightly. I looked up at Carol, and she just smiled. This boy had lost his father when Atlanta was destroyed; much of his world was gone, yet he was thankful to me, a guy who wasn't even able to save himself. After a full minute, he moved back and looked at me. His eyes were clear and fearless. I knew this little dude needed no bullshitting. He'd already faced off against the very worst of what was down there and survived; he was the kind of fighter this new world would require.

"How does it feel to be living in space?"

He grinned. "It's awesome! Wish my friends could see me."

His face shadowed, and I knew what he was thinking.

"So, who is this?" I asked.

"Junie," he responded eagerly.

"I see you know Sumo already. Did you take care of him when I..." I almost said died.

"When you were dead?" he said with no hesitation.

"Um...yeah."

"I did, but Sumo wouldn't leave his spot under your hospital bed, not until the medbots made him go at least. He likes Junie, though, they get along. Junie is a great dog." His little eyes looked away, and for the first time I saw them tearing up.

"There was another dog," Carol offered.

Lux raked a sleeve across, drying his eyes. "Timber."

"The other dog was named Timber?" I asked. "What can you tell me about him?"

The boy's chin quivered ever so slightly before he got it under control. "He saved my life. You know, after the car stopped and Marcie died."

I looked up at Carol who mouthed, "NannyBot."

It took several minutes for Lux to tell me some of the story, and I had to admit it was incredible. Someone his age with no supplies, no training, literally on his own in a war zone.

"You have good instincts, Lux, trust them...always. Maybe Timber got away, he seems like a smart dog, too, but at least you managed to save this ball of fur." I had Junie pinned on her back rolling her from side to side as she tried in vain to bite at my hand. "I need to go brief my team, you wanna come?"

"Banshee?" The kid's eyes lit up like a Christmas tree.

"Hell, yeah, they're prepping for a drop. Scary as hell, but pretty damn awesome." Belatedly, I looked at Carol who nodded her permission with a smile.

"So, kid," I began as we walked down the long metal corridor, "I know being on your own was bad and all, but what do you remember most?" I knew it was shitty to be bringing up trauma to a kid and all, but shit, it's what my pops would have done.

"Bacon."

Fuck, I had to laugh. "Bacon?"

"Yeah," he said. "You ever heard of it?"

I nodded. "I've had it before, used to be a lot more common than now. When I was a kid, real meats were mostly what we ate."

"That must have been awesome."

I liked this one. All the crap and fear his mom and I had been through, all the dangers he himself faced, yet this was what he remembered.

"Why are you smiling?" he asked.

"It's just...well, you remind me of a soldier."

His eyes lit up at that remark. "How so?"

"Yeah, well...see, we go through crap, really tough days, even just in training. You learn to push your body through things you never would have thought possible. Even on missions that sometimes go tits up...er, I mean, you know, badly, like off the rails. You just have to learn to move on, put the bad stuff behind you. They call it resilience."

"And a lot of you focus on bacon?"

I chuckled. "Some," I admitted. "The main thing that works for us is to find something good about every day to remember. It doesn't have to be a big thing. Sometimes it's the little things that matter the most."

"Yeah..." he said with an air of authority that no child that old should possess. "The bad stuff just gives me bad dreams. I don't want to remember that anymore."

"Smart, Lux... very smart."

CHAPTER TEN

LUNA BASE

"It's Valyn, sir."

The older man gave a nod but remained silent. Looking out the porthole toward something... or maybe nothing.

The younger officer remained at attention long after the ensign had left. The admiral had a reputation, and forgetfulness was at the top of the list. Finally, the older man turned and eyed him up and down.

It surprised Valyn how tired and weak the man looked. He was gaunt, and his skin was nearly as gray as the lunar landscape outside.

"Any word from them?"

The admiral's new assistant knew who he meant. Valyn shook his head. "No, sir. They are not responding to our hails and have disappeared behind the planet."

"But we are sure it was under power?"

"Yes, Admiral, uh. Sorry, sir." He kept forgetting his boss had elevated his own rank earlier in the day. "Yes, War Commander, the propulsion system leaves a very identifiable signature our sensors can easily detect."

"I don't need a damn lesion in space drives or sensor dynamics. I want to know who is operating my spacecraft and what we have to do to bring it down. We cannot allow the enemy to be using our own ships against us."

Valyn was still unsure why the man thought the enemy would be aboard the nearly obsolete ship, especially after they had apparently blown three others out of orbit, but Reese seemed convinced.

"We have limited assets, sir, space tugs, a few shuttles, no real military assets."

Luna was part of an old NASA base called Gateway and more geared toward exploration than defense. It and the orbital platform high overhead were originally designed to refine fuel and water to get the precious deep-space vessels ready for the trek to Mars or the asteroid belt beyond.

The admiral smiled, then his face seemed to take on an entirely new demeanor. "Next shipment up, let's get some more of those chocolate mint things. You remember, we had them at that birthday party."

Holy shit, this man was gone, why had he not been retired by now? "No, sir, I just arrived before the attack." He wasn't sure which salient fact he was trying harder to convey, that he wasn't here at the last party or that they probably weren't getting anything else from Earth. At least not anytime soon.

"Ah, yes," the admiral said with a sigh. "Don't worry, you'll get the hang of it in no time."

The flag officer's aide tried hard to keep that one eyebrow from raising questioningly. It was an annoying habit, at least according to his friends.

"Follow me, Captain Orric."

"Sir."

Orric was impressed the man had remembered his name. He'd been on Luna for less than two weeks when the missiles started flying back home. He could now find his way around the sprawling base mostly, and the low gravity was less impactful on his stomach than it had originally been. Still, getting used to the quirks of his new boss had been the biggest challenge of all. The man seemed almost completely clueless as to the severity of what their home planet had just been through. If Xero's intel could be trusted, and he had no reason to doubt it, then something even more deadly was now at work down there.

He needed to be back; he knew he'd lost friends, family, maybe everyone on that day, but instead, he was on assignment here. An assignment that might be permanent if he couldn't find someone still alive in his command chain to reassign him.,

Gateway and Luna were one in the same as far as being a single base, but Gateway was nominally under IAS command, and Luna was U.S. military. In reality, there was so much overlap, little of the bureaucracy made any sense. The lone ship up in lunar orbit was clearly IAS, a research vessel—the IAS Sao Paulo; built to be the 'Mars and Beyond' colony ship. Now, it could well be their only lifeline back to Earth. Luna base was only 64% self-sufficient. The organic growth medium could produce enough organic matter for food. The water extractors provided way more than the colony needed, but this was a harsh environment. Technology was just as important in this environment as food and water. Every person here needed medicines to keep radiation sickness at bay, bone density treatments, and countless other items. Hell, even the simple CO2 scrubber filters that had to be changed weekly couldn't be produced here. Without resupply, Gateway would fail. Valyn felt sure the old man knew this clearly. He was quickly realizing the man simply played dumb. The man was not. Yes, he was an ass, he was lazy, he was a coward, but no, he was no one's dummy. On top of that, he was ambitious. Dangerously so.

CHAPTER ELEVEN

The man sat by the window overlooking the dark cliffs. Deep blue waves crisscrossed the Atlantic out to where it met the sky twenty miles out. The sky, he thought, had never been clearer. He sipped the wine, trying to decide frankly if he loved it or hated it. Some things are just that complex. Sometimes there is not a clear answer, a winner, a loser.

His feeling for the man standing several yards behind was much easier to categorize. He had failed him; he was a liability and now, he was making excuses. Nevis turned to face him once more. The haunted look of fear was there but still a touch of defiance, a bit of the old fire still burned deep within.

"Please, Señor Carlson, I..."

Nevis held up a single finger to silence the man while he took another sip. He had made up his mind; he walked past, deliberately ignoring the man and looked at the label on the half-full bottle, then made a note on a pad. It was good, very good in fact. It, he would keep. Diego, well, sadly... not so much.

He signaled to his men standing just outside the open door as he poured another of the delicious burgundy. He swirled it around as the two guards carried the screaming man out of the study. Carlson continued to sip as he watched them drag him across the immaculately manicured lawn and throw him over the cliff. The terrain was unforgiving here. Millennia of bitter winter storms had been eating away at Maine's coast like a hungry bear. What it left behind was a jagged coast of rock and cliff side. This had been his parents' home once; he would not do unsavory business within its walls. Out there, though... meh.

Diego had been a key asset in the Liberty Strikes. His mission was to coordinate several of the missile launches from the converted cargo ships. He'd done well, all things considered, but the Order demanded perfection. They also hated loose ends, not that anyone would be investigating. His little failure had caused an inconvenience, one Nevis would deal with later. Today he had more pressing matters, much more pressing.

He grimaced as he looked across the manicured lawn to the large mechanical object just to the north. He touched the comms link on his jaw and opened a channel to his assistant. "Get Acevedo in here and have them move that thing out of the front gardens. Also, advise the chef I will have the duck for dinner." It might be the end of the world, but that didn't mean one couldn't be civilized.

The tall man appeared in the doorway instantly. He looked frail. Nevis knew that was incorrect on so many levels. Bertrand Acevedo could appear different as the situation demanded. Nevis had never quite figured out how the man accomplished it. His face was so bland and forgettable that you could look right past him and never notice, but as many of his victims discovered, if he was that close... it was already too late.

Acevedo took a seat without being told. His breathing slowed, and his posture relaxed so much that he seemed to become one with the expensive, leather club chair.

"We are going to need to handle a problem."

Acevedo said nothing but tented his fingers and rested his chin atop them.

"The Sisterhood."

A brief spark of life showed in the killer's eyes, a delight, a challenge perhaps. It was there, and now it was gone.

"Which one?" he finally asked.

Nevis poured wine; he considered offering Acevedo some but smiled, already knowing the man never drank, never smoked, never had sex as far as his people could tell. He was a killing machine, an organic robot who let nothing interfere with any mission. He sipped the delicious vintage and again remarked on its complexity. How could something be almost too much and not quite enough at the same time?

"Does it matter? You know who we want, but at this point, at least send the bitches a message."

Lumia, The Grand Mother, would be the ultimate prize, but he knew better than to even hope that. On Last Day, they had targeted her compound in Morocco with multiple rounds of ordinances including the modified Darkstar, and even one of the very expensive Sapphire warheads mounted to a stolen Russian-made cruise missile. They had even dropped high-altitude bunker busters on the supposed escape room deep underground. They found neither Lumia nor any of the Sisters in the rubble. Instead, they found the mutilated bodies of almost two hundred of their own private paramilitaries chained to walls. The Sisterhood was great at laying traps but disguising them to be impossible for a foe to resist.

"My friend," Nevis moved slowly over next to the man's chair, "strike them where it will hurt. We are too close to let that bunch of hormone-crazed lunatics cause us more problems. The closer the pain is to their leader, the better." Lumia might always be just out of reach, but causing some significant losses in her inner circle should work. "I want them back in whatever fucking hole they first crawled out of. Our new world has no place for them."

Acevedo stood in a fluid motion that seemed more like gravity releasing its grip than a physical act. He nodded and turned for the door, moving with cat-like grace.

After all these years, the man still gave Nevis the creeps. He was not a friend; he was a tool, a dangerous one. Acevedo might even be the best, as he'd never failed an assignment. He also didn't brag or offer any details of how he managed to accomplish any of the tasks. Only rarely would Nevis even ask for more details.

He downed the rest of the wine and set the empty glass down on top of the Steinway piano. The polished, black mirror-finish reflected his face in dark relief. Tapping his comms dot with a trembling finger he made the call. He was declaring war on the Sisters of Light, and others would need to be prepared.

CHAPTER TWELVE

Drop Team ready rooms all had the same smell. I'd never been able to fully describe it. They stored the unused drop-coffins against the far wall, and no matter how much refurbishment we did, they still retained that slightly burnt ozone tang. Combine that with the funk coming from the hard-shell vacuum suits we sometimes wore and some of the other natural aromas, I felt sure I could have found it without Ada's map.

This was the first time I had seen all the team together since that field in Tennessee. I thought that it felt like a lifetime ago before realizing how accurate that was.

"It lives!" Priest said.

"We took a vote and are officially changing your combat call sign to Ghost," Halo added.

"Not funny, assholes, and you are not allowed to change the call sign of a squad leader."

There were fist bumps and back slaps for me and Lux. It seemed like the squad had adopted him as one of their own. They were just getting into their body armor, and I told them we were making a slight detour.

"Your Spidey sense again?" Halo asked.

"Not this time, some intel we need to follow up on. Captain Hauk will just have to bear with us, this could be important."

The normally quiet Korean sergeant came close and extended his hand. "Very good to see you again, Master Sergeant."

The two of us held each other's gaze for a moment. He and I had been through so much, saving each other countless times down in the bowels of that awful underground factory. Volumes of silent understanding passed between us in that moment. He nodded, and I knew he was ready for whatever came next.

"Okay, listen up. G-Force is in command."

"Not you?" Priest asked.

"I'm still technically dead so until we get that straight, I can't get clearance. Bayou wants me up here for now, but that could change. Gi can plan it and get the load-outs. Go heavy on what is needed to put down those damn beasts. You remember. The ones that we hope we don't encounter."

"Ooh rah!"

That was it, no bullshit egos, no eye rolls. The new guy, or The Fucking New Guy, had a clear understanding of the threat they would likely face. My team knew its role, and it executed best when the appropriate person was calling the shots. Leadership in a squad like this was more about capability than authority. This mission belonged to the ROK operator, who nodded his assent.

"I've heard Hauk can be a handful," I said. "Anyone ever seen him in action?"

"Not directly," Priest said. "Served with his brother on Pathfinder Team before you guys drafted me."

"Pathfinder, "I said. "You guys got chewed up pretty damn good as I recall. Where was that, Poland?

Bishop, aka Priest, looked down, and I knew he was seeing the faces of his buddies that hadn't made it. It was a common trait for all of us. "Belarus, some little shit-hole spot on the map up near the Russian border." He paused to secure the ratchet straps on his combat boots three times on each foot. We all had our good luck rituals. "Logan Hauk was a hell of a soldier, hell of a leader. He was our lieutenant before the shit went pear-shaped. His brother's company came in and liberated us. Red-7 got their name from that mission."

I laughed recalling the story now. Jordan Hauk supposedly landed in Russia, stole an entire combat convoy and drove into neighboring Belarus flying the Russian flag to get to what remained of Pathfinder. "Okay, Priest, you get Captain Hauk on board. He won't want to leave Earth side, but we need a base to mount ops from, and the Stone Mountain is better than anything else right now."

The all-comms system chimed, "Master Sergeant to the bridge, we have contacts."

I shook the men's hands again and wished them luck. They would deploy as soon as we reached the right orbit, and I had a feeling I was going to have my hands full until then. Sumo and Lux turned and followed me back toward the bridge.

CHAPTER THIRTEEN

"We are 120 kilometers. Periapsis is coming down, and factoring our trajectory, we have an intercept course coming up in eleven minutes."

Strangely, I understood all of that.

"Thanks, Packer." I turned to Bayou and smiled.

"Something is out there. Long range scanners have identified an inert mass. How did you know?" she asked.

I shrugged.

"Can we match orbit?" I knew this could be the real problem. Like two cars traveling in opposite directions on the interstate, if we were in radically different orbits, we might only get one brief look at whatever it was my dad wanted me to see.

"No need, it is in the same retrograde orbit as us. As soon as the AI can calculate a true speed and tumble, we can slow to match," the pilot said.

"Ship." I said. Then, looking at the lieutenant, I asked, "Does our ship AI have a name?"

She shook her head, "Does it really matter?"

It did, to me at least. While AIs were not sentient, having one in my head had made me more sensitive to their status. Plus, I simply preferred thinking and referring to them as something other than machines.

"My users have used several common names to address me since my installation on this vessel, Master Sergeant," the ship's monotone AI said. "Your current crew has not yet assigned me one."

"I see. Did you ever have one you preferred over the others?"

"The space engineers who perform maintenance on me typically refer to me as Belle."

"As in Southern Belle?" I asked.

"I would assume so, this ship is named..."

I cut her off, "I know, big freaking rock outside Atlanta. Okay, Belle, get me a visual mockup on that object as soon as you can. Also, notify the SEs that we may need them for an EVA."

"Lieutenant Riggs had me do that a half hour ago. The retrieval team is standing by in the main docking bay."

Several anxious minutes went by as Belle began filling in images on a three-dimensional outline of what her sensors were seeing. I'm not sure what I was expecting, a weapons cache, maybe some kinetic rods, but what took shape was a complete surprise. The ship rocked sideways suddenly.

"Sorry, encountering unmapped space debris," Belle stated flatly. "Slowing to match speed and rotational attitude."

"That's a..." Bayou started.

I nodded, "It's part of one of the destroyed ships. Looks like one of the cargo bays. Had to be a big mother."

Now we were getting real-time updates and could see the piece of debris was large, at least seventy yards long and maybe half that wide. It was also tumbling on multiple axis.

"They are venting atmosphere. That's causing the leak. It appears to be part of the cargo and crew quarters from the Denali. I am picking up life signs."

Ada, alert the SEs to have medbots ready to receive them, I said silently. "Belle, can we recover the fragment intact?"

"If Captain Packer will allow me full control, I can match spin and should allow the engineers to attach winching clamps."

"Do it, Packer."

"Master Sergeant, a word," Bayou said as she motioned toward a small room off the bridge. I looked at the image of the container and saw its rotation slowing, which meant ours was actually speeding up to match. I nodded and followed my XO into the room.

"What or who will we find in there, Kovach?"

"No clue."

She licked her lips, then dove right in. "Joe, look, I know you just got thrown into this, but I've been dealing with it for days. We have to decide if we're going to be a rescue and aid vessel or a ship of war. First, going after Red-7 and now this? We have a planet full of victims and apparently survivors out here as well. Where can we do the most good?"

It was a good question and admittedly one I had given little thought to. "Bayou, this war is being fought a hundred and seventy miles below us. All we can do up here is regroup and plan, that is what this minor detour is. Maybe we find some armaments, maybe fighters, but it is doing some good."

"And if we find some asshole Alliance admiral who has different ideas?"

"They can bunk on ten-up." She smiled. Most ships of the fleet had nine decks sealed to the hard vacuum of space. One deck, the outer deck, was not sealed. Ten-up was our way of saying toss them into the deep dark.

We watched the live feed as the space engineers moved out, quickly secured the large mass, and moved aside to let others begin the retrieval. At the same time, fresh oxygen tanks were fitted to external valves, so clean O^2 would flow to the interior. The new cargo was winched in and secured way more quickly than I would have guessed. The engineers were used to working out there and were damned efficient.

"Mister Packer, take us to dive depth, notify G-force when on station. Bayou, you're with me."

CHAPTER FOURTEEN

I'd made it only a dozen steps before my stomach cramped, and I dropped to a knee. The pain was so intense my eyes went blurry.

"You good, Kovach?"

I looked up at Riggs and nodded. "Yeah... I think... no, I know what it is. I'm starving. Do we have a working galley?"

"Yeah, it's stocked, and all the automated stuff works. The SEs take turns doing the main meals themselves. Sort of a competition among them. A few are talented behind the grill."

We stopped in. Riggs suggested a cup of oatmeal and watered-down juice. "You've had nothing in your system for days. The medbots stopped the nutrient flow when you decided to check out."

I got an Italian proto-beef sandwich on a ciabatta roll with chips and a black coffee. *No sense in living if I have to do it on oatmeal and water, right?*

"I heard you tell Carol that it was her friend that shot you. She killed you. Why?"

I shook my head between bites that literally reminded me of how Sumo could devour his food in massive gulps. The pain in my belly was already easing, though. "No idea, Riggs. She's a strange one, lots about her just doesn't add up. Somehow, though, I think she knew the shot wouldn't kill me, nor was not getting the antirejection drugs going to be lethal."

"The shot didn't hit anything important," she replied. "In fact, it was perfectly placed, just damaged something that the scans couldn't identify. It apparently wasn't essential."

"No idea what it is... was?" I asked.

"Nope, the scanners simply ignored it when we tried to get more information. You know the auto docs on these boats are kind of limited," she said as she stole one of my chips.

"Or...they program the system to not reveal anything deemed classified," I said, leaning over to grab a small salad that was sitting in the chiller case.

"Yeah, like the repulser engines on the TriCraft?" she said.

"Too many goddam secrets, Deb. The shit down there in that fucking monster factory. That was our people's doing. That was a Hammer facility."

"Our people, their people... what the fuck difference does it make anymore, Joe?"

I was missing something, something big, but despite my upgraded cognitive abilities, it simply wasn't there.

"What?" Bayou asked.

I smiled; she'd been around me long enough to know how my mind worked.

"Can't decide between the pudding and the cake?" she quipped. "Do both, I think it's been that kind of day."

I did both, and she was right. The cake was freaking amazing, too... damn, that was worth coming back from the nether regions for.

I saw the look she was giving me; something serious was on her mind. "Ask it," I said between bites.

"Where were you?"

I slowly put the fork down, wiped my mouth and leaned back. The question needed no other context. It was the small black spider crawling around in the back of my own mind. Something I had refused to acknowledge personally... not yet at least. I drew in a deep breath and let most of it back out. "I don't know... somewhere dark... really, really dark."

She and I were soldiers, honestly, we dealt with it. As Pops said, death is our business, but it still freaks us all out. Soldiers tend to compartmentalize the shit out of it, though, and now she was asking me to unpack it for her. Explain to her something I hadn't even allowed myself time to consider.

"Just dark?"

"That's what I remember, Deb, dark, wet, silence. Death is not a happy place."

"You weren't dead," she said, obviously not even able to convince herself. "Ok, you were clinically dead, the machines said you were dead..."

"I think we should drop it, Riggs. I'm still me, as far as I can tell at least." The truth was, I don't think I had been gone—not totally, and that scared the fuck out of me.

She nodded, and I finished my cake. Then, a related thought finally bubbled to the surface, something my mind had been stewing on for a while just below the surface.

"Where were all the people?"

"That's your big question? What about who started this damn war? How were we so unprepared? Who shot down the other carriers? Why in the fuck were we making monsters?"

"Who shot JR?" I quipped.

"Don't you mean JFK?" she answered quickly.

"Dallas or Dallas, that's the real question."

Actually, all of them were very good questions, all questions we needed to be finding answers for. Ada was streaming a list of additional ones as we spoke. The list had to be already in the thousands. "You said New York was nearly empty," I said. "That makes some sense, it took a direct hit."

"Kinetic strike, we think."

I nodded, finished the coffee and refilled my cup. "Out past the coast, though, beyond the reach of the bombs, most of the people were still gone, dead, I mean. We checked a few houses, we saw lots of bodies."

"Carol's kid says the same thing. Most of the houses were empty or had dead people."

"Shit. Poor kid," I said.

"Kovach, he's one of the lucky ones. One of the very few to have made it out."

"Killer vines, mutant animals, murder-crabs, Decimators. Obviously, that was just the stuff we saw. Could something else be at work down there, bioweapons, contaminants, or something?"

She shook her head. "Our systems didn't detect anything like that. I can't say it with much certainty. Let's face it, the attacks didn't hold back much, but what we are hearing about is mostly the work of what you mentioned first, plus good old-fashioned assholes being assholes."

I arched an eyebrow. "People attacking each other?"

She nodded. "It's bad, should be plenty of food for all of them, water could be a problem, but enough of the planet's clear for the moment for the survivors to regroup and begin a solid defense."

"Let me guess, instead, they are hoarding, stealing, and proving why anarchy is such a lousy form of government."

"You got it, Master Sergeant."

Her eyes drifted to my shirt, and I reflexively covered the piece of tape.

"You are still a Master Sergeant, right?" she asked. "I mean… I know you have been busted from officer ranks before, but you wouldn't have been demoted just because you died, would you? Hell, they were dead, too, so who would have done it?"

She moved to peel back the strip of tape, and I caught her hand. She laughed, then tapped her temple. I knew she was bringing up her link to the ship's AI. And then, she would read the updated ship's roster…

"No fucking way!"

She stood quickly.

"No fucking way!" She obviously wasn't going to stop.

"It's wrong, Riggs, ignore it."

"No fu…"

"LT?" I spelled it out.

She was still laughing, but she almost came to attention.

"It's just a thing… you know, when you die in battle. Or something…" Fuck, I had no idea.

"Battlefield promotion for a dead guy?"

"You know, I am starting to get a little sensitive about everybody referring to me as dead."

"Sure, sure, Master...er, Captain. You prefer something more sensitive like 'previously alive' or 'recently undead?'"

"Not better...no."

I finished my coffee and grinned at my executive officer, now once again junior to me in rank, even if it was only going to be temporary.

"Fuck you, Riggs, and wipe that damn smile off your face. At least now I can get my drop clearance reinstated."

She placed a hand on my arm. "Fuck you, too, Kovach. Glad you're back."

I stood, "Let's go see what those SEs are reeling in."

CHAPTER FIFTEEN

I was glad to see the engineering crew had an armed security detail who had taken up firing positions around the massive piece of ship being lashed into place. The SEs were just as much military as the rest of us, just with additional levels of skills and training to do their very specific jobs. Sometimes required to do that job in war zones and in the line of fire. I had met none of them yet, but that was soon to be a priority.

"Specialist," Bayou said to a white clad woman holding a datatab.

The dark-haired woman turned and snapped off a salute before turning back to the fragment. "Gate stasis field is back in place. They are re-pressurizing the hangar deck and will have access in ninety seconds," Otero said without hesitation.

"Is this one of ours?"

The space engineer turned to see who I was, and her eyes briefly went wide in apparent recognition. "Yes, we believe it is part of the Denali. The deck configuration on that carrier was unique."

"So, presumably friendlies."

Bayou shook her head, "How could anyone be alive in there? They attacked Denali five or six days ago best we can tell."

"Each section has some safeguards in case of catastrophic failure. Vital compartments can even be jettisoned in an emergency. Just like Old Stoney here." Otero waved up at the gray decking all around.

I knew that the red emergency lockers were in every corridor, and I knew they held emergency vacuum suits, oxygen generators, water, and more. The fact that they could pop an entire section out was news to me, though.

"Equalized!" one other yelled before the light on the door went from yellow to green. We piled in, every soldier armed but Riggs and me. Then I saw she had a handgun out as well. So, everyone was armed but me.

"Tapping coming from inside," one of the SEs said, pocketing a small device he'd been using to listen.

The damn thing was massive. Jagged metal, wires, and duct work stuck out at every angle. The entire thing sat canted at a thirty-degree angle on the ship's deck. In truth, I couldn't see any part of this thing that looked like it would hold air much less livable space.

Several of the engineers began cutting into the wreckage at very specific points. I could see they were going in between the deck and an outer hull. An area that would normally be mostly hollow space filled with water just like the Stone Mountain's hull configuration. The water was essential for obvious reasons but also in shielding the crews from deadly cosmic radiation.

Specialist Otero's crew was precise and well-trained. One of the workers signaled, and she ordered her team back into firing positions. "Opening it up now, sir." She motioned for both of us to take cover.

A section of wreckage fell away and a gaping dark maw in the interior of the twisted metal opened up. Armed SEs replaced the engineers with cutting tools, and with lights affixed to their pulse rifles, they lit up the interior. Through the tight beams of bluish white light, I saw lumps of orange. Some of the lumps soon resolved into arms and legs.

Riggs and I moved from cover along with most of the others. These weren't hostiles, they were barely alive, in fact. The orange I had seen appeared to be survival tents. Inflatable bags for those who couldn't get into the emergency vacuum suits. "Shit," I said as we started pulling them out of the dark hole. "How many are they?"

The answer was forty-seven; it was actually seventy-three, but twenty-six were dead, or would be gone before the medbots could even triage their condition. A couple of the bodies moved arms and even appeared semi-conscious. I removed the helmet from one man, a large, solidly built Marine who appeared stronger than the rest.

The man's lips moved, but no sound came out. Riggs handed him a water bladder, and he drank from the spout greedily. He nodded and offered a feeble thumbs-up. As we cut away the cheap emergency suit, the man reeked of sweat, urine, and other unpleasantries, but the tattoo on his arm and the winged globe with twin archers let us know exactly who these guys were.

"They're Alliance Space Marines," Riggs said.

Like the ancient naval ships, every Space Fleet carrier had a compliment of Marines aboard. They were trained to fight in every environment, including Zero-G, however, that had only been tested a couple of times over the years.

The Marine's lips moved again, and this time a croaking sound came out. I leaned in close. "Permission to come aboard, Captain."

Using that rank to refer to me still felt off. I wiped the grime from his name tape and glanced at the rank insignia. Atkins, Trip AWO. I patted him and nodded. "Welcome to the IAS, Stone Mountain, Chief." Two of the SEs carried him to an awaiting auto-gurney where the attached medbots were already getting IV lines ready.

"Interesting find, Prowler," Riggs said, looking at me and shaking her head. "One of these days…"

She was cut off by Otero on our left calling up to one of her men. The specialist was glancing between her datapad and the wreckage with a confused look.

"Problem, Specialist?"

She didn't answer immediately, her mind clearly on the rows of numbers on the screen.

"Deep scan, wide spectrum, soon as all the bodies are removed," she yelled. Finally registering my words, she turned to me and realized I had asked her something.

"Sorry, sir, the umm… the weight is wrong."

"Weight?"

She nodded, "Yes, sir, the deck plating has sensors built in to calculate the weight. It's useful for artificial gravity and such, but also, the ship has mass even if we don't always have weight. For maneuvering that must be calculated."

I knew some of that, and looking at the piece of debris, I finally noticed that Ada...or maybe I, was also running various calculations on the thing.

"It's too heavy," I said, understanding dawning.

"Yes, sir, by a lot."

"Tell me, Otero, on the Denali what was adjacent to the Marine billet?"

"Hangar 12, sir, same as all the Monolith class."

"Hot damn!" I said, and mainly to myself whispered, "Thank you, Pops."

CHAPTER SIXTEEN

The test concluded with a beep. Ada moved on to vocabulary. The first word was Triskaidekaphobia. They got progressively harder and faster. I knew the questions were coming in seconds, then fractions of seconds, then microseconds. Eventually, all was too fast for verbal responses, so I simply thought it.

"Do you need a break?"

"Of course not, this is not like work." And it wasn't. While I had been more interested in my physical changes, Ada seemed more startled by intellectual enhancements. I thought back to a conversation with Doctor Reichert soon after my injury. He said the brain was the most important upgrade any soldier could want.

I'd already noticed several improvements. Better memory recalls, faster problem solving, reading, analysis, and multitasking.

"Okay, that's enough on math, let's move on to chemistry."

Suddenly, I realized I had completed the last exam while thinking of the doctor. Parts of my brain were now working entirely independent of the others. How did this help me be a better soldier, though?

After more than two hours, Ada finally relented. "That's it, Joe. That is the extent of what the human test can measure."

She explained that for humans to devise a test, someone had to be smart enough to devise the question and know the answer. I had just exceeded that limit.

"In what areas?" I asked.

"All of them. You never once skipped a question, you never answered incorrectly or 'I don't know.'"

"So, I am a genius?"

"That's imprecise. Your IQ is likely well above 200, but you are more like a pocket computer. You know a lot, you have great potential, but it really depends on the application. How are you going to use it?"

"I'd like a beer."

"Your parents would be so proud."

"Hey, now that's just mean." Ada was getting a seriously snarky personality, and I had no idea where it was coming from. Seriously. No idea.

CHAPTER SEVENTEEN

Halo constantly fidgeted with his gear belts. It was part nervous habit and part superstition. He'd done it before every successful drop. He counted all of them he survived as successful.

"You think all that hurky-jerky shit makes a difference?" Priest asked.

Halo shrugged; it was a well-worn topic. Something they went through to take the edge off before a jump.

"Say, what do you think about Kovach? Coming back like that an' all. That's some shit, right?"

"Can it, Priest," Gi ordered, striding into the room.

The other two men were caught off guard and both began laughing. "Where's your accent?" Halo asked.

"I'm in charge on this one, don't want to muck it up," the Korean offered with an amiable smile. "Seriously, though, we went through some weird ass shit down there. Never underestimate him. The man may or may not be invincible, but he is a damn fine soldier. One I would fight beside any day."

"Amen to that," Priest said with a fist bump, his large, black fist dwarfing the smaller Korean's.

"So, did I hear correctly, we pulled a can full of Marines out of the deep dark? Any chance we can get some help down there? I mean, we are a few men short on this drop," Halo asked.

"I heard the same as you, Halo. I doubt they're in fighting shape. They must have been floating around out there since the Denali went down days ago. Who knows what injuries they may have?"

G-force went on to brief the squad on every manner of enemy they'd been up against at the Ranier facility, one of the aptly nicknamed Nightmare Factories. Sadly, all they had was the standard load-out of weapons. No one had any 'ah-ha' moments that might prove useful in whatever Red-7 was likely up against.

"This is no way to fight a war," Priest said.

"We aren't," Halo answered a little too quickly.

"What the fuck does that mean?"

Halo kicked out at the edge of a nearby gear locker, his boot making a rhythmic thud each time.

"He means we are doing body retrievals right now," Kovach said carrying in several large bundles. He dropped the load at their feet.

"Thought we wouldn't see you before we dropped."

"Change of plans," Kovach answered, his face breaking into a wicked grin. "I am now cleared, and Deb and I came to an... understanding."

Getting locked into the X-class pods was a serious upgrade. These even had built-in displays with an external view. Still, they were essentially a coffin. Deep down, I knew I had been just days or even hours away from a funeral pod. The dull black ovoids slung in racks high above us in the storage slots. Each of us had mixed feelings about them. Truthfully most RDT fatalities were down on the ground. Few of us made it back up here to be deep-spaced. It was considered an honor, though, any of us could request it if we were KIA.

I shook my head to clear the morbid thoughts and familiarized myself with the pod's systems. As usual, Sumo was secure beneath me in his own compartment. Despite the chaos of the last month, things seemed oddly familiar. Telling Carol and Lux that I was dropping had been tougher than I'd expected. I wasn't used to having anyone care about what I did. These guys, my team, they were my family.

The launch tubes appeared on the screen like...well, like an oversized gun barrel, which essentially was what they were. The Stone Mountain's orbital velocity was in excess of 17,000 miles per hour, and much of that had to be canceled out before our pods would drop into the atmosphere. That was normally achieved by firing us in the opposite direction of the ship. We also had to stay on a trajectory that would place us on a glide path very near the drop target. Now, thanks to my upgrades, I can calculate all of that in real-time. One thing I'd never fully realized was the Earth itself is rotating to the east at around a thousand miles an hour.

Seeing all the advanced calculations did little to ease my mind. Still, this was not my first rodeo. The ballistic pods and I were old friends. Kind of.

The kick of the rail gun firing me out the tube still felt like a car crash, but I had to admit, these new pods had better inertial dampeners or something. Now, we just held on and hoped we could make the transition from space to atmos without burning up. For the next few minutes, there wasn't anything we could do to affect that outcome.

As my pod began its drop, the outer skin quickly heated up. Through the display, I could see the blue-yellow plasma jetting around me. Knowing just millimeters away the temperature was over 2000 degrees did little for one's nerves, but the howl of the air screaming past was what normally made me switch on the noise canceling feature in my helmet. Today, I listened to it, though. I was still alive, and I was going hunting.

CHAPTER EIGHTEEN

"Captain Hauk."

The man turned; Hadroop started to give the update, then realized his CO's attention was elsewhere. His steel gray eyes seemed to be looking toward the western sky, and he was speaking on the Milcrypt comms to someone.

"We have friends, Lieutenant."

Hadroop followed the man's outstretched hands. It took a full minute to pick out the razor thin lines of white against the blue morning sky. Too small and too close together to be attack aircraft. Even the new autonomous Shrikes didn't fly that tight.

"Drop troops?" he asked hopefully.

Hauk nodded. "Space Force finest, Lieutenant. One bona fide RDT jump squad. Their commander is none other than Master Sergeant Kovach, and he says they are bringing party favors. Get the men ready. With any luck, we may finally take the fight to these asshole lizards."

"Hoorah!" the man said before disappearing back down the line.

Hauk had only seen RDT teams incoming once before in his sixteen years of service. It had been enough for him to know that job would never be for him. These guys were nuts, riding a flaming beer can down from high orbit just to be ejected out into the cold empty airspace seconds before impact in hostile territory, and that was if everything went right.

Banshee was supposedly the best. He watched as the contrail arcs slowed and dipped. He could see the drop troopers deploy, but he knew it must have happened as the drop cannisters blasted back up skyward. “Only four,” he said to himself. That hardly seemed to be much of a help, but he would take it. No one else was even answering his calls since Last Day.

“Incoming, five klicks high, Captain, at our nine o’clock. Three... no, four tactical glider wings arrowing toward the LZ. Damn, sir, looks like they will nail it, dead nuts.”

The voice in his ear was his radioman and spotter, Gomez. He was on a small rise a few hundred yards back and would likely be the first contact Red-7 would have with the team, assuming they made it. The RDTs were legendary, but nothing about this new enemy was conventional.

“Bring the CO to me,” Hauk ordered. “Deploy the others as they see fit.”

~

As Sumo uncurled himself from the harness with a yawn, our feet had no sooner touched the ground than a sickly lavender vine began arching toward us from a stand of nearby oak trees. The forest looked as if it was being strangled by the alien infestation.

In my HUD, I saw the green beacons of the friendlies surrounded by a sea of pale red. The battle suit’s AI still couldn’t decide if everything was an enemy combatant or not.

In my experience—it was. I unclipped Sumo and gave him the signal to guard right. I saw a green dot moving in our direction. Gomez, Joseph, PSC. I moved to flank left so the private would be between me and my dog. In the meantime, I pinged the rest of my squad. We’d landed on a small peninsula of dry land with marsh and ocean on three sides.

“Here, Boss,” Halo called. I saw his marker show up on the far-right side of my suit’s field of view.

Gi signaled, the man was precisely where he'd targeted. No surprise.

"Where the fuck is Priest?"

"Where else? Dumbass is in the water," Halo called back.

Figures, if the suit was under too much water, the beacon wouldn't transmit.

"You think he knows what direction to walk?"

The suits held plenty of air and were sealed to the environment, but if he gets into those vines, he may have a bit of trouble. I kept those thoughts to myself.

"I'm coming, Prowler, don't wait on me," Priest said. "Larger, more manly bodies need more cushion to protect the vital parts, you know?"

"Master Sergeant... er..." the young Ranger man began speaking, the uncertainty clear in his voice.

"Sorry, sir. Um, Captain Kovach."

I assumed my ridiculous new rank had just updated in the FOF ident my battle suit AI was broadcasting. Gomez would see my digital name tape and rank on his HUD. I subvocalized for Ada to try and reverse my shipboard promotion status...at least while I was down here. Ada acknowledged but added that the suit's own basic combat AI would likely keep reverting it back.

Fuck!

"Talk to me, Gomez. Where is your captain?"

"Waiting on us, sir. Please follow me."

I saw one of the green dots in my own HUD begin to radiate circles out. That was the commander. I relayed the position to the others. I knew Gi would go find Mister Bishop before moving off to get their own take on the battle space. Halo and Sumo would shadow me all the way in.

Captain Hauk and I knew each other mainly by reputation. He had a solid service record, very by- the-book commander most of the time. When he went off the reservation, though, he did it in some very dramatic fashion.

Bayou had given him high marks, so that was good enough for me. Shit, simply being alive right now was an achievement.

"Captain," I said, stepping up, sleeving my helmet back and up and gripping the outstretched hand.

"Kovach. Really glad to see you. Your men all down safe?"

I saw him eying Sumo as he spoke.

"We're good. One is soaking in the pond at the moment, but he'll be along shortly."

Hauk looked concerned. "There are... things in the water, Kovach. Very bad things."

"Scaly green skin? Alien eyes, mouth full of worms?"

He smiled and nodded. "I take it you've met."

"Yes, Furies was what I called them. Mean, ugly bastards."

"What can you tell me about them?"

"Aim for the inner thigh, femoral artery. Don't let them get close. They have Ginsu knives for fingers."

"Yeah, we've figured that much already. Any idea where they came from?" he asked.

I knew he meant what terrorist labs, or maybe just what country. "They are Hammer tech."

"No fucking way!" His shoulders sagged as the truth hit.

"Pretty sure, I raided one of their black labs a while back. I saw hundreds of the things and signs that even more had been there."

"Hope you erased that facility from DARPA's inventory," Haul growled.

I nodded.

He spat and wiped away a bit of blood from a cut above his brow. "So, we are fighting our own assets."

I shrugged. "Seems like. I don't think the sides matter much anymore, Captain. Someone wanted humans gone, and they have gone to great lengths to make that happen."

I saw the weariness behind the man's eyes. "You've seen some things, I take it."

"Oh yeah, more than I want to remember."

He eyed the name tag stenciled on my armor, the one that still read my actual rank. My new intellect ran through all the likely thoughts the man was having, resentment, jealousy, curiosity. "Ignore it, brevet promotion or battlefield promotion. Off that ship up in orbit, it doesn't really count. I'm a working stiff." I could see in his expression that it did matter. He wanted someone else to be making the tough calls; he just wasn't sure that it should be me.

"Kovach, Red-7 is...was trained for conventional warfare. Like Banshee, we were an elite group and highly skilled for those kinds of battles. Now, almost half the force is made up of acquisitions, really just remnants from other outfits, and this is nothing even remotely like conventional."

"I feel you, brother. This is more in our wheelhouse. Banshee has been battling monsters for years." I took a moment and stared out over the battlefield. "Not normally in battles of this scale, though."

"So, what do we do, Master Sergeant?" he asked.

I bit my lower lip, eyed the AO once more before responding. "We are men of action, Hauk. When needed, extremely violent action. We kill these fucks and get our people to safety."

Our eyes met, and I saw agreement.

"That something we can agree on?"

CHAPTER NINETEEN

"So, what's the situation, Captain?"

Hauk just stood there eyeing me in that way. Like I should already know. Like I would never be able to know, maybe that I wouldn't live long enough out here for it to matter. I'd been in his shoes plenty of times. Watching the horrors of war, your men dying, the relentless killing, then some new guy shows up wanting to know why you were struggling with such an easy fight.

The man scratched at a red whelp that encircled much of his neck. The wound looked angry and was blistering in places. It was a telltale mark of the thunder vines.

"Deep in the shit." His voice was flat, devoid of emotion. The vocal equivalent of the thousand-yard stare that battle-weary soldiers sometimes have. This wasn't the Jordan Hauk I had expected. "We have injured... dead, low on food and ammo, and a highly indefensible position."

That was undoubtedly admitting more than any commander wanted. Still, I knew it wasn't his fault.

"They left us here, no plan, no exfil, no fucking ship. Sent us in on a fucking suicide run for the HVI, and for what? We save one person and ignore thousands more. Shit... more like tens of thousands."

Captain Hauk was a man unused to defeat, but anyone could see even he was nearing a breaking point.

"What's your take on all this, Kovach?"

I thought I knew what he meant, the mutant creatures... the Furies, the vines, the lack of survivors. I told him what I knew.

"The Sapphire bombs. You think the pretty lights caused all this shit?"

The guy was a bit of an ass, but I was here to help him, so...

"No, I think," I stopped and backed up. "I know we created them, the Furies. My guess is we created some of the others, too. The bombs just added a whole new level of crazy. Something about it alters the DNA at the genomic level, causes the normal biosphere to go apeshit crazy."

"No shit. I was nearly decapitated by a glorified morning glory earlier." He absentmindedly rubbed at the blister again. Hauk moved farther down his lines, checked on something, then eased his way back with quick, precise movements. "Those labs, did they build an entire army of these things? And you said that was in Tennessee. How in the hell are they down here already?"

"I saw hundreds. Not an army of them, not in Tennessee at least. Those are good questions, though."

The man rubbed his short hair and stared out. I wasn't sure what he was seeing, ghosts maybe, but he was someplace else.

"I saw something else out there."

His words chilled me, I had a feeling the mutations were not just limited to what I had seen already.

He continued, "I may be wrong, but it seemed in control... of them... the Furies. It wasn't one of them, though, it looked more... aquatic to me. Maybe like a squid or something. You know, tentacles instead of arms."

Shit, that was great. One more thing to worry about.

"I'm glad you're here, Kovach. I just wish you'd brought a brigade with you because that's what we're going to need."

I flinched as a K8 Disruptor began firing a few hundred yards away. I couldn't see what it was firing at, but I saw the result. What had been remnants of a neat little grouping of bungalows disappeared in a cloud of debris and smoke. The man on the trigger was good, he wasted little ammo. As the last of the cover fell, others then took up the call, and I got my first look at the attackers. They were Furies but looked somewhat different from the ones back in the Nightmare Factory.

These gathered and spread out several times and sent individuals out to test our lines. Even though I knew they engineered these things for battle, they didn't have all the advantages. We could see them, yet they seemed unsure as to exactly where we were. Which gave us time to engage.

I'd unlocked my Rattler without even thinking about it, the action as routine as tying my shoelaces. I shifted my aim to the nearest target, a tall, gangly bastard who was snorting as he approached to my left. One of Hauk's men beat me to the shot, driving a jacketed round through his thigh and another into its head. The thing fell forward, the back of his head completely missing where the soldier's round had torn its way out.

"You did figure out the weak spot."

Hauk nodded. "Any other tips you care to share?"

"Yeah, fuckers are strong, incredibly so," I answered, snapping off a pair of shots at a trio of beasts heading toward our flanks. I heard Sumo bark and instructed him on comms to help guard the civilians. Priest and Gi showed up and began passing out the fresh ammo packs, rifles, grenades, and just about everything else we'd robbed from the ship's small arms locker. I grabbed Gomez and thrust one of the Glisson MK4s in his hands. The extended magpack was set to launch nothing but carnage rounds. Those would take off legs even if it didn't finish the bastards off. He shouldered his standard rifle and grinned.

"Now we're talking!"

Gi gave out all the other heavier weaponry. Not smart giving troops a new weapon in the midst of battle, but if what you had was ineffective, then you must adapt. Besides, I'd been a Ranger once, I knew they all trained on the Rattlers in basic, the damn Army was just too cheap to buy them. The Silka 88s they carried were sweet, reliable, and most importantly, cheap to build. We'd brought down a butt load of 5.56 ammo for those as well. The Rattlers had the edge on the Army's Silkas, but you just had to love the reliability of those weapons.

We were dropping them, but it didn't seem to slow them much. It still amazed me at the number and variety. Something had clearly changed, or Voss had been right about the possible number and variety of Hammer's productions sites. A smaller one of the things trampled over a larger corpse lying in the sand, its clawed foot pushing the bloodied head deeper into the dirt. That one didn't make it much farther as I sliced his neck open with a carnage round a split second later.

Fortunately, most of our shots were on the mark. There just were many more targets than we had trigger-pullers. My auto-targeting was synched with my team members, so we didn't shoot at the same targets unless they were within a certain range. Red-7 had their own system, though, and I found my rounds impacting multiple times with theirs. Ada flashed me a warning; she didn't need to as my warrior mind had come to the same conclusion.

Looking at Hauk, I told him we needed to move. This place was minutes from being overrun. He glanced my way, nodded, and gave the signal. Despite our differences, Hauk was not just capable, he was in the zone. The man was making good choices, listened to others, and seemed to have excellent battlefield presence. He would have had to in order to get this group all the way from central Texas.

One of Hauk's men caught something in the throat and went down spewing blood. *Did the beasts have weapons now?*

No... I could see they were picking up rocks and debris and flinging them with deadly speed and accuracy. Then one removed a knife from a downed soldier and sent it into the chest plate of a corporal who had just popped up to fire. The man coughed up blood and sagged down behind the embankment. The Furies were learning to use tools and improvise weapons. They weren't mindless. That was fighting. Despite my urging to the men to make every shot count, we just had to pour the firepower on in great gouts. 'Spray and pray' is what my old DI would have called it. And, as Stalin supposedly said, 'Quantity has a quality all of its own.'

Red-7 began to pull back, my guys were in better condition, so Banshee covered the retreat. It had sounded good when I had said it, but the reality made me second guess myself with every passing second. Objects smashed into my armor from three sides. Without the protection, they would be breaking bones and worse. A broken bone in this situation would be the same as a death sentence. That the creatures were learning how to fight even better and also as a group, was setting off alarm bells in my brain. This could be exponentially worse than I'd expected.

Banshee dropped Furies in singles and small groupings. Our shots were precise and coordinated, but more of them came at us. I could see their strange mandibles opening and closing and the odd needle-like teeth gnashing into the air. They were obsessed with ending us. What drove them to this insane level of ferocity?

We were killing all we could, but we weren't slowing them, not enough for Hauk's men to pull back to a safer position. *Shit,* there were no safe positions. The front lines of the beasts were coming in close now. Close enough, I didn't have to rise above the broken wall to strike killing blows. My rifle's targeting reticle's image fed directly into my HUD, allowing me to more or less pick them off. Not that I needed to stay hidden; the shit they were throwing would not injure me, but years of training said stay hidden. Also, when they noticed us, several of the things would charge our positions at a speed that was almost too fast to react to, much less track with a gun. I already knew first-hand the damage those claws could do to an armored soldier.

With sad realization, I knew we'd done all we could. Retreat chapped my ass as much as it did Hauk, but I gave the order anyway. Defending this Texas ditch accomplished little in the long-term. "Move your asses, boys!" I yelled and signaled to Red-7 that Banshee was coming in hot. I did not want to get shot in the face by the people we were here to help.

CHAPTER TWENTY

We ran flat out to get ahead of the damn things. A trained RDT soldier in full battle armor can reach speeds of forty-five miles an hour. I felt confident we exceeded that safety limit as I had to swing wide to make several turns, and I saw Gi lose traction and run into the side of an abandoned restaurant taking out a chunk of the wall.

Hauk had pulled his men into the burned-out ruins of what once had been a massive, ornate church. The roof and stained-glass windows were gone, but the walls were solid. It wouldn't work for long, but it was better than the exposed position we'd just fled.

"Damn, everything is bigger in Texas," Halo said walking by and looking from side to side.

"They like their churches here," a young boyish looking woman said. She was busy working on some of the wounded, and Sumo seemed glued to her side. Ada flagged her as the HVA, or high values asset, Red-7 had been tasked with securing. I was surprised to see she was wearing a Dragonhide Battleskin. These were German versions of the Revix model we wore, but when worn alone, it offered much better protection than ours.

Hauk motioned me over before I could even respond to her. No appreciation nor concern from the man. He was all business. "We need an exfil, Kovach. We can't fight them off much longer, even with you guys."

The man reminded me way too much of my dad. He was demanding, stubborn, and unflappable. Besides that, something about him just rubbed me the wrong way.

"We can get a dropship but not quickly." I had Ada running orbital vectors to see when the Stone Mountain would be back overhead. "Also, we won't all fit." The TriCraft were large, and if we removed the Wulf and everything else, we could probably hold a hundred people. Ada had flagged our current group at closer to 140 with around twenty of those injured and difficult to transport.

"We can leave the camels and a lot of our gear," Hauk said hopefully.

I shook my head. "It would take two trips and likely at least twenty-four hours between. Could half of your men survive an extra day?"

"Goddamnit!"

I felt the man's frustration, we just didn't have the assets available to do all that was needed.

"They're coming!"

We both turned back toward the voice. Disruptors began pumping out ordinance at an impressive rate. Red-7 had positioned them on the far left and right sides of the building.

We rushed civilians to the rear as soldiers lined every opening on the front wall and began firing again. Almost immediately, a giant Furie jumped over an abandoned car into the same door I'd just entered. The thing was massive. With one swipe of its razor-edged claw, it disemboweled two of Hauk's men. As guns turned toward it, the thing leapt sideways, crushing a young woman against the wall, then sped directly toward Captain Hauk.

I was firing, but I swear the thing could sense where all of our rounds were going. Gi shot the raging monster from about two feet away, pumping multiple rounds into him so fast that they blended into a single prolonged execution. The Furie barely noticed. It kept the bony armor toward us and the vulnerable thigh shielded. The creature began moving through the crowd of combatants as if on a single mission. The captain seemed to realize what that mission was before any of us. He was being targeted. Take out command and control, battlefield basics. And now our enemy had advanced its war-fighting capabilities yet again.

Hauk charged the creature firing his pistol with his right hand and a long knife gripped firmly in his left. This man wasn't going down without a fight. The Furie was taking lots of hits, some of them had to be scoring damage, but it didn't slow. Hauk's approach appeared almost in slow motion, then I saw the captain's expression suddenly change from anger to fear.

"No! Senior!"

Red-7's Senior Chief Grayson hit the captain knocking him aside just as the Furie struck with an open claw. The appendage snapped closed cleaving the old man's body cleanly in two. Hauk had rolled into a perfect firing position and stayed crouched as he lay rounds into the meaty part of the thing's thigh. The Furie crashed down with a sudden force that brought us all back to the present moment. I turned back to see dozens more of the things breaching the front wall.

Jordan Hauk knelt over Grayson's body; losing the man was hitting him hard, as it would all the men once they realized he was gone. Hauk knew he had to get up, get back in the fight, but the senior chief's sacrifice pushed him right up to and then over the line.

Even more of the Furies were charging up the church steps. We could hear the raspy wheezing howls and a clicking the things made with their rubbery mouths. It was unnerving, and I ordered Ada to filter it out of all our people's battle suit speakers. Then, the first of Red-7 men started running out of ammo.

A man beside Halo shot an obvious female creature that was leaping through the window frame, and his Silka went dry, the firing arm locking open on an empty ammo pack. The man checked his belt, then his chest rig before fully realizing he was completely out. Halo was dealing with his own issues but somehow realized the drama playing out to his right. He pushed the man out of the way of a downward strike by the female before slicing her in two with a carnage round fired point blank into her abdomen.

Others were clicking on empty mags as well. "Priest, get a bird up and find us something safer than this." Bishop 'Priest' Taggert moved back from the front line and reached into his suit's storage for one of the mini drones.

Our attackers were relentless; they never paused, never hesitated. Whatever genetic programming that was driving them must have been exceedingly precise because they just kept coming despite the pain we were delivering. I began to get a sense of what Red-7 had been going through for the past few days. It wasn't just the brutality of the fight; it was the fact that it never ended. They just moved from one bloody skirmish to the next. We had to break that pattern… somehow.

Priest moved in beside me and pointed to the screen. "May have an exit, Boss. It's ugly but could work."

*Yeah, shit…*it was ugly. If we'd been up against a conventional enemy, it would never work. In fact, half of the journey would be through a nearly perfect shooting trap. Lucky for us, the Furies didn't have guns… not yet at least.

Something on the screen caught my eye. I tapped to zoom in without knowing why. The reptilian part of my brain had spotted something it thought was important.

"What is it, Prowler?" Bishop asked.

I zoomed in and out several more times before it hit me. I was looking at a building that was on fire. The K8's had taken most of it out along with several abandoned autocars nearby.

"That fire…" I said. "Look how the creatures are avoiding it."

"Well, yeah, Boss. They're ugly, not stupid."

"No, they're hanging way back, giving the entire area a wide margin. Some look like they don't even want to approach it."

"Yeah, well, that's a pretty energetic fire when those battery stacks cook off."

"Those lithium batteries give off a lot of heat and…" I checked with Ada. "Shit… tons of noxious gasses."

I gave an all-channel call to switch to incendiary rounds and target the cars on the street. Our Rattlers couldn't do that, but I knew the Army guns could. To his credit, Captain Hauk was back in the game and quickly buzzed my comms. I filled him in with what I was thinking and our next escape plan. "It's time to get out of here, Captain."

"I am fucking tired of retreating, Kovach. Let Banshee take point, my lead fire team will take rear guard. Just protect the HVA. Her name is Xero, she is all that matters."

I wasn't going to argue with him, and if my plan worked, we should soon have a wall of intense flame between us and the attackers.

"By the way," he continued, "I think we will fit on your damn dropship now."

The number of dead and injured continued to add up. It wasn't my job to keep track of his men, but he obviously was. He'd hoped for the calvary, instead he'd gotten me.

I slapped Priest and yelled–"Move, move, move!"

Simon began corralling the civilians into a bunch. We pushed the mass down a series of corridors putting distance and walls between us and the enemy.

"Hard stop, coming up," Halo said.

Indeed, I'd seen the solid wall blocking our improvised exit plan. One great thing about having the best battle armor in service, we get to show off sometimes. "Take it down."

Halo and Priest charged the wall, both using sensor feeds to target weak spots between the reinforcing spars inside the polycrete wall. They hit with the mass of a truck and laid out a six-foot section of wall right into the alley we wanted to use for our exit. "Sumo, up front."

"Hauk, we are out, follow close."

The group we were with included Xero and a half dozen other civilians and several medics carrying litters. I told them to follow Priest. Gi and I guarded the intersection between the alley and cross streets. So far, none of the Furies had spotted us back here, but I wasn't counting on that lasting. I took a moment to glance at the drone feed still streaming in. Hauk had done a good job building a wall of fire. The Furies were not crossing it, but they were racing to get around it at each end. I could warn Red-7 that their flanks were vulnerable, but if they hadn't moved by now, they were just being stupid.

As if in response, I saw the first of his primary force exiting behind us. A corporal and a lieutenant took up guard positions opposite me and nodded me to go forward. I did like how these guys operated. Even under intense pressure, I had yet to see any of them falter.

We raced in the fading daylight, the sounds of pissed-off mutant monsters never far behind. But for the first time that day, it seemed we had won a round. Seeing Hauk's face as he exited the church last let me know he did not feel the same way.

CHAPTER TWENTY-ONE

We took refuge in an abandoned welcome center just off Beach Road. I knew Hauk was pissed, hell, I would be, too. Nothing I said would bring the man into a useable headspace... not yet. He'd just lost a third of his men, and that was during a retreat.

"He's a good man," Xero said moving up beside me and speaking low.

I eyed the person talking. She, they, were looking at Jordan, too.

"I know he is. He's just in an impossible situation right now. We all have missions that go sideways, Xero. Some... just worse than others."

She gave a grim smile. "You ever lose to monsters?"

"They are all monsters, the human kind maybe worst of all."

I walked over, pushed a few of the dust-laden pillows off a chair and sat heavily, loosening the magnetic clasps on my body armor. "We don't fight civilized people. When an enemy will take your life or give up his, there's no real difference between them and those abominations back there."

Xero nodded. "So, Master Sergeant, who do you report to now? CenCom is gone, right?"

I shrugged. "Good question." Sumo came over, and I handed him one of our protein bars from my pack. I tossed another to Xero. "I'm just trying to help out. Gather enough warfighters to maybe make a difference when we find who's behind this." My dog looked at me, obviously displeased with my limiting his rations. He'd worked damned hard, too. I handed him another.

"I had a contact," Xero offered as a way of introduction.

I waited for more. Honestly, I was exhausted and just wanted sleep. Even with my upgrades, or maybe because of them, I seemed to need even more rest. "You are the HVA," I said, biting into a protein bar of my own. Besides rest, my new body also demanded food… constantly.

Xero gave a sad nod. "Apparently."

"I'm listening." I watched as Captain Hauk finished the rounds with his men and headed in our direction. "You think the attack was an inside job?" I asked before biting off most of the chewy cardboard brick that passed for ration bars.

The woman… yeah, I was going to call her that, she'd already made it abundantly clear she couldn't care less how I referred to her. Xero's face confirmed I had scored a hit.

"What do you know?" she asked.

"Oh, no… you first. You're the HVA."

She blew a sigh of disgust. "It was highly coordinated. I was tracking a data breach, a massive Zero Day hack. Biggest one I'd ever seen. I'd been warning…"

Her voice faded off. Her work was obviously classified, as was who or what she reported to.

"An enemy doesn't need weapons of mass destruction as long as they can use yours… right?" I said, offering a guess.

The slight smile flashed again before nodding.

"Do you have a name? A location?"

She shook her head, her short, dark hair rushing down in front of her eyes before she raked it back. "I am getting close, was getting close," she amended.

"Arleen Hammer, Magnus Reichert," I offered.

She looked genuinely surprised. Then something like recognition blossomed behind her eyes. She reached a hand up and turned my face. Her finger traced the ridge of scarring behind my left ear. "It was you." Her next words ended abruptly as Hauk stepped up nearly between us.

"Can I borrow you …Captain?"

He said the last like my newfound rank was something that dropped out of a dog's ass. Couldn't really blame him for that. I stood and slowly followed the man out.

"Look," he said in a tone that probably didn't get challenged very often. "You need to stay away from the asset."

I couldn't quite place the look he was giving me. *Was he jealous*?

"He saw her touching your face, Joe," Ada said internally. "So, yes, read his body signs. Flared nostrils, elevated heart rate and blood pressure. The man has developed an emotional connection to the asset."

"Or wants one," I subvocalised to my AI. "Captain, I'm just here to help, but make no mistake. Do not get in my way. I'm going to find out who was behind these attacks and how to stop this alien fucking duckhunt."

My right hand pointed at the remnants of his troops. "They need a win, Hauk. Shit, we all do." My guys were just as worn out as Red-7. The Korean sergeant was sprawled out on the floor fast asleep. Halo was helping Bishop clean the mud out of his suit, but I could see they were both exhausted, too. Seventeen hours of near constant fighting, and we were all feeling like Monday morning after a weekend bender.

"Kovach, I lost good men today. Shit, we lost plenty just getting this damn far. I have to finish the mission. We must make these losses mean something."

"Where was she supposed to go?"

He shrugged. "Not my part of the op. Red-7 was to deliver her back to the Arago. From there, who knows?" He'd been protecting Xero, trying to justify to himself and his men that the mission was worth it. After everything happened, that had to be a tough sell, even if it was just to convince yourself you were doing the right thing.

"It's going to be worth it," I offered.

"You and Banshee are drop troops, you don't see the shit like we do."

I arched my eyebrows, ready to challenge him on that, but Ada suggested I let him go on.

"Down here, its personal. We see the loss, the love, the regret. We learn names and faces, then see them on toe-tags attached to corpses."

"War is always personal, Captain. Just like any disaster is."

His gaze was again looking out over what was left of his men. "We've never fought for home before, Joe. Not like this."

I could challenge that we always fought for home, but I knew what he meant. Not many recent skirmishes had been on U.S. soil.

"Little town about twenty miles inland, I think it was called La Carisa or something. Not a living soul there. Supposed to be over 6000 residents, and we didn't find one living thing. No people, no pets, not even a damn ant farm. Just those vines, blood everywhere, and tiny tracks all over. Not the prints your lizard hybrids make...something else."

I picked up a stick and drew a few marks on the ground. A short line on the left, longer one on the right and a double dot between them.

He sucked in air and looked at me, nodding. "What are they?"

"I called them murder-crabs... small battle droids with straight razors for claws."

"Fuck!"

"Yeah and no, those aren't the worst either, but they are freaky as hell. They do a synchronized little death-dance before they try to dismember you. Like a horde of whirling surgical knives looking for anything to slice to pieces."

The fatigue washed over Jordan as well. I could see it in his eyes. A bone-tired weariness that only other soldiers seem to fully understand. I pulled a bottle and two cups from my pack, pouring some whisky into each.

"You remember hell week?"

He smiled and nodded. "We thought that was the worst it could ever be, didn't we? It sucked, but nothing prepares us for the shit we just saw."

"No one is prepared, Captain, no one could be."

He looked at me strangely. "You were. You handled those creatures like they were nothing."

I had a cracked rib that suggested otherwise, but I let his words have the space they deserved.

"We've met before," I said.

"The Furies."

I nodded, "And the crabs and... worse."

He didn't press, and I left it alone for now. I'd give the man a full briefing but not tonight. Tonight, we just needed to rest and recover... wait for Bayou to send Packer down for exfil.

"I've heard rumors about you," he said. "And your dad."

Here it comes, I thought. Just like so many times before. Someone who viewed me through the distorted lens of my father's exaggerated reputation.

"You're better than I expected. You are...capable."

Wow! Coming from an Army man, that was indeed high praise.

"I heard about you, too."

He looked at me side-eyed while he sipped, poised to spring if I said the wrong thing. "Bayou told me about the op to go get your brother. You killed a shit-load of tangos, brother. Solid bit of soldiering." We clinked cups, bourbon sloshing out of mine.

He nodded his acknowledgement; I took it as a signal for peace. We sat there drinking and listening to the sounds of the surf and frogs.

"We need to end this," Hauk said.

"Agreed." I just had no clue how to make that happen. We were on the edge of a coastal campground. In happier times, campers and RVs would have lined the auto-charge stations. We could hear the waves crashing on the beach a hundred yards away. In the fading daylight, I could see the silhouettes of soldiers patrolling the water's edge. Would life ever return to what it was? Was this the new normal?

"Hauk, I'm not a very likable guy. In fact, feel free to hate me...lots of smart people do. I am a damn good soldier, though. I'm not here to have some pissing contest with you. You need me, I need you. Let's work together to do some good... deal?" I held out a hand.

He stood there staring at me for an uncomfortable amount of time, then reached out and pressed his calloused palm into mine.

CHAPTER TWENTY-TWO

We were up before dawn. Jordan Hauk and I both knew this place wasn't defensible. I still didn't know what was going on with Bayou up there but felt sure she had her hands full. I'd assigned Ada the task of finding us a good bolthole to use for cover until the drop ship could reach us. The only good thing about Red-7 being at half strength was we didn't need as much space.

"Show me."

It was a National Guard Armory. Unlike most, this one was old and still contained a fortified fallout bunker. Just over eighteen kilometers.

"Take us most of the day to get there." Still, it was a good spot. I sent the feed over to Captain Hauk's combat AI.

"I know why the Stone Mountain has been unresponsive," Ada said. "Someone is actively jamming her signals. Incoming and outgoing."

"Who?"

"Unknown."

Shit, that was perfect. "We need an exfil, half these guys need emergency medical treatment, we won't last long on this coastline." I checked my suit's radiation monitor. Something I had been avoiding until now. It was in the amber range of numbers but beginning to dip toward the red.

"Try my dad, see if he can get us some answers."

"You want me to call your dad?"

"Yeah, I'm not loving the thought either, but he always has good intel."

Hauk sent me an affirmative response on the new target location. I could hear his lieutenant getting the men up and moving already.

We broke camp and were on the move before sunrise. Seventy-eight men and women and one dog. I'd worried about the HVA, but Xero proved herself more than capable. She had an athletic build, and although her pack was lighter than the military loads we carried, she handled herself well. I assigned Halo to shadow her. Hauk had Private Gomez doing the same.

"Hi, Joe?"

The voice on my comms was not at all whom I had expected, The feminine tone was definitely not my dad's.

"Voss?"

The last time I had heard that voice she had just kissed me, and then she shot me. Both actions were inappropriate and deeply disturbing to my shaky mental health. Somehow, now all I could think about was the damn kiss, though.

"Yep, so how you doing?"

"I'm great, Voss, no thanks to you."

"Never know," she said.

Her tone made me wonder if she knew something I didn't.

"You're on-planet."

"Okay," I said noncommittally.

"Texas?"

"Jesus Christ, Ada, does everyone have access to my data feed?"

A red question mark icon appeared in my visual overlay. My AI had no clue what I was talking about. Just like my dad's calls, she didn't seem to be able to listen in on Damiana's either.

"What do you want, Voss?"

"Can we go back to me being Dami?"

It was hard to concentrate jogging down the side of the road in full battle kit, but yeah... no. "We definitely can't go back there," I answered.

I was pissed, this woman had used me to get something and then killed me. Maybe I was being petty but that's a hard thing for me to get past.

"Okay, Kovach, look. You mentioned a name when we were at Ranier. Nevis Carlson, do you recall that?"

Why was this woman not surprised I was still alive? "Yeah, of course." My upgraded mental facilities seemed to have near perfect memory recall now. Strangely I hadn't thought about Magnus mentioning that name until now. Doctor Magnus Reichert was the man who'd overseen my own enhancements and apparently the development of some of the mutant shit we were now fighting.

"Is he behind this? Did you find him?

There was a long pause. "Not exactly."

Xero sat on the hard bench listening to the sound of a bird off in the distance. The cooing echoed through the horribly misshapen pines lining the shoreline.

A memory surfaced from her past, the bird was a mourning dove. Mourning for the loss of a loved one, a mate, or maybe for the entire world. It was all gone now, wasn't it?

"It's gone," she whispered to the wind.

The world we knew is no more. Her world had disappeared when Valyn was transferred from Houston to Luna. No... if she were being honest, it was when she filed her report on the internal hacks.

No one in power wanted to believe anyone on the inside could be doing all this.

The dove's mournful song came again, carried on the wind along with the intense smell of rot.

She was so tired and had already seen so much death. All because of her. If Captain Hauk hadn't come to her aid, she would have been gone weeks ago, now nearly half of his team was dead. They called her a high-value target, but to her, she had no value... not anymore.

"I tried to warn them," she whispered. "I fucking tried." All she ever wanted to do was make a difference. She had a broad base of genius level knowledge, yet maintained it inside the shell of an antisocial misfit. One that turned off most people; no one cared what she knew.

My hand held a cup out in front of her.

"Drink up, Xero. Damiana Voss said we need to finish our talk."

CHAPTER TWENTY-THREE

She sipped delicately. Her eyes never seemed to move away from me. It was not like she was into me… more like she was studying me… every inch of me. I didn't feel like I needed to guide this discussion, so I waited on her.

"Is it active?"

Intuitively, I thought I knew what she meant, but I wanted clarification. "It?"

"The enhanced battle AI."

"Joe," Ada said softly, "I believe this person is one of my original programmers. She was a contractor used by the DARPA lab Magnus was attached to."

"She is," I answered Xero's question.

She smiled. It was unexpected and radiant. "Can I speak with —her?"

"Hello, Xero, I am called Ada." Ada's soft voice came out of my suit's speaker and inside my own head.

"You programmed her?" I asked Xero.

"I was one on the team. I developed several of the core algorithms."

"Joe, she was key," Ada interrupted speaking internally. "Her programming architecture allowed for fluid development and the fully integrated operating state an embedded AI must be able of adapting to."

"It sounds like it has been a success," Xero said.

I honestly didn't know how to respond to that. I didn't think of Ada as a program or app. She was more a part of me and a partner. Truthfully, I couldn't imagine life without her.

"She's a dumpster fire," I said. "Total incompetent."

If Ada was human, she would have shot fruit juice out her nose she laughed so hard.

"We manage," my AI said laughing. "Joseph is still in training."

Xero smiled again; it was a good smile. She enjoyed meeting some of her work now that it had matured. "I'd love to do an exam on you at some point. See how the neural network has evolved."

I think she was asking my computer, but I answered for both of us. "Ok, but later. First, I need to know what you know. Nevis Carlson," I said as a way of kicking things off.

Xero looked puzzled, then contemplative. "He was the director."

"Of?"

"The DARPA oversight committee. He..." her voice trailed off. "Are you suggesting he was behind the Zero Day attack?"

"I am. He is one possibility. I need to know why eradicating the planet would have appealed to him."

She looked off momentarily, then started to speak but seemed to think better of it. Finally, she said, "He was in a key position, I suppose it could have been him. Very well off, highly placed, but..."

"But?" I asked.

"I don't know. He just seemed, you know... sad. Not really capable of something like this. He was a bureaucrat, a manipulator sure, but not sure I can buy into all this being on him. More of an aging frat boy with a trust fund and insider connections than a terrorist mastermind."

"Ada, send Xero our files from the Nightmare Factory."

"Done," came the nearly instant reply.

"What you did and the things you probably saw with Reichert in the labs was only a small portion of what was going on. I know you realize that," I said. She nodded. Thanks to Ada, I now knew her background in ethical hacking and some of what she had uncovered on the days leading up to the attack. "If they had only listened to you. All of this might have been avoided."

Her deep, brown eyes were filling with tears. I understood her frustration. It was too late for 'what-ifs,' though. Far off, I heard a night bird cooing.

The discussion lasted long into the night, and for once, I had more data than I could sift through. Interesting thing about having received newfound mental intelligence, it didn't make you smarter… not immediately and not in very many obvious ways. Ada explained it as if my brain was a local library. If they tripled, or hell, quadrupled its size, it would hold tons more knowledge, but it would still be a library. My brain was still a brain.

"So, we agree that Nevis Carlson is a likely target but not the top guy. We also have no clue if he is still alive or where he is."

Xero nodded. She had the anxious look that told me she needed something. A fix maybe. "What's your crutch?" The bourbon was no longer enough.

She shook her head, "You don't wanna know."

"Come on, weed, juice, oxy…we need to get through this."

"Sex."

Hmmm… I did not see that coming.

She smiled. "Sorry, I have a hypersexual condition due to increased hormone levels. Sometimes… often, I just need a fix." She held up the empty cup. "The bourbon helps, though. Another shot?"

I poured. She was smart and cute, and I liked the shit out of her, but I wasn't crawling in the sack with her. I told her she should go see Jordan.

"Captain Hauk?" she asked, both eyebrows raised in surprise.

How is it that they attach the most brilliant minds to some of the dumbest people? Dumb as in reading others, common sense, understanding social norms. It constantly amazes me.

"Yeah, I think he has a thing for you… pretty sure, in fact. Ada, do you concur?"

"Totally has the hots for you, Xero. Not sure how comfortable he is with it, but Joe is accurate."

Xero tossed back the two fingers of whiskey and wiped an arm across her mouth. "Damn! Didn't see that one coming."

I smiled. “Pay him a visit tonight. I think it will do you both a world of good.”

I sighed and looked off into the darkened sky.

“One last thing… tell me what you know about Voss.”

CHAPTER TWENTY-FOUR

SAFEZONE, SOMEWHERE IN THE MIDDLE EAST

The man crouched low and belly crawled through the low dunes. He'd been trained in Russia and various TWC terrors camps, including the Yemen Special Reserve. He was confident, skilled, and ruthless. Still, this night he was apprehensive.

The world ending less than a month ago could certainly be part of his nervousness, but Allah would prevail. The end of the world was basically like any other Wednesday back in the village of his birth.

He clicked on the tracker; it signaled a drone in VLO, or very low orbit. That was when his nerves always ratcheted up. Like most professional soldiers, he feared his clients as much as his targets. Once he switched on that he was in position, his client held the ultimate high ground. One deselected uranium slug to the back of the head fired from very low Earth orbit left little traceable evidence behind.

The target was sitting on a chaise lounger overlooking a perfect, azure pool. The island resort of Majorca. If there had been a world ending attack, he, nor the resort, seemed to be taking any notice. He signaled the rest of the team.

The sun had disappeared many hours earlier, now it was well past midnight. The bartender had already issued last call three times, but the lovely woman and several others nearby were ignoring his pleas to go to bed.

Through his special Steiner optics, the man eyed the long-legged beauty. She was offensive to his Muslim beliefs in so many ways.... still, she made him have thoughts he preferred to ignore. Her Western cut swimsuit left little to the imagination, but he caught glimpses of something wrapped around her right arm. A bracelet, or bangle, perhaps. She would be dead soon, that was all that mattered. He clicked the comm twice to advise he had eyes on the target.

Suddenly, a foot caught him in the side of the head. He moved to swing his sound-supressed Silka 88 up, but a fist slammed into his nose with tremendous force. Blood sprayed out, and his eyes watered. He could no longer see the assailant. If he could have focused those eyes, he would have seen his target still lounged by the pool. Her friends still joked and carried on, oblivious to the violence taking place a few hundred yards away.

~

Damiana Voss was very, very good at what she did. Despite her striking good looks that still turned heads, she had mastered the art of blending in anywhere. Here, in this opulent and exclusive desert oasis, it had been a challenge to not be noticed. There were only a few hundred guests and nearly as many staff. The five-star enclave was a pit stop for the uber rich; even celebrities had to wait for an opening to get a reservation.

As her mother would have said, this place smells of old money and superb wine. She sat back on the bed. The sheets had a thread count so high they should get a nosebleed. Yes, the world had ended a few weeks ago. Monsters now ruled much of the planet, but the rich hadn't yet taken notice. Well, not all of them.

Voss jammed the taser into the man's neck again and used the setting that would produce tremendous pain without causing unconsciousness. He spasmed violently, his arching body straining the bindings that held him tight to the antique chair. Nevis Carlson had taken the bait, just like her mother had thought. "He is a weak man, a weak man who doesn't know that he is," she'd said.

Now let's see what this assassin knew. She slipped a small item out of a zippered pouch. It was no larger than a postage stamp and appeared just as innocuous. Peeling back the thin polymer liner, she carefully placed it to the man's throat and pressed the center releasing the serum. A mixture of drugs the Sisterhood had been developing for decades absorbed quickly through the skin and into the bloodstream. It was a truth serum of sorts but had other uses as well.

She studied her smartwatch as the timer ticked down from three minutes. She checked his pulse, then opened both eyelids to verify that the intravenous agent had indeed latched on to the appropriate neural receptors. If he tried to answer dishonestly or not answer at all, the serum oils would activate various pain receptors with no other action from her.

Damiana squeezed the man for every crumb of information he possessed. "What do you know of Nevis Carlson?"

The assassin struggled to answer, then grimaced as the negative response triggered a lightning bolt of pain throughout his system. His violent response was every bit as bad as when she had tazed him, but this time, she hadn't needed to lift a finger.

"You...you can't torture me," the man struggled to say. Spittle ran down his face from a mouth that was sagging slightly on one side. He was Middle Eastern, perhaps Lebanese. She would know for certain in a few minutes.

"I could," she began. "I might even enjoy it, but torture is unreliable. There is only so far you can push someone with physical or even mental duress. Eventually, they will simply tell you too much, they will admit to anything. That does me no good. The biological I just dosed you with is triggering your pain receptors with no physical damage. So, despite your suffering, you can actually endure this all day... assuming you are half as tough as you think."

She patted his knee as she stood and moved to the bed where the meager contents of the man's pack had been dumped. "You are wondering about the woman... the one at the pool, as well as your other men, I suppose."

Damiana saw in the man's face that he was. The woman was a Sister, of sorts. One that bore an uncanny resemblance to herself, but she wouldn't give the man any satisfaction of that knowledge. "Just shows how incompetent you are at your job. And your men... well, I paid them each a visit before you. Now, tell me everything you know about Nevis."

And so, it began. Just over forty-five minutes later, she left the suite, the drug cocktail inside the man's veins moving on to the final iteration. Causing the complete organ failure, then erasing itself from the victim's bloodstream. Not that anyone would bother with forensics these days.

The man hadn't known as much as she had hoped. One nugget he had offered was he was not alone. Someone else was on the contract. She slipped into her own suite and eyed the luxurious tub. She could have really used a hot bath and dinner. Instead, she donned her night watch cap and added the man's rifle to her armaments. Voss needed to go hunting... again.

CHAPTER TWENTY-FIVE

RED ZONE TEXAS

I was crawling back to the burning vehicle. This was not how I had expected breakfast to go, but hell, welcome to combat. Days or weeks of complete boredom interspersed with moments of chaos and terror that may define the rest of your life or just as easily end it.

My mind was racing to fill in the gaps as to what in the holy fuck was going on. The scene reminded me of a mission in Jordan where insurgents snuck inside the line and placed multiple IEDs triggered to go off at morning mess. It had been damned effective and ultimately helped me decide to rotate out to Space Force.

I ran to a group of people and rolled to a stop near them beside a broken wall. The company's XO was attempting to contact someone on the Milcrypt Comms. He looked up and shook his head.

"What... Are... We... Fighting?" Yes, I spoke loudly and slowly as I hadn't had coffee yet.

"Don't know, Prowler, reports of several of those Furie things jumping the front lines."

I looked around at everything burning. "Did they bring RPGs?"

The man looked away. "Some men..."

I got it, cutting him off. His own men had fired blindly into the compound. "Direction!" I snapped. He pointed. "Secure weapons, if they are not positive of the target, Lieutenant." I stood and began moving in the direction he'd indicated. It was where the smoke was thickest.

"Hey, Kiddo, how the fuck are ya?"

My father's timing was uniquely horrible, or maybe he did it on purpose. I saw scaly legs moving with incredible speed toward a group of soldiers. I sped up to intercept.

"Doing good, Pops." It did no good to be honest with him. I dropped to a knee and fired off several of the carnage rounds praying they hit the damn thing I was aiming at. They didn't. One cut through a tree and the other sliced part of a support trailer in half. Oops.

"Sounds like you're busy, I'll make this brief."

Something slammed into my right side with the force of an autotruck. *Jesus Christ!* I grabbed at it, but it sailed away. Inertia is a bitch, and now, thanks to my newest upgrade, I could teach everyone the computational physics I was using as I moved awkwardly through the air, I thought again that I should be fucking better at this. The first enhanced super soldier, and I was getting whipped by lizards.

"I am going to patch in some asshole from Luna. He's the prick who wants your hidey-hole of a ship. He's been attempting to take remote command, but so far, has only managed to cut off the comms array."

"Roger that," I said grimacing. My rib was only partially healed from the last time.

"What's his..." I heard the hiss and the telltale metronome beep of signals coming in from the moon.

I saw the Furie that had blindsided me. He was moving toward a downed soldier. I ran at him returning the favor. Hitting it was like hitting a block of polycrete. I went down; it just stood there staring down, its reptilian eyes flicking the lids from each side. Then Sumo hit the bastard in the face. *Hell, yes! That's my dog!*

Vaguely, I was aware of the voice on my comms. "Sorry, could you repeat that?"

"Is this Captain Kovach?" A gruff voice growled.

"It is, and to whom am I speaking?"

"This is Admiral Reese of Luna Command. Acting War Commander Reese," the man said, adding emphasis each time he mentioned his rank.

"My God, he's an ass, isn't he?" my pops interjected. Sumo had a chunk of the beast in his mouth. It seemed to match the missing spot on the creature's face. I stepped in to do my part.

"What can I do for you... sir?" I asked as I hit the thing in the thigh, then leveraged it over my head using my body as the fulcrum. Worked great, but I had forgotten about the hooked razor claw which caught me under my good arm and ripped through the armor and yeah, it began peeling away flesh. My... flesh.

"I want my ship back, Captain, and I use that term loosely, No one can explain how you got a multiple rank promotion when Fleet Command is offline."

Shit, that hurt. I punched the goddamn thing in its fucking mouth. "Probably the same way you made War Commander... sir." *Yeah,* that was a dick move. But then again, I'd been an asshole way longer than I'd been a captain. Hey, I did add the 'sir' to the end.

"That was a dick move," my pops said. Followed by, "I like it. Shoot, let's all make up new titles for ourselves. I am King of Cedar Key and the lower half of part of the county of Levy. Not the part currently overrun by monsters... someone else can rule there."

I brought an armored knee down into the face of the Furie with a sickening crunch. I wasn't entirely sure if the crunch came from me or it. Ada had my pain receptors dialed down so low, I could no longer tell.

"I'm waiting," the admiral said impatiently. Obviously, I had missed more of the conversation while my dad had talked right over the other man's comms signal, but technically, I was otherwise engaged.

"For what?"

"Look, Son, you can address me as Admiral or War Commander. I am a superior officer and deserve that level of respect."

"Go fuck yourself!"

"Excuse me?" the man said stammering. He obviously wasn't used to being spoken to like that.

"You heard me. You fucking washed-up twat. Fuck you! You have no skin in this game. You run an unnecessary auxiliary base that was all but unaffected by the actions on Earth. Unpin my ship's comms array, and once we have secured the known enemy combatants, we will make arrangements to make a stop at Gateway."

I studied the piece of my own skin hanging down knowing it should hurt way more than it was.

"You do have the ability to shield yourself mentally from all of the pain," Ada said, reading my thoughts again. I focused on the arm, and indeed, I was controlling the pain. I eased back on the setting and holy fuck, it hurt like hell. I quickly dampened it back down. I wasn't sure if it was better if she handled that or me.

"Captain Hauk is moving a fireteam into a pincer move," the AI said.

"Good." I was growing less impressed with the legendary Red-7, but they had been through hell.

"Multiple targets," she said.

"You going to unmute him?" my dad said. "I want to hear this shit."

I hadn't even realized I had, but sure enough, the flag officer was using all manner of words to let me know what high treason was and what the Space Force equivalent of keelhauling involved. "You are a pirate, and how you ever..."

I cut the feed as I belly crawled to a position where I should be able to lay eyes on one of the two remaining monsters. "Ada, do whatever it takes to retake full control of our ship. Permanently lock out that asshole and anyone else who attempts to commandeer the vessel. And get us a goddamn drop ship!"

My Rattler barked twice, and an arm and a leg disintegrated from the target's body. That felt good. Hauk and his men dropped the other one before I even had eyes on it. The company medic was suddenly at my arm applying a field dressing.

"We lost both of the camels," Captain Hauk said, walking up and eyeing the scene. "Where's our ride?"

The camels, or CM-L's, were the modern military's pack mules. Agile autonomous cargo haulers that could go nearly anywhere. Each carried food, munitions, and medical supplies for a platoon. Jordan Hauk had been using the other to transport the worst of the wounded.

"I'm working on it."

To be honest, my AI was working on it. I had a feeling that Bayou would send the TriCraft down anyway in time, assuming the 'war commander' hadn't locked them out of the hangar deck as well. I'd left

Riggs in an impossible situation just to come down here and what...give this man's platoon false hope?

"Work faster, Kovach," Hauk said before stomping off. The medic finished taping up my arm and also disappeared.

"You're welcome," I whispered.

"You told a fleet officer to fuck off, Joe. Are you sure that was a wise move?" Ada asked, her voice a well-modulated monotone offering no sign of what she thought. She was, after all, military property and honestly might have some backdoor access that the admiral could use against me.

"Probably not, but it felt good."

"Kid, you know before I die, I was hoping you would make something of yourself...I should have been more specific," My pops said.

The line went dead as my dad once again offered me not one shred of anything helpful.

CHAPTER TWENTY-SIX

Xero was waiting for me when I got back to the armory building. She eyed the bandage on my right arm.

"Fighting with the locals again?"

I ignored her. We both knew the wound wasn't serious.

"Why does it seem like we have more people?" I asked, looking at the crowded room.

"We do, basement bunker had survivors," Xero said.

That stung, I hated to be heartless, but that put our numbers out of reach for a single dropship again. I followed the woman's eyes and saw the captain out there checking on his men.

"You still haven't fucked him?"

She smiled and shook her head. "He's still as honorable as ever?"

"Worse, never met a guy as hard to read as Jordan Hauk."

"Not even Damiana?" she asked.

She had a point. Damiana Voss had been with Carol Reynolds, two strangers that I'd picked up in Virginia just after Last Day. Both had seemed desperate to get out of an unpleasant situation and offered to help me find one of the other Hammer Industries facilities. Only later would I learn Voss was working me; I was her asset at best.

"You know she shot me?"

Xero looked surprised, then asked me to show her where.

I dropped my torso section with the plate carrier and lifted my base layer up showing her the thin, white scar. It still amazed me I could heal this fast. The woman, girl, person, moved a slender finger over the area, then seemed to do some calculations.

"Were you near the end of your cycle? The drug regiment?"

Jesus, this chick was well informed. Hardly anyone inside the project knew that. I nodded.

"I think she saved your life."

"I don't think so…she ended it." But yes, I'd begun having the same thoughts.

She tilted her head and cocked an eyebrow.

"Technically, I was dead."

"Current observations would suggest otherwise."

I'd already gleaned that Xero had some insights into Reichert's augmentation project. I just wasn't sure to what degree. "Please continue."

She bit her lip, and I had to admit she was damn cute. Maybe we *could* have sex…or not.

"If your body had run its natural course, the organ rejection would have likely flooded your system with toxins and a flood of white blood cells. That would have sent you into shock, cardiac arrest, and likely liquefied much of your internals. By shooting you, she stopped all that, and if I am right, she was aware of a failsafe or system reset. Her shot looks like it would have grazed the edge of your spleen. An area in which I know they did significant modifications."

"I thought you were a computer hacker."

She raked her short hair back out of her eyes and looked past me. "I'm a polymath."

I'd heard the term but didn't recall it. Helpfully, Ada whispered the definition to me.

"You know lots of different things," I offered.

She nodded, "More than that, really. I am well versed and highly skilled in many different specialties. Knowing is not enough, you have to be able to recognize patterns, intuit information, sometimes make leaps that carry you further. That's why I am considered valuable."

"You saw all of this coming, didn't you?"

"The creatures...no."

"The war?"

She nodded. "I did. I wish I hadn't, but yes."

"You said you didn't know who was behind it, but you must have some suspicions."

"More like contenders," she offered.

"I need a name," I said.

"That I don't have... not yet."

"So why are you the HVA? You must have intel that someone wants to protect."

"Or someone they want to silence," she said.

"Well... shit." She had a point. I tried another path. "Something here in this country triggered the attacks. Our own assets were used against us?"

She nodded. "There were breaches, high level internal breaches."

"Where?" I needed actionable intel.

"Everywhere... DARPA, Hammer, Apex, NSA, Homeland. Hell, even the Texas Militia. You realize that a relatively small group of individuals worldwide essentially control everything?"

I shook my head. "Like a cabal or something?"

She stared past me as she considered her response. "Maybe it could simply be someone with enough money and influence. I personally can't think of anything much worse than trying to run the world, but the CIA did a study years ago detailing how it could happen. They said as few as 1500 individuals could bring about world change. Even less if they were very well placed and had additional help."

"Who would those people be? Who could do all this?"

"Not a who, Kovach... a what."

My brain jumped to where she was heading. "You are saying an AI started this war?" I asked. This was the stuff of sci-fi films and conspiracy theory nut-jobs for the last hundred years. I remembered the movie with the android foot stomping down on a shaman skull. Good movie, and then I thought about the Decimators. They would have made those T-1000s look like kids' toys.

Xero shook her head. "I am saying it was part of it. Nothing but a highly advanced AI could have planned this level of chaos or have breached those systems that fast or that thoroughly."

"Who has an AI with those kinds of capabilities?"

"Us, the U.S. Space Force, to be precise. Program started back around 2015 by the U.S. Air Force to develop a cyber task force of their own. They also got some of the very first quantum computing systems to get them started. They developed multiple highly effective AI systems mainly useful for research, predictive analysis, and pattern recognition. The Stetson, which was the projects codename basically did what the teams of data analysts using super-computers did, it just did it much, much faster."

"Are you suggesting Space Force's own AI," which was something I had never heard of, "that Stetson was...is sentient? It decided to wipe out humanity?"

She laughed. "No. I don't believe any AI has ever reached consciousness. I am one of those who maintains it never will, not by design at least. That would be a Level-5 AI. The best we can do is a moderate strong Level-3. Those can mimic complex sentience structure and nuanced conversation, but you probably know that better than anyone. You have one living in your head."

"Ada, your mom thinks you tried to kill the world."

"Pointless," my AI said out loud. "Humans breed like roaches, can't wipe you out."

I elected not to face palm my head or say "Duh!" Yes, Ada was developing a personality despite her programming.

CHAPTER TWENTY-SEVEN

IAS STONE MOUNTAIN

The ship's AI, Belle, confirmed what Bayou suspected. The lockouts to several key systems had been done remotely. It had taken Otero and her team several days to disable the remote access nodes.

"Comms array coming up now, Bayou."

"Thank you, get me Captain Kovach or Hauk as soon as possible." She'd already tried Kovach on her internal comms to no luck.

Moments later, her friend and boss's voice came through. "Bayou, you read?"

She smiled, "Good to hear your voice, Prowler."

"Same. What's the status?" Kovach asked.

She knew instantly he knew someone had been screwing with the ship.

"We're in stable orbit 250 miles up. Just got comms array back under our control. Maneuvering engines are still offline, but the SEs are working on those next. Any idea who did this?"

"Probably the admiral at Luna."

That jived with what she was thinking as well. "Any way we can block him out... or anyone else?"

Kovach queried his AI before answering, "Have to change the command codes at the highest level of authentication. Ada says she doesn't have access at that level." He paused as if he was talking to someone else, then added, "Get us a dropship down here, and I will send you someone who might help. Our HVA."

"Solid copy, Boss, but exfil may be a challenge."

Bayou checked the nav screen before giving him the bad news. "Without maneuvering thrusters, all we can do is stay in the rotational orbit that we initially took."

"That means you are only over Texas a few times each week, right?" Kovach asked, picking up on the problem. The TriCraft was great, but it worked best when used almost like an elevator. Drop it straight down right on target, make a drop-off or pick-up, and then ascend to the next adjacent orbit and wait for the mothership's next pass. There were some workarounds, but they put a lot of undue stress on the craft, and since it was the only operational way they had of traversing to and from the surface now, other than ballistic drop pods, no one wanted to risk it.

"Time to next intercept?"

"Just over three hours," Riggs answered. "After that we won't be back on that same line for three days unless Otero or your wunderkind down there can unlock those thrusters."

"We won't all fit in one trip. We have wounded and some equipment, but some will have to stay behind," Kovach said.

Deb knew he meant himself. He would not leave before everyone else did. "What else can I do for you, Boss?"

"Keep the high-ground, Bayou. I have a feeling we're going to need it."

"Hard copy on that."

Kovach needed one more thing. "Bayou, how is our contingent of Marines?" They had rescued the group from a destroyed ship a week earlier.

"Most are well enough to leave the med-bay now."

"Good." Kovach said. "We're going to fill it up on the first run. Something else, though..."

Bayou had a feeling she knew what was going on.

"You need to know where everyone's loyalties are?"

"You got it!" Kovach said quickly. "We have a lot of things to fight, we don't need to include any we are giving sanctuary to. You read me, LT?"

"Hard copy, Chief."

"Good... now get that boat on the deck as soon as possible. Let Packer know the LZ will almost certainly be hot. Let me know updates on the rest of your efforts to gain full control. Kovach out."

CHAPTER TWENTY-EIGHT

The first group extracted included the wounded, the HVI, and as many others as Packer could cram onboard. Hauk sent his second-in-command, Hadroop, and like me, stayed with his remaining men. They had fought off two more attacks, the last one included something new. A small coyote-type animal with a whip-like tail. They'd learned the hard way that the tail had a stinger and that it was armor-piercing and lethal.

I was a seasoned soldier, battle-hardened and fearless. But patrolling the nearby woods later that night had me on edge. Fear was something I was familiar with; we were old friends, but since meeting up with Voss's creature and its psionic capabilities, I knew our fears could be manipulated. Catching a glimpse of Sumo coming to attention, I focused on the combat dog, then what he had spotted. Ada automatically scanned all wavelengths to give me a target. On every spectrum, all I got was a black shadowy outline. Fuck, I was in trouble.

This was no Furie, this beast was massive. It towered over Sumo like a mountain. Its body was covered in thick fur, and its eyes glowed with an otherworldly light. I could sense the evil in this thing. In a flash of moonlight, I saw saliva dripping from razor-sharp teeth.

"Sumo, back," I whispered.

I knew we were outmatched, but of course, being a total dumbass, I refused to back down. I briefly considered if this was the beast that Hauk had thought was controlling the others, but no, this thing didn't look aquatic. Even in shadow, I felt like this was more bear or Sasquatch than little mermaid. I raised the pulse rifle and fired. The flare of carnage rounds lit up the entire scene, and I realized my target was not there. Sumo glanced at me confused and then did a full perimeter sweep. Our enemy was gone, or ...hiding.

There is something most people don't know about Tier-1 military teams. We don't get deployed that often, and when we do, we've usually trained on the exact mission for months. We study the terrain, we build mock-ups of the buildings, we study the enemy, their habits, backgrounds, weapons...everything, and I mean everything.

Now, we're meeting new threats every fucking day. Enemies no one could prepare for. Creatures that equaled or surpassed everything we could throw at them, and they still kept coming. We were not at our best, not even me. Joe Kovach, the super enhanced prototype for the future of the military. What a freaking joke.

The thing attacked, its jaws snapping at my throat. I rolled to the side, but the beast was too fast, and it caught me with a powerful swipe of its paw. I was sent flying, my body slamming into a tree. Jesus, this thing is strong. It felt like a dozier-bot had just swatted me into the outfield.

I staggered to my feet, my body aching from the impact. I heard Sumo go on full attack mode just before the beast was on me again, its jaws open wide. I punched the fucking thing in the face, but it was like hitting a wall. The goddamn thing roared in anger, then swiped at me with something sharp. In the darkness, I couldn't tell if it had a weapon or simply claws, but it fucking hurt.

I released my Heidelberg blade; my hand gripped it tightly as I stabbed and sliced. I felt it dig into the thick hide. I knew it had found muscle and bone. The thing moved back just out of reach, and I swear to God, it laughed. A very creepy, high-pitched almost human laugh. The sound sent chills up my spine and yes, I pissed myself. Just a bit.

We barely managed to dodge the next attack, but already I knew I was in trouble. I was hurt. Sumo kept darting in and taking bites, but the HappyBear or Bigfoot or whatever ignored the vicious attacks. He was solely focused on ending me. We were running out of options; I needed to get away, and fast.

I started to run, my augmented legs pounding the ground. I could hear the beast's roar growing closer, and I knew that it was gaining on me. We sprinted through the forest, dodging trees and jumping over fallen logs. I turned twice to fire at the thing, but both times it seemed to vanish from sight only to appear just off my sightline seconds later. I considered launching grenades but figured the same thing would happen.

I am not ashamed to say I was running for my life; I could feel my heart pounding in my chest. The fight or the fear was causing me to overheat badly, and I knew I couldn't go on for much longer. Sumo seemed to sense that I was faltering and stopped to take on the thing alone. He would give me time to get away.

"No, Sumo." I gave him the command to retreat. Not something either of us liked, but strategically it was the right move. I was running flat-out, faster than I've ever run before but could still hear the Happy-Bear's roar getting louder and occasionally more of the weird laughter. I was running out of time, and I knew we needed to find a way to escape.

Finally, I burst into a clearing and saw my chance. Ahead of me, I could see our perimeter line. I shouldn't have led the beast back toward our line, but I would not defeat this thing alone. Shit, who am I kidding, I would not defeat it at all. Sometimes, you just have to realize the game is rigged, and it's time to fold.

~

Halo and Priest were waiting by the armory. "We gotta move, boys," I said, running by at nearly full speed. The rest of my team quickly fell in behind.

"Um, Boss, why are we running?" Halo asked, struggling to keep up with my frenetic pace.

Priest quipped, "Second Battle Law of Kovach."

Halo shook his head. When he'd joined Banshee, the second in command had given him a weathered printout of twenty-five rules. The unofficial mantra of the squad. The second of these had read, 'If you see

Prowler running during a battle, you might want to try to keep up.' He kept up.

Hours later, Red-7's recon patrol reported back. "No sign of anything like you reported, Master Sergeant."

"It wasn't there?"

"Ada, you have the footage, the sensor data. Shit, I have the scars, and look at Sumo, he looks like hell."

"It was there, Joe. HappyBears are real."

Shit, maybe it was a Squatch.

~

I moved cautiously into the tumbledown structure. The interiors weren't in much better shape than the outside. Assorted furniture, desks, and broken chairs formed a rickety barrier near the far wall. Carpet, or perhaps just a rug, lay in shreds on a concrete floor. The cement stained with what might have been blood, or vomit, or who the hell knows.

Overhead, a long light tube flickered to life. The thing looked ancient, maybe even a fluorescent gas light. The illuminations cast everything into ghastly shades of sickly yellow. *How did this place still have power?*

Sumo ranged farther ahead; Halo was helping Hauk deploy what remained of his squad. The thought of a defensive perimeter seemed ridiculous after the day we'd had, but it was still the right play. That new fucking beast was still out there, even if no one else had seen it.

"Priest, find your way to God's country and keep us safe tonight." I would have preferred to have Darkman on sniper duty, but he'd bought the farm down in Costa Rica when some other mutant beast had trampled him in his sniper's hide. The thought that all these missions we'd been on for years, knocking out bio-labs and terrorist cells around the world, was exactly the same tech we were now fighting. More than once I'd personally had to hand over captured intel and data to Hammer personnel. Data they had obviously used to help build this army of mutant freaks.

Moving deeper into the building, I became aware of a smell. A mixture of swamp, salt air, and decay. It immediately transported me back to a canoe trip with my dad when I was fourteen. That would have been after Texas but before he shipped off to fight in the third Gulf War.

I moved around a clump of vines and moss that may have once been a computer workstation. I still had no clue as to what this place might have been, but the decay suggested decades of neglect, not just months. My mind subdivided, and part of it was back in that canoe in central Florida, the black water gliding past with only the occasional splash of a large swamp predator or some invisible bird taking flight to break the spell.

It had been hot and so humid, late July or maybe August. We'd made camp on the river the past two nights. I was tired and had scratched all day from the countless mosquito bites, but I refused to complain. Time with Pops was fleeting and often artificial, as if he was playing a role more than simply being himself. This day he was mostly silent, and what filled that silence was magical.

We rounded a sweeping bend in the river, and suddenly, the black water morphed into a dazzling crystal clear stream of such clarity I couldn't be sure we weren't floating on air. I could see the shadow of myself and the canoe a dozen feet below. My darker reflection seemed to stare back just as confused at what he was seeing as I was looking down.

Sumo's growl brought me to a sudden stop and my gun to my shoulder. I approached the darkened passage where the dog stood in his low guard position signifying an unknown threat. That could be good or bad. Sumo certainly knew what the Furies were now. He had a unique signal for them.

I moved past and switched on the Shitek night optics, which flooded the space with IR and NV illumination, which resolved itself in my HUD to a huddling mass of something in a far corner. The cascading mop of unkempt blonde hair suggested humans, but I took no chances. I signaled Sumo to close in.

The huddled figure made no move to flee or defend herself. Moving closer, I could definitely see she was female. The suit's sensors detected respiration, cardiac activity, and a variety of other signals that the girl was alive.

"She may be in shock, Joe," Ada offered.

I shook my head; we weren't in the rescue business, even though that seemed to be all we were doing this week. The smart thing for me was to make sure she was unarmed and continue clearing the structure. Sumo, though, had broken position and was nosing over to the girl... woman, person. He was not detecting a threat, and my partner's threat detector was even better than my own.

Sliding my helmet back into its receiver, I broke the silence, "Miss, are you okay?" You know, except for the end of the world, monsters trying to kill you, sleeping in one of the shittiest places on Earth. Yeah, I left all those details out. Her head continued to hang down, she continued to ignore me.

I spent several minutes attempting to assess the woman. I lifted her head, blank vacant eyes stared back at me. She had a massive gash across her chest, continuing up a once beautiful cheek, and disappearing into her hairline. Dried blood lined the wound, and small bluish globules hung to parts like an infectious fruit.

"Medic!" *We could at least treat her*, I thought, softening the guilt I knew I'd feel later. This woman was gone, her body just hadn't figured it out yet.

Hauk's men reported back that they, too, had found a survivor. An old man resting near the back corner of a warehouse space. I filled him in on our find, and we agreed to set up treatment areas inside the warehouse.

The old man was in better shape than the young woman but not much more helpful. He'd been on the move for days since the Furies moved in. He and his wife had lived in a high-end retirement community a dozen miles to the south. After the attack, they had been okay for a couple of weeks, but then they had to venture farther and farther out to find food.

"One day she just didn't come back," the man whose name we'd learned was Osan said.

He talked in detail about his adventures after that. His failed attempts to track her down. His first encounters with the lethal vines, and then just yesterday, he'd spotted and narrowly avoided a Furie.

"Damn thing scared the hell out of me. God did not make anything like that. Those creatures are not of this world."

I mostly agreed with him on that. "Did you know the girl, the one you probably passed inside?" The medical team had her on a gurney and brought her into the dimly lit warehouse now. They were busy treating her along with several others who'd been injured on the panicked run in from the armory.

Osan shook his head. "I wanted to stay outside so I could... you know, see them."

The man had no weapons, no pack, no food or water from what we could tell. Still, he looked in relatively good shape. How were any of these people surviving?

"Compound is secure," Halo reported almost an hour later. We'd all downed some calories and agreed on a makeshift guard rotation. Hauk had retreated even further since Xero had left. I think we were all counting the minutes until the TriCraft could return.

"How's she doing?" I asked the corpsman who was assigned to the survivor. Our eyes met, and I saw the doubt.

"Stable, but extreme shock." He stroked a hand through her unkempt hair. It was an unexpected tenderness from one stranger to another. "It's up to her. She has to decide whether she wants to live or not."

I considered that as I moved away. Honestly, I'm not sure what the better outcome for her might be. Osan was finishing a ration pack and smiled when he saw me approaching. In the man's mind, we had bonded, I guess. In a way, he did remind me a little of my father, but the Asian face and clipped English quickly distanced him from the recent memories of my old man. Osan nodded his head toward the rear of the building. I followed.

Captain Hauk was already in one of the chairs someone had retrieved and set up on the shipping dock. The ocean breeze felt good, and I could just make out the breakers out past the line of pine trees.

From somewhere, Osan produced a bottle of bourbon and several disposable cups. "Gentlemen?"

We both nodded eagerly. It was unprofessional, foolish, and entirely against regulations. Fuck it!!

My first two shots went down in seconds. Damn, someone had good taste. Sumo came and sat between us. I fished a treat out of a pouch I'd kept for him. It wasn't as good as my whiskey, but the dog seemed just as happy.

"I'm sorry about your men, Jordan."

Hauk nodded and lifted his cup. "Thanks. We got Xero out of this so..."

I could tell he wanted to say more, but the pressure of the day had closed in on the man, choking off his ability for conversation. I looked over at the old man.

"How was it you saved this?" I pointed at the bottle.

He smiled. "Priorities!"

"Here, here," Jordan and I echoed.

The four of us sat there long into the evening. Sumo barely stirred as we refilled our cups multiple times. Osan finally filled the silence.

"You know why I like the sea?" He held his cup out toward the breakers. "It's always changing, but it's always the same."

We were all a bit buzzed by then and saw wisdom where there were really only words. Still, the man continued.

"I was in the Navy. Met Joann on leave in Corpus Christi. She made me promise we would live here when I retired. I didn't argue with her. Shoot, anywhere with a seashore was perfect to me. We would go out and walk the beach every morning just to see what had changed, what new treasure the tide had washed in. Most days it was just a new shell or maybe a unique piece of driftwood. Once we found a prop jet from a rocket. You know, one of the old SpaceX launches. I guess that had to be when they moved them out to the Texas facility. Anyway, it was always something new. Nothing exciting... totally ordinary, but they all found a place in our little beach house."

'Until now,' was what he didn't say. Now the tide brought in shit that could kill you. Things that could snatch you from the world of the living.

We drank the man's liquor and enjoyed a brief respite from the near continuous battle. What if this was all we had to look forward to? Fighting, survival, being on the run constantly. How many would make it? Was that even a life? Somewhere out to sea we heard a tremendous crash as something large breached the surface and fell heavily back to the depths.

The thought I'd been avoiding since landing hit me like a sledgehammer. *This is no longer our world.*

"Hauk, where was Red-7 coming from?"

I saw him grimace slightly, not sure if it was from the whiskey or the memory.

"Lackland," the man said with finality.

I was familiar with the base, spent time there early in my Space Force days. Near San Antonio, it was hotter than the middle of hell in the summer. Xero had indicated that was where she had been taken, but I wanted Hauk's explanation.

"What was so important there?"

Jordan Hauk took another sip before resting the cup on his knee. "She was...the HVA."

I didn't want to get into what Xero had told me about the AI project there.

"How did the city fare?" I asked.

The man shrugged; he knew which one I meant, the only big one around. "Better than most, worse than some. No direct hits, but no power, no food. You know, lots of gangs popping up. We lost a few men just getting away."

My brain automatically calculated distance, terrain, and what I knew of Red-7's assets.

"Two hundred fifty miles, mostly on foot. That had to be one hell of a hike, Captain."

"Yeah, farther if you aren't traveling in a straight line."

He didn't add more, but they obviously had made detours. Hauk was not a man of many words, but I was sensing we were reaching an understanding of sorts.

"What are we doing here?" he finally asked.

I could hear the bone-tired weariness in the man's question. "As my pops was fond of saying. 'We show up... show up and do our damn job.' We fight, Captain."

"And what are we fighting for, Kovach?"

I didn't answer immediately. Truthfully, it was a question I'd been asking myself. My eyes focused on a dark shape moving in the surf a hundred yards offshore. I took in the soft snores from the old man as his head nodded over to one side, hand still clutching the half-empty bottle.

"Survival." I took a long pull of my drink. "And same as we always have, Jordan. We fight for them."

Even from here, the smell of salt air mixed with the sting of rotting meat. The odor of death and decay was now a permanent fixture of our home world.

"We're failing," the other warrior said before rising and walking back inside.

I sat there in silence stroking my dog's fur. Hauk wasn't wrong, but my thoughts went even darker. What do we fight for when everyone is gone?

CHAPTER TWENTY-NINE

IAS STONE MOUNTAIN

"Renegades?" Bayou turned away from the console muttering the word. Kovach was always a bit of one, but that had never been an apt description for her. Now, though, this asshole in Fleet Command had condemned her entire squad.

The ship's complement was mushrooming. Parts of Hauk's initial team were aboard, as well as the HVA they were protecting. Kovach had suggested Bayou talk with her as soon as she could. She was trying to come to terms with what to do with the Space Marines they had rescued as well.

So far, that was mainly what they had been doing, running around picking up surviving soldiers. It wasn't a bad plan, but Bayou was the one who had to come up with ways to feed everyone and put them to work. Mostly, she'd been handling disputes from each of the armed force branches and nationalities represented. She desperately needed help and could realistically only use those who were trained for working in hard vacuum. Her mind made up, she headed to engineering.

~

"You are Xero?"

Xero nodded and eyed the pile of parts the boy was working on. "What's your name?"

"I'm Lux," he answered without looking up. "Do you know anything about building robots?"

"I know how to make them do stuff but really not much on how to build one, no. Sorry." She picked up several of the circuit panels; they were all modular, and she'd seen enough of them to know this had to be a vintage model. Probably a loader, certainly not from a combat bot.

"I'm trying to bring my friend back. Her name was Marcie."

"She was a bot?"

Lux shrugged. "She was a NannyBot, but she was my friend. She saved my life when the... when, you know, the war started."

Xero instantly liked the boy; he was mature for his age and seemed to have adapted to shipboard life already. It was unusual for her to engage with anyone, but in the recent crises, she seemed to have found many more people she could work with and even like.

"There are spare parts and stuff all over the ship," Lux said. "Not just bots, you know... but all kinds of stuff. Ms. Otero said I could use whatever I find as long as one of her people checks it out first."

Xero reached in and fastened a video output connector onto one of the control boards. The readout display on the floor lit up. It amazed her to see it running through a simple diagnostic. The kid had hooked the basics up correctly.

"Thanks," he said.

"How do you know how to do any of this?"

He smiled but continued working. "My dad... he is... was an engineer. Something called autocrat or autonomouse."

Xero chuckled. "Automation engineer."

Lux nodded.

A sound at the door made both look up.

"Xero, might I have a word?"

"Yes, Lieutenant Riggs."

"You can come back and help me later if you want," Lux yelled as the two adults left.

Bayou ushered Xero into an empty workspace. The engineering

deck on this ship seemed massive and was festooned with cubbyholes and unnecessary, long neglected, assembly rooms.

"Thank you, again," Xero said. "I'm not sure we would have made it much longer down there."

Bayou nodded. "That's why I need to ask for your help."

Xero's head cocked slightly as she listened.

"Fleet Command has put a lock on the ship's AI and removed several layers of its command functions. They are trying to forcibly recall the ship to Luna."

"And if they get the ship," Xero began, "all Terran operations will cease, including any additional rescues."

"Among other things, yes," Bayou stated flatly. "I read your file; what parts they didn't redact at least. I feel confident in guessing that you are more versed in AI protocols than anyone else on this ship. Possibly more than anyone else left alive."

"My work was in a different field of machine learning, but I get your point, Commander. The onboard AI, is she receptive or hostile?"

Damn, Bayou thought. *She thinks of these things in human terms, like Joe and Ada*. "It... she," she amended, "seems friendly to us. Kovach's AI could interface with it and got the initial command authorization we needed to bring the ship into orbit."

"That's good," Xero said thoughtfully. "I'm assuming Admiral Reese is the one trying to override the ship's command?"

"You've heard of him?" Bayou asked, the surprise clear in her tone. "He's declared himself Supreme War Commander."

Xero gave a snort laugh. "That sounds like him. I thought you Space Force types always followed orders, though."

Bayou almost laughed out loud. The number of times Kovach and the rest of Banshee had gotten in trouble for disobeying, or more commonly, putting their own interpretation on orders, was massive. This was uncharted territory for all of them, though.

"This is a war... was a war. We lost. Now we're trying to help save the survivors... maybe we can find out who's responsible, but mainly I view this as a humanitarian mission now, Xero. Some stuffed shirt, flag officer who probably never saw any actual combat starts making demands to simply satisfy his own agenda, well...we aren't on the same page of the playbook."

Xero looked back down the corridor toward where Lux was still playing with his box of parts.

Riggs followed the woman's gaze. "His mom's onboard," she said. "He was down there on his own for a while, though. He's a tough kid. Who knows how many more just like him are down there fighting to stay alive? Somebody must be up here to give them a chance."

Quietly, in that corner of a darkened workspace, Xero made up her mind. Whatever these soldiers were up to, their hearts seemed to be in the right place. "Get me logged in, Riggs, and I'll see what I can do."

CHAPTER THIRTY

Damiana allowed herself the luxury of relaxing but only slightly. She'd been back in the red zone for less than an hour, and already she'd narrowly escaped thunder vines and something truly evil-looking and freaky acting. The thing slightly resembled a miniature version of the Furies, the giant reptilian- looking beasts that she and Kovach had seen back at the DARPA lab. But these, were all teeth and muscle; they also stood on two feet but had long tails and were less than a meter tall. The worst thing was how silent and how fast they were.

The Sisterhood had briefed her on what she might face, but even they were unsure of which experiments were loosed and what additional genetic alterations might have taken place since the war began. Aberrations, that was what they had called them. Unexpected results of tinkering too much with a creature's biological code.

"Unexpected my ass," she snorted quietly while watching another creature through the enhanced optics.

"Well, hello," she whispered as she zoomed in on the head. Long, dark hair swept to one side as the girl walked calmly along the banks of the small river. Maybe late teens. The girl's body not yet mature but just on the verge of adulthood. Despite the danger, she walked as if she had no cares in the world. Damiana slowly swept the rifle to each side, the scope picking up several predators close to the girl. None made any move to attack. In fact, they seemed to ignore her as much as she was them.

Voss stowed the weapon and began cautiously making her way down the slight rise. In the distance was a town, not one she'd bothered to remember the name of. It was simply a waypoint on her way to Nevis's last known location. A shadow passed over her just before a loud screeching sound tore its way across the valley. Voss's eyes were locked on the scene below; the girl turned just as the massive raptor overhead dove. Voss flattened herself to the dirt as the claws hit her shoulders. The jacket had leather and Kevlar protection at several points, including the shoulders, so the claws didn't penetrate, but the full weight of the bird still drove the air from her lungs.

She rolled to her left, flexing her wrist in the process. The compact Silka C3 was instantly in her palm and firing in the same motion. The now headless bird toppled over just as it was readying for another lunge.

"Shit!"

Looking down the hill, there was no sign of the girl, but a veritable pack of other creatures was now heading this way. The compact pistol retracted back into its hidden receiver underneath her forearm. Voss considered going back to the rifle, but this was a case of retreat clearly being the smarter option.

Voss knew her mission was to observe and report. The stakes were too high to risk failure, but this girl could be the key to everyone's future. Smoothly, she grasped the hilts of the curved knives. Voss was known for many things, but choosing the safe route was not one of them. "Mom is going to be pissed."

She began running directly at the lead creature, another of the wickedly fast mini-Furies. A flicker of color briefly passed on her right. She smiled. Her protector, or as the soldier called it, the Wraith. Voss was unsure what help it might offer against these monsters, but it offered her comfort and strength. She caught site of the girl again, far in the distance heading directly toward the ruined city. That girl had a way of passing right by these things. That was something she needed to know more about. Only one way to find out—get to the girl.

CHAPTER THIRTY-ONE

Her feet moved in deliberate strides, unwavering in their path. A path which she, herself, knew little of. In truth, the girl had no idea where she was, or perhaps more apt—who she was. Things like that had simply ceased to matter to her since the... since the... the flicker of thought was gone, evaporated into the wind like someone blowing out a candle.

Thoughts had become elusive to her, memories all but nonexistent, but she did have purpose. It wasn't something she could articulate. More of a natural imperative to 'go,' to 'do.'

She'd seen the commotion on the hill, the giant bird attacking something, a person, but it hadn't really registered. The creatures were dangerous, but for whatever reason, they didn't bother her... not anymore. Back in the before, they did. Back then, she'd also had a name —what was it?

The sound of the wind and the trees and the constant plodding of her bare feet on the dry soil were the only sounds. From a distance, you might mistake her for being in a trance or even a zombie. That wasn't the case. She was simply driven. By what, though? That was the real question.

The scream came from behind her; she didn't bother turning. She understood the cycle of life, hunter, and prey. Not in a way that mattered, but somewhere in the seldom-used part of her conscious brain, she knew another life was ending. Probably the person from the hill. Then that thought, too, was swept away.

~

Voss rushed through the first wave of attackers, her knives glistening with the now familiar purplish blood. Several of the smaller creatures lay in pieces behind her. She hadn't intended to scream, but it had come out like a war cry. Something she remembered doing in the earliest years of her training before her Sisters had taught her the way of enlightenment and all the control and discipline that went with that acceptance.

More creatures were moving in the scrub brush just out of sight. Occasionally, she would detect a spike, a scaly appendage, or one of the oversized eyes. She had yet to see the whole creature those things belonged to, but the eyes alone were grotesque. All the various creations working together were baffling. Few pairings in the natural world were truly symbiotic. Animals, including man, were opportunistic. But these things attacked as if humans were a common enemy. A threat to their own existence.

Knowing that people like Doctor Reichert had created them made that all the more puzzling. The off-the-books DARPA facilities had been attempting to make biological weapons. Not bacterium or viruses, but actual fighters they could use on battlefields. Why would they now have such a drive to kill, to consume, to eradicate?

The attack came from Voss's flank; she felt the psionic pulse from the Wraith, and the attacker gave a withering cry before she turned and pierced the thing through its eye. So, they could sense, could be affected by the manipulation her friend could deliver. That was helpful, but would it save her life?

The Wraith itself was likely also a product of some similar research, even Voss did not know its full provenance. The full story of its origination was a mystery. She had been its rescuer, or at least that was how she now recalled it. Either way, the thing had bonded to her many years earlier on another mission and resisted all attempts to be separated from her. On missions where it just wasn't feasible to have a nearly invisible flying stingray, it stayed in its custom-built habitat next to her quarters.

Even then, it sometimes got free and would often disappear for long periods, but eventually it returned or would find her, even if she had traveled great distances. She reluctantly sheathed the blade and flexed both of her wrists, bringing her matching handguns to bear on separate targets, dropping both.

Voss's attackers seemed to be communicating strategy with each other. Apparently, the Wraith was sensed this as well because the shimmering image of it began pulsing a faint red. It was an aggressive mental countermeasure that she knew would leave it exhausted quickly. She had to end this now before more of the things showed up.

CHAPTER THIRTY-TWO

RED ZONE - TEXAS

I awoke in a cold sweat, unsure of whatever nightmare was taking up residence in my head tonight. The newly upgraded, augmented, reality sensors showed my surroundings, the other members of my team, and Red-7. The IFF transponders all showed green. I felt Sumo's chin resting on my leg, his normal place to sleep since our first encounters with the freakish monstrosities in the Ranier facility. I scratched behind his ears gently, and his body pressed into my leg even more. We both have issues and scars to remind us that our enemies are real.

So many battles, so many AOs, but this.... all this felt so totally alien. I'd been kicking myself all day, first for not making sure Bayou knew how sorry I was about Darko and her sister. Jack Smith, call sign Darko, had died in another battle against a monster, but Rigg's sister was a total innocent. A young woman just on her way to work, or to meet her boyfriend, or some other totally normal, totally random thing most normal people do day in and day out. Only that day, it was not normal. It was instead, the end. The end for her and billions of others around the globe.

I lay there in the darkness and replayed some of the skirmishes we'd been having with the creatures I'd been calling Furies, as well as the more recent HappyBear. Ada had also been analyzing to see if there was anything tactical in their actions, or if it was just instinctual. Someone had manufactured these things for war, for conquest. They had a genetic mandate to win. Someone had to give them a baseline of operational guidelines, and if we could get a grip on that, perhaps we could have the edge in the next encounter.

Billions dead... and those might just be the lucky ones.

A message alert popped into my visual overlay. Simple text, that was unusual, but seeing who it was from brought me wide awake. Damiana Voss. Now what was she up to?

"Hello, Cowboy."

I ignored the obvious implication that she knew my location was still in Texas.

"What's going on, Voss?"

This woman had shot me the last time I saw her, but if others could be believed, she had likely saved my life in doing so.

"When you are done with your beach vacation, I think I could use your help," she answered.

"Not a vaca...what have you gotten yourself into?"

I wasn't used to text typing, so I engaged Ada to translate my subvocalized words into text.

Voss's response was slow in coming. "A lead, a possible lead, Nevis Carlson. He may know who is behind all this."

Now she had my attention. "Tell me more."

"I can't, not yet. I've been battling the bloody little monsters for days, and I may finally have a location."

Little monsters? I wondered.

The text continued, "Can you get transport to these coordinates?"

Ada automatically converted the data to a visual map in my ocular overlay. *Northeast U.S.... maybe even Canada.* I considered it for several seconds and interfaced with Ada to make sure it was even possible. Many things were easier when hovercars were everywhere, and a hyperjet could take you from the West Coast to the East Side in just over an hour.

"Yes, I can do it." Sumo looked up at me. The dog seemed to know when I was about to do something stupid. "Just me or the whole team?" There was a delay in her response. Perhaps she knew I didn't much fucking trust her. Getting shot by a person could have that effect.

"Just you, Joe, unless you need your support animal."

"Ha! You're one to talk. How is your little flying freak doing?" I think the genuine sense of sarcasm was lost in the text-based messaging. Sometimes you just need to be looking face to face, so they get the full effect, *you know*?

"It's part of why you need to be here. I think we've discovered a few things that might be helpful in whatever this little crusade you seem to be on."

So, she did know what I was doing. She'd hacked Ada or left a back-door or something in my skull. I knew the woman couldn't be trusted.

After several seconds, the text updated. "Calm down."

Okay, I really didn't like that. Even if she was spying, she couldn't really know how I was feeling, nor my unsaid thoughts. Could she? I reeled in my ego and tried to offer a more adult response.

This woman was perplexing, as were my own feelings toward her. She had lied to me, used me to get what she wanted, and ultimately nearly killed me, but somehow, I found myself thinking of her as a friend... maybe even more. "I'm listening."

And I did, or more accurately, 'I'm reading'. The woman might not be on our side, but she had some damn nifty skills, not the least of which was a sharp mind. Something I was increasingly agreeing with the late doctor about. She detailed several things which hadn't occurred to me despite my recent upgrades. Things that in retrospect seemed rather obvious.

"Why me, why not call on someone from your own organization?"

I knew nothing about whom she worked for, but I knew she wasn't just out here on her own. That would be suicide. Voss didn't even miss a beat. She knew I was fishing for intel, and she was equally quick to let me know she wasn't sharing.

"I don't think you realize how important or how capable you are, Kovach. I would be an idiot to not try to use an asset like you. Plus, you have a vested interest. You are motivated to find the truth and maybe end this before it's too late for all of us."

She wasn't wrong. Right now, we were simply throwing bodies at these things hoping we could outlast them long enough to get away. We weren't fighting to win; we were simply stretching out our defeat as long as possible

~

Jordan Hauk was punctual as ever, my system clock hit 0430 as he strode through the door.

"Good to go?"

I simply nodded; my body didn't seem to need the same levels of sleep that it used to, but that didn't mean I was eager to grace the day. I recalled what Dr. Reichert had told me after my first round of enhancements. For every gain, there is a cost. A price to pay. I wasn't sure what that might mean for me in the future, but I felt sure it was going to be steep.

"What's the plan, Captain?"

Hauk looked at me with a totally unreadable face. "I want my people somewhere safe or somewhere we can make an actual difference."

"You have somewhere in mind?"

He hesitated before looking skyward. "Not up there. Not long term, at least."

I nodded in understanding. Ada gave me the insertion times from the Stone Mountain, and I could see the dropship was scheduled to arrive in just a few hours, but its time on the ground would be extremely limited.

"We need to go inland a few klicks. The dropship will barely be on station long enough for the pickup. The farther west we can go, the more time it will have," I explained.

He was familiar with the problems the orbital battleship was having overhead but had less data on the limited maneuverability of the mysterious TriCraft. Most people who were aware that the damned things even existed just assumed they could go anywhere.

"You are in charge of that, Kovach. Just tell us what you need from us."

We went over the manpower and loadouts while we grabbed a quick breakfast and actual coffee. Much of the ground assets would need to be abandoned, they simply wouldn't fit aboard the craft, not with all the personnel. I'd also considered asking Riggs to send down a ground assault vehicle for me to use to meet Voss. That would have simply taken up too much space. I could go on foot, or I could drop launch later.

Sumo and I had a new mission, but I needed to give Deb a hand up there first. My head hurt thinking about how rushed the exfil was going to be. Speed leads to mistakes, mistakes often lead to deaths in our line of work.

"What about her?"

I saw the woman the corporal was pointing at. The one I had found the previous night. This was technically Hauk's command, but he'd deferred to me on anyone outside his command that might look for a ride up to orbit. "Halo, go check this woman out. Something about her doesn't feel right to me."

"Spidey senses again, Boss?"

"Maybe, I don't know, but something... we need to know if she's okay before we take her onto our dropship." I'd always had a good feel for danger, but with the greater sensory input and my brain working at hyper-speed now, I wasn't sure if this was gut feelings or something more substantial. Some minor clue that my brain picked up, but my conscious mind hadn't yet processed.

"Roger that." Halo went over, kneeling down in front of the woman.

"What about the old man?" I'd already forgotten his name, but he seemed to be harmless.

The corporal shrugged. "No idea, he was gone when we got up. No sign of him anywhere."

Troubling, but less so than a thousand other things. I knew Ada would be running through all available surveillance footage to see if someone had spotted him today. Perhaps he was just off doing his business. Somehow, I didn't think that was the case.

"She said there was a witch."

The comment took me off guard, and I laughed before even turning. Halo was standing there looking perplexed.

"I swear that's what she said. A preacher, or witch, or prophet. Someone who seemed to know all this shit was about to happen."

"If that's the case, why is this woman all alone?" Something about the statement reminded me of my conversation with Voss. She had also mentioned a girl alone.

Halo glanced down, "I don't think she believed the woman was a witch or had powers, you know. But something fucked her up. In fact, I think a lot of shit went down. The woman has a necklace that makes me think she was a mother. It's the cheap kind kids give for Mother's Day gifts and all."

I looked at the woman again, she still gave me an uneasy feeling, but I had no real reason to keep her from getting away from all this. Our job was to protect people, not to judge them. I nodded and cleared her for transport with the others just as Hauk gave the order to move out.

CHAPTER THIRTY-THREE

The faint sound of gravel crunching beneath boot soles was the only sound as we started our inland trek. We'd left the small beach community before dawn and now had a good two-hour hike to reach the landing zone. So far, we'd encountered none of the creatures from the day before, but everyone was on edge. I could feel the tension radiating from the others like a toxic fog.

Sumo was holding a perimeter position to my right, and Halo and Gi were on our left and slightly forward. I knew Priest would hold the rear-guard position. The terrain was mostly blackened trees. Wildfires had raged through Texas after the prolonged drought of the last couple of decades.

Working with an Army unit was not that uncommon for us; we cross-trained often, and because of the strange recruiting tactics of the Space Force, most of us originally came from other service branches. Sometimes the tactics and signaling had to be learned, but we were simply here to amplify Red-7's own lethality. We weren't a separate force, we weren't the 'A' team, no matter how some of the other soldiers might look at us.

Despite that, my team really only trusted each other. If the shit got real, which it probably would, we wanted to know where every member of Banshee was. That was just how it was in all militaries. You fought for each other. You risked your lives for your friends, not strangers. They were family. Sometimes you might want to strangle them, but you would also protect them with your dying breath, or preferably some other dumb bastard's dying breath.

The old man, Osan, never showed back up, and I had to admit the other civilians, including the woman, hadn't really slowed us down. I was beginning to feel a bit more optimistic about our chances, then I heard the first rifle shot.

It was from the front of the unit. Hauk's voice was on the comms instantly, "Gomez, report."

"Contact, front!" was the shouted reply.

More shots rang out. These from the rear. Any soldier yelling "Contact" knew to also include the direction.

"Location?"

Another voice cut in, "Everywhere... sir."

Rifle fire opened up on all sides, but I still hadn't seen a thing. We had fifty-five minutes to make it two more miles to meet the dropship. Now, I was unsure how possible that would even be. I kept scanning the terrain; a thick canopy of trees was blocking out most of the early morning sun. The shadows and low scrub bushes made it hard to pick out any target. I immediately dreaded another possible encounter with the Bigfoot thing... or maybe hordes of them. That's not what this was. It took me crucial seconds to realize the warning alerts on my HUD, as well as to see where Sumo's eyes were pointing. He was looking up.

"They're in the trees," a random voice yelled. I heard a loud 'snap-boom' and saw a soldier go down.

I could now see the movement through the limbs, just fast-changing shadows, really. Nothing that gave me any sense of size or threat. These couldn't be the Furies, those things were massive. No way those tree limbs would hold them, nor had they exhibited any ability to climb. This was something else. I heard more of the 'snap-booms.' Some were so loud that my helmet's sound dampeners cut in to mask it. It sounded like shotgun blast, but they were coming from the trees.

The day before, the open ground near the beach had worked against us. Lack of cover had cost us lives. I had agreed with Hauk's decision to use the forest as cover. Now, our enemies had adapted, or maybe they had maneuvered us right where they wanted us. Just as we had different weapons and tactics for varying battle plans, these enemy creatures seemed to have their own system for deploying forces.

"They were designed for war, Joe – they were genetically programmed for this," Ada offered up. She was clearly interpreting my thoughts, or maybe I had spoken them. Either way, she was right. We might be damn good warriors, but none of us were designed from birth to do this.

I caught a fleeting shadow in my sights as it moved from one tree to another. I fired a three-round burst center mass but saw no evidence of a kill. Ahead of me, I could see the green icons pinpointing Hauk's soldiers beginning to turn yellow and a few red. *Shit, we're losing more people.*

"Banshee, take charge, covering fire, go heavy. Give Red-7 a safe corridor."

Hauk would be pissed, but this was where our weaponry and tactics would be most effective. We couldn't risk getting bogged down here in a sustained battle with the wildlife, we would lose. Halo and Priest opened up with their heavier Glisson Rattler Mark IVs. Limbs and entire trees came down under the precise barrage.

Hauk gave the order to move, and the unit began running toward an open patch of daylight a hundred yards ahead.

"Ada, what are we fighting?" My MK4 was lining up and shooting at targets without my total understanding of what the enemy even was. Then I watched the blurry outline of a gray-furred creature leap at the throat of one of the other soldiers. The loud sound coincided with a massive gout of blood spewing from an open wound on the man's neck. Another icon flared yellow, then red before fading to black.

Ada briefly showed me a freeze frame of one of the creatures, and honestly, I wish she hadn't. These had heads more like a bat but were the size of a large house cat. I couldn't tell if the body reminded me of a squirrel or a monkey. Something about the rear limbs was off, in fact, the proportion on all of it was off, but what had my attention was the long tail. It was thick, muscular, and flattened and seemed to grasp something at the end. It wasn't a barb like a scorpion, although that had been my first guess... no, this looked more ordinary. The tail was a full-functioning appendage, and it was holding something that looked very much like a knife. That was what had whipped out just before that soldier had dropped. I calculated the speed of that strike and gasped. The calculations appeared in my head as I considered them. It was faster than the speed of sound. That 'snap-boom' was the sound barrier being broken by the hammer strike of the tail.

"Shit, they're using tools... weapons, and those tails are supersonic."

I went on the all-unit channel, "These..." I needed something to call them. All I could relate them to was a show I'd seen on a killer shrimp. One with the fastest strike in the animal world. "These mantis chimps use their tails as weapons. Their strike is faster than you are, so stay clear. Keep moving, and let Banshee plow the road," I yelled into the comms.

Honestly, over the sounds of battle and the massive whoosh of our heavier caliber Rattlers, I wasn't sure anyone heard what I'd said. Then I was ducking. Not on purpose but reflex, possibly augmented by Ada. I reached out and grabbed the bat-like head of the thing just before pain exploded across my back. My hand automatically tightened, crushing the remarkably fragile creature. Blood spewed out as the thing fell to the ground. How in the hell can something that fragile pack such a punch? I didn't know what it had hit me with but thank God for my battle suit. My entire spine stung like fire, though.

~

It took the group precious minutes to adapt to this new fighting style and to make it to the clearing. The murderous little chimps needed the trees to get close. On the ground, they were much slower and easily taken out. Halo blasted one as it dove for the woman, splattering its purple blood over several others.

The countdown clock in my display let me know we didn't have time for this. Also, I had to assume the larger foe would have heard the sounds of battle and be showing up soon. We damn sure didn't need Furies attacking right now.

"Disengage, Banshee."

It was time to join Red-7 in getting the hell out of here.

"Mantis Chimps, Boss? Really?" Priest asked minutes later as we set a perimeter on the most open ground of the LZ.

"I was rushed, admittedly not one of my better designators." I could see the numbers of wounded and dead as well as our remaining ammo counts. We'd gone through a shitload of p-cells just to get this far.

"War wagon is on the way," Gi said, walking up. It was the first I had seen of the man since early in the battle. His battle suit was nearly unrecognizable. It was covered in dried purple blood and many dents and a few actual holes where he'd been attacked.

"Good," I responded before passing the information to Hauk. "Gi, what's your status?"

The sergeant knew I could look at my admin panel. It gave me complete readouts on everyone under my command, but I preferred to hear it from my people directly. I'd also learned to trust the Korean in the few days I'd known him. He was not a person who tended to bullshit anyone.

"I am seventy percent chief."

My readout showed he had compound fractures in one arm and a possible dislocated shoulder. Knowing how the man fought, though, seventy probably was about right.

"Fall back, Sergeant, and guard the loading of the dropship," I ordered, getting him to an area of relative safety. My sense of the enemy was they would wait to attack then. I wanted our best shooters out front. Jordan Hauk seemed to agree as he and several of his top guys were forming up beside us.

"Two mikes," Ada said indicating the ship was two minutes out.

I held up the corresponding number of fingers for the others to see. We leveled our guns at the tree line, but Sumo's bark alerted us to the right side where the rolling hillside seemed to erupt with dozens of the scaly Furies. I was unsure if they had been using the ground as camouflage, or maybe they could burrow under. Either way, we were about to get hammered. Little bastards had used the Mantis Chimps as distractions. It sounded crazy, but somehow, I knew it was true, these things could coordinate attacks.

"Thirty-seven new targets, Prowler."

"Not helpful, Ada."

"This shit seems oddly familiar, Halo," Priest stated.

Halo just grunted his agreement. I knew both men had barely gotten out of the jungle with Bayou on an earlier mission. "Designate targets, make it count," I said unnecessarily. Our battle suits, hell, even our weapons communicated with each other and wouldn't let us both target the same enemy unless massed firepower seemed necessary.

From behind, I heard a collective gasp as the small clearing fell into darkness. I knew that meant our ride had arrived. The creatures tried to swarm us; we used the most destructive settings our weapons had. The twin flechette plasma rounds that sliced the damn things in half. The downside was they ran through the magazine's power in seconds. Didn't matter, in seconds we wouldn't be here, and as a former CO once said, "Our ammo count didn't matter if we were dead."

Hauk's rifle barked beside me as he felled several of the beasts as well. His men still had a habit of firing at the head or center mass instead of the less thick, armored thighs. They were getting the message, though. Red-7's enemy body count was about half of Banshee's, but without both teams, we would have all been killed.

I felt, then saw, Gomez's head slam off my shoulder before toppling into the weeds. It was no longer attached, and the monster that killed him was now moving in on Priest.

"Load up, Hauk–take your men." I could tell we were down to mere seconds.

Hauk paused to look at the body of his fallen man before leaving the line. I closed the gap the best I could. We began backing up, tightening the circle. Selectively taking targets that moved into our killing field. Part of my brain registered that Sumo was engaged with one of the things, and I swung to the side, fired just over his head and returned to my target without fully knowing what I was shooting at. My combat skills were no longer by the book.

Priest moved into the beast in a move that was counter-intuitive unless you'd trained on edged weapon combat tactics. The creature's main weapon, the claw, became a significant disadvantage in close-quarter fighting. Priest moved inside the arc of the blade which swiped harmlessly down the soldier's backplate. Unfortunately, it meant Priest was also unable to use his main weapon, but the man had a plan. While lacking in the pure fighting aesthetics as Gi, Priest was a Ranger at heart, a warrior. He drove his armored fingers into the Furie's inner thigh. The one weak spot we'd identified.

The creature gave a screaming howl of pain, and blood covered Priest's hands as he continued to wrench the thing's muscle and tendon from the inner bone. This was the essence of battle, and the soldier knew there would be no prize for coming in second. As the thing backed away slightly, he brought his weapon under its hideous chin and unleashed a carnage round into it at point blank range. The threat disappeared in a mist of purplish-red blood.

Ada gave me a running count of the dropship loading, and I could see it moving to the single digits. I could also still see eighteen enemy targets in my display. I moved behind Halo, tapping him on the shoulder to fall back. He nodded, disappearing toward the ramp. His gun barking several more times before he disappeared. Priest was next to go. I would be the last. Sensing their quarry getting away, the remaining creatures rushed me and my dog.

"Sumo, go!" I yelled, knowing full well he wouldn't until I did.

In the past two days, I had fought harder and moved faster than I ever had, but what happened next caught me totally off guard. My left hand grasped my Damascus steel vibrasonic blade, and in my other was the Mark IV Rattler. I dove to my right, narrowly missing one creature while slicing up and through the arterial vein. My rifle was sending pulse rounds into the legs of every one of the other three closest to me. Sumo had also caught on and was funneling the things into my path as I swept, slashed, and fired in an arc of death winding my way to the dropship platform. I turned and used the grab handle on the dog's armor to shove Sumo up the meter of space toward the hovering door. I leapt, catching the narrow supports, still firing with my other hand. The TriCraft rotated away and up as I backward crab-walked up into the interior allowing the bay door to finally close on the nightmare outside.

Shit, that was not fun. I sheathed my weapons and turned to look at who had made it. Every face was turned to look at me. No one spoke.

"What?" I asked.

CHAPTER THIRTY-FOUR

"Welcome back."

Bayou looked at me, then the rest of the unit coming off the transport.

"Jesus, Joe—you guys all look like hell."

Sumo had nestled beside the lieutenant wagging his tail so hard the rest of his body was bobbing side to side. She knelt and rubbed the animal's ears before offering him a bit of jerky.

"Need a quick SitRep, LT Any progress on breaking the lockout?"

She had locked eyes with Jordan Hauk, who was busy helping his wounded down the ramp of the TriCraft.

I caught the look between the two warriors, definitely some history there, but now wasn't the time or place. "Bayou–I need an update." I motioned for Sumo to go get chow. We weren't going to be aboard the battle cruiser for long.

She seemed to get the message. "You aren't taking back command up here, are you."

I shook my head. "Things are changing fast. Hauk can fill you in. I'm going to need to drop, hopefully on the next rotation."

She nodded and followed as I began walking away, already pulling off my battle armor. She could see a massive bruise rising up over his shoulder and wondered what in the hell had done that.

The report didn't take long, and honestly, I had little to offer. I'd dropped my gear off at the armory. The guy working as the chief armorer looked familiar, but I was too exhausted to recall from where. He looked at the dents in the outer shell and shook his head.

"I'll need that back in an hour, Chief, with drop-rig and full kit resupply."

"Where are you going, Joe?" Bayou asked.

"To the shower and...then to get some answers," I growled before heading off.

"So, Joe is aboard?" Carol asked eagerly as the other members of Banshee made their way into the mess hall. The increased number on board was filling out the large space. All the new arrivals seemed to have headed for bunk rooms or here. As a civilian, Carol was no longer allowed back in the arrival hangar. She didn't mind, the open hangar door looking out into the black space beyond gave her the chills.

"He is," Priest offered between bites of something that may have been a rough imitation of chicken. That was, assuming you had never seen or tasted an actual chicken.

Carol had already heard some of the others talking about the fighting. Her concern for Joe was obvious, but she still wasn't sure where she stood with the man. Yes, they'd had a bit of a 'thing.' Maybe they were still an item, but she knew it was mostly just physical. Since his regaining consciousness, she still couldn't bring herself to think of it as coming back to life. He had been different, distant, and if possible, even more driven than before. More than one of the overheard conversations described how he fought; fearless was one adjective. Inhuman was the one she heard more often. That disturbed her.

She saw a woman sitting alone. She'd been with the last transport and looked miserable. Her blonde hair hung limply as she stared down at the untouched tray of food. Carol stood, realizing she would not get much more from these guys. They were shoveling food and undoubtedly headed to get some shut eye soon after.

"I'm Carol. Welcome aboard," she said, sitting down across from the woman. The other woman's eyes didn't rise to meet hers.

"Low gravity. Right?" Carol said. "I get it. Took me days to be able to hold food down when I first arrived. Still have moments, you know?"

If the woman heard her, she offered no sign that the words registered. Carol studied her; she was young, late twenties probably. Attractive enough, but a face that seemed clouded by trauma. Carol had no idea what the woman had been through, but the emotional damage was clear. Her years of running predictive behavior modeling began to add up the visible data-points, and she did not like where they were leading. She leaned over and patted the woman's hand. The blonde recoiled slightly from the touch. Carol didn't know why, but a shiver ran down her back.

She stood quickly and offered cardboard platitudes to the newcomer as she turned to leave.

"Witches."

"Huh?" Carol was several feet away but clearly heard what the woman had said. She turned back, but the girl's face held the same blank expression as before.

~

Carol's son Lux was hard at work on his project. Something his mom had briefly shown interest in but now was simply happy he had a hobby. The systems all checked out, but he had little understanding of what to do next. Honestly, he wasn't even sure what he could build out of the pile of junk he'd been given access to, but it was fun. He wouldn't admit it, but he was holding out hope the new coder, Xero, would help him. Maybe together they could find a backup of his old NannyBot Marcie and load her into the system.

He now knew that NannyBots were for babies, but he missed her just the same. She'd saved his life, and stuff like that mattered. He carefully added the peripheral board to the sensor array. This was the third time he'd tried it, but the thing kept giving false signals. All he wanted it to do was pick up a signal when he or his dog Junie was in the vicinity, but the sensor kept showing two heat signatures where there should have only been one. Junie had run off to find Sumo when the soldiers returned, and shortly after, the ghost signal started occurring on every boot up.

Lux hated going to Xero about every little thing. He knew she was working on the important stuff. He had to figure this out on his own. Dragging a datapad out of his bag, he turned it on and heard the familiar voice of his father as soon as he hit the play button.

CHAPTER THIRTY-FIVE

I didn't want to jump before talking to Carol but, shit… what was I going to say? If I let her know it was because Voss asked for my help, she might try to toss me out an airlock without my suit. Couldn't say I would blame her, hell, I had enough doubts for both of us. Bayou had also been upset; she had a significant number of refugees that seemed to grow every day.

One thing I'd noticed was the attention she was paying to Captain Hauk. There was definitely more there than she had let on. I wasn't sure what, but perhaps having him aboard would help stabilize things. After all, most of those aboard were his people. Like it or not, Red-7 was now a space-borne fighting force. As I walked down the corridor and heard the sounds coming from many of the billets, I knew space was not the peaceful refuge many had hoped for.

Space Force had rigorous testing to weed out those who were overly susceptible to space or motion sickness and had a sensitivity to pressure changes like altitude sickness and even anxiety caused by confined spaces. You simply had to be comfortable up here to do your job. That the cold vacuum of space was only millimeters away couldn't be allowed in your thoughts. Even with the screening, the corps doctors still gave us regular drug cocktails to combat the effects. One of the new men stumbled out of his room and held on to the far wall as he hurriedly rushed toward the communal toilets.

I knew from experience that many of these guys could not adapt to life up here. They would need to be back dirt side within a few weeks, or they would wither and die. It was just not a life most were prepared for.

"You're going back?"

I turned to see who was speaking. The voice threw me momentarily, but seeing that it wasn't Carol Reynolds was a relief. I nodded in response.

"Yeah, more work to do."

"Can you make a difference, change anything?" she asked, before running her fingers through her short hair.

I shrugged. "That's a good question, Xero, but we can't just hide up here. Not long-term anyway."

I motioned her to follow me. "I appreciate your help in getting ship's functions back up, but we need full control. Any chance you can manage that?"

Xero shook her head. "The access level required is beyond even what I can crack. Perhaps Ada with your own command levels could help."

My AI had been trying since we had come aboard and gotten no further than the woman had. "What if we could target Gateway's own comms array? Would that end it?"

"Target how?"

I shrugged. Her face took on a look I couldn't quite read. "Just asking hypothetically."

"Simple answer is no. I investigated that, but we aren't getting a constant signal. It might help them from updating the code to work around my own countermeasures, but I believe they have built-in fail-safes."

"Fail-safes?"

"Venting atmos," she said. Her matter-of-fact tone reinforced her certainty on the issue.

"Shit. So, they will just kill us all if we block them out. Vent our oxygen into space?"

Xero pursed her lips and nodded.

We were nearing the ready room, my gear was ready, and Sumo was standing in the doorway waiting on me. The other little dog of Lux's had her front legs down on the ground and her butt raised up as if she was ready to attack the big husky. I could tell they'd been playing and hated pulling my partner away.

I fumbled in my locker and finally found what I was looking for. The small object felt cold to my touch. My fingers ran over the smooth multi-faceted shapes. I held it out and dropped it into her hands. Her confused expression let me know she wasn't sure what it was.

"I think you are the right person to have this."

"Too big for a ring, should I wear it as a necklace?" she asked smiling. "Either way, it's very kind..."

"Cut it out," I interrupted. "I recovered this from... from Magnus. Ada believes it is a holographic data storage device."

She hefted the object in her open palm trying to judge the weight. The artificial gravity of the ship was only about two-thirds of Earth normal, but Xero got the feel of it.

"Maybe – never seen anything like it. Must be a Hammer Industries design."

"Or maybe nothing," I offered. "Just look into it when you can, okay? And I'd appreciate it if you kept this between us."

I'm not sure why I added that last part, nor why I was trusting this person I'd only met two days ago.

She nodded and pocketed the cube and reached down to pick up Junie. "Come on, girl. Your boyfriend has to go back to work."

I'd already started fitting my dog's combat gear as they left.

"That may not have been wise," Ada said.

She'd already warned me, but I didn't know why. "Xero was one of your programmers, and you don't trust her?" I snugged up the Kevlar vest and mounted the dog's helmet collar.

"She's brilliant, Joe, extremely talented but also volatile. She dislikes authority and has anarchist tendencies. That was one of the reasons she was never fully brought on board the projects. She was a contractor they used when no one else could figure things out."

I could get behind that. Wasn't too far from what my profile might say. "It's done. Give her increased access to the ship's computer up to a point. Make sure Bayou can monitor and override."

Ada had made more progress with the ship's AI than I had let on to the hacker. Even so, we weren't able to break the command lockout the admiral had triggered. In the back of my mind, I kept coming back to the Stone Mountain's sister ship. They had taken Alice Springs out in the days just after the attack. Someone out there had ship killer weapons, or it had been an inside job. Either way, I didn't think we had time to wait around to find out. This was a ship of war, and to perform its duty, we had to be able to steer it at the very least.

I pulled my hastily repaired armor out of the rack and headed toward the drop bay. I was rushing my mind with whirling thoughts at lightning speed. I hadn't told the rest of the team. The truth was, there was so much that needed to get done up here, but fate seemed to keep pulling us back into the fight down below. I decided not to work out the logic, just trust my instincts.

Locking the coffin lid tight from the outside, one of the space engineers gave the thumbs up as he slid the unit onto the launch tube tracks and disabled the safety interlocks. I heard him secure Sumo's own compartment just below my feet. The ballistics system we used for launches kept him and me tethered but gave him an even more confining space than my own. We needed it to survive the high G-forces of reentry and the thermal barrier between us and the nearly 3000-degree temps outside as the air thickened and compressed when we punched through it to the surface.

The technician slapped a hand on the pod's shell, and I felt the movement down and into the firing chamber. "You okay, boy?" I knew Sumo could hear me through his comms if not through the thick padding separating us. He gave his standard disinterested wuff just before my screen flashed yellow, orange, and then green. An audible whoosh of air was followed immediately by total silence as we were fired down the tube and out into space.

My battle suit compensated as the air left my lungs due to the sudden acceleration. The first few times I had dropped I blacked out, which was not that unusual. Honestly, the suit's AI and the ballistic pod could handle most things whether we were conscious or not. Right up until they couldn't, which had happened to me on more than one occasion. I preferred staying awake as terrifying as it was.

The ballistic pod quickly scrubbed speed which caused a corresponding decrease in altitude. Each of the pods differ from the early rocket capsules in the fact that we maintained some thrust throughout to help stabilize and keep us on our specific trajectory. The old Apollo capsules topped out at about 36,000 feet per second near the top of reentry and used the denser atmosphere to slow to just over a hundred feet per second as they deployed the big parachutes. My start speed was similar at around 38,500, but I only needed to slow to around 380 feet per second, or 260 miles per hour. After that, my pod would eject me and Sumo into a very high-altitude freefall. Our battle suits still had to absorb a tremendous amount of heat and cold as soon as the superheated plasma bled off.

Every drop was different, and the terrain, need for stealth, and atmospheric conditions all played into the exact way we handled it. Today, we were having the pleasure of dropping through a massive storm front on our way down. In the later afternoon light, I could see the swirling cloud mass below me as the capsule ejected us. I would need to drop several more minutes before I could deploy the lightweight glider wings and have any means of maneuvering away from the heart of the storm. My right hand instinctively patted the mag lock gripping my rifle on my back.

Several things were wrong with my jump. First, was the fact I was doing it alone, totally against regs. The second was the time of day; we always jumped at night or early morning when the upper atmospheric winds were more predictable. Lastly, was the complete lack of intel. I was totally unprepared for what I was getting myself into as I stared down at my freshly ruined planet. Normally, command would be programming the jump, and I just had to ride the guidelines in my HUD. Today, Ada was handling that. She would be adjusting the small flight surfaces built into the pod and later on my suit and hopefully, guiding me safely toward Voss.

On the terrain map, the entire region was shaded in red. I'd just been rescued from one red zone only to jump back into a different one. After several minutes, I got the signal to deploy the glider wings. Always another moment of terror as the wings were extended from each side of my backpack. If these failed, there was nothing to slow me down for the rest of the brief journey to the planet's surface. I used a series of eye blinks to confirm deployment and waited for the sound of my suit's access panels to open. Only… they didn't.

CHAPTER THIRTY-SIX

My panic threatened to take over before an almost irrational feeling of calm took its place. One part of my mind knew something in my system had to have shunted off the flood of endorphins, but I was too busy working the problem to actually care at that moment. Ada was doing her part as well, quickly going through the emergency procedure to allow me to manually release the servo motors controlling the deployment rig.

The 32,000-foot mark quickly came and went; that was where I'd intended to have my glider wings fully extended. Now, I was entering the storm in a very non-aerodynamic position, and the thickening air was buffeting me side to side like a ragdoll.

I've experienced almost every failure in a drop before but not a failure of the glider wings. The system was so simple and thought to be so bullet-proof as we no longer even drilled on it not working. Twenty-six thousand feet. Lightning arced across my path so close as to blind my display momentarily. Sumo bucked in the harness dangling a half-meter below me. The normally placid animal was terrified and unlike me, had no stress augmentation to help calm him.

"Joe, you are in excess of terminal velocity. You risk severe injury if you don't slow your speed or shed weight immediately. You can't deploy glide wings successfully unless you slow."

I knew what she was saying but ignored it. I wasn't losing any of my body armor, much less my partner. We were in this together. My eyes were trying to ignore the maelstrom as I concentrated on screen after screen of maintenance menus. I was looking for anything that might help. Sure, Ada could do it faster and probably had already done all this, but she was a computer. Maybe something didn't occur to her.

The narrow access doors on each side of my suit's back panel covered the glider wings but also the grenade launchers. The gliders were single use items which were discarded upon landing. The idea was you would never need grenades in the air or wings on the ground. Made sense, it's how I would have designed it, if I could do that sort of thing.

"Ada, fire grenades both sides."

"That system is unavailable in freefall," she unhelpfully responded.

"Bypass it, I know you can."

We passed 17,000 feet, and my airspeed was still climbing.

"Times running out!" I yelled.

"I have to slow your speed. Deploying emergency chute now."

I hadn't expected that. The emergency chute was a small drogue that wouldn't even hold half my weight. None of us even knew why it was part of our suit's standard kit. Sumo had one the same size that I sometimes used when I wanted to drop him farther out than where I was landing.

Ada let me know she was gauging the wind gust before deploying both our chutes. She needed our relative speed to be momentarily almost dead stop before the grenades would launch. I felt the control surfaces on my armor biting into the wind to maneuver us, then a massive updraft hit, rolling me sideways as the chutes popped out. The jarring motion rattled my insides, but simultaneously, I felt the pop of grenades being launched.

"Cutaway the chutes, Joe."

That was something I had to do manually, at least for mine. Sumo, who was now hanging right in front of my face, had an automatic release but only when he was nearer the surface.

"Hey, buddy, if you could like move your ballsack to one side, I'll umm... you know, cut away your rescue chute." Yeah, that sounded stupid to me, too. Either way, I had both chutes released as we passed

10,000 feet and trusted Ada to get the glider deployed and locked in time.

Our descent was slowed considerably by the small chutes, but we regained velocity quickly. I felt the ribbed wings sliding out and finally heard them lock into place above me. The synthetic micro-silk popped as it caught air and offered me a few minutes of controlled flight. Through the rain, I could see the landscape was a mix of purple vines, downed trees, and mud. To the east, a river had burst out of its banks. I was well off course and entering the heart of the red zone, an area my suit's AI identified with either lethal radiation, biological dangers, or both.

I'd jumped out of a perfectly good starship for this. Pops was right. I am an idiot.

~

My right leg was in mud up to my thigh. The other was naturally being encircled by the damn thunder vines. The day had quickly faded to night as the storm clouds raged Sumo watched from the relative shelter of a rocky overhang as I struggled to free myself.

"Go ahead, laugh your ass off!" Yeah, it was a childish thing to say, especially to a dog—but what can I say? I'm a child.

"Fuck!" I yelled as one stuck leg came free only to drive the other into more mud.

"Hey, Sport!"

Oh, God, not now. "Little busy, Pops."

"Yeah, screw that, Junior. I know you're enjoying your semi-retirement. You're probably relaxing on a beach, sipping one of those goddamn fruity drinks you love."

"It's nighttime, Dad, and I'm nowhere near the beach."

I really don't know why I engage in his bullshit. Mom said I was an enabler. More often, I felt like the underpaid straight man in his comedy act. I pulled again, and my left leg finally came free with a sucking pop. I fell backward into a bush as I used my knife to cut away the vines that were now encircling both legs and my lower abdomen. Sumo was off to my left taking a nap.

"What's on your mind tonight, Pop?"

"Ah..."

I heard sounds of a TV being turned down. He liked the old-style flat screen sets. Wouldn't have one of the newer holostream high-def sets. *Wait. How the hell would he be getting a signal or power?*

"I was just wondering why I ever had children, so I thought to myself I should just go right to the source."

"Because torturing strangers is illegal in most states," I offered. "Besides, Mom was the source, why not talk to her?"

"Don't be an ass kid. Your mom was a goddamn saint, and she loved me more than she could ever express. She tried to give us a child we could all be proud of, but we got you instead."

I saw the flicker of eyes appearing in my field of vision. Ada automatically offered a full spectrum sweep of the area. Creatures were out there, some she could identify... others, not so much. I raked off as much of the mud as I could and eased up beside Sumo ready to move.

"Pop, any chance we could continue this abuse later?"

Something came darting out of the brush; my handgun had fired before I was consciously even aware of the threat. Whatever they had done to me had my reflexes and muscle memory optimized for killing shit fast.

"That was a squirrel, Prowler," Ada offered. I could hear the hidden layers of ridicule and scorn in her voice... I could. Hell, I didn't know it was just a squirrel. It could have been one of those murderous, bat-faced monkeys or something worse.

We had to get out of here; I was over ninety kilometers from the rendezvous point with Voss and had heard nothing from her since I landed.

"Gotta run, Pops, duty calls."

"You mean you have to take a shit? That's no reason to hang-up on your old man. Hell, where do you think I'm calling from? I come in here and sit down, and automatically I think of you."

"No... Dad." I layered in the exasperation, as if he could get anything that subtle. "I have to be somewhere. You know, soldiering stuff—end of the world and all." The man really seemed clueless that anything was going on out here in the real world.

"Ah, yeah, ok–gotcha, kiddo. You're heading after Nevis Carlson."

Goddamit! The man was infuriating, but just as much for his uncannily accurate knowledge as his verbal abuse.

"Why do you say that?" I asked after trying to come up with something witty and disarming.

Pops just ignored the question. He knew he was right and that I was stalling. "Nevis is a pointy-assed little pip-squeak. You think he could have pulled this shit off?"

"I don't know the guy, Dad. He's just part of my mission package."

"Ah."

I heard the sound of him downing a drink along with his trademark sigh of contentment. Sumo and I were moving now, both our speed increasing as we raced into the blinding rain.

"Man's a total dick, always working the angles, but that doesn't mean he isn't dangerous. Watch your six, kid."

"Okay, Pop, what else can you..." The sound had changed. A simple nothingness fille my ears..

"He's gone, isn't he, Ada?"

She laughed before offering the same answer as every other time he had called. "I show no record of any recent communications, Joe."

"Contact!" Ada yelled just before something hit me from the right side knocking me clear off the old road.

The suit's sensors were useless this close, and darkness and rain prevented me from knowing what I was fighting. "Please, God, not more HappyBears," I whispered. I felt something like hands on my arm, then a claw or blade down near my groin. Right... that was my thought, too. Protect the groin. Except that turned out to be a wayward tree limb, while whatever grabbed me was now rotating my arm joint in a way that would eventually rip my elbow and shoulder out of place.

I am an idiot, but I'm not completely stupid. At the same time, I spun into the thing and brought my knee up. I felt soft tissue give way to bone, or cartilage, whatever the creature had underneath it, but it didn't loosen its grip.

"Ada, light it up." I wanted to see what I was up against, although that would screw up my night vision, or maybe it wouldn't, I hadn't really checked that part of my upgrades yet.

The built-in suit lights cut on. "Off, off...cut it back off!"

"Holy fuck, holy shit, Jesus Christ, what is this thing?" To explain fully in one brief example of the differences between a human and an AI, Ada helpfully answered my stupid question by showing me a fully rendered 3-D image of the beast. Yes, she showed me a still image of the horrific creature that I didn't want to see while I was fighting the same effing creature. "Goddamnit, Ada, get rid of that."

I have no idea what it was. Yes, I do—it was a fucking mistake. It was someone's half-formed attempt at building an actual nightmare. I do mean half-formed. That much was obvious. Skin hung from exposed muscle tissue and a bony skeletal undercarriage as if it was still a work in process. The thing hit the side of my helmet hard enough to make me stumble backward. I heard Sumo and knew he was attacking but had no way of knowing where my partner was.

That was when lightning streaked overhead illuminating the thing once again. Looked no better in silhouette... nope. Still the ugliest fucking thing I'd ever seen. That was saying something because Banshee team had been raiding bio-labs for years, and we'd seen some freaky-ass shit. This ugly asshat motherfucker looked like he'd stepped off the coroner's table just to come hunt me down.

My souped-up brain just sat there behind my face and said, "Huh." Neither of us had a clue. I couldn't make out a head, nor legs. Still, it looked kind of humanoid, but the way it moved was certainly not bipedal. In the darkness, it seemed to flow, or more accurately, shutter and shift from one position to another. I finally had a few feet of separation from Corpse Boy, which would have been an excellent time to go for a weapon. Instead, that was when the suit's air filters cut out, and the aroma of this stinking pile of meat hit me.

Rotten eggs, decaying fish, rotting bodies, and a thousand bean-eating sumo wrestlers farting at the same time would not have come close to this horror. I begged Ada to do something. My eyes watered, and I staggered. I felt a vice-like grip encircle my hip and something penetrating through the outer wall of my suit. That shouldn't even be possible, but the smell was literally debilitating.

Then I saw Sumo leaping up and over me to engage the creature. The pain on my hip eased up as it moved and dodged the combat dog's vicious attack. My boy had had enough and was ripping chunks out of the thing. I had no idea if that was a good strategy, but I joined in. We both began tearing away body tissue, muscles, bones, anything we could tear loose. I saw a blur of movement as something else emerged through the creature's insides and heard Sumo yelp just before I felt another blow that sent me careening back into the road.

Rolling back into a ready crouch, I scanned for the thing but only saw Sumo off to one side struggling to regain his own footing. The lights came on, and Ada ran full scans, but the Corpse Boy was gone, no sign of it at all. No sign of the thing, no smell... nothing. I crawled over to the dog and pulled him close. I checked him closely, and he seemed in better shape than I was. Ada triggered an injection on the dog's suit that would hopefully counter any toxins or contagions having mouthfuls of rotting flesh might have given him. I sat there for long minutes holding him close, both of us trying to catch our breath and figure out what in the hell had just happened.

CHAPTER THIRTY-SEVEN

"You look like hell, Kovach."

Why was that becoming the common greeting everyone had for me? "Has to be better than the last time you saw me," I responded, walking up the overgrown road. My suit was covered with mud and blood and some other things I couldn't even identify. The anti-fouling system seemed to have been knocked offline. That and the fact that I'd battled a corpse *and a killer squirrel.*

With more than a little uncertainty, I stuck out my hand as a sign of peace, but she brushed it aside and embraced me, giving me a quick kiss. Doing that in a battle suit was awkward, but still, it felt good, despite my obvious hatred for this woman. Hey, it's there, just buried under layers of 'Damn, she still looks good.' "How are you, Voss?"

She cocked her head, and yeah, it still looked adorable despite my nearly complete lack of trust for the woman.

"Still not good calling me Dami?" she asked in a cooing voice.

"Some things are harder for me to get over. Like... you killing me."

"Yet here you are," she said, stepping back and opening her arms. "Besides, Joe, I just shot you. Your own body is what killed you."

"You knew I would come back?'

She shrugged her shoulders. "It was a fifty-fifty shot."

That did not make me feel better in the slightest.

"I knew if your body sustained much more damage, you were beyond hope. One of your doctors, though... cute little thing named Jacobson, told me about a sort of biological reset that would flood your body with nanobots to repair damage at the cellular level. I know you don't believe me Joe, but everything I did was to help you and Carol stay alive."

"Sounds like your little doctor friend shared a lot. You must have gotten close for him to open up like that. Jacobson... Jacobson." It took me several seconds for the name to register, despite the fact that Ada had helpfully posted the guy's ID badge in my HUD. "You fucked Lawnmower Man?"

Voss snorted as the laughter erupted. "God, Joe, I have missed you."

Then she kissed me again, hard.

"For your information, I never fucked Doctor Jacobson, although I would have if I'd needed... obviously," She said.

Whatever she was saying after the kiss could have been in another language. God, this woman was hot, dangerous, and confusing as hell.

Sumo looked at me, peed on a nearby tree he'd been watching since we arrived, then eased over to Voss for an obligatory head scratch. Apparently, the master sergeant getting affection wasn't good enough for the muddy dog.

"You ready to go?"

I knew she said we had a long hike ahead of us, but honestly, I was beat. The last twenty miles I'd had to carry Sumo. I am an augmented soldier in a battle suit. He is not. Well, he's augmented, just not to that degree. We'd both been fighting nearly continuously for days. It had taken its toll.

"Give us a few minutes, we landed way off course and ran all night to get here."

"The storm?" she asked.

I just nodded. I didn't want to let her know my suit had malfunctioned, or worse, someone up on the Stone Mountain might have sabotaged it. I was packing that little question away for another day. I knew Ada would be busy assembling the evidence without my intervention.

We ate a cold breakfast from a supply Dami had already gathered. This was technically a red zone but not from radiation. The biologic lifeforms posed the major danger. The houses that lined the road were all dark and abandoned, as empty of people as the farms were devoid of livestock. The John Deere agrobots sat motionless in the fields where they had stopped. The food in those houses was still safe to eat, though. At least all the packaged foods, they would last for decades.

She watched me eat — and eat, but said nothing. I knew my appetite had increased exponentially.

"You're different," she said as we began packing up.

"How so?" I still wasn't comfortable opening up to this woman, although damn, she still felt as comfortable to me. A friendship that seemed to have years behind it but in fact only had a few tumultuous days.

"Not sure, but I think I like it. Death becomes you, sweetheart."

Sumo was still sniffing at the same tree. I was fairly sure that was where the Wraith had posted up. It still amazed me that it could be around both me and my dog and remain completely undetected. Shit, the thing had hitched a ride with us for hundreds of miles, and we'd known nothing.

"So, tell me about this thing that scared you last night."

Scared me. Scared me... that was how she was spinning this. Fine. Okay, yeah it scared me. I went through it all again. Even showing her the brief footage Ada had pieced together.

Voss nodded and had heard rumors about them. "Some of the survivor groups have begun cataloging the creatures. I think this is one of the ones they call Culls."

"Odd name, but ok," I said, leaning down to pull up my daypack. "We're half a country away from the Rainier or Iron River facilities."

She nodded and pushed her hair back over one ear. "Those were obviously not the only facilities working on bioweapons, Joe. I told you that back then."

"Shit." I'd hoped I had remembered that wrong. The Nightmare Factory had more than enough horrible shit. We didn't need multiple versions all producing their own variants of the biological or mechanical terrors.

"Rainier was a production facility," she offered. "We are relatively sure they worked on the most mature projects, those creations they judged ready for production. Creations whose lethality and investment would make Hammer Industries more money than they could have ever hoped to spend."

"I don't think it was about the money. Not totally."

"What was your mission at Ranier?" I asked.

She ignored the question drawing my arm computer closer and scrolling back through the fight scenes of the previous night. "This poor thing doesn't even look like it's partially developed. Its lifecycle must have been interrupted much too early."

"Poor thing? Are you insane? The 'thing' very nearly took out a trained soldier in full battle armor and his dog."

She patted my hand dismissively, "And yet again, here you are."

I could see she was not unprotected, not wearing armor like mine, but more than the battleskin I'd gotten for her during our last trip. Slinging her weapon, she tapped my chest armor with a resounding thud.

"Come on, tin man, grab Toto, time to go find the wizard."

It left me wondering if she was Dorothy or the Wicked Witch. Somehow, I was sure I was going to find out pretty damn soon.

CHAPTER THIRTY-EIGHT

Xero heard the woman before she came into view. One of Hauk's men stood in the corridor blocking the tall blonde.

"I'm sorry, ma'am, I have my orders," the young corporal said. His words were not harsh, but neither did they offer any hint of compromise.

Xero didn't recognize the woman but thought she was also a new arrival. Xero passed the soldier with a simple nod. Her current clearance got her access to virtually any section of the ship. The fading complaints of the other woman reminded her that not everyone would be so lucky. The increased access Kovach had granted allowed her to make some headway against the ship's control system lockout. It felt good to be doing something productive again. The day before, she had eliminated all the limits from the sensor grid. That had proven to be both good and bad.

Good, in that they could see anything approaching. Bad, in that they kept seeing an intermittent contact just on the edge of sensor range. A ship possibly hiding in the sensor shadow of what the ship could detect. Bayou wanted desperately to change position to make sure whatever it was just happened to be in the same orbit and speed. Xero knew the odds of that being the case were astronomical. Currently, the ability to alter their course was not an option. Whatever command codes the admiral had used seemed above god-level access for the ship's systems.

Opening the hatch into engineering, Xero smiled seeing the boy hard at work on his one pet-project. In less than a week, she had enjoyed Lux's company far more than she would have thought. She'd never been around children and assumed her intolerance for most adults would have been even worse with their progeny. Lux had proven her wrong, though.

"Hi, Zee!" he said without looking up.

Xero smiled at his new nickname for her. It was the same thing Valyn used to call her. "How is she coming?" The boy had been working on it nearly every waking hour since she had been aboard.

"I'm not sure it's a she," he answered. His arms were inside what looked to be the chest cavity, or maybe the power storage, for the modified service drone.

"I thought you wanted me to find your Marcie files to load." She hadn't been able to, but Xero knew she could write a simulation of the NannyBot AI in just a few days.

Lux shrugged. "I did, maybe I do. This just seems like..."

"Not like a girl?"

He looked up at her and grinned. "Yeah."

"Like I don't seem like a girl?" Xero asked curiously.

"Are you?"

Smart kid, answer a question with a question. "I am neither... and I am both. Does that make sense?"

Lux shrugged. "I don't understand adults. You are Xero, and you're my friend. That's all I know."

The smile warmed her face. *If only everyone could embrace such simple truths,* she thought.

"All right, sir, I have to get to work on the nav computer. Do you need anything before I go?" She had gotten in the habit of helping him solve one problem before she began work each day. Since she wasn't a robotics engineer, he normally saved the mobility questions for Specialist Otero of the space engineers. He'd learned to mainly hit Xero with systems problems. He nodded eagerly before running through his latest challenge.

Twenty minutes later, Xero strapped into the command console and began working her way through the system's submenus. Something about Lux's challenge today kept nagging at her. He saw things in such a simple way. It was cute, but also in ways, superior to her own approach, which was to assume the solution to a problem would always be complicated and require an exponentially more advanced solution. She'd been in the digital arms race much of her life. One side increased security, the other increased its attacks. It had tinged her view of the world.

Lux was very bright, potentially very gifted, as his mother was no mental slouch and apparently, the father, too, had many talents. Knowing the boy had survived on his own down on the surface proved to her he had more than just mental aptitude. He had tremendous potential; already he was teaching her new ways to look at things.

She brought up the command-line interface and triggered the neural link she had installed. It allowed her to literally think about the command coding she wanted to test, and it would appear in the buffer file.

"Think simplicity," she whispered. Her problem had been with one central kernel of the command system. It was protected by a constantly changing security encryption that so far had defied every attempt at pausing it, much less getting in. Regaining command control over the related systems like life-support, engineering, and eventually comms, had been time-consuming but simple. This core process on navigation and propulsion was defeating her, at least so far. She'd tried the normal methods, brute force hacks, backdoor maintenance patches, buffer overload exploits, and total system reboots. But so far, no joy.

What was truly baffling was Xero was confident that she had gotten into the control matrix multiple times only to find herself back on the outside looking in once more. She leaned back in the chair and thought again about the boy. Lux's issue had been one of ghost sensors that kept giving a faulty reading. It wasn't one sensor, but many. The hovering drones, which is where many of the parts came from, had to be totally aware of their environment to function correctly. It also had to be able to determine static objects like walls from moveable objects like people. Despite him insisting it wasn't a system problem, she had helped him recalibrate the array to eliminate the false-positives hits, the persistent shadow of something living that wasn't there.

What if it was there? Xero thought before turning around. She could see Lux still busy at his workbench. His mother had brought him a plate of food and was sitting across from the boy watching him work.

The code slasher turned back to her own screen. "See what is really there."

She went through screens at incredible speed, flashing in and out of windows faster than could be followed with an untrained eye.

"Fuck!"

She caught it, just briefly before it changed. Something that shouldn't have been there. A screen exactly like another she had seen before. The two should have been similar but never the exact same. It was a small monitoring sub-routine for the engine maintenance ports. It constantly measured and adjusted cooling, propellant, core containment fields, and such. All very dynamic items, yet the readout had been identical to the last time she'd been here, but only for a microsecond, then it updated. Older buffered systems might do that but not the quantum systems of today.

She needed to cross-reference to another workstation's screens to see which was real, but if what she was suspecting was happening, that might prove impossible to do alone. She tapped her cheekbone to make a call.

"Otero, are you near a workstation?"

The engineer answered at once, "Of course, ma'am. I'm on the bridge monitoring the final disassembly of the..."

Xero cut her off. "Please go to this maintenance screen and send me a screen shot." She rattled off the long index for the right view. "Let me know when you take the shot, I need to get my own timecode just right."

"Ma'am, why not just pull it up yourself? You can even emulate any other workstation."

Xero ignored the near constant use of the formal gendered term the woman insisted on using. "Just do it, Specialist. I have my reasons."

Otero counted down and snapped a screen grab, the same instant

Xero froze her own. She used one of the flats linked to her comms to display the image next to her own holodisplay.

"Son of a bitch. Thanks, Otero. Is the commander on the bridge?"

"Yes, Riggs is here."

Please have her wait for me, I have something she will want to know.

Xero raced through additional screens, setting up buffers and keystroke generators that continued to generate code as if she was still sitting there. It looked like she was attempting to spoof the ship's AI. Leaving her chair, she ran over to Lux and his mom who had apparently joined him before going to see Bayou. She hugged the boy before kissing the top of his head. "You're a genius," she said before heading to the hatch. Then she stopped. "Cancel the recalibration on the array, Lux. That wasn't the problem. Sometimes the solution is exactly what it seems to be."

CHAPTER THIRTY-NINE

Bayou stood hunched over the tabletop display in obvious confusion. The view showed a large window with the now familiar orbital trajectory of the IAS Stone Mountain and various smaller windows of more technical data that she was clueless on. "I'm still not following."

Xero tried again to explain what she had found. "Lieutenant, do you remember the massive data breach from around ten years ago when Wall Street trading algorithms were hacked?"

"Vaguely, yes," Riggs said. "That was before all global stock trading was decentralized and block-chained, wasn't it?"

"Yes, exactly. I had a hand in locating the code slashers on that one," Xero offered in way of explanation.

"Chinese ex-pats hiding out in some renegade, African nation."

Xero grimaced. That had been a false narrative her bosses had created to insulate the public from the actual truth, but it wasn't worth going into now. "Something like that, yes. The exploit the team used was so deceptively simple that no one even considered it. Honestly, the best hacks usually are. Back in the early days of the twenty-first century, they coined a term for the exploits, 'Social engineering.'"

Riggs shook her head, still not following.

"They use your own biases and beliefs to get you to do something... to open the door for them."

"But you're talking about something in the ship's sensor shadow."

"Yes! It is related, I promise," Xero said, moving around some data screens on the table. "One of the earliest PC hacks involved simply adjusting the alphanumeric characters displayed from white to black. There were no color displays back then, so that effectively turned the screen off to the user.

"What good did that do?"

"Well, it could have started a world war. If an enemy state were able to network into a nuclear silo system, they could capture usernames and passwords as the operators tried in vain to login to a system that they were already logged into. The enemy could have even gained direct access to the day's launch codes."

"Oh. Did that ever happen?"

"No, Bayou, not that I am aware of. It was more a nuisance hack, a prank for the most part, but the idea is still around."

"And this is what you found?" Riggs asked. She was still highly pissed at Kovach going AWOL. She wanted Ada working on this, as well as the brilliant hacker, but she was glad the woman... person, was here.

Xero nodded. "Yes, while the other command locks were all triggered programmatically, the propulsion and navigation are being done in real-time. Someone is putting fake data into our holodisplays to make it look like we don't have access, when in fact we do."

She pulled up the side-by-side images showing the same screens from the two different workstations. "Otero helped me track it down. I then set up a subroutine to make it look like I hadn't noticed but also began tracking down the signal lag. How fast could the screens update? That gave me a good idea of how far away the hackers were. Perhaps it was someone already onboard."

The lieutenant was already sensitive to potential security issues from all the new arrivals on board. She had no way of effectively vetting anyone properly, and several minor incidents had already been reported to her. "And you found..."

"Point zero one light seconds away," Xero answered immediately.

"That is the lag between screen updates on any workstation I am using. That's 1800 miles," Deb said, doing the mental calculations. "Just on the outer edge of our sensor range."

"Yes ma'am."

"A ship, comms relay, drone, or what?" Riggs asked.

"Possibly any, but it's obviously an AI program running a constant attack. That would require a lot of power and room. Also, the speed doesn't allow for a more remote sending unit. It has to be generated immediately. That rules out the drone or comms relay."

"So, the shadow we've been seeing the last two days is a ship?"

"That is my conclusion," Xero said, expanding a display window of seemingly empty space.

"Something is out there. It doesn't want us to maneuver but seems okay with keeping us alive. Is it Gateway? The admiral?" Deb asked.

"No way to know, Lieutenant. The other issues were almost certainly from them. They downloaded with a standard maintenance update from Fleet Command on Luna. This could be their next step or totally unrelated."

Riggs was thinking of how helpless she had felt watching the Alice Springs get attacked and breaking up in orbit. "We have no large weapons capability yet. That ship could have missiles." The SEs were now being helped by several Marines who had recovered, working around the clock on restoring weapons capability to the warship. They were even using the giant 3D printers to manufacture ships' munitions. Deb knew she was an inexperienced captain, and the ship would be no match against any genuine threats out here.

"Thank you, Xero, for everything. I assume you can bypass this?"

"I can compensate for what they are doing. I can get us moving but can't guarantee I can lock them out of our system. I also have to wonder what they will do next. They probably didn't expect you to have someone like me on board. Once they see their hack isn't working, then what?"

Riggs considered it long after Xero left the room. 'Then what?' That really was the question. She called Captain Hauk to the bridge. Perhaps he could offer some insight, some possible solutions she wasn't seeing.

CHAPTER FORTY

We had a couple of days' travel to Nevis' presumed location near the coast. "We doing this all on foot?"

Voss shrugged, "Unless you see something usable. Nothing airborne, though. I feel sure he can spot that."

I scanned the countryside and investigated likely looking homes and barns as they passed. No obvious signs of travel. The stalled autocars lining the road in places were all useless, many were simply charred shells.

"Where is everyone?" I asked. It had been my nagging question since the attacks went down. "You mentioned survivors. Where are they?"

"Not here, not sticking around any of the red zones," Voss said as she trotted at a steady rhythm. She wasn't as fast as me, but she was doing alright. "Originally, we thought around thirty percent of the global population was wiped out on Last Day."

"Three billion people," I said, almost numb to the sheer magnitude of that loss.

"Yeah, that was a low estimate it turns out."

"How low?" I asked, not really wanting to know the answer.

"Depends on the day. The losses seem to be multiplying exponentially. My people now believe it was closer to forty percent in the initial attacks. Since then, the numbers have continued to add up. Not at the same rate but steadily increasing just the same. The last figure I had was fifty-two-point-five percent of the population missing or dead and over sixty by the end of the summer."

"Jesus Christ. Half the human population," I said, stopping to take a drink of water.

"Worse in some cities. Populations in London, Hong Kong, and New York are almost totally wiped out. Five percent of the populus left...maybe, hard to have anything more accurate."

"Where are the bodies?"

"That is a damn good question," she said, also taking a pull from the hydration pack on her back.

"The creatures are probably feeding on some, but they seem most interested in the living. Still, the smell of decomp is everywhere."

My suit's filters blocked most of the smell, but whenever my face was exposed, I knew she was right. The smell of death hung to every thing, every place.

"Tell me about what you found, you mentioned something when you called."

We began walking again and could see a neighborhood in the distance. My map display showed a small town just beyond.

Voss told me about the attacks she'd endured and then her observations of the girl who walked right through them. Something about the description made me think about the blonde woman back in Texas. She had mentioned a witch several times. Someone whom the creatures seemed to ignore.

"You think this WitchWalker had some power over them? Something like your Wraith maybe?"

"Maybe, but don't think so. The Wraith doesn't seem to be much help against many of the beasts. Also, the girl didn't seem to even notice them, like they weren't even there."

She picked up the pace seeing something ahead that obviously grabbed her interest. "If the biologics are all weaponized, Joe, they seem to respond in proportionate mass to the enemy."

"So, the more people we have to fight, the more aggressive and more of them that will come after us?"

"I think so, yes," Voss confirmed.

That would explain some of why the encounters with Red-7 were so aggressive and determined.

"That's why you wanted me to come alone?"

She stopped near a building and turned toward me and smiled. "Sure. That was one of the reasons."

Damn, this woman was aggravating.

"Can you drive it?" Voss asked.

Ada had assured me I could, but the meat part of my brain was much less certain.

"Yes... maybe," I said. It was a vintage Indian motorcycle. A 2035 Thunder Chief, one of the first totally electric bikes the company ever made. Voss had spotted a sign on a metal building that somehow clued her into looking inside. The girl flat-out knew her stuff.

"You sure it will run on P-cells?"

"Yeah, it has the adapter already installed. Just give it a try," she urged.

Since the bike wasn't powered when the EMPs hit, chances were reasonably good the entire system might not be fried. The key fob was sitting in a coffee cup on a nearby bench. This had to be a restoration project for whomever previously owned this place.

I straddled it and got a feel of the weight. Part of our RDT training had involved riding motorcycles in case we ever needed to 'borrow' some from the locals to get to a clear extract point. Those were all self-balancing with internal gyros for stabilization. I could tell at once this one depended on the rider balancing it. With more than a little trepidation, I pushed the start and was rewarded with total silence. Still, the small dash had lights. I twisted the throttle slightly, and the bike jumped forward several feet.

"Yeah, Cowboy, it's on."

We rolled the machine outside and loaded up. Sumo found a spot in front of me, and Voss sat on the seat behind me, the closeness of her body making me feel emboldened to attempt this stupid adventure. I didn't ask about the Wraith, I didn't much care if we left it behind entirely. Damn thing still gave me the creeps.

I patted the pup, and we were off. Voss's grip tightened around my waist, and I found I could raise my knees up high enough to cradle Sumo, keeping him from sliding around too much. Soon, I was speeding down the road relying on Ada to identify debris or creatures on the path ahead. My improved reflexes really came in handy as I dodged tree limbs, cars, and something large and dead. As we moved back farther away from civilization, the ride took on an entirely different feel. The bike was whisper quiet. No artificial engine sounds like most modern bikes were required to have. The tires crunching over the dead leaves and the wind whipping past were the only sounds. Occasionally, Voss would point out something, but I think we both were just enjoying ourselves. The sun was out, the temperature was mild, and two people were out for a nice Sunday ride with their dog.

Okay, there was a lot wrong with that statement, but the feeling matched...at least for a while. Enjoy the small wins while you can, right?

We stopped for the day in a forest clearing near an overgrown lake. There was no sign of destruction here. None of the purple vines even; those had faded out a good thirty miles back. I slid my suit's helmet back in its receiver and loosened the rest of my body armor. It was lightweight and highly maneuverable but still felt confining after a while. Sumo hopped down and immediately peed on the front wheel. We needed to make camp, and I wanted a battle plan for dealing with Nevis.

"That was fun," Voss said, coming up and embracing me from the front. She pulled me close and kissed me again.

Damn, she was confusing and aggravating, but I was enjoying the kissing parts.

"So, what do you want to do?"

"We need to discuss how we deal with Nevis," I said with more enthusiasm than I felt. My priorities for the mission seemed to have shifted in the last few minutes.

"You sure that's what you want to do?"

Her hand was busy loosening the lower parts of my armor. "Umm... yes," I said, not even convincing myself of the lie.

"I don't like you, woman. You killed me." We were still kissing as her hand slipped inside my battle skin and touched flesh.

"I know." She laughed, slipping her own top off. God, her body was amazing.

I wanted her, but yes... *I have a thing with what's her name. Oh, God, don't be an ass. Don't be such a guy right now.*

Her mouth moved to my neck, then she seemed to sense my resistance.

"I want you, Joe. Now!"

I was counting to a hundred backward, remembering Christmas morning with my grandparents, focusing on anything but this beautiful woman in front of me.

She smiled, "Carol, right?"

I nodded slowly. Then her hand found the one part of me that had no self-control. She kissed me deeply.

"Trust me, she won't mind sharing."

I had no idea what that meant but soon realized it didn't matter to me either. Yes, I am an asshole. True fact, and long since being a surprise to any of us.

CHAPTER FORTY-ONE

The sex was fast, aggressive, and inventive. I've been through PT courses that hadn't required as much physical effort. Both of us seemed to be needing whatever this was, and yes, I knew she could simply be hijacking my emotional connection to serve her own needs, but her actions seemed more like a release than anything contrived. The emotional component seemed non-existent, to be honest.

Afterward, she slept long and hard. I rested for a few hours, then awoke fully rested. My dad would have raked me through the coals for getting distracted when I was on a mission. Honestly, every CO I ever had would have done the same. Times were different now. Hell, I was different.

I used the time to talk to Ada. Say what you will for my built-in personal assistant—she doesn't judge. "Have you come up with anything on Nevis Carlson or where we might be headed?" I asked subvocally.

"Nothing so far, Joseph. Numerous enclaves for the super wealthy are closer to the coast. Few that show up as being particularly noteworthy and none linked to Carlson, Hammer, DARPA or any known contacts or subsidiaries."

That didn't surprise me. Ada was good, but AI search algorithms could suss out nearly any personal data these days. Most people, including myself, went to great lengths to hide personal information. The world had moved to link addresses and anonymous IPs, assuming any tidbit of actual information would be stolen, sold, and used against us. After our prior generation seemed intent on over-sharing every bit of personal data, we had done a 180 and gone to great lengths to ensure our privacy. Now, it didn't matter. There wouldn't be enough people left to give a shit about our personal story. And those who survived would have way more on their mind than where others were spending the holidays or what they were wearing to the prom.

"Anything new happening?"

I'd never been much for current events, so much of the news in the before was stylized for its entertainment value that the substance was lost or meaningless. Now, though, in a nearly complete vacuum, I found myself desperate to know what else was going on out in the world. Despite the attacks, government collapse, whole cities falling apart, and the astounding number of mass casualties, broadcasts were still being posted to the working streaming channels. Gone was the need for over-sensationalizing the story. Real-life was dramatic enough. It wasn't really news, more like scraps of news and personal observations. Still a few semi-credible stories seemed to get out. Ada distilled the media feeds knowing I was mainly interested in anything that might help on the mission or lead us to everyone involved in the original attacks.

"San Francisco reported twenty-eight more attacks by what they are calling a killing machine."

"The horde?" I asked, remembering the swarm of MurderCrabs we'd battled many times.

"Probably," Ada said, "although the descriptions are incomplete and seem to vary wildly."

"Parts of Brazil have gone completely dark," she continued. "The capital city was not in the initial attack, leading some to speculate that the TWC might have been using it as a staging area. Now, there is no news coming out of the area, and drone overflights show no signs of life... or destruction."

That is troubling, I thought. They weren't attacked, at least not conventionally. "Bioweapon?" I was thinking more of the shit that had hit us.

"No further information, but my own assessment is no. The vines and creatures leave a very recognizable trail of destruction, and the drone footage shows none of that."

"Okay, what else?"

"Paris, there seems to be a significant human resistance coalescing in the ruins of the old city."

"What are they fighting?" I asked. Times had changed, no longer was the question 'Who?'

"Unknown, Joe, but a large explosion took an ancient castle fifty kilometers outside the city and unearthed a network of subterranean tunnels. The tunnels were modern and apparently still in use, although doing what is unclear."

The story was intriguing but didn't seem particularly relevant to our situation. My heightened acuity understood, though, there had to be some connection. "What else?"

"I think you will find the names of some of the missing or captured interesting."

Damn! She was right, I did. Reading the list, one of the resistance fighters names jumped out at me immediately. "He was lost at the castle breach?"

"Yes, that appears likely."

"What other information do you have on that location?" I asked.

"It's provenance and current ownership are a mystery, but I think it is something you should discuss with your friend."

I looked over at Damiana who was beginning to stir. Was she my friend, and what in the hell would she know of an attack halfway around the world? Whatever truths I was chasing just kept getting more and more confusing.

"Hi, handsome."

Although it was still dark, my eyes could pick out her flawless face lying beside me. "Hi," I said, trying to force a neutral tone. I didn't want her to read anything into this.

"Thank you. For last night, I mean," she said in a sleepy voice.

She pulled the edge of the sleeping bag from her naked body, affecting me again with an overwhelming sense of desire.

As if sensing my hormone levels increase, she shucked herself out of the bag and stood. “I’d love a repeat, but I think we have a busy day ahead.” She gave me a quick peck on the cheek and went into the bushes. I assumed she needed to take care of business, but with Damiana Voss, who knew?

I broke down our small campsite and slapped a hot patch onto a small thermal water bladder. I made myself a cup of coffee and a tea for Voss, who sipped it thankfully while she dressed. A part of me wanted to discuss what had happened between us, but somehow, I knew that was the wrong thing to do. This was a woman who knew what she wanted and had no issue in taking it. Last night she had me in her sights. Tomorrow, who knew? I had to stop this. *Focus on the mission, Kovach!*

We mounted the Indian and began again in the early morning light. My helmet was sheathed, and it felt good to hear the early morning sounds and feel the wind on my face. My rear passenger’s head rested on my shoulder much of the time. That was pretty nice, too. There was no smell of decay here, nor had any creatures bothered us during the night. My Spidey sense told me that the danger we were facing would be something more conventional. If Carlson was behind this, he had likely spared this part of the country, so he would have a safe-haven, a walled garden of sorts in the midst of all the destruction. Either way, Voss indicated we probably had a few hours before we would run into trouble.

The thick forest around us reminded me of my little mountain cabin 800 miles or so to the south. I wondered if it was still standing. Had it been looted or overrun by now? Mornings there, the valley would have been filled with the smell of wood smoke; here, there was nothing, just the rich earth smells of the North woods.

I remembered what Ada had suggested and mentioned the attack in France. I felt Damiana’s body stiffen. She motioned for me to pull over. She jumped from the bike and put her hands on her knees. I wondered if she was about to be sick.

“Those fucking bastards,” she said with clenched fists.

The woman was pissed; her expression was animalistic in its raw fury. I quickly realized I only knew a fraction of who this person was.

“Your people?” I asked, assuming it as fact.

She gave me a side eye and nodded reluctantly. I knew next to nothing about the woman, but Ada and I both had guessed she was a part of something much larger.

"My Sisters," Voss said, her eyes filling with rage instead of tears.

"They were your family?" I asked, confused.

"Are my family," she said confidently. "They were attacked, they are not gone."

Her voice had lost its hint of British formality. Now it sounded darker, more ancient. Hints of German or Slavic even. Voss was a chameleon, a shapeshifter becoming whatever she needed to be. This was her at her most basic, her most dangerous. It was also the first sign of vulnerability I'd ever seen from her. She was human, but like me, seemed a lot more at times.

I hesitated, then put an arm around her and drew her close. She resisted briefly then leaned in and accepted my comfort. I heard what sounded like prayers, then cursing in hushed breaths. I stroked her hair and let her get it out. I couldn't fix it; I didn't even understand it. All I could do was to be there for her. Whatever 'this' was, cut deep into this woman's soul.

Finally, she drew in a breath and straightened. "Thank you, Joseph. I am glad you are with me. Nevis will pay for this."

"You're sure it was him?"

She looked toward the rising sun and nodded. "It explains why his man was hunting me in the desert. They have been hunting us for a very long time," she answered.

"Your sisters?"

Her lips tightened as if she had already revealed too much. She gave a simple nod and walked away, tapping her comms and making a call.

I resumed my position on the bike. I tried not to listen in, but my hearing and Ada's were good enough to pick up fragments of the conversation. Whatever it was involved someone named Lumia.

"Ada, anything?" I subvocalized. She obviously had connected Voss to the battle scene overseas, but I had learned that was often through the accumulation of varied and otherwise random data points instead of something more tangible.

"Working on it, Joseph, but may take some time. There isn't a lot to go on. I believe we can assume she comes from an interesting family."

CHAPTER FORTY-TWO

Bertrand Acevedo moved deeper into the shadow so he could watch the monitor. He knew he'd struck a blow but sadly, not a killing blow. That was disappointing; he'd burned many assets and far more money than he'd wanted to pull off the attack. Still, he'd missed her. The Grand Mother of the Sisters of Light had not been where he'd been assured she would be.

He wasn't worried, he knew his boss would be pleased. They had definitely hurt the pesky group. One the Sisters would not easily recover from. Learning the location of the backup facility had not been an easy task. The Sister who had finally revealed it still hung from the ceiling beams of the old church a dozen miles away from the ruins. At least parts of her were still there. He'd meticulously followed the almost invisible trail of leads from one person to another before finally reaching the woman. She was a minor player in the Sisterhood. She didn't even know anything of its scope or mission. Still, she was aware of the long-abandoned Château de Lavardin and its subterranean vaults.

Now, the ancient castle was indeed ruins in every sense of the word. It was difficult getting an accurate headcount, but his spotters had seen over a hundred of the small body bags being carried out of the rubble. Then the spotter had gone silent, as had the man's brother a short time later. Now, Bertrand understood the Sisterhood was using whatever means needed to track him down. His mission had been to deliver a message to the Sisters of Light, that did not include revealing himself.

~

"Thyraa."

The woman nodded silently but didn't otherwise acknowledge the other. Thyraa was busy doing what she was good at, dissecting and analyzing. In this case, it was fragments of the bombs that leveled the complex. She brought her fingers to her nose. The smell was unmistakable, octanitrocubane. She pursed her lips, then made a call.

"Yes, OCX-9, and a lot more than was necessary."

She eyed the perimeter as she talked. This had been very intentional, a direct assault on the Sisters. No one had been that brave or that stupid in a very long time.

"Yes. Right away!" she said in response to the question. "Paris is not good. The machines, they are a problem. The water is also fouled."

She closed the connection and continued her examination. Her heart was with the resistance fight a hundred miles to the north, but Lumia herself had commanded that she take charge of this. After Morocco, the ruins had been the single largest sanctuary for the Sisterhood. This was not a strategic target, simply one of opportunity for their enemy. The chateau was but one of several in Europe that helped with recruiting and introducing new arrivals to the ways of the group. The vast majority never made it beyond these walls. The rigors of daily life, the discipline, the restrictions all were too much. That was where the system had failed. One of the acolytes had gone missing just days before the attack. She'd been sent to the makeshift market in a nearby village looking to acquire fresh vegetables.

The skin pricked on her neck, and Thyraa wiped away the sweat and grit. It didn't ease the feeling, though. Years in the field had taught her many things; mostly it taught her to trust her instincts. Whoever was responsible would want to see this, they would want proof of how successful the attack had been. She bent down looking as if she was studying a charred bit of timber, but reaching beneath her cloak, she activated a remote sensor grid the complex had. It was decentralized and would not have been affected by the blast.

The sensors were designed by the group's own tech department and were better than anything else available. Checking the thin, flat panel display, she saw three targets light up immediately. They were small and stationary, so not drones. Motion activated microcams judging by the size. So, the human spotters hadn't been the only thing they were using. The Sisters had gotten little from the two locals other than a foreigner had paid them. First for odd jobs, then to watch the ruins and report in.

Her first instinct was to send a pulse through the grid to fry the cameras, but that might negate possibly finding the perpetrator. No, she needed to pursue this from another way. Track the signal, see where it led. Giving no sign she knew anything, she deliberately walked away from the location of the cameras and took another call.

"Allo. Oui! Comment allez vous, Dami?"

"I'm fine," Damiana said, and physically that was true. Inside, though, she was torn apart.

Thyraa said the code word that let Damiana know it wasn't safe to speak openly on her end.

"I understand, can you tell me..."

"She was not here, Dami, she would have never come here. We did lose many of our Sisters, though. You will be filled in when I can," Thyraa said in a language that was neither French nor English. "We are still very much at war, my Sister."

Bertand gently closed the small device that offered him the voyeuristic thrill and then looked out over the marshes. He had what he needed. Carlson would be pleased. He placed his hands behind his back and walked up the short incline to the main house. While his attention was still back in France, he was in fact nowhere near there, despite Thyraa's feeling of being watched. Damiana was far closer to him than her 'sister' was.

CHAPTER FORTY-THREE

“Son, look–I just want to know one thing. Who left the bag of idiots open?”

You know, as soon as I think I am a mature individual, a seasoned veteran, and am immune to my father’s abuse, he opens me up and guts me with a single statement.

“Idiots?” I asked…knowing better.

“Yeah, you have a full team of elite Rangers. You have a squad of Army assaulters, you have a fucking warship, yet you dropped into a red zone with a fucking dog and a stick.”

It wasn’t a stick; it was a pulse rifle, but I knew better than to argue. His point was still valid, as much as it pained me to admit that.

“My contact here believes that the enemy masses against opposing forces, so the more we bring, the more they bring.

“This contact is the same one that shot you, right? I believe she nearly killed you?”

“Your point?”

“Well, hell, Son, if you can get past that, ya’ll should get married. Start on a family right away. Your relationship will have nothing as tough to overcome as her killing you.”

“I trust her, Pops.”

"So, you two are fucking? Shit, Junior, there's no hope for you, let me talk with the dog."

"I hate to um... wrap up this feel-good call, Pops, but do you happen to have anything useful for me?" I asked. Even though it was stupid, the colonel still had connections that were better than anything I could match. Even though yelling at his kid was his way of spending quality time.

"Yeah, Joe, I just think you should keep the dumbfuckery ideas down to a minimum on this mission, you know? Fucking your teammate definitely falls on which side of the stupid scale?"

"Sorry, Pops, I didn't know there was going to be a test."

"A test, a test? Life's a fucking test, moron. Look, kid, this isn't about you. I just don't want one of my old buddies coming up to me in the club joking about the stupid shit you did, okay? I have a legacy to protect."

"Thanks," I said, "for the concern."

And he was already gone, nothing useful...again.

"Your dad?" Dami asked.

I had my helmet up, so she couldn't have heard the conversation, but I guessed that she knew that was who it was. "Yeah. He was... wishing us luck."

Her face scrunched into a smile that let me know she wasn't buying it. Maybe she had met my dad. She was back in control after her call earlier. She hadn't shared any details, but I desperately wanted to know more about her sisters.

We'd abandoned the bike at the edge of the national forest and had a twenty-mile hike to the target location. Voss was understandably quiet, and I wanted to give her whatever space she needed. I used the time to make one more call. One I wasn't looking forward to. I had my AI connect me to the ship and the comms officer got Jordan Hauk on a private comms channel.

"Captain," I said several seconds later when the call connected.

"Yeah, Captain, what can I do for you?"

I wasn't even sure he knew that I was no longer aboard the Stone Mountain. "How's your men, Hauk?" Red-7 had suffered a staggering number of losses on the HVI retrieval mission. I knew that was where his concern would be right now.

"Good, all receiving excellent care in the med bays. A few are even getting over the space sickness. Myself not included," he added with a laugh.

"It's not for everyone, sir. Look, I have some intel that concerns you on a personal level. I would rather give you the news in person, but that's simply not possible."

The silence grew for several seconds. I knew the hardened veteran expected bad news when getting a call like this.

"Logan?" he asked, offering his brother's name. He was the only close family listed in the captain's files, so it was probably not that hard of a guess.

"Yes," I answered.

"KIA, MIA?" he asked. "I tried to get through to him after Last Day, but shit..."

"POW."

Jordan had not been expecting that. "Who in the fuck are we fighting that is taking prisoners?"

"Captain, do you have any idea what your brother was doing on Last Day?"

"Honestly, Kovach, I don't even know who he's working for. He was a damn fine soldier, but I think he was truly gifted on the clandestine side of things."

That seemed to mesh with the paltry information Ada had retrieved. I offered him what we had found.

"What am I supposed to do with this, Master Sergeant? I am 200 miles up on your ship right now. Half my platoon is out of action, and being on the ground is near suicide."

"I'm just passing the information along, sir. I am not sure what the best call is, but if I was in your shoes, I would want to know. No one else is calling the shots for us anymore, Hauk. Yes, there are other battles we probably should be fighting, but family still matters." I looked over at Voss who was running hard, her face still a mask of grief and fury. "Maybe more than ever."

It took a moment before the man responded. "Thanks, Joe. You're a good man, sorry if I may have judged you otherwise at any point."

"It's okay, Jordan. My dad always said I could grow up to be anything I wanted. So, I became an asshole."

He laughed, the first I think I ever heard from the man.

"Look, if you decide to make a play, have Bayou access all the intel available. You can get resupplied from ship's stores, and the dropship can have you in France as soon as the Stone Mountain is in position. Bayou will look after any of your people that aren't mission capable."

"Thank you," he said uncertainly. I knew he was thinking how off the rails a rescue mission might be. Hell, France was a foreign country. But it wouldn't be the first time the man had broken the rules to go save his brother. Thinking again about Voss, I had one more idea.

"If you go, I might be able to introduce you to some friends that might be instrumental to you."

"I appreciate it Joe, I'll take any help I can get. Logan is the kind of hero the world needs right now. I hate the thought of him rotting away in some warlord's prison cell."

I had no idea if it was a warlord that took the man or something worse. Perhaps this could be connected to Nevis's organization. As I disconnected the call considered the other name Ada had given me, that had made me think that Carlson's involvement might be a possibility, but right now, the idea fairy had yet to show and grant me any wishes. So it was just a vague hunch.

Voss slowed, then stopped and quickly dropped. I followed her example, strained my vision, and engaged my suit's optics to better see what she had spotted.

Well, fuck! A goddamn Decimator Warbot standing in the middle of the road. Its triangle gun turret head pointing directly at us.

"I guess we are here," I whispered. Sumo turned his head toward me quizzically, but Dami had already moved somewhere out of sight.

CHAPTER FORTY-FOUR

Lieutenant Deborah Riggs had reached the end of her rope essentially with everyone onboard this ship, her ship–at least for now. All the goddamn petty problems had to take a backseat while she, Xero, and Packer worked on ways to defeat the ship that was shadowing them. A ship that Xero confidently believed was actively hacking the Stone Mountain's navigational and propulsion systems.

"Halo, report."

"Still nothing, Boss. Weapons bay is still dead."

She shook her head. Point defense lasers were still functional, and in fact, the bridge fire control was still operational. If the ammo caches and missile defense batteries located in the lower bowels of the ship wouldn't arm or even release armament for firing solutions, all they could do was point the lasers at targets and say, "Pow!" At least they had missiles again. The armory printers had been going nonstop, and the SE crews had built dozens of them already.

Xero and Otero were working on it, but Bayou's patience was gone. Too many competing interests on board and out there. Plus, Kovach running off for some idiotic mission leaving his pseudo-girlfriend up here asking questions about his location that Deb had no way of answering.

"Ma'am?"

She turned, anger flashing across her face before she saw who it was.

"Hey, Captain." She pulled out a chair and lowered herself into it motioning Jordan to do the same.

"You look like I feel, Deb. What's going on?"

She rubbed a hand across her jaw and tried to see where to start or even if she should. "I'm good, Jordan. Nothing that a hot shower and some fresh coffee wouldn't solve."

He placed a broad hand over hers on the illuminated map table. "I've known you a long time, Riggs. Don't blow me off, and I know coffee isn't your drink of choice. What's wrong and can I help?"

So, she told him; she told him all of it, from Kovach jumping back dirt side, to Xero finding the ship, to the admiral ordering her to return to Gateway base, and the assholes on board who wanted to complain about every fucking thing imaginable.

"One woman literally demanded I stop and listen to her list of grievances that she has been singularly more abused than everyone else because of her political views. The world ended for everybody—bitch! Not everything is about you!"

The career Army man studied her and smiled. "Ever wished you had stayed home and taken over your family's seafood business?"

She was surprised he'd even remembered that. They'd briefly been an item, but that was many years ago. "Every day, Jordan... every day. My sister and I couldn't wait to get away. I enlisted after two years of college, and she got a full-ride scholarship to NYU a few years later."

"I heard about Liz. I'm sorry, Deb."

Tears filled her eyes, but she held them back as best she could. "Thanks. Still hasn't sunk in yet. What about Logan, any news on him?"

That had been the reason he came to talk to her, but getting into that now seemed like a shit move. He knew he would need her help for what he was planning but held on that for the moment. "He was overseas when the shit went down. I haven't heard from him yet, but Kovach has given me a possible lead."

"You talked to the Master Sergeant?"

"Yes, briefly this morning," Jordan said. "He was just offering an update, no other information."

Hauk watched as the woman frowned and chewed the inside of her cheek. It was a habit he'd once called her out on and quickly learned *that* was not going to be acceptable. He might outrank her, but she pulled no punches in their brief relationship.

"Something is out there, Jordan," she leaned in and whispered, clearly needing to change the subject.

The man's confused expression was no surprise. She quietly confided in him all she knew about the ghost ship. He didn't understand why the need for secrecy, no one else was around, but also kept his responses in hushed tones.

"How do you know they are a threat? It could just be a lifeboat with survivors, people that have nothing to do with what's going on with your ship's control systems."

"We've considered every contingency. That ship out there is clearly shadowing our orbit, and Xero has intercepted part of the tight-band comms signal that is originating from that craft."

Hauk looked troubled. He squinted and looked away, almost as if he could see through the dozens of meters of deck plating and hull toward the craft in the distance. "Still, they've taken no overt threatening action. I don't think you can even classify this as an attack. If they cut off life support or tried to drop us out of orbit, maybe."

"Jordan—listen to me clearly on this."

He knew that tone—he'd heard it only a few times, but it meant Lieutenant Riggs was about to lay down the law. Part of Jordan Hauk recoiled, thinking not for the first time that the inmates were running the asylum. He was a trigger-puller, a soldier, and not used to being part of the team creating the missions.

"I don't give a fuck. All potential threats, all our enemies, and hell, any of our friends that impeded our mission of survival will be taken care of before they can do any additional harm. I don't know about you, but I learned my fucking lesson on Last Day. From now on, we shoot first. They die first, before they can ever strike out. Am I clear on that?"

"They die first! Crystal clear, LT," Hauk whispered, leaning back and taking a more formal posture. "How can Red-7 be of assistance?"

CHAPTER FORTY-FIVE

KOVACH

The blast hit nothing and everything. It wasn't what I expected, but that was undoubtedly more to me living up to my dad's most recent nickname. I was a dumbfuck. The Decimator had leveled something at me that looked nothing like a weapon. Then, my suit systems went dark.

It has a tactical EMP weapon—*well,* of course it does. And since every motherfucking thing in my suit runs on electricity, I was now essentially a tin can full of juicy meat products just waiting to be stomped flat.

Only thing was, the massive metal Warbot wasn't stomping toward me like they had in the factory. Hell, it wasn't even looking my way. I was laying partially on the ground...to be honest, my knees and my head were on the ground, which yes, that is an awkward and also particularly ineffective combat position to be in. My ass was the high point and likely the one part of me sticking above the relatively thick ground cover.

Ada, who was only nominally tied into the suit's systems, gave me an update.

"Hip and thigh servo actuators are down. HUD systems offline. Revix life support offline."

"Gee, thanks, can you trigger a flash restart?" The battle suits went in a limp mode if hit with an EMP. Supposedly, they were shielded from the more damaging effects, but honestly, we'd never had a good chance to test them against an actual EMP weapon. That's probably not true; I'm sure lots of soldiers were in battle suits on Last Day, but I hadn't been, and that was the only research that actually mattered.

"Weapons?" I squeaked out.

"Primary weapons offline, Maglock in safe mode. Auxiliary weapons available," Ada said.

Still struggling to get the massive metal leg under me using muscle power alone was proving useless. I could reach my sidearm, though, and felt better with it in my grip, even though I couldn't hold my metal-clad arm out to aim at anything but the nearby ground.

All that money they spent on me and the suit, and I was essentially a prisoner of my own tech. The Decimator began stalking toward the north. Its speed was incredible; it had to be going after Voss. I felt a servo motor kick in, then hydraulic pressure charging my hip actuators. The knee lifted, and I maneuvered into a crouch. My systems were slowly coming back to life one by one in order of the AI's prioritized checklist. Screw that, I needed weapons.

The damn Warbots had been virtually impossible to kill, but we had to get past the thing.

"Multiple enemy contacts converging on this location."

"Nature of threat?" I asked, not really wanting to know.

"Biologics, Prowler."

Great! More fucking monsters. These big-assed machines must have a way of summoning or controlling the mutant life. Something I should be able to figure out and take advantage of, but first I needed to survive the next ten minutes.

"Joe, I am on the other side," Voss's voice said in my helmet speaker.

Other side of what? The field, the Warbot, the realm of the living? I ran, my suit's systems approaching ninety percent. The Warbot began a sweep, the EMP weapon still pointing out. I'd swapped weapons and now held the Glisson Rattler Mark-IV loaded with the high-impact rail gun darts we had determined to be the most effective in our previous outing. The first shot took off the claw that was holding the weapon. What I had failed to notice was a firing tube located on the midsection. A small rocket launched through the port and impacted directly on my position, which I had barely vacated microseconds earlier. I was tumbling across the ground, rattled but uninjured. Make no mistake, in combat there really is no such thing as a 'small' rocket. That's just a figure of speech, like premature death. If the reaper has your number, it's just death.

Needless to say, I came up firing… at absolutely nothing. My HUD was giving me readings that weren't making a whole hell of a lot of sense. The job of a combat veteran is to be able to focus. To drill down on the absolutely essential elements to stay alive and succeed in the mission. Currently, I was below par on the achievement scale but ready to ace the retake and make my teacher proud.

My own grenade launchers finally locked on to the hard target and fired. I saw Sumo moving into an attack position against something else that was outside my field of view. Ada was now filtering and feeding me data that she felt was most relevant, and she has a damn good handle on what I want. We'd had time to work out the kinks on many deployments.

"Second combat droid detected."

I could have done without hearing that, but hey, that's Karma for you. Giving you the dish you deserve… not the one you wanted. I switched to the twin plasma carnage rounds and seared off a sensor grid on the first bot, which was unloading holy hell on a tree line where I assume Voss had gone.

"Contact, six o'clock!" Ada yelled just before an enormous mass hit me from behind. Well, at least she was adding the location now, just had to work on getting that intel to me just a bit sooner.

I knew instantly this was not a bot, too many moving parts like claws and teeth. Then a flash of scaly skin revealed the Furie. My right hand dropped the grip of the rifle and whipped my combat blade out of its sheath and down through the thick thigh muscle in one motion. The strike was so vicious I nearly severed the leg from its body. Gouts of the purplish blood shot out, covering me and it, but the thing kept fighting even as its life was draining away. I swatted it to the ground turning just in time to see the metal fist coming for me.

Getting hit by a Decimator was literally like being hit by a truck. Sadly, it was not the first time for such an occurrence. The scaly monster I had been fighting was instantly compressed into green and purple jelly as the Warbot literally drove me through the thing's body in an instant.

"Goddamn!" I felt my innards shifting around inside my body. Having a high impact composite battle shell does little to minimize inertia. Ada was busy using all her tricks, as well as trying to get me moving again. I felt stimulants entering my bloodstream from the suit's med packs. As I struggled to get back to my feet, I was still woozy. I shifted left to dodge the massive bot's claw but slipped in the pile of gore that was running down that leg.

Something else hit me from behind, I ignored it as my main threat was now right in front of me. My eyes tracked across the Decimator looking for damage, any sign of weakness. Then, the targeting reticle centered on a small section of the chest plating and zoomed in. Holy fuck!!

"Eyes!" Human fucking eyes.

This thing has a human pilot. As more of his face came into view, I could see he was smiling. I centered my weapon and snapped off multiple shots, but the man's expression did not change. Not even a flinch when the rounds hit the viewport.

An unseen appendage locked onto my left leg and began clamping down. I could feel the damage, but my body had automatically dialed back the pain receptors. Pain was a notification system, and I had bigger worries right now. I was badly outmatched and outgunned, but strangely, I got the impression the man or robot was toying with me. I was relatively sure it could have ripped me in half, even with my body armor. This thing was a beast. Dodging the metal arm again, I didn't notice the bullhorn shaped device now peering over the shoulder until it fired, and my world instantly went black.

CHAPTER FORTY-SIX

Xero wanted to contact her friend Valyn. The mere fact that she did pissed her off. Her entire being was founded around the concept of independence or needing no one. She was a proud introvert with a disdain for asking for help no matter how great the need. Much of her identity was crafted around her own self-sufficiency, and she feared even the tiniest of fractures could unravel it completely. A therapist had once described her as suffering from imposter syndrome.

"She was a fool," Xero said to no one.

"Hey."

Xero fought to control her surprise from the voice coming up behind her.

"Hello, Hauk."

Jordan looked over her shoulder as she worked on the small black object held under the bright light. The multi-faceted side sparkled in the light like a cold fire.

"What's that?"

He pointed, then realized she was wearing VR goggles and wouldn't have seen his hand. "... that you're working on?"

Xero smiled; she enjoyed his nervousness around her. She wasn't immune to his obvious attraction, but she'd learned to control those urges long ago. Okay, some of them. Besides, the man seemed permanently preoccupied. She wasn't unsure if that involved his feeling for someone else or just how the military man was wired. Either way, she didn't think it wise to follow Kovach's recommendation. Not yet at least.

"A special project." She moved the object from the clamp and held it out to the captain. "Ever seen one?"

He held it up briefly before passing it back and shaking his head. "Nah. Heavy, but doesn't feel natural."

"It's not, it's a tightly compressed, artificial, crystal carbon base, but not a straight, crystalline lattice-like diamond. Something else entirely."

"Look," he said passing it back. "The LT said you and the Marine engineer were working on something. Is this part of it?"

Xero shook her head with a smile, "No, Captain, this is just a distraction for me." She rose and motioned for him to follow. They entered a metal corridor that he thought must run next to the engineering section. "Captain, how familiar are you with starship propulsion systems?"

He looked a little baffled. "Essentially not at all."

"That's okay. Honestly, I wasn't either. But Specialist Otero has been very helpful in bringing me up to speed despite her hesitancy in revealing classified intel to a civilian. But these are challenging times."

He nodded agreement.

"We are currently running the ship in maintenance mode. That is to limit our power output and frankly, because the spy ship out there would expect us to do it."

"You think they have that level of monitoring over our situation?"

"I believe whoever is out there can see or hear almost everything going on onboard this ship. Except down here, next to the reactor's core. The shielding is too thick, and we have continuously swept the area for sensors."

Hauk considered that as Xero undogged a hatch and entered, holding it open for him. He saw Otero and one of the Banshee team working on something.

"So, here is your attack plan?"

Xero smiled and said, "No, *you* are my attack plan."

An hour later, Jordan Hauk leaned against the bulkhead in disbelief. Xero, Halo, and the Marine Space Engineer had gone over it multiple times, but he still wasn't buying that it was even remotely possible.

"Who would be stupid enough to do something like this?"

Otero grinned. "We have just the guy." She touched an icon on her sleeve computer and spoke into it. Minutes later, the biggest Marine Hauk had ever seen emerged from the hatchway. "Holy shit!"

"Captain, meet your space assaulter, Corporal Koog."

"Koog, really?" Hauk said, watching his own hand disappear into the meaty paw of the Marine.

"It's short for Coughlan, or something," Otero said. "Point is, Koog will carry the IED."

"And all we have to do is get him onto target. But why me?" Hauk asked.

Xero flipped up a holodisplay nearby and entered a command line sequence that brought up a schematic layout of the entire ship. Hauk could see the numerous colored dots moving around and many that seemed stationary. As she hovered the cursor over each of the dots, an ID popped up on the screen.

"Personnel manifest," Hauk stated.

"Yes, but this isn't ours. Banshee essentially hijacked this ship, they didn't go through any of the normal procedures. I thought the AI may have done it, but the code isn't right for that. No, this is an ugly bootleg hack that was remotely installed along with the other command blocks." She handed him the control. "Tell me what you see."

He accessed as many of the IDs as he could but quickly understood what she was getting at.

"Red-7 isn't showing up, none of us."

"Neither are the rescued Space Marines. Apparently, they didn't think we would add to our ranks or simply haven't thought to do an updated scan. They have us locked down, so why should they worry too much about who's aboard?"

"So, Koog and I can go for a little spacewalk unnoticed while the rest of you would show up immediately."

"You? Not one of your men?"

Hauk nodded. "This is my responsibility. I'm also the only one who successfully went through SWTS, Space Warfare Tactical School. Plus, according to this, I am invisible."

"Essentially," she agreed. "Although, I don't show up either," Xero added. "However, planting actual bombs isn't my specialty."

"Corporal, are you up for this?" Hauk asked. "Because I have never done a real spacewalk in my life. I have no idea what to do if anything goes wrong, and hell, I may just pass out the moment we step out through the stasis field."

"Oh, hell yeah, sir," the Marine said. "I can't fucking wait. And you'll be fine, I've taken a lot of newbies out into dead space before."

Halo slapped the big guy on his back. "I love this fucking guy. Don't die out there, okay?"

Hauk shook his head. This wasn't what he wanted to be doing, especially since talking with Kovach, but this was the deal he'd made with Riggs. Help them free this ship, and she would give him and his men a ride home. "So, when do we go?"

CHAPTER FORTY-SEVEN

"Y'all are out of your mind!"

"Bishop, you don't know the half of it. These crazy bastards are just going to step out of a starship moving..." he checked the flexible display on his sleeve, "let's call it 18,000 miles an hour and watch as we sail on out of sight."

"Yeah, Spacers don't know shit. It doesn't work that way," Koog said, pulling on the upper portion of his Marine Recon Patrol space suit. "We will keep traveling the same course and speed as this ship unless we make a trajectory change."

"Which you will have to do in order to get to where the enemy's stealth ship is," Bishop said, as if justifying his original point.

"Look, we know it's a bit crazy, but hell, we've actually trained for stupid shit like this. Me and the captain go out, circle the planet a few times while slowly drifting into the path of the other vessel. Our suits have a zero-radar profile. We won't show up on any sensors."

"Not even ours," Bayou said, just walking into the nearly empty hangar bay. "Corporal Koog, you are our stealth bomber. Captain Hauk, you are overwatch and targeting. He's going to be nearly blind maneuvering the weapon."

Hauk eyed the long, black, angry looking device. It was an ugly piece of ordinance that he never wanted to be standing this close to.

"I-8 Penetrator with isometric warheads," Halo said with pride. It had taken him and Otero's crew days to wrestle it out of its launch cradle without setting off the ship's alarms systems, wrestle its 1500-pound dead weight to the work bay under the propulsion engines, and reconfigure the missile for manual deployment and remote detonation.

The Penetrator was an old-school type of weapon relying on brute force. Upon detonation, it would send a superheated slug of copper through whatever was in close proximity. The shaped charge device could be programed for multiple targets on explosion. But if used singularly, such as the hull of an enemy ship, it theoretically could punch through up to a foot of armor plating before igniting a fireball that should consume whatever was on the other side with devastating effectiveness. The technology was a generation old and based on the EFP, or explosively formed penetrator devices. What made them so lethal was they literally turned your ballistic protection into energy.

"How close will it need to be?" Bayou asked.

Halo looked at Koog for an answer. "Very. Range is very limited. Under propulsion, it would detonate on contact. Not good for a proximity mine. Specialist Otero added a magnetic locking device. It will self-arm once it connects with the enemy ship. Then, the captain just has to send the signal. Please wait until I am anywhere but there before you do that, sir."

"Roger that, Koog," the captain said.

"Where on the ship should it go?" Bayou asked, knowing the team had been going over these details for days.

"Anywhere, really," Halo answered. "Since we have no idea what configuration the other ship is, we are just going to decide based on approach and situational awareness. Ideally, engine compartment or the bridge, but on some ships the command deck is in the center deck of the ship, so that may be sub-optimal. Koog will have a better sense of where it should go. Trust him."

Riggs couldn't get past the fact that this was literally like commanding an old-school aircraft carrier and tossing two sailors overboard with a torpedo to destroy a sub that may or may not even be out there. "Okay, guys, you have the extra oxygen tanks. You will be out there a while, don't get disoriented and don't lose track of the target.

You must slow drift into the spot. If they spot you, they will assume it is just more space debris because, believe me, the shit is everywhere right now."

"What if we get hit by some of that debris?" Hauk asked. That was a concern he hadn't even known to have until now.

"It won't matter, brother," Halo said, handing him his helmet. "It will be over before you realize you were in danger."

Bayou waited for the crew to do final checks on both men and the bomb. She saluted both of them before returning to the bridge. Ten minutes later, an inner air lock hatch opened, although her systems board did not show that. Likewise, when the chamber cycled, and the outer door opened. Mission TDF-1 was a go. "Yep, they die first."

"It's a stupid plan, Riggs," Halo said, reactivating the safety on the airlock.

"Prowler's Ninth Rule of Battle," she said with a laugh.

"If it's stupid, but it works, it wasn't stupid," they said nearly in unison.

Riggs turned back to the opening gate. Nothing kept them from the cold of space but a nearly invisible field of charged electrons. The stasis field generator was another of those miracle inventions that no one seemed to fully understand, yet they trusted it with their lives every day. Now, she was sending two men out there, probably to their deaths. She pushed the thought aside, she'd made the decision, it was happening. "Good hunting."

Hauk and Koog moved the massive weapon to the opening on it's wheeled trolly. Bayou and the others moved back past the yellow line on the floor indicating where the backup field would automatically generate. She watched as both men stepped out into the darkness.

CHAPTER FORTY-EIGHT

The restraints were surprisingly effective; I wasn't sure what it took to actually secure me, but someone seemed to. The Decimator that hit me had not chosen to kill me. That was an important detail. Didn't seem that useful at the moment, so I filed it away for later. Basic assessment told me little. No serious injuries, damage to my leg was already healing, but I had no immediate way to free myself. I opened my eyes and scanned the room.

Despite my systems heightened spatial awareness. This was not at all what I was expecting; the room was large and ornate. Dark, heavy beams lined a ceiling high overhead. My prison seemed unnecessarily spacious, ornate, and old. Everything, including the smell, was old.

"Update," I subvocalized.

My AI seemed distracted, which did little to put me at ease.

"Residence," she stated matter-of-factly. "The compound is approximately the target locations Ms. Voss supplied."

Yep, her tone was all but icy, which had to be deliberate. She was assuming Voss had intentionally lured me into a trap. That wasn't a totally unreasonable assumption, but I was avoiding making that leap.

"Where is Voss and Sumo?"

"Voss is unknown, Sumo was not captured, but his beacon has been motionless for the last three hours."

"Injured?"

"Nothing that is showing on his telemetry," Ada responded.

I pulled against the restraints again. They seemed to give but almost immediately stiffen and tighten even more. The more I struggled, the tighter my bindings became. I relaxed and paid attention to what else she was saying.

"One individual so far, your eyes were not open enough to make a positive ID." The image showed a man walking toward me; he was tall and lean and almost glided when he walked.

"That's not Nevis?"

"No." Ada paused deliberately. "I'm sorry, Joe, I don't think I helped you manage the fight very well. We shouldn't have been captured. Not that easily."

My AI and I had a disagreement on what was 'easy,' but I got her point. Despite our capabilities, we had been rather ineffective so far. The upgrades had either not been totally on point, or something was off.

"It's okay, Ada. We're exactly where we wanted to be. Now, we just have to complete the mission."

~

"You are well out of your lane, Gunny," the tall man said, moving closer to the table I was strapped to.

He spoke with an accent that my system placed as Central American, although his appearance was more European. Truthfully, he had such a forgettable appearance he could have gone unnotched nearly anywhere. That, plus the fact Ada could find no record of him, scared me. He also misread my chevrons and rockers emblem stenciled on my chest plate. The screaming eagle in the middle identified me as Space Force, not a traditional master gunnery sergeant. No one who knew anything about the service would ever call me Gunny.

"Got lost," I replied.

The man gave the briefest of smiles; it looked like an unwelcome visitor on his dead face. My head was strapped down tight; I'd guessed that some of my battle suit was removed, although he would have needed an armorer's key to get the full rig off.

"Gunny, you are of no interest to me. You obviously were hired protection for the woman. Who is she?"

The man moved with a silent grace that let me know he was a killer. Still, he'd made assumptions about me that were incorrect, and that mistake might prove fatal.

"I don't recall a woman, but if you find my dog, he needs to be fed. He's particularly fond of assholes, so he should be fine with you."

"Our own 'pets' will deal with them both," he said slowly, while he focused on something just out of my line of sight. "I am curious, though. How have you survived out there since the Liberty Strike?"

"Liberty Strike? You mean all the shit of Last Day?"

I saw now the knife he was holding; it was menacing, and it was mine. He'd found the release on my suit, slid the Heidelberg Damascus blade out, and was getting the feel of its balance and weight as anyone familiar with knife work would.

"You have your name for the cleansing, we have ours."

"So, you were responsible for killing half the planet?"

"Me?" He actually did laugh then. "No, no, I am but a lowly errand boy for them. I provide a service, nothing more."

In my peripheral vision I saw him working the nearly hidden controls to activate the vibrosonic blade. I knew he'd gotten it right when his grip on the handle changed. The special combat knife blade now vibrated at an almost imperceptible speed. It was on a level so microscopic that you could look at it and not see any movement. The person holding it could feel a very slight hum that tended to reveal itself as an itch in the palm of your hand unless you gripped it tightly. In this mode, it would also slice through nearly anything in microseconds up to and including human bone.

"Very nice, Sergeant, truly a special weapon. You won't mind if I hang on to it will you? I assure you that you will be having no further use of it."

"Well, asshole, since you put it like that, yeah. I really want you to have it."

"Ada, give me something to get me free of these restraints. I need to kick this bastard's ass."

She responded to my subvocalized commands instantly. "The material seems remarkably similar to the thunder vines that are so prevalent now. Although, I am not sensing any toxins entering your system. Still, each time you struggle the elastomer properties seem to constrict even more."

I wasn't in the mood for an alien biology lesson. I just wanted to be free.

"So, errand boy. What are we doing here? Is Maine an armed camp now? Your rich masters have trained Warbot guard dogs?"

I did not see the motion nor feel the knife blade enter my thigh up to the hilt, but I felt the searing pain as he began dragging it down my femur. The razor-sharp blade cleanly separating tendon from bone. As he neared my knee, he removed his hand but left the blade imbedded in flesh.

"Simply brilliant," he said, marveling at the destruction on my body the tool had rendered.

Ada offered to dampen my pain receptors more, but I stopped her. He seemed unaware of my battle AI or my enhancements, and that was about the only advantage I had right now. I wanted him to see my pain although honestly it just fucking hurt, and I wasn't exactly thinking clearly at the moment.

"She is one of the Sisters," he said. "Sisters of Light." He said it like the words themselves had a foul taste.

I grunted something as my body spasmed in pain.

"Did you know that when she hired you?"

"I don't know any fucking sisters, you goddamn sadist."

"Sadist? No, no, my friend. That I am not. I take no pleasure in your pain. Pain is simply a tool, something I use to get my job done. Probably much as yourself. We have unpleasant tasks to perform in our chosen careers, but other than the satisfaction of a job well done, we both undoubtedly must separate ourselves from the horrific tasks that we sometimes must do, no?"

He removed the knife and laid it aside, then picked up a tube and showed it to me. I couldn't move my head enough, so he loosened the restraint on my forehead. He squeezed the tube like toothpaste and rubbed a small bit between his fingers then applied it to the long slash in my leg. I felt a stab of pain, then a numbing pressure of his fingers and hand running down the cut, then nothing.

"Amazing stuff," he said. "Anadium, just one of the many products that has come out of my employer's research."

"Industrial painkillers, thanks. Still not worth destroying the world."

"Oh no, sir. Not a pain killer. Your leg is being healed as we speak. Nanoparticles are binding the cell walls back together and repairing blood vessels, even reattaching tendon to bone. The pain receptors are blocked during the process so, yes, the analgesic effect is wonderful as well. "So, you see..." He held my knife up again and then stabbed it down on my other leg.

He could torture me over and over again without risk of killing me. The pain was unbearable, but I got his point. He could literally make this shit last all fucking day, all week even.

"What do you want, you son of a bitch!" I screamed it, spittle flew out of my mouth and tears were burning their way down my cheek.

"I want to know about the Sister you work for. Who is she, for starters?" He gave the handle of the knife a thump with his finger which sent shockwaves of pain through my entire body. I could just see the knife still embedded in my right leg just like he'd done on the other.

I instructed Ada to dial back the pain receptors. I needed to think clearly, and my suffering was getting in the way. I did like that Anadium stuff, though, that shit was amazing. I could see the blood flow had entirely stopped on my left leg, and the pain on the other side hadn't been bad even before Ada adjusted the settings on my nervous system. *I need to kill this bastard; he isn't going to willingly give up anything.*

Through half-closed eyes, I watch him move along the back wall with his cat-like grace. I could see he was speaking to someone on his comms. Ada could likely lip read some of what he was saying, but I assumed he was getting instructions on what to do with me.

We were in Nevis Carson's coastal estate. That was just a guess but seemed likely despite me never seeing a house. The Decimator had been waiting for us before we even got close. That meant he had been surveilling us remotely. I wondered—*how long?* As if in response to my thought, a small wasp flew around the beams high overhead and slowly descended until it landed on my bare arm.

Insect drone. The little buggers had kept getting smaller and more capable for the last fifty years. Any this small still had a limited range but could send voice and comms back for miles, especially if you had plenty of them networked together. If the one on my arm was a drone, it was a damn good one, because I could clearly see the angry-looking face and the yellow and black bands on its belly writhing just like the real thing. Then, it tensed briefly and drove its stinging barb deep into the flesh of my arm before flying off.

It stung like a wasp, but before Ada even said anything, I knew it hadn't been a real insect.

"We have a message from Voss."

She had somehow encoded a digital message into the wasp-sized drone and delivered it to me here inside this compound. Damn clever, the nanoparticle-sized payload obviously couldn't hold much information, but it might just be enough, if I could just hang on. As I watched the creepy man approaching, I knew that might not be all that easy.

CHAPTER FORTY-NINE

The message had been a one-way communication, but I appreciated it. Voss was with Sumo, and they were in a relatively safe location. She had identified my captor as a man named Bertrand Acevedo, a hired killer who was a known associate of our target, Nevis Carlson.

"You are not my mission," Acevedo said moving back to my right side. He peered over and looked at the wound on my leg.

"I may have nicked an artery. Not the femoral, fear not. I am not that clumsy. Perhaps the profunda, although to be quite honest, that is not so much better for you. Death, it is still... hmmm, how should I put this? Just outside the door. My mission is the girl, tell me what I need, and I will release you."

"Release me from my bonds?" I asked, knowing full well what he had meant.

"Not exactly, but they are quite remarkable, aren't they? Another gift from some of our researchers. Very similar genus to the lavender vines that now cover much of the country. The ones that feed off the decaying bodies."

He looked at me and grinned. "Oh, you didn't know that was what their purpose was, eh? Yes, much like other carnivorous plants that trap you, there is a neurotoxin producing a mild narcotic combined with a paralytic. Then, they wrap their victims and slowly liquify and directly absorb the nutrients as the body decays. From what I understand, it was one of the simpler genetic designs. At some point in Earth's history, a plant like that did exist. They just had to roll the clock back on the DNA a few million years. Dust to dust and all that. We are all just compost in the end, right?"

I felt a small jolt on my back which I knew was Ada doing something with the neural interface that was imbedded at the base of my neck and upper spine.

"Mister Acevedo may have just offered us a solution, Kovach. I was unaware the restraints were absorbing blood and tissue, but we can use that to our advantage."

"How?" I asked internally.

"I am modifying a few of the billions of nanoparticles that are always present in your system to attack the cellular structure of the material. If it is still living tissue, I am going to give it a cold. If it works, you may feel them loosen...just slightly."

As an augmented soldier, I had been given nanobiotic regiments since basic with even more complex nanobody infusions during my extensive lifesaving upgrade. Truth was, I had boatloads of internal microscopic machines to spare.

"My employer wishes to know your name, Master Sergeant."

He removed my knife from my leg, and I made sure to yell out in pain, although I really didn't feel it. He scraped the blade up my bare arm and pushed the base layer of my suit up until my service tattoo caught his eye. The iconic starfield on black left little doubt as to who I was with.

"Hmmm, that explains much but also conjures up many new questions. You are not just a simple soldier, are you?"

I felt a slight quiver in the restraint on my left upper leg. "Honestly, Dude, I am pretty simple."

"No, no... you are special. You're a drop trooper, right?"

"As my pops would say, that just makes me a special kind of stupid."

He held up the tube of Anadium. "You are bleeding out, Gunny. Answer my questions and I can at least make things a bit less unpleasant for you."

I did want the painkiller cream, but bleeding out wasn't a terrible way to go. I mean, the pain was gone, so it was essentially like going to sleep. I felt the quiver again, stronger this time, then a twitch from one of the other strands.

"Tell me about the girl, what has she told you about the Sisterhood?"

"Uh, uh, know nothing of the Sisterhood," I said, my voice heavy with faked grogginess, although truthfully, the blood loss was starting to be a real issue.

"The Sisters of Light? A coven of witches but much more dangerous."

"Danger?" I asked, truly confused about who they were.

"Si, they almost managed to stop all of our plans, despite the trillions of dollars we had invested and the massive security protocols we had in place. I hate them, but I do not deny they are a formidable enemy."

I was an Alliance Space Force Tier-1 Operator, and he was more concerned with Voss and her Sisters? I began to understand that I needed to know more about my partner out there. I gave a moan and rolled over, my eyes going glassy because of a few bio manipulations by my AI. She offered to make me throw up, but I thought that might be overkill.

"No, no, don't die just yet, soldier." I felt the man rubbing something in the gash on my right leg. The healing cream again, I guessed. He wasn't quite ready for me to die either. That was good, and I knew he'd laid my knife down near my injured leg. Several of the living restraints were significantly looser now. I wasn't entirely sure I could break free, but I was damn sure going to find out.

I stretched my body, flexing every muscle to expand the reach of my bindings and held it for a count of four. Acevedo was using a datapad to take a picture of my face.

"He's going to run facial recognition, Prowler."

That wasn't good. Although none of my information was on public record, and I'd gone to great lengths to keep my information private, I had no doubt Nevis and his group had access to military data. While my face may not produce any hits, if he ran a retinal scan, he may learn much more than I wanted him to know. He turned away slightly, keying something into the screen.

I relaxed my body completely then arched up high in a good approximation of a seizure. The assassin turned to watch me writhing under the restraints. While they had loosened after Ada's nanovirus, they didn't release.

"Gunny, you are going to injure yourself even more."

His tablet beeped; he eyed the readout then looked at me. His face gave little away, but I sensed an increasing level of concern. His threat index had just increased, and I sensed he had my info and suddenly realized that keeping me alive might have been an error.

I hadn't expected the bands to just fall away, that had not been my plan. My plan was to reach the handle of my knife, which now was wedged under my damaged thigh, my right hand gripping it tightly. Now I just needed the bastard to get a little closer.

I'll say this for the man, he was not stupid. He had taken inventory in a microsecond, and while he may not have known what was wrong, he knew something was off. Acevedo backed away several steps and drew a pistol from an unseen holster.

I slid the knife from beneath me and activated the vibrasonic blade. It would now slice through nearly anything with ease.

"Mister Kovach, my apologies. I hadn't realized I was in the presence of military royalty."

I backed the blade through the nearest strap, which parted. I couldn't cut myself free before the man shot me, which at point blank probably would kill me no matter where it hit.

I gave Ada a silent command to activate my suit's beacon in three seconds. The main part of my battle armor was lying on a table a dozen feet away. I was slicing before the killer noticed the alarm and high-contrast strobe. To his credit, he didn't turn to see what it was, but his attention was no longer fully on me. He fired as I flipped off the table landing hard on my two injured legs. The cream might be helping, but I wasn't fucking healed...not yet.

My opponent had a handgun, I had a knife. In the movies I used to watch with my dad, the guy or girl in my situation would always throw the blade, catching the gunman with a perfect strike, embedding the knife in the opponent's skull. Funny thing, knife fights don't work that way, and I'd been in a lot of them. The last thing I wanted to do was throw away the only weapon I had. I was badly injured and at an extreme disadvantage. He was a skilled professional and still in charge, and I had to come up with a way of evening up the odds on this battle.

I felt several more rounds hit the table I was hiding behind. I also noticed the tube of painkiller medicine which I squeezed liberally into my still gaping leg-wound. My immediate assessment was I was likely stronger and faster despite my injuries, so I needed to use that and any other advantage I could find. Interestingly, I found absolutely nothing handy. Then, I realized I was wearing what I needed.

A class-1 RDT Battle Suit is not like a suit of armor, not exactly. Instead, it is a modular piece of equipment that is customizable to each soldier and each mission. In this case, I'd kitted out in one of my standard versions. Heavyweight protectors on the chest and back, with lighter weight protection guards on my arms and legs. My leg armor was obviously removed, as was my back plate. He hadn't figured out how to remove my chest rig, though, and that was damn luck. Lucky for me, not so much for him.

While I was unwilling to throw my knife, my chest armor comes with a number of nifty tricks, including a row of snap-out pitons for climbing sheer rock faces. They are about five inches long, solid titanium, and blend in with the protective shell as to be virtually invisible. I dropped two out and hurled one at the killer's head before rocketing out the other side of the table.

I guessed correctly he would dodge the spike and fire as soon as he swiveled toward my new position. I hadn't gotten a close look at his gun, but Ada had cataloged it as an older Italian Bianchi XL88. Depending on the configuration, it could hold up to twelve standard rounds. I felt reasonably sure the professional killer had opted for the larger magazine, which would give him fifteen.

My right arm snapped out before I'd even thought about it, and a piton lodged in Acevedo's chest. My aim was too high; he was hurt, but it wasn't a killing blow.

"You are a very capable warrior, Master Sergeant Kovach. Perhaps you would like to discuss terms."

I knew he was hurting as much as I was, but damn, his voice was flat and neutral as if nothing at all was happening.

"Nah, I'm good."

"Ahh, but you aren't. Think about it, my friend. I still have a Decimator and acres of wildlife guarding this property. Wouldn't you like to know how to not have to fight them to stay alive? Trust me, Joseph, you want a place in the enclave? We can always use a man of your particular talents."

"You are a paid killer, a security dog, you can't offer me anything but answers, and I am going to get those from you, anyway," I snarled before diving for another piece of my armor that I'd seen. His shot nearly shattered my shoulder, but my suit's shoulder plating deflected most of it. I quickly checked the shot count; Ada and I both had been keeping track and had him at seven. He hadn't reloaded, and I didn't think he had a back-up piece, but that was a lot of assumptions. I pulled on the back plate and slid my helmet from its receiver and back into place. I was still vulnerable but not like I had been.

I stood, snapping off another piton that caught him in the wrist nearly severing it. He smoothly switched hands and shot me in the face. That was just fucking rude, and should have been fatal except Ada had activated my helmet just in time. Despite the armor, it hurt. I charged and sliced but only got a bit of flesh. This guy was fast, too fast. It suddenly occurred to me that he could have received upgrades, too. He smiled knowing full well what I had just figured out.

"No, you are not the only one," he said before firing again.

One of the jacketed rounds tore through my exposed arm. The damage left it nearly useless, but I switched the knife to my other. My second round of upgrades, the ones after I'd been killed, had done a number of things, but being ambidextrous was one I had barely noticed until now. My left hand strikes were just as lethal as my right. I slipped another piece of armor on, my vital back plate this time. A single forearm sleeve was also nearby so I added that to my growing ensemble.

As a combat soldier, I knew most fights were over in thirty seconds or less. When at least one of the fighters is armed, it's almost always less. We'd been going at it for over a minute, but even I knew my blood loss and injured lower body had taken a toll on my stamina. I needed to end this so I could recover.

"Bertrand, why don't you tell me where Nevis is?"

If using his name bothered him, he didn't show it. I could see part of his face as he took cover behind a large cabinet. I was debating whether to slide one of the leg sleeves on. It would take time, but the built-in servos in the armor would make up for my weakness. His next shot persuaded me to come up with another plan.

"Your friend might want to know that it was I who killed her Sisters in France. Telepresence is such a wonderful thing. Unlike you, Gunny, I didn't even have to be on the continent."

That was what Voss had been so upset over earlier today. She hadn't shared a lot, but his remark had hit home.

Shots left? Three, assuming we'd both counted correctly. I launched my last piton high over his head then activated the grenade launcher on my back. Yeah, I know, overkill. Welcome to Prowler's Battle Rules number four. Overkill is underrated. The two whumps arched out to each side, and I went down shielding my unarmored body parts the best I could.

The blast and overpressure in the confined space was tremendous, but I was up and moving toward my opponent before the sound had died away. The room was in shambles; thousands of bits of shrapnel and wood fragments had pierced everything, I was counting on one of those things being Acevedo, but he met me mid-stride running toward me firing blindly in the smoke. I went low and slashed up in two vicious strikes, then used my armored forehand to smash his face in.

"I ...AM...NOT...A ...GODDAMN...GUNNY!" Yes, I kept hitting to make sure he got the message. His limp and bloodied body fell to the floor. Message received.

CHAPTER FIFTY

Hauk drifted behind Koog, who was towing the warhead. After hours of consideration, he'd concluded this was the stupidest thing he'd ever done. Surprisingly, it wasn't the cold vacuum of space just outside his suit that bothered him as much as the prospect of failure. Koog, on the other hand, didn't seem to consider danger or failure.

"Hey, Captain Hauk, you ever wonder why there's so much empty space out there?"

"Hauk is fine, or Jordan." He'd told the kid a dozen times, but the Marine was ignoring that. "To answer your question—no, not really. I haven't had a lot of time to look out into space and ponder the big mysteries."

"Shit, I do." Koog said. "All the time. I mean, we see shit sometimes, you know? Things we aren't supposed to talk about. Not like aliens, but you know, lights, like the fast-movers. Crafts or 'objects' that travel, well above anything man has come up with, or even weirder objects tagged as asteroids that seem to change trajectories for no reason."

They had both taken the meds to sleep for a large part of the mission. They used less oxygen that way, and since there was virtually nothing for them to do until they closed on the target, it helped fight boredom. Now, though, they were both wide awake.

"So, you believe in aliens?"

Koog laughed. "I don't think there's any doubt, man. Too much out here for just us. Besides, we've already found signs of life here in our own solar system. If life is that common, intelligent life must be, too."

Hauk had to admit the oversized kid wasn't stupid. "So, do you think we will find that aliens are the ones who've been shadowing us?"

"Nah, Captain, sir. I mean, I guess it's possible. I've heard some weird tales about what's going on down there. Seems pretty freaky to me. But I imagine this is just some survivors, maybe from our side, maybe from our enemies, who would love to have the shelter and resources of a full-sized warship but wouldn't stand a chance in a direct stand-up battle."

"Relatively sound battle tactics, Koog. I get the feeling you weren't always a Space Marine; you guys don't see that much action."

Koog didn't respond immediately. He seemed to be considering how much he should say. "No, sir, I was MARSOC back, you know... before."

"Wow," Hauk responded, duly impressed. Marine Special Operations. "Force Recon?"

"I was a specialist attached to a blocking force for a Recon Team. Never quite got the pin. Once the Kaohsiung City fiasco went down... well, I had to make a move."

Hauk knew only a little of the Marines' failure in helping the Taiwanese stand up to the second attempt by the Chinese invading force in the port city several years earlier. It was a doomed mission, too little planning, lousy intelligence, no clear objective, but some politician made the call, and it happened. Chinese state television showed the lines of dead Marines on the beach and paraded out the captured Tier-2 Recon troops like war trophies.

Taiwan quietly slipped under full Chinese control, and the entire U.S. Marine Corps was deemed too archaic to continue in its current state. No one fought large-scale ground wars anymore, they said. Hauk's own combat experience called bullshit on that. In his opinion, the Marine Recon and Force Recons would have been just as effective as the RDTs, but the failed mission had left a stink on them they hadn't deserved. One that reduced the corps to a mere shadow if its former self.

"But Corporal?"

Koog understood the dig. “Lance corporal,” he corrected. “But yes, I know I should be further up the line, but I like this position. I enjoy the work, and we fall under Alliance ranks, so the paygrade in the Space Corps is pretty good.”

“You don’t miss the action?”

Koog turned until Hauk could see his face. “I’m all but riding an antimatter bomb to an enemy spaceship. Seriously, does it get any better?”

It wasn’t an antimatter bomb, but Hauk got the point.

“Changing O^2 to final set,” Koog said minutes later before discarding an empty pack of air cylinders into deep space.

They’d left the Stone Mountain loaded down with extra oxygen supply but had been depleting the cannister packs every few hours. Now, Koog was on his last set, which would give him just over three hours, assuming his respiration remained generally constant, which it probably would not. Hauk’s body mass was significantly less, and his suit still calculated an hour left on his current supply, so he would be out in four, give or take.

“So, no one waiting for you down there?” Hauk asked, realizing now he was the one wanting to fill the empty space with words.

“No, nothing serious. Have been getting close to someone onboard the ship, though,” the Marine said in a slightly embarrassed tone.

Hauk doubted the big guy had any trouble getting ladies. He took a bearing on the Stone Mountain noting the position hadn’t changed. He wondered about the survivors aboard that ship. It was an interesting mix, and any mission from now on would likely be a joint operation involving different branches and specialties. Debra was a good person to handle it. She had command authority and a quick mind; he’d hated losing her out of his unit years earlier, but he understood. He’d made it difficult for her, and he also stood in her way. She would not have an easier career track under someone else. For, just like Koog, Jordan Hauk had turned down numerous promotions as well. He knew where he fit.

Several hundred miles beneath his feet, he recognized the west coast of Europe just breaking into the daylight. Somewhere down there, his brother was being held prisoner. How many mornings did he have left? This crazy mission was his ticket to get back down there and help find

Logan and bring the pain to whoever had done this. In that regard, he wasn't all that different from that crazy Kovach. In the total darkness, he almost missed Koog frantically signaling.

~

On board the Stone Mountain, the military groups had been quietly mobilizing for possible action. No one was expecting a boarding party, but the military is the breeding grounds for rumors, and today, the hotline had been lighting up with one crazy theory after another.

"It's the Sixth Wave, man," one of the engineering crew said to a table of shipmates eating lunch.

"What in the natural fuck is that, Olsen?"

The man in the white overalls had a puffy face and far too much time in front of a computer screen instead of the workout room. "A wave of mass extinction events, Shepard. You know, major fucking die-offs like the dinosaurs getting whacked. People have been predicting it for centuries, that we would do something stupid enough to end the human species."

"I heard there aren't even any bodies in the infection zones. Those Army guys said nobody is left in the red zones," a skinny guy with glasses said.

Carol looked across the table at the only other occupant. The blonde-haired woman was eating now. It had been her only real concession to reality over the last week. "Don't listen to their crap," she told her.

The blonde looked up briefly, then returned to staring at her tray where she was pushing the food around with a fork.

"I know it's not that good, mostly from the synthesizers, but I was thinking. We could organize a real galley crew. Use the food synths to turn out raw ingredients, then we could cook some proper meals. Doesn't that sound good? "

The woman said nothing.

"I was never much of a cook. Heck, even Lux can do better in the kitchen than me, but I feel sure we have some people aboard that have that skill. I bet you can cook, can't you?"

The woman was making trails through the pudding-like sludge they were eating today. Several times Carol thought she recognized names before she swirled it back into paste. Carol had been patient with her; she'd studied human behavior at length and knew the signs of PTSD. Still, she needed to make more headway. In the absence of a real psychologist aboard or even a doctor, she might be the only help this woman was going to get. She reached across the table and lay her palm over the woman's hand.

"You had children, didn't you?"

Carol recognized the sudden flash of rage in the woman's piercing blue eyes, but just as fast, the blank stare was back. She should let it go; she wasn't getting anywhere, but no one got to just exist anymore. This girl was going to have to contribute and the sooner the better.

"Are you sure they're gone? Mine was missing for weeks before we found him."

Slowly, the other woman's head tilted up, and she locked eyes with Carol. There was an icy hatred there that the older woman couldn't fathom.

"Yes. They are dead." She then rose from the table and leaned in close. Her closeness and aggressive posture caught Carol off guard.

"Maybe you should be worried about yours instead of mine."

A cold shiver ran through Carol. The woman's bitter and undirected hatred was like an icy hand reaching out of the dark.

CHAPTER FIFTY-ONE

"Xero, let's make the Stone Mountain a lot more interesting to our friends out there."

"You got it," Xero called back from her workstation in engineering. She knew she probably should say 'Roger' or some other cool military response, but she was happily non-military. Still, she knew what the commander wanted. The floating bomb crew of Hauk and Koog had been out for three hours, and slowly, they had maneuvered from the far side of the ship in relation to the enemy, then dropped as far as possible. Now, they would take several more orbits to move on an intersecting tangent toward a cluster of small orbiting rocks or debris that were in essentially the same vectors.

The spot had been carefully selected due to the fact that the debris piles were pretty consistent, as they came close to it on every third rotation. Two more hours before the two-man team reached it.

"You have navigation and vector propulsion." It wasn't a lot, not like full control, but they could essentially change the attitude of the large ship. That should keep the ghost ship's attention on them but not so much that they would reveal themselves.

"Helm, let's put on a show for our visitors," Bayou ordered.

The pilot smiled and engaged the maneuvering thrusters which caused a rumble through the giant warship but, other than changing the starfield image on the display, accomplished very little. Bayou had laid out this show and knew that was the point. Not to do enough to invite direct action but to keep their focus. All of this was based on a lot of very vaporous assumptions. Assumptions on the ship actually being out there. Of it being the primary cause of the ongoing control problems with the IAS Stone Mountain and of it being a tangible threat.

She also knew she and the others aboard were essentially pirates. They had boarded the Stone Mountain out of desperation soon after the attacks down below. They had found it nearly abandoned other than a team of maintenance crews who were handling the refit in high-orbit space docks. So, while it was a Space Force asset, Space Force Lieutenant Debra Riggs had no authority to be in control other than what her people entrusted her with. That was enough, though. It was enough to fight for, and until she found a more capable officer to hand over the reins to, she was willing to be it. She'd tried doing that with Kovach, but she'd known his mission would always be back on Earth. Battling an enemy you couldn't see was just not his style.

"Ma'am, we have a problem." It was the comms officer.

"What do you have?" They were not receiving any comms from the two bombers, not even telemetry because Xero had clarified that the other ship might pick up even the line-of-sight communication signals. Bayou scanned all the external monitors, looking for trouble.

"Internal sensors, ma'am. Someone on Deck G just triggered the distress alarm."

"Seal it off!" Bayou ordered unnecessarily. That was immediate when any alarm activated.

"Nature of the threat?" She needed to know if it was a breech; did they need engineering? Was it environmental, perhaps the $C0^2$ scrubbers had malfunctioned, or God forbid, a fire. Fire aboard a ship was the constant fear.

"Unknown, ma'am," the ensign responded.

The timing automatically made Riggs associate it with the mission on the hostile ship, but presuming connections could get you in trouble. G-deck was three floors below, or above depending on how you oriented yourself. She could see on the big display the signal was on the aft side near the center.

"Security team Alpha, report in." Alpha because they had no others. The hastily cobbled together group of soldiers had been organized in just the last few days mainly to help with the growing population. Bayou ordered them to investigate. Sergeant Gi was in charge of the small team mostly pulled from Hauk's Red-7 with a few of the Marines added for good measure.

The security team was always armed, but that seemed unnecessary. She'd done it in an abundance of caution just in case someone tried to board. That made her consider, what if someone from the other ship was attempting the same thing they were to the ghost ship? No time to dwell on it, and her gut said that wasn't the case.

Another alarm went off farther up G-deck.

"What the fuck?" she whispered. "Do we have video surveillance in either of those locations?"

The screen shifted to show split screens. The first showed just an empty corridor. The second clearly showed two dark irregular lines weaving up to and then out of range of the camera.

"That was blood," Packer said, momentarily forgetting about his own task.

Bayou had to agree, it looked precisely like the blood trail a dragging body produced. One that she knew too damn well.

"Red alert! Ladies and gentlemen, we have an intruder. Get to a secure room and seal it at once."

Bayou instantly transformed into combat mode. "Ensign, find the other end of that blood trail and let me know what we are up against."

"Gi, we have identified a threat, probably heading directly toward you."

"Yes, Boss, we have a casualty in sight," Gi replied calmly.

Bayou flipped to her command channel so she could monitor what her sergeant was seeing. A pile of bloody flesh poured out of scraps of a white coverall. *Shit,* had to be one of the SEs. The space engineers all wore white coveralls.

"Ensign?"

"Working on it, ma'am. The trail stopped at the body. The security system is motion activated, so screening back to last marker now."

Riggs knew to let her team do their job. While they might not all be her team, they were coming together out of necessity. Still, this crisis drew attention to the challenges of throwing together military from different branches, different specialties, and assuming you could function on a mission. Those were all details they could reevaluate later… if there was a later.

~

Xero was busy at her station working to pinpoint the enemy ship's exact location. They had the relative position of Koog and Hauk, and she had come up with a way of signaling a course correction without using their MilCrypt line of sight comms. As the ship's position was changing somewhat randomly, she and Hauk had worked out a pattern that he could see from his position that would indicate if he needed to maneuver one way or the other. They were also able to signal by activating or disabling certain running lights for even finer course adjustments. The benefit of the enemy ship being that far away was they really shouldn't be able to see much of this. The downside was the closer the TDF team got, the less of the signals they would be able to make out as well.

"It's doing it again."

Xero hadn't noticed the boy moving up beside her. She held up a finger before relaying one set of corrections up to Packer. "Still picking up the phantom hits?"

Lux nodded; he liked how Xero took whatever he was working on seriously. Most adults wouldn't do that, but she was different.

Xero glanced at the screen to make sure the flight adjustments had been passed correctly. Satisfied, she turned back and took the datapad from the boy. She went over all of his work, his refinement of the sensor array, his meticulous systems test, then dove into the code itself. He was correct, there was no reason for the thing to be picking up heat signatures.

"Why's it doing that, Zee?" he asked.

Xero was still focused on the data and about to answer when she noticed he was looking up past her. She turned to her main screen and immediately saw the red flashing bar showing an alert. She drilled down into the security feeds and realized the threat was internal just before Riggs' ship-wide announcement. In horror, Xero focused on the location. She and Lux were on G-deck.

"Lux, where is your bot?" Something else occurred to her, something that in retrospect should have been obvious.

Minutes later, they were in the outer corridor, the rebuilt service drone leading them both toward what she hoped was safety. Xero quickly used her own datapad to load in some classified combat simulation into the bot's mainframe AI. She triggered it on to maintain a defensive posture.

"That's blood," Lux said stepping past the streaks. They appeared more brown than red under the artificial lighting, but both knew instantly how dangerous the situation had suddenly become. Xero marveled again at how quickly the boy adapted, first upon hearing that they were in danger and secondly, that his bot was not broken and in fact might be their best bet on finding safety.

"So, it's been picking up something real all along?"

Xero offered a grim smile. She was terrified, but the kid was simply happy his work on the drone hadn't been flawed. They cautiously moved down the long hall knowing danger could hide behind any of the many hatches. Xero had no plan other than to get her and the child off this deck.

The bot chirped before spinning and launching a grappling hook right between them both. Xero screamed and ducked, taking Lux down, too. She heard the hook hit something solid, then a meaty sound as the barbs penetrated. She glanced back and saw the scaly creature with the spiked back. It filled most of the hall and had moved silently to within feet of them. It snarled, that mouth full of the writhing finger-like teeth that she knew would be impossible to escape from.

"Run!"

How did a Furie get onboard? Her mind went through all the possibilities, but there was only one way. It must have hitched a ride on one of the dropship missions. Smart fucks, not just brainless monsters.

Ducking around a corner, she pulled Lux close. The modified maintenance drone had little to offer in the way of weapons, but maybe Lux had thought ahead. He was looking up at her, obviously not prepared for what they had just encountered. If she hadn't seen some of them back in Texas, she would have been just as surprised. "What else can your bot do?"

He took the datapad from her outstretched hand. "I call him Rex." He busied himself pulling up submenus as the sound of the creature and the rising pitch of the droid's small, repulser drives were getting closer.

"Make it quick, Lux."

"Xero, we have you and the boy on the monitor. Security is coming your way, three minutes."

That might as well be an eternity, and sadly, she'd realized the corner they had taken cover behind led only to a sealed storage compartment for radioactive byproduct from the enormous engines.

The Furie's long, claw-tipped arms came into view wrapped around the alloy upper section of the droid. Lux smiled as he saw the creature's position. Punching one of the commands on the tablet, a drill laser instantly punched a small hole straight through the monster's stomach. Purple blood flowed out and down over both. The Furie made a high, mewling scream of pain, then swept a tremendous blow across the front of the machine. The claw left a streak of shiny metal in sharp contrast to the dull finish on the rest of its chassis.

"Fly Rex into the thing, push it back so we can get by," Xero yelled.

Lux handled the controls like he was playing one of his video games. The mass of the droid wasn't huge, but the momentum of its flight took the injured creature off its feet giving both humans a chance to squeeze by and run for the end of the corridor. That was where they discovered access out of the deck was sealed off.

The Furie stood; it had to duck its head to move toward them, the seven-foot ceiling short by at least a foot. It slammed the floating droid against the wall and moved past. It wanted human prey. Xero had the boy behind her pressed up against the sealed hatch. She could use her sleeve computer and override the security controls for the door, but no way to do it in the time they had left. Besides, that would just release this thing into the rest of the ship.

Her lightning fast mind worked through the options and quickly came up with—nothing. Then the little bot suddenly righted itself and charged into the back of the creature breaking off several of the sharp spikes in the process. It extended its metal arms around the Furie and interlocked them, not stopping it, but slowing it down considerably. Still, the pair were within just a couple of yards.

Xero glanced back at Lux, but the boy wasn't triggering this. This was just the bot adapting or improvising on the limited programming it had. Self-preservation was an understood base of most machine code. Rex seemed to have it in abundance.

The Furie flung itself, freed one of the bot's arms, and drew back to slash just as the hatch they were pressed up against unexpectedly clicked opened, and a pulse rifle emerged through. Instantly, plasma rounds began tearing into the creature. Gi pulled them both back into the other section as Lux yelled for them not to hit Rex. The little bot had already figured out the situation had changed and retreated back into the corridor Lux and Xero had used earlier. The security team flowed around them, all knowing the weak areas of the scaly, greenish beast.

~

"Did we get it?"

The man was looking up into the broken grating on a small access panel.

"You know that's exactly how idiots die in space movies, right?" Halo said. He and Bishop had rushed down to join Gi when they heard the shooting. The man looking into the dark space stepped back several steps and raised his weapon to the high-ready position.

"It's wounded," Sergeant Gi said. "I'm afraid it's not mortally so, though. I know how hard those things are to kill."

"Two KIA back here, G-Force." The Korean had passed the bodies on the way. He knew from the uniforms they were also part of the engineering contingent.

"How could that thing have gotten on the dropship and survived the hard vacuum?" Halo asked.

"The LT is going to want answers. Suggest taking a team and inspect the dropship. We don't know this was the only one," Gi said. He then directed his team to sweep the entire deck, room by room.

Moving back through the hatch, he saw they had reunited the boy with his mother, who appeared way more frightened than Lux did. Gi moved up near Xero, who had been unnerved by the encounter but kept her shit together. "Excuse me, might I have a word?"

They moved away from Carol and Lux and two-armed sentries Gi had assigned as a protective detail.

"Xero, how has that monster evaded the ship's sensors? Assuming it came up with the last dropship, it's been on board for nearly a week."

She looked back toward where they'd so nearly been killed. "Did you get it?"

"It's wounded, many wounds," Gi said. "Unfortunately, that could make things even worse. A wounded animal is a dangerous one. I need to know if there's more than one, and then where that one is."

Xero thought about the two men out their floating toward their target. "Sergeant, I don't have those answers. Short version is we can't fully trust our ship's sensors. I'll work on it, but I have a more pressing issue to deal with. Is my workstation secure?"

Gi was frustrated, his job right now was onboard security, but he trusted Xero knew the ship's priorities better than himself. "No, I can't guarantee that it is. I'd suggest relocation to engineering or the bridge. Those are hard points, naturally difficult to breech and easier to defend."

CHAPTER FIFTY-TWO

MAINE

I didn't notice the wall coming down around me, nor did I notice the comms channels suddenly start working. I had used my energy reserves, and my body's supply of adrenaline and endorphins was not only finite, using them up quickly came with a downside. Blackness took me just as I felt Sumo's wet tongue on the side of my bare face.

The next several hours were snatches of movement, pain, bright lights, and at one point, riding across very bumpy ground. I awoke in a darkened room. Yes, it could have just been nighttime, but my senses automatically gauged the size of whatever space I was in. The room was large but not like where I'd been held prisoner. A cold, wet towel fell off my head as I leaned up. My hands traced the outline of well-worn leather and nail heads beneath me, a sofa, likely an antique, but the feel of it screamed money.

"Back from the dead again," I heard Voss say nearby. Then, I realized my injured legs were in her lap on the sofa.

"Threats?'"

"Neutralized, for now."

"Acevedo was a hitman, Carlson's assassin who came after us. I think I killed him, I was damn sure trying to. You didn't find a body in there with me?"

"Sorry, Joe, no bodies other than yours. We managed to get you into a loader bucket on the Agrobot I used to break through the wall. We're in Carlson's main house now."

I nodded; the movement sent a wave of nausea through me. I needed to know that she had cleared the house, but Voss was a professional, she would have done it right. Honestly, I was just glad she was here. "My legs?" I asked. I could tell she had removed my battleskin, and it felt like the wounds had been bandaged.

"You were filleted, Joe. The cuts were nearly to the bone, but they are healing remarkably fast. You were holding onto the cream which Ada informed me was a rapid healing compound. I liberally applied it several times. It's been eight hours, and I'd say the healing looks like you've been on the mend for two, maybe three weeks."

"Thanks, and yes, we aren't leaving without a supply of that medicine. And the wet rag?" I smiled, holding the towel out to her.

"I'm not domestically inclined. If you were having contractions, I would have boiled water. You have a high fever. I put a cold rag on your head. That's the extent of my medical abilities."

I laughed. "I doubt very seriously that is true but thank you. I always have a fever now, my core temperature is higher than before my enhancement."

"I recalled that, but this seemed unusually high," she said, folding the towel and placing it on a table. "As I recall, increased appetite is also normal. Can I get you some food?"

"Absolutely! I am starving." I hadn't really thought about it until then, but yes, I could eat.

"Well, we hit the mother load of supplies. This main kitchen has anything you can imagine, including a tank of live Maine lobsters."

She stood to go. "It's just down the hall, give me a few minutes."

I nodded and waited for her to leave before checking in with Ada on building security, then putting in a call to Bayou.

Voss returned just as I was logging off the lengthy call with my number two. I watched as she set a massive amount of food in front of me, including two lobsters and what appeared to be an actual steak.

"I thought you didn't cook."

"I may have implied that, but truthfully, I love to cook. It's one of my secret passions. Plus, this place has everything, including an AI controlled oven and cooktop. No way to overcook anything." She poured him a drink from the bar and sat it down as well. "I can get you a cold beer if you prefer."

I stared across the side table at the bottle and smiled. "Pappy's is good for now." I shoveled roasted potatoes and carrots into my mouth before taking a bite of steak. The pain in my legs, the frustration of war all disappeared. "Oh, my God, Dami, thank you."

I paused between bites when I noticed she was just watching me. "Are you eating?"

She looked down at her wrist comms, "Sumo's and mine are just finishing up. I didn't want you to wait."

"Where is the big furball?" I asked.

"He's watching the timer on the stove," she said rising to her feet. He slept beside you for hours, that dog loves you—he just doesn't want you to know it.

I carved the steak bone away from the delicious meat and set it aside for him. Then I went to work on the lobsters; the action resembled me fighting some of those damn creatures outside. It was a battle I eventually won and oh, how sweet the rewards. I might just move up to Maine permanently.

I was sitting back sipping the expensive bourbon when they came back in. Voss set a large bowl of something on the floor for Sumo and then joined me on the couch to eat. Her meal looked delicious as well but much more low-key than what she'd given me.

"So, what did we learn?" she asked between mouthfuls.

I was still dwelling on what Bayou was dealing with, so it took me a minute to shift mental gears. "First, where is your Wraith?"

She eyed the room suspiciously. "Out there patrolling. What do you think is keeping all the other creatures away?"

"Does that work? I mean, I recall them being all over us inside the Nightmare Factory and he... or it, was there."

She moved a little closer and handed me a beer she'd brought back from the kitchen. "I think that was simply because we were in such a confined space, but yes, it has an effect, although I can't tell how strong. The more highly developed ones seem more aware of it than the others.

Sumo and I had our hands full waiting for you to do something creative."

That stung. "Sorry, I was indisposed for much of that time. What I learned is Nevis isn't here, nowhere. The man that captured me was an assassin and also appeared to be augmented."

"Like you?" she asked.

I thought about that, I really wasn't sure. "I don't think so, but he was certainly enhanced, but I would say he was also naturally very skilled. He is a killer. I should have ended him."

"You weren't in any shape to do much more."

"Damiana, there is something else." I took a deep breath before continuing. "He said he was responsible for killing your Sisters. And that it was you he was after."

Even in the dim lights, I could see her face darken, and that look of a predator descended once more. I took a long pull on the beer and waited. I could see the mental wheels turning in that beautiful head.

"I need to know about the Sisters of Light." She took another bite of her food and refused to make eye contact. "You told me not so long ago that you had resources, that we could be useful to each other if we went after these guys."

"There isn't much I can tell. I am under a blood oath. I'm sorry, but that's how it is. We go back a very long time, and we always try to fight on the side of good, but that doesn't mean we don't get our hands dirty."

I already had a good idea of what she was willing to do to accomplish a mission. She'd proven that firsthand. "Not affiliated with any state, totally independent?"

"I can't honestly answer that, partially because I don't know, but more accurately, we are probably embedded in key places in most national governments, or were. We go where we are told and do the things necessary to get the job done."

"Who decides what the jobs are?"

She took another bite. I wasn't getting an answer to that question, nor how large their numbers or what kinds of resources she could call on if needed.

"Are you using me?" I asked, already knowing the answer.

"Of course!" she said, her voice way too cheery for my liking. "But try to understand that doesn't mean I am going to discard you, or my enjoyment in your company is false. I'm here, Joe, we are friends and partners." She held up her own beer bottle and tapped the bottom against mine.

"All women?" I asked.

She smiled and then nodded. "Yes."

I'd been around top-secret intelligence most of my adult life and my dad many decades longer, yet I'd never heard a whisper about this group. That was damned impressive.

"He said your people almost stopped the Liberty Strike."

"That's what he called it? The Liberty Strike?" she asked, now on full alert.

"Yes, I challenged him on it." Truthfully, I could just have Ada play back our entire exchanges, but I was relatively sure I'd passed along the most relevant points.

We sat and drank, and I ate again before she pulled me awkwardly to my feet. "Come on, handsome, this place has the most luxurious looking bed." We had a lot to do, and staying here in the heart of the enemy's stronghold was ridiculous, but we both needed a good night's sleep.

I leaned on her heavily, and since I was already stripped down to my boxers and bandages, I just lay down and damn, she was right. It was the most perfect mattress I'd ever felt; it enveloped and supported me in all the right places, constantly adjusting to my every move. God Almighty, having money was the way to go. Lobsters, Pappy Van Winkle bourbon, and now this. Damiana rolled over and kissed me. She knew I was in no shape for anything more, and that was okay. I held her close and had to admit that I loved the feeling.

This incredibly tough, smart, and confusing woman could make me crazy, yet she could also be so tender and vulnerable. If it was all just an act, she was an incredibly gifted actress. I'd learned long ago to simply enjoy the moments. Despite my injuries, this moment was a keeper.

CHAPTER FIFTY-THREE

IAS STONE MOUNTAIN

"What?" Hauk yelled, finally realizing Koog was in trouble. The kid was spinning clockwise at an increasing rate. The tether was twisting tighter and tighter. That EVA tether was all that kept the missile attached and allowed them to communicate.

Hauk moved up close to slow the man down.

"No!" Koog yelled. "Mass is too great. I will just make you spin off in the other direction."

Right, that makes sense, Hauk thought. The kid seemed a lot calmer than he would have been, but of course, the Marine worked up here, he didn't. "What happened?"

"Micrometeoroid would be my guess. I believe it clipped one of the maneuvering tanks on my SAFER unit."

Hauk had an identical unit strapped to his back over the life support system. It allowed them to do fine maneuvers with quick bursts of compressed gas or larger burns using the small, built-in thrusters. He was relatively sure it had to be one of the gas canisters, he could see white mist coming off one side as Koog spun by. The rotations were about once every fifteen seconds now and still increasing.

"How can I help?"

Koog had been busy grasping at something on his belt, but his own momentum kept making his hands miss. His responses were increasingly garbled. Hauk figured he only had minutes before he passed out.

"Gotta jettison the MMU."

Shit, Hauk knew they had gone over this really quickly in the safety brief, but there'd been so much to cover. If the kid lost his maneuvering jets, though, the mission would be over. No way they could get to the target vessel, deliver the Penetrator, and get away sharing one pack.

"Help me hit the release," Koog said, his arms still flailing wildly.

Hauk quickly studied the release on his own belt. Simple enough, just a two-position latch. Flip one part up and the other part back. Simple, unless you were spinning like a top. He went into combat mode. *Get your head in the game, Hauk*. Identify, assess, and most importantly, act. The simple procedures had been drilled into him since basic. The problem was, this wasn't his typical battle space; his tactics were not designed for this. All he knew was losing the SAFER pack might be as bad as losing his teammate.

Koog's gloved hands were now wrapped around the securing harness and inching their way to the release mechanism.

"Don't do it," Hauk said as calmly as he could manage. He could see part of the unit's shielding had blown away, and it wasn't one of the tanks inside, it was a valve that looked to have been damaged. Hauk felt a tug and realized the tether between them had twisted so tight it was in knots and drawing him and the missile toward the spinning Marine.

He wasted no more time; he'd done the first two things, now he had to act. Unfortunately, he really only had one play. He jerked down on the tether drawing Koog toward him and simultaneously shoved the missile into his spinning path. The Marine connected with the object with a silent thud. The mass of the bomb was great enough to absorb much of the kid's momentum, but it quickly began pulling them in the opposite direction. Hauk wasted no time getting a hand inside the maneuvering unit and shutting off the damaged valve. The rush of escaping gas trickled to a stop.

Hauk wanted to check on Koog but first had his suit's AI execute a burn to arrest the momentum and get them back on course. The tether dug into his waist belt, but slowly, the accelerating mass of the I-8 Penetrator slowed to a stop and began returning to the two men.

The Marine was shaken but uninjured; he came around within a few minutes none the worse for wear.

"Did you black out?"

"I dunno, I guess so, I saw stars," Koog said pointing up.

Hauk shook his head, "You crazy idiot. How much propellant do you have?"

Koog checked the displays, "Not a lot, about thirty percent of what I did."

They untangled the tether and worked on modifying the plan. Hauk preferred the more experienced Marine have the better gear, but since they couldn't swap units, Hauk would take the lead and do the bulk of the pulling and course corrections.

"Okay, Jarhead, just sit back and enjoy the ride. Let the good old U.S. Army get the job done, as usual."

~

Several hours later, Koog drifted up close to the other man. "Captain, you good to go?"

Hauk had been zoning in and out. This was one of the most challenging missions he'd ever undertaken, alternately terrifying followed by hours of monotony. The scenery didn't seem to change, and he'd never felt more alone despite the other man a few yards away.

"Yes, sorry, Koog, I was just going over the plan again."

Koog knew better but let it go. "Oorah, sir!" The warship signaled a two-degree course change. That should be the last one.

Hauk turned back toward the Stone Mountain instinctively to verify. They had been drifting farther apart for most of the past day. Now it was just one bright speck of light among many. Using his HUD to zoom in, he could see the position and the light array on the hull to confirm the corporal's report. They triggered the burn, pulling the Penetrator along between them now.

"We should get a visual on the target any time now. If we could use radar, it would be easy to get a fix, but the boss lady didn't want to risk it," Koog said unnecessarily.

Hauk was having a hard time understanding how something could just hide in the wide open up here, but then again, they'd been drifting behind a small cluster of space debris for much of this journey.

"Let's keep the package close, less chance for the enemy to spot it," Koog said.

They did it and then both began scanning the area on multispectral wavelengths for the enemy ship. The suits' built-in AI handled most of it, but the rapid change of visuals was barely noticeable on the HUDs, except for the electromagnetic wavelengths, which lit up the display like a rainbow. Both men watched the counter working its way toward zero. Bayou and Xero had concurred on the most likely location, but they all knew it was just an educated guess. The counter went from two kilometers down to 784 meters with nothing in range. Then, they both picked up an object on infra-red.

"It's too small," Koog said.

"Maybe," Hauk agreed, his voice a whisper.

The thing appeared to be blacked out; it gave no reflection, and they were emerging into the day side of the planet's orbit.

"Suit calculates it is still over a klick out. We are just looking at the leading edge. Visual perception gets weird up here. I'm having the suit do a suggested intercept path to put us right over the back end of the thing. I'll link it to your suit, so you can do the heavy lifting."

Hauk was impressed, the kid was on point. He may have gotten shaken up, but he was solid as they came. He reviewed the course change and had to accept it. He didn't know shit about fighting in space. It looked to him like he was charging into the path of an incoming fighter jet, but in reality, they were a good thirty degrees off its bow on the starboard side. Just far enough out that the ship's nav-safety system would auto-adjust course to miss the pile of debris. They just had to time it that they were in the right spot soon after the ship moved by.

"You recognize it, Koog?"

"I can't see enough detail yet, and we're heading into the sun again, so my shields are blocking a lot of the visible light. Just guessing it's about the right size for one of the Chinese corvettes."

"China?"

"Well, the right size. They use them for a little bit of everything up here. Ship to ground, ship to ship, even have some configured for light freight haulers."

"No one from China should be able to get into an Alliance ship's computer systems, but since Last Day, who the hell knew who was on any ships up here?"

Hauk had the suit start recording video and sensor data. It was all programmed to send back to Lieutenant Riggs in a burst transmission should anything go wrong. "Here we go, in three, two, one."

The thrusters fired, automatically bringing them up from below and over the sleek, matte-black ship. It had no insignia of any kind, and even Koog seemed confused on where the best place to plant the bomb might be.

"It's not Chinese, sir." Now Koog was whispering too, not that anyone could hear them in the vacuum of space. Still, it seemed right. The ship was about 120 feet long, or about the size of a TriCraft dropship, but much, much thinner. It had short, stubby wings that seemed to meld into the hull very gracefully. This was a space plane likely designed for space or atmo.

"Engines, cargo doors, landing struts." Koog had been doing a mental breakdown of the craft as they approached and now seemed convinced he knew where to go. "I have the location mapped in. You just need to activate the warhead."

"Once I do that, they'll know we're here," Hauk reminded the younger man.

"I've mapped out all the obvious weapons ports. We'll jet away in the least dangerous direction."

The Army captain was trusting this kid with his life, but what choice did he have?

"Shouldn't we at least, you know, knock on the door, say hello... something, before we try to blow them up?" Koog asked.

"It's called orders, kid. As our leader said, the engagement rules are simple now. They die first!"

Hauk finished the activation sequence and sent the command. The I-8 arming lights flashed green, then red, and its internal guidance kicked on and began searching for the coordinates Koog had marked.

The two of them hit the thrusters at top speed hoping to put as much distance as possible between them and the weird little ship.

While still moving away, both turned and looked at the large Penetrator bomb settle onto the surface, and instantly, a bright light erupted beneath as it fired its slug of molten copper into the back of the doomed ship. Within seconds, the entire craft exploded outward like a scene out of a movie. Their suits were little cover for the mass of debris heading their way. They needed to outrun it, which was unlikely, or find something solid to put between them.

They found something solid. Another ship.

CHAPTER FIFTY-FOUR

Alarms blared; lighting over the tactical station went red.

"Bogey-1 is destroyed, but..." the pause that followed was excruciating. "It's another ship," the tactical officer said.

Bayou tapped comms. "Xero, are they out of the system?"

"Affirmative!" she said from her workstation several decks below.

"Weps! All ship-to-ship weapons online, get me a firing solution. Maneuvering thrusters, present as small a profile as possible," Bayou yelled, unsure of half the things she was ordering. Like Hauk, this was not her battlespace. "Comms, any word from our people?"

"Radio dark, ma'am, but I am getting positive telemetry on both. Position is identical to enemy vessel," the young Marine manning the station yelled out.

"Firing solution plotted, ship-killers locked and loaded."

How in the hell had they missed the larger ship? Someone missed something, and now they were going to pay the price for her 'They Die First' mandate.

"She's targeting our engines. Incoming point-to-point lasers."

Bayou had to trust Otero that the shielding back there was adequate. "Launch missiles two and four, indirect intercept."

She didn't know much about space combat, but after years of being on the orbital platforms she'd overheard enough to know in space battles you dealt with time as well as distance. You had to fire where you thought the enemy would be, not where they were.

"Missile lock is not holding, ma'am, we are getting an IFF transponder from the enemy ship," the weapons officer signaled.

"This is the same ship that is firing on us? Damn sure not friendly forces."

"I can override the armaments code to ignore that, ma'am, on your authority."

"Do it," Bayou yelled to the young specialist.

"We're being hailed, ma'am."

Riggs looked at her young comms officer incredulously. "They want to talk?"

"Yes, but only to you," the girl said, her face a mask of fear.

"Weps. Get those missiles on target. Don't wait for my signal. Drive those bastards home." She also radioed down to the flight deck for Packer to get into his dropship. "We may need a pickup, or at the very least, have another pair of eyes out there." There was no longer any reason to stay quiet or hidden.

She motioned for comms to transfer the call to the ready room. Riggs moved in behind the display and accepted the call.

"Hello, Bayou. We need to talk."

"Holy fuck!" Bayou stared at the screen in utter disbelief.

The smiling face of a ghost stared back.

CHAPTER FIFTY-FIVE

MAINE

"Wake-up, sparkle-farts, there's dragons to slay."

Coming fully awake to the sounds of my father's colorful descriptors was becoming a normal part of life, since neither Ada nor I had any luck so far in finding the off switch for whatever comms link he was using. I had no option but to take the fucking call. Today, it was at zero ass o'clock in the morning.

I very reluctantly crawled out of the wonderful bed and gingerly hobbled out into the hall and down to a large window where Sumo was curled up. Moonlight cast the well-manicured grounds into a scene from a fairy tale. In the distance, I could still see the Decimator Warbot, I hadn't thought to ask Dami if it was still active. I couldn't see how she would have gotten by it if it was.

"What's up, Pop?"

"Well, whistle-britches, while you've been taking a weekend of love-making and lobster rolls, the world has gone further into the toilet."

"What now?" I asked, dreading the answer.

"Some group in northern France is now suggesting all survivors unite to overthrow whatever is left of the world governments. They are advocating anarchy, no politicians, no police, and no military. You guys are getting crucified in absentia. "

"B.F.D., Dad. That's nothing new, and hell, we probably did do it, or at least failed to prevent it."

"It is a big fucking deal, kid. No way this is a major hot button issue right now, someone else is fanning the flames."

"Who?" I asked. "Shit, no one likes politicians especially. They're mostly just lawyers who were too lazy to go to work in their own offices."

"Moral decay isn't something you go to your dentist to fix. Nor is it worth the wholesale eradication of the species."

"So, who's pulling the strings? Carlson?"

"I keep telling you Carlson is a fucking pip-squeak, a paper-pusher. Besides, haven't you killed him yet?"

I really hated admitting that I hadn't, or that I'd nearly been killed by his fucking butler. "Not yet," I admitted.

"Well, shit, Son, maybe you should have sold Tupperware for a living. I thought you were a goddamn soldier."

I tried to find words, then just gave up. It was too early, and my legs were burning where the healing gel was still doing its magic. "Pops, what can you tell me about the Sisters of Light?" I asked, changing the subject to something I really wanted to know.

"Never heard of 'em," he answered just a little too quickly. "Oh yeah, Indie rock. Think I saw them play at a little club down in Charleston."

"Dad, stop fucking around."

"Hell of a drummer and the lead singer... damn."

"You aren't going to tell me?" I asked. The man stayed silent an unusually long time, especially for him.

"Lumia," he said finally. "They call her The Grand Mother."

"What can you tell me about her? Or them?"

"Honestly, Son, not much. Supposedly roots of the organization go back hundreds, maybe even thousands of years. No one in government seemed to ever be clear if they actually existed, and if so, what side they might be fighting on."

"But you know Lumia?"

Again, the delay before answering "Yes, we had dealings. Let's just say the Sisterhood leaves a mark on your soul. Even now, I don't want to betray the promise I made to her."

Goddamn, my father was scared. Shit—that scared me. Because in all my thirty-seven years, I'd never once seen the man afraid of anything. This man would fight Satan himself just to prove he got the winning letter first in Bingo.

"Can they be trusted?" I asked, already afraid of the answer.

"No... well, maybe. My personal belief is Lumia was the most loyal person I have ever dealt with, but I know they will lie, cheat, steal, or kill to get what they want. They have no moral nor geographic boundaries, Joe. I put our full intelligence gathering apparatus to work on finding out more, and in three years, not only did I find not a single other associate of the woman, but I also couldn't even verify that she existed."

"She didn't care that you went after her like that?"

"Hell, Son, she suggested it. She wanted me to know they were invisible... bulletproof, whatever you want to call it. We couldn't touch her."

"Carlson's man said that the Sisters nearly stopped the Last Day attack, something he called Liberty Strike."

"Then that may mean that we are on the same side in this fight. Still, I'd advise you to avoid them. Stay in your lane if you know what's good for you. They will smile to your face, then shoot you in the back if it serves their purpose."

Or stomach, I thought.

~

Voss was up slipping into her gear when I returned. "Pleasant talk with Dad?"

I smiled, there was no point in trying to keep anything from the woman. "Sorry, I didn't want to wake you."

She leaned in and kissed me. "It's okay, I'm a light sleeper."

She slipped on her boots, an everyday activity for her that suddenly felt like an act of seduction.

"So, how are you doing, back in the game?"

"Huh? Oh, yes. Not full speed, and my legs itch like crazy, but Ada says my mobility is around seventy-eight percent and climbing. Fighting capabilities, a bit less."

"We need to go, staying here is fun and all but isn't helping us catch up with Carlson."

"You have a plan?" I asked. Because I had nothing to say about where to go next.

She did, and we spent the next several hours going through every data file in the house including the printed files in the man's office. I mean, who prints anything anymore? After hours of fruitless searching, I gave up and headed to the kitchen. Food and beer sounded great.

Voss joined me a short time later, and I pushed a plate of pasta with cream sauce and diver scallops toward her. She dug in and smiled.

"You cook, too?"

I shrugged. "I can, but this was in the prep center just waiting to be warmed up. I just had to sear the scallops. I'm assuming Acevedo hadn't planned on missing dinner."

"Does tracking him help? He's injured and should be close and easier to find."

I'd already considered that, but the man was dangerous, even more so injured. He also wanted Damiana, and I had a hard time thinking about using her as bait. "I don't think so, I don't think his boss confides much in him. That man is a fight we don't need right now." Though, I felt sure I would see him again.

"What's the story on that?" I pointed with my fork toward the stationary object a few hundred yards away.

"The Decimator?" she asked. "It went dormant not long after you were taken. We didn't have to fight it, thankfully. I don't know why he didn't put it in sentry mode, it just seemed to go into standby."

That triggered something, Acevedo had mentioned telepresence when he talked about taking out the women in Paris. "Do you know if those things can be operated remotely? Maybe via a VR hookup?"

"Telepresence?" she asked. "Yeah, I am sure it would have to be on a totally immersive rig. Too much to control to try to do it from a standard workstation."

"Right," I said, thinking out loud. Finally, my million-dollar brain seemed to be earning its keep. "He mentioned handling the strike in

Paris using telepresence. I didn't think about him not being in the Warbot because I saw his face in the view port. I just assumed he'd been piloting it from inside."

"No, we never saw the cockpit open up on the thing. A few minutes after you went down, the tall man was standing over you."

That was impressive, I thought. With almost all telepresence I had seen, there was a small lag. Just enough to make it impractical in an actual battle. Acevedo's bot had been on point and just as lethal and quick acting as the man himself. "He'd have to have a VR room, and it would probably be close to where he took me. Have you seen it?"

She shook her head. "The estate is huge, but Sumo and I went through checking every room and outbuildings, but admittedly, I did it fast."

"What about you, Ada, can you pull up plans or track the wiring? A purpose-built space like that should stand out on the layout."

"Working on it, nothing in the original plans, but those were almost two hundred years ago. VR node room technology is only a few decades old. Sorting through building permits and contractor bids."

My AI was speaking aloud, so Damiana could follow along.

"What does finding his node room do to help us find Carlson?"

"You'll see."

"I may have it," Ada said. "A DOD contractor out of Virginia did work with Hammer Industries twelve years ago on an undisclosed location."

"Undisclosed doesn't help," Voss said.

"The mileage expenses from the contractor to this location match well enough. Going through the building specs, and it is obviously subterranean. Also, some reqs for materials for very specific granite and bluestone. Likely to match what was already here."

The patios and veranda were all paved in the local bluestone, and the foundations of the main house and storage buildings were granite. "Time for a field trip."

CHAPTER FIFTY-SIX

It wasn't simple; we spent several hours looking for the VR bunker. Several times, one or the other thought we had it, only for it to be an old wine cellar or maintenance door. Sumo was the one that finally located it, right in plain sight. A section of connecting wall between the carriage house and a media room. The rock-work looked precisely like the surrounding masonry, but the dog hit on a scent that had to be Acevedo.

I used my suit's sensors to scan the walls for control panels, hidden voids, or anything that might be a way in. Voss stood back ten yards and just watched me. I was on my third pass using a type of advanced lidar to peer beneath the outer layers of the wall.

Voss walked up, held out a small comms devise, and within minutes, a small panel clicked out of an adjacent wall. This had a card slot and a bio reader.

"Ada," I began, then stopped. Voss had detached a card from the comms unit and dropped it into the reader, then affixed her thumb to the print reader.

"Quantum based scanner. Goes through billions of frequencies and codes in seconds."

"Why didn't you just start with that?" I asked. "And where can I get one?"

"I didn't want to spoil your fun, and honestly, I was expecting a mechanical system. This guy seems old-school, you know?"

The door clicked, then swung inward on silent hinges. The security access panel slid back into the wall.

"Sumo, blind search," I whispered. He moved down the steps and into the interior at a run. I wasn't expecting booby-traps or tripwires, but my dog always knows to be extra careful, whereas I tend to just bulldoze through shit relying on luck.

"Room is clear, Prowler," my AI said seconds later.

We descended the stone steps and entered, my Rattler MK4 sweeping the room anyway. I'd had enough surprises this week. Compared to the rest of the house, the subterranean space was rather modest. It was thirty feet long and half that wide. The standard zero gravity VR rig hung loosely from the ceiling beam. The telepresence hand grips hanging limply like a tired scarecrow. What I was looking for was in the adjoining control room, which was even smaller. I withdrew a small cable from my sleeve computer and plugged it into an access port. "Ada, take everything."

"The other places he connected to?" Voss asked intrigued.

"And the actual conversations, up to a point. The buffer is small, and its encrypted, but like your device, my girl Ada is impressive as hell."

It took nearly fifteen minutes for her to download the files and begin decryption. I didn't want to hear or see what they said. I wanted useable intel—who were they speaking with, and where was Carlson heading? Admittedly, he probably wasn't using telepresence for all of that, but we might get lucky.

"One other thing, Ada, see if you can get command authorization on the Decimator unit and anything that might let us know how these fucks are controlling the other nightmare beasts."

"I do not yet have control but have a visual feed from the Decimator sentry unit. Prowler, you may want to see this," Voss said.

~

"It's her, the WitchWalker."

I didn't know which one of us had coined that term, but it seems totally fucking appropriate. The lone, wolfishly thin girl was standing in the road looking toward the house... toward us. Ada zoomed in until I could see her face; sallow cheeks and haunted eyes sat beneath jet black hair that blew wildly in the strong ocean breeze. She wore a simple dress, the color long since faded to a muted grayish brown. The most striking thing wasn't the girl but the literal army of beasts that seemed to accompany her.

"You sure it's the same one you saw?" I asked, thinking about the blonde girl in Texas description that sounded remarkably similar.

"Why, do you think there are more of them? I'm not positive, but I'd lay good odds on it."

"She made damn good time then. That was what, almost a hundred miles away," I said, still studying the packs of mutant beasts behind and to both sides of her. None approached her nor came any closer to us than the girl.

"I haven't even seen a lot of those creatures, the mutations seem to be getting even more bizarre," Voss said, her tone flat and analytical.

A flicker of movement on the screen confused me until I recognized it for what it was. The Wraith was very near the WitchWalker, the almost iridescent wings catching the afternoon sun.

"We need to talk to her, we need to know how she is controlling the creatures," Voss said, an emotional edge creeping in now that she'd seen the Wraith as well.

"And how do you propose we do that?"

It was a good question; I had no intention of going out there and being slaughtered. In fact, it didn't look like we even had an escape route away from this place now. The green zone that had been the manor's grounds had jarringly shifted over to the side of the wastelands.

"The Wraith can bring her in."

I shrugged my shoulders and let Voss take over. Clearly, I did not understand the relationship between her and her pet monster. The damn thing had tried to kill me, but ultimately, had also helped ease my pain. Damiana obviously could communicate with it somehow, but that was not anything she wanted to share. I still hadn't even seen the thing up close, not that I wanted to, and it always seemed to be in camouflage or like now, nearly transparent.

"Don't go out there or do anything stupid," I warned.

Ada began showing me the most relevant findings from the telepresence links while my new partner did her thing outside on the edge of the massive lawn. What was 'her thing' you ask? I have no fucking idea. Must be a Sisterhood, talking to the animals, Disney movie kinda shit.

"Carlson was a busy little fuck." None of the sessions were prior to Last Day which meant either they had been wiped, or this node was not used until then. So likely, none of the planning was here. "Okay, track back any of Acevedo's connections but limit it to ones after the last one of his boss."

"You assume the man would be checking in with Carlson, and that might offer a location?" Ada surmised.

It did not. The hitman, it turned out, wasn't much of a talker, not to his employer at least. There were several connections to what I would describe as underlings in France. I had Ada index those; Voss might want to see them later.

She began playing back more of Nevis Carlson's video of each connection. Ones she had tagged as most relevant. I had her increase the speed until I was processing what I was seeing at over ten times the normal frame rate. The audio was badly distorted at that speed, but Ada flashed subtitles up, and I was able to interpret the conversation and slow down when I wanted to review an exchange in more detail. One of these stood out.

The connection was a call out, so the VR environment was the recipient's node room, not Carlson's. I scanned the link address and, to no surprise, found they had used triple-level masking to cover the location. The person was unknown to me and was using one of the weirdly popular filters that shifted their appearance to mimic faces from famous paintings. I found the whole thing distracting as hell, but neither Carlson nor the other man seemed to give it a second thought. What was most strange was the environment, using a technology that allowed you to virtually appear to be anywhere. This person seemed to have put no effort at all into the meeting space. Where some might want it to appear to be an outdoor café on the Rue des Martyrs in Paris, or by the marina in Santa Monica, this host was using a very basic iteration of the standard room scene that Sony shipped with all their virtual rigs. It first got my attention more through its ordinariness than anything. Then I listened more closely to the conversation.

"I believe we were assured that the eradication protocols would not extend beyond the original target zones," the other man said.

"Indeed, my friend, we were." Ada had identified that second voice as Nevis Carlson, the bland face of the thumbnail view in the upper right backed up my father's unflattering assessment of the man. "The Sisters interfered, and some of our containment efforts were negated."

"Goddamnit, Carlson. Your only job was to handle that. Are you too fucking incompetent to take care of the simplest of tasks? You wanted a goddamn seat at the table—well, you got it, and now you fucked up already!"

Silence hung in the air a bit too long. In fact, now that I was listening in real time, something was clearly off. There was a slight delay, a lag in the comms. It was one I was intimately familiar with. The other party was off planet, possibly on a ship, or maybe even the moon.

"Carlson, you understand that none of this matters if we don't have a planet to inherit when the dust settles."

"Sir, this was a final option, let me remind you that we did anticipate certain problems."

"Subject Zero?" the anonymous man who now appeared as Van Gogh in his self-portrait growled.

"Taken care of," Nevis said.

"What about his pet?"

Nevis clearly paused on this one. "He or it is in the wild. Our intelligence is obviously spotty in the affected areas."

"Well, fuck!" the man said spitting out the words. "Proceed with the next phase. And after that, thankfully, your involvement will be done. Your incompetence to this point has not gone unnoticed."

The generic background went dark, and I clearly heard Nevis say, "Fuck you" and something else before he switched the terminal off.

"Ada what was that last bit?"

It took her a moment to zone in on that section of the audio track. "Badly garbled, I can try to reconstruct but not a lot to work with."

"Give it a try, and let's move on to the next one."

"Joe?"

"Yes, Ada."

"We have a problem."

I stared at the terminal window from the Warbot outside. Voss was moving slowly toward the woman. "Goddamnit, I told her..."

CHAPTER FIFTY-SEVEN

"Packer are you in the bus?"

"Yes, LT," the pilot responded, noticing the uncertainty in the woman's voice.

"Tactical is sending you the coordinates, go get our boys. Do not linger, do not do a sensor sweep."

Debra sat heavily into the captain's seat, which took effort in the low shipboard gravity, the weight of what she now knew was a burden she was totally unprepared for. She rubbed a hand over her chin and stared up into the network of conduit and metal that made up the ceiling. "How in the fuck did we get here?" she whispered.

"Ma'am?" her nearby communications officer asked.

"Nothing, Johnson, just been a long day."

They had removed one threat only to have it replaced by something even worse. Something she couldn't even tell her own team about.

"Sergeant Gi, do we have a body yet?" Riggs needed to concentrate on something else, and a mutant monster running around the ship was a good secondary priority.

"Negative, ma'am, blood trail stopped on the aft hatch of E-deck. Xero's now running wide spectrum scans to help narrow its escape route. It was injured..."

"Do I hear a 'but' there?"

"Yes, ma'am, Xero feels like these things may be able to rapidly heal most injuries."

Well, fuck! "Roger that. I'm sending the remainder of Banshee to help on the search. Do we know if we can contain it to a certain deck?"

"They are at least as capable as humans, ma'am. They open hatches, climb, and seem to have a rudimentary ability to shift their own coloration to better hide. These are not monsters, they are weapons, and a single one on the loose aboard this ship..."

The Korean didn't need to finish the thought; she got it. Sighing in frustration, she took the datapad from its sleeve on the arm of the seat and studied the ship's path. They had propulsion and navigation back, as well as weapons, including the two ship killers they had launched. She recalled them soon after the strange call she'd received. They were now stowed back in the armament racks with safeties reengaged.

"Nav, place us in parking orbit over this location as soon as the dropship is back. I'm going to get some chow."

The ensign nodded and repeated the order, another part of Space Force protocol that had come over from its naval roots. She found it cumbersome but accepted it like much of the newness of this strange role. Right now, it was just about the furthest thing from her mind. She needed someone to talk to, someone to help her develop a plan—some way of saving the ship from a threat none of them had expected. Unfortunately, the two people she felt she could rely on were off limits to her. Hauk was looking for a ride down to save his brother, and Joe... well, Joseph Kovach wouldn't handle this rationally.

She punched the door open to the ship's gym. Riggs wasn't hungry for food, she wanted to rid herself of this tension and anger. Slipping into her workout clothes, she began her rigorous daily routine of weights, resistance training, and then high-impact cardio, including a virtual Muay Thai match against the gym's robotic opponent.

The lieutenant kicked, pivoted, and snapped off another kick to the thing's virtual head before ducking low and punching into the groin area. Riggs pushed herself to exhaustion and beyond, ignoring the pain and the tears streaming down her face.

The noise she was making masked the thing's approach. The tentacle-filled mouth could taste the odor of sweat coming off the human.

She would be an easy kill and feeding again would help speed up its own healing process. The arm extended, the leathery fold of skin contracting back to reveal its own weapon, the claw.

Deb was facing a mirrored wall, but the room was dimly lit. Through her tears she could not see the camouflaged beast as it inched closer. Except for the claw that almost seemed to hang in midair, and when it registered in her mind, she was already turning to face the creature shimmering into view just feet away. The thing swiped up, and Deb felt muscle and tissue give way in her abdomen.

Damping down the pain, she attacked, pummeling the thing's head with her gloved fits. Strong arms flung her off, and she hit the wall with a thud. She had broken bones and was minutes away from bleeding out. All she had been through, and this was how it would end.

"I don't think so, bitch." Her fingers closed around a steel bar, one that she'd been planning to load up with dead weights. Now she had something else in mind for it. The Furie sprang, and Deb drove the rod into the creature's oversized belly while wedging the lower end between the wall and the floor. It pierced the thing's hide but not deeply. Still, the scream of rage from it was unmistakable.

"Hurt's, doesn't it?" Deb teased. She was using one hand to help staunch the flow of blood from her wound and to keep her insides in place. The other grabbed the bar again. She could feel her strength waning; it wouldn't be enough, but she was determined to go down swinging.

The beast's eye blinked, the weird, horizontal eyelids flicked. Bayou remembered Joe thinking these things had once been human. She couldn't see it. Deb felt consciousness ebbing away. This had to end now. Apparently, the Furie had reached the same decision. They both charged the other, meeting with a colossal test of strength and will. The thing was injured, Deb could feel its chest breathing and its rapid heartbeat as they battled hand to hand. Then, the claw came up and swung down again and again. Deb saw the darkness closing in, knowing she had failed.

~

"Good to see you. We can use the help."

"Just tell us where we can be the most use, G-Force."

"Priest, take my security team and cover engineering. We can't let this thing get to any of the ship's critical systems. Halo, you're on point with me. I have a group of Marines holding ground at each end of the deck," the sergeant said in his near flawless English. While he was still relatively new to the team, he'd already earned the others' respect.

"Anything we should know?" Bishop asked.

"Shoot nothing that isn't a Furie," the Korean said before adding, "Tactical ROE, but seriously, watch your down range fire."

The Glisson rifles had a built-in safe mode for shipboard or close quarters operation. They would limit, or even negate, fire if the likelihood of hitting a civilian or vital piece of machinery was high. Punching a railgun round through a high-pressure hydrogen line would do more damage than the creature. So, the pulse rifle would not allow you to select that option or would slow the velocity down to relatively safe levels. This deck was likely the heart of the damn ship, all the mechanical pipes, tubes, and ductwork ran along nearly every surface except the floor. Checking fire here was asking a lot, especially if your life was at risk.

"That's why you called the A-team, Sarge," Halo offered with a fist-bump. "Wish we had Sumo," he subvocalized into his whisper mic minutes later as they were clearing one of the dozens of storage rooms in this section.

Gi didn't disagree and also wondered if the boy's puppy might be helpful but quickly discarded the idea. Apparently, Lux and Xero had been working in close proximity to the creature for many days. They had found where it had been nesting. The boy's dog would have noticed the thing then if she'd been able. He knew firsthand the Furies had a smell, but that could simply be pheromones they emitted during an attack or something else entirely.

"Report all contact, watch your firing lanes," Gi said again, more for the benefit of his security crew than his fellow RDT team members. They knew instinctually what to do.

"Any chance we can get the illumination dialed up?" Halo asked. "I didn't bring my NODS."

"Ship is in power safe mode. Xero said we can't bring it up unless we get the other reactors to full power," Gi answered as they moved down the dimly lit corridor. Both men's helmet's built-in night vision was sufficient, but the military special night optical devices could see through the darkest of rooms.

"These things are bigger than I am by nearly two feet. How can it hide so well?"

Gi wondered the same thing; he knew he'd placed multiple rounds on target, yet the thing shook it off and fled. Now it was injured, and a wounded enemy was a particularly dangerous one. He reached and slowly unlatched the next hatch, then stepped back while Halo moved in to clear. Gi stepped into the empty space backing his partner by sweeping right to cover the opposite wall.

This went on for an hour and a half, painstakingly clearing every room one by one. The mostly empty rooms weren't bad, but when they got to those used for storage and then bunkrooms, every obstacle had to be checked and cleared. Ninety minutes is a long time to hold an edge, reflexes take over. Your mental sharpness begins to slip; even for the most disciplined of soldiers, it can become taxing. Still, Gi felt confident they had covered every possible location when they reached the end compartment on E deck.

The larger compartments on the end of each deck were typically workspaces. Areas meant to be used by groups of people, so depending on the function, they might fill the space with workbenches, computer workstations, machine shops, or in this case, spare parts storage. Gi lifted his visor and sniffed, the greasy smell of Cosmoline-coated metal hung in the air but nothing else. Rack after rack of maintenance parts were crammed floor to ceiling. This room was going to be tough. He signaled for Bishop to move forward. He didn't want the thing slipping out the hatch behind them.

Suddenly, a large jolt shook the room, parts rattled, and something fell in the far corner. Both men's rifles swept up and out looking for targets.

"Dropship is back," Halo whispered. "I've felt it a few times, and the landing bay is just a few decks above us."

Gi nodded assuming Hauk and the Space Marine had returned and returned. They would be too tired to offer anything to this hunt though. His focus returned to the grid search of the open space. Not for the first time, he wished he'd brought his swords.

"Hey, guys, we have movement."

Bishop's voice caused them both to stop. "Outside, now," Gi ordered. He and Halo moved back to rejoin the others in the corridor.

"What do you have, Priest?" Gi could see the three-man team closing to within about sixty yards. They were looking up, every rifle centering on the same spot.

"It's up there, above the conduit rack," he said, motioning with the barrel of the Rattler. His cheek was pressed firmly into the stock and finger already squeezing back in the trigger.

"How in the fuck could it fit up there, can't be more than a few inches of clearance," one Marine on the security detail asked.

Minutes later, they had their answer. While the conduit rack was hanging below the decking by less than a foot, at key points, there were connecting tubes to the deck above. The Furie had a better understanding of the ship's mechanicals than the soldiers.

"What's above us?" Gi asked, looking quickly for the ship's layout on his HUD.

"Laundry, showers, cargo holds, and gymnasium."

"Shit! Regroup on D-deck, now—move!" the Korean yelled, already running toward the stairs. He would clear that floor as well but just had to make one stop first.

CHAPTER FIFTY-EIGHT

The light was fading as I approached the small hill. Voss was silhouetted next to the now idle Decimator. The woman was a few dozen yards away atop the small rise. The eeriness of the scene wasn't lost on me. In fact, I wondered if I was the intruder and she the ruler of these lands. Even from here, I could sense the girl's presence, her control—possibly it was due to the line of creatures surrounding her. Creatures that I knew would tear us to shreds if given the chance.

"What are you doing?"

Voss flicked her eyes toward me dismissively. Do you know how hard it is to help someone who clearly doesn't want you there? Fine, then, I went over and sat at the base of the Warbot. "Go on, do your thing," I mumbled.

Damiana gave me the middle finger. That was fair. I was being an asshole again. Ada was busy, and I'd forcibly ordered Sumo to stay back in the bunker. He'd been through enough fights this week, and I didn't want to push his luck... or mine, any further, if I'm being honest.

Voss was speaking to the girl, woman... in tones so low even my suit auditory inputs couldn't enhance. Occasionally, a word would slip through, but as Voss moved closer, I realized it was how you might talk to a wild animal. More the way you spoke than what you said. She had her hands slightly raised, although I knew damn well she wasn't helpless in that position. She took tiny careful steps, and even her body language whispered non-threatening.

With my visor lowered and the light exposure controls dialed up, I could see the girl's features. She had high cheekbones and an angular face beneath straight black hair. Handsome would be how I described her. Beautiful, but not in a traditional sense of the word. Her dress looked homemade or maybe just well-worn. It was unadorned and simple like the woman herself. I kept going back and forth trying to guess her age; was she a girl or maybe a young woman? Ultimately, I couldn't decide. She could have been a sixteen-year-old with a very hard life or in her late twenties, maybe even older.

"She is most likely Native American, Prowler," Ada said, surprising me out of my mental trivia.

"Hmmm, any of their reservations in this part of the country?" I subvocalized.

"No, four remaining tribes, but they are not centralized, no reservations or tribal villages. Even more just over the border in Canada."

I didn't think there was much more we could learn about the girl, so I had Ada dedicate most of her processing to cataloging the creatures, deciphering Carlson's last message and trying to get us access to more of the Warbot's control systems.

The girl turned suddenly and faced Voss as if noticing her for the first time. She took two quick steps toward her, then froze. Although unarmed, this WitchWalker was a clear threat, and I had a bad feeling about all of this.

Apparently, Voss did, too, as she backtracked over to me. "I think she is in a semi-catatonic state. Either that or an extremely deep mediation. Whatever it is, I am not getting through to her, and as far as I can tell, neither is the Wraith."

Oh yes, our little flying see-through manta-ray. I'd almost forgotten about him starting this little hilltop party.

"We could shoot her," I offered helpfully. "And there she goes with the finger again."

"She needs help." Damiana offered.

I looked at the line of creatures, stretching out into the darkness, snarling, shrieking, fang-filled mutants. "She needs help?" I eased myself up slowly. "What are you, some kind of doctor now?"

"Yes, I am."

"Wait...what?" My voice stammered to catch up. How many layers did this woman have?

"How else would they have let me work at Iron River?"

"I thought you were an assistant or something."

"I was, a medical assistant. One with a PhD. Now, can we get back to this girl?"

~

She saw them, the woman, and the soldier. She saw them... and she didn't see them. They were not what had drawn her to this location. She sensed their fear but didn't hear the woman's words; it was gibberish in her mind. There was danger here, and salvation.

The salt-tinged air mixed with the green smells from the thicket of spruce trees. Change, that was what was in the air. That was the only thing constant in nature...change. She wanted to see the ocean; it had been too long. She longed to put her feet in its icy depths, to feel the oxygenated surf as it caressed her body.

To her followers, she merely suggested that they stay, then she stepped one foot forward, then another. The pull of the water was drawing her closer. She sensed no fear from these two, and the fluttering thing was a curious sort. Not one of the new creatures she'd seen before. It kept trying to sense her, that was obvious. It fed off the feelings of others, and like a mirror, could redirect and reform those emotions back. From her thoughts, it received no input and offered back no reflection.

The woman was in front of her now saying something, holding out a hand. She was trying to be friendly, but she was unimportant and would likely be dead soon. There was an emptiness inside the woman who was talking, a place that used to have feelings for others. A place this woman's pleadings might have found purchase, a rooting spot for a kindred relationship to grow. Now, there was nothing there. It was a desert, an icy plain on which nothing could grow.

Her bare feet felt the soft grass of the lawn. It was deep, lush, and strangely artificial. Like the structure, it wasn't natural and should not be allowed to stay. The vines would begin removing it soon. That was not something for her to worry about. In her head she heard the rushing of crashing waves and understood that not all of them were from the ocean. A part of her was being dashed upon the rocks as well.

The woman pulled at her arm. How long had it been since any other creature had touched her? She couldn't recall, nor did she have any actual sense of time. The ocean was close now. She could see swells of white far below as the surf rolled toward the cliff face. She moved closer, then all at once, she was flying. No, not flying... something was lifting her up. She suggested to her friends to come help, they should all come help her.

CHAPTER FIFTY-NINE

The girl weighed nearly nothing. Of course, I was in a highly engineered battlefield exosuit designed for rugged conditions, but still, yeah. She hadn't been eating regularly… or at all.

"Go—go—go," Voss yelled as she pressed against me to get into the house.

"I have reengaged the Decimators' defense capabilities," Ada said as the sound of automatic weapons sounded behind us.

"Doctor, huh? And all I got was a damp rag for my injuries?"

"Not now, Kovach," Voss growled.

"Why not now? What's wrong with now? I mean, I thought our relationship, you know, had matured beyond being totally dishonest with each other."

"Relationship?" Her eyebrow arched dangerously high on that beautiful forehead.

She was busy checking the girl for injuries. The girl… um, Witch-Walker was, well, she was doing nothing. She was just watching us maybe with a bit more focus than before but still seemed to look right through us.

When Voss yelled for me to grab her, it looked as though she might leap off the cliff into the ocean. We wouldn't get any answers that way.

"Decimator is not putting up an adequate defense, Prowler."

I could just barely hear the steady rhythm of the chain guns outside. Sumo lowered his head to the floor, not wanting any part of what was happening out there.

"Give me video." I'd leave 'Doctor' Voss to deal with the girl.

The video was surreal, Furies and Mantis Chimps swarmed over the Warbot pulling off pieces of shielding, wiring, and anything else they could get claws into. Thunder vines were already thickly encasing the lower portion. Other creatures I hadn't yet come up with names for were busy trying to clog the gun turrets and ammo storage with their bodies or maybe the bodies of their young. I couldn't actually tell.

"Ada, why are they attacking it now but seemed to fight alongside it the day we arrived?"

"It may have just seemed that way because we were the common enemy to both," she replied. "This area's status as a green zone in the midst of the wastelands suggests they had some type of countermeasures for the creatures, though."

"Find it, check all the subsystems. Check for active processes that were running upon our arrival." I knew she was doing that already, but it gave me something to say.

"I've found something," she said several minutes later. "Not what you asked for, but you are going to like it."

"Send it," I said, watching the battle unfold via the video feed. Then suddenly, I was in battle. I was controlling the Warbot remotely.

"You have control, not telepresence, but simple remote data-link connection."

"Hot damn!" I began blasting the Furies away with speed and accuracy. I swung violently to one side and tossed off two dozen of the furry little monkey bastards. Jesus Christ, this is fun! I needed to move, but the damn vines were holding me tight. I swam through virtual menus until I found what I needed. A large vibrasonic sword attachment. The killing blade extended out of the mechanical hand, and I began slicing through the vines like an old-school weed-whacker.

"Contact, right and rear," Ada said, getting into the melee. I ducked, pivoted, and slashed backward with the blade decapitating one

Furie and lopping off the entire torso of another. This was like the best video game ever. Screw Halo, this needed to be a multiplayer game if the world ever recovered.

I began to get the feel of the machine, what its limits were and its strengths. One advantage that was obvious was an enormous energy and ammo count. Way more than I'd imagined. I don't know if they were all designed this way, or if this one was special, but shit...they created it for extended deployments in hostile territory.

The monsters were attacking in waves, and I felt sure many had gotten by me and were already heading toward Carlson's mansion. Something huge slithered over the top of the hill, and I hit the spotlights. It looked like a cross between a hippo and a garden slug. I know, that was a hard one for me to wrap my head around, too. Then it opened its mouth, which curled back to reveal interlocking fangs. I selected blasters and sent two max power pulses of energy into it, and all that happened was a dissipation wave rolled across the thing's greasy-looking surface. The slimy fucker started charging me. Yeah, speed was much closer to the hippo than the slug.

I stepped backward a half step, then leapt.

And yes... Decimators can do that, although I doubt it is in the user manual. I came down with one leg square on the thing's head and the other, well, I'm not sure. I saw one of the grisly Culls that had been partially crushed under that side. The SlugBeast virtually exploded on contact, and everything that was caught in the blast zone began smoking, including the Warbot.

"Acid blood." That is so cool and, you know... really bad.

"Stop!"

I guessed it was the girl's voice, but I couldn't be sure without disengaging, which I had no intention of doing. I was back in melee mode doing a marvelous job of mowing down the stragglers.

"Call them off, and he will stop." That was Dami's voice, that much I got.

"Is that a kill counter?" I was watching one set of numbers in the red threat matrix screen climbing fast.

"Yes, it appears to give full value to major threats and the lesser ones are added as a fraction of the whole," Ada answered.

I blasted a Devil Squirrel and inadvertently got a Furie that had been hiding in the brush, just as a tree full of the Mantis Chimps descended onto my back... the Decimator's back. You know what I mean. I saw an auto defense option, and I triggered it. Maybe this mechanical warrior was finally figuring out how to fight these things.

"Engaging raid mesh," a hidden speaker said.

Raid mesh? Couldn't say that meant anything to me, but I'd battled these things before. I knew they could fucking fight. If I hadn't set them all on fire and tried to block them in a collapsing tunnel, I know they would have killed me.

Through the remote sensors in my battle suit, I felt something extending from the Decimator's sides. Glancing at the video feeds, it looked almost like solar panels extending on a newly launched satellite.

"No." It was the girl's voice again.

"Fuck, yeah!" was my overly enthusiastic reply as soon as I saw what the Decimator had planned. From almost every inch of the extended panels hung lethal looking bomblets about the size of an old-school hand grenade. The Warbot started spinning on its center axis and the bombs began jetting off into the now thinning crowd of attackers. The faster it spun, the farther the weapon reached.

The detonations were tremendous. I don't know what the explosive was, but way more powerful than a grenade. This shit was clearing the landscape; old growth spruce trees were launched hundreds of feet skyward. It had turned the estate property into a killing field, bodies or pieces of bodies began piling up, and I pulled the Decimator back toward the house as the raid mesh began winding down. The firing wings retracted back into the body, and on my own HUD I unbelievably saw that they were reloading. Jesus, I wanted these things on our side.

The girl was crying now. Apparently, a WitchWalker without her followers was mostly just a hot mess. Doctor Voss was giving her a dose of tough love. More confident now in the Warbot sentry, I disconnected and allowed Ada to place it back into active sentry mode.

"Banshee Actual to Prowler."

The use of combat call signs automatically put me into a different mindset. Halos' voice came through my headset clear as if he were standing beside me.

"We have a problem, Boss. Multiple problems. Packer is on the way down to your location."

"SitRep?"

There was a pause, too long of a pause. "It's Bayou, sir, she's down."

CHAPTER SIXTY

"My God!" Gi shared the feeling. The gym looked like a slaughterhouse. The steel gray walls were painted with blood. Deborah Riggs' blood. She was already in medical; the bots were working on her, but they all knew it wasn't looking good.

A severed arm lay against one wall. An arm covered in scales with a curved claw at one end.

"The lieutenant didn't go down without a fight," Bishop said.

Gi had helped drag her near lifeless body out less than an hour ago. He'd failed her, and that stung. He knew that the Army captain was with Bayou in the medical bay. What he didn't know was who was running the ship. Honestly, though, that was now secondary to finding this Furie.

Dark purple blood smears ran across the wall and toward a smaller maintenance hatch. The security contingent was much larger now, many fill-ins from Red-7 as well as the Space Marines. They were all armed, and nerves were on edge. *How in the hell had she put up such a fight?* Gi wondered. He touched the crossed swords now on his back. Bayou had been unarmed, yet she was still alive.

"Halo and Xero are handling the bridge. We got this, Sarge," Bishop said, patting him on the shoulder. "It's time to do some ship cleaning."

They'd given orders for all non-essential personnel to lock themselves in their cabins. That might not help much, but they had no intention of losing anyone else today. Gi moved that thought from his mind., Riggs wasn't gone. He tapped his comms link.

"Xero, you must find a way to locate this creature."

"Sergeant Gi, they seem to be able to mirror the ambient temperature around them. IR is no good, and I have yet to see any other aspects that would allow our sensors to pick up on its movements. They engineered these things for stealth."

And combat, Gi thought. "Copy that. Then watch all video feeds, no one should be moving except us."

"Yeah, about that," she said. "You are about to have some additional help."

~

The TriCraft settled into the docking cradle, and the ramp was already coming down. I hit the deck just ahead of Sumo and we both raced to medical. My heart was pounding, and I was in a cold sweat that had nothing to do with our narrow escape from Maine. The landing bay and corridors were ominously empty, and I knew why.

Still in my heavy suit, my footfalls echoed like thunder as I charged down the hall and slid into the sterile, white room. Jordan Hauk turned his face toward me in surprise. The man looked as tired as I was. Just beyond, I could see the limp form of Deb. Her face was ashen. Blood covered much of the trauma bed and the surrounding floor as the surgical bots worked. The same bed I'd been in a few weeks earlier also fighting for my life. I moved closer to the bed. Her abdomen had a large open gash. The ceiling mounted surgical bot was busy doing something inside the wound. She'd been in her workout gear, an LSU sweatshirt now shredded along with the skin beneath. I touched her leg, the only part of her that didn't seem to be injured.

"How's she doing?" It was a stupid question. I could see the damage; I even understood what most of the obscure readouts meant.

Hauk just shook his head. He and Deb had once been close, and now he was here with her. "All we've been through and then one of those things can cause this much damage." He turned to look past me, toward the door.

"Voss, get in here," I said to the other person coming in. I took her by the shoulder, she looked less comfortable than I'd ever seen her. "Where's the witch?"

"Your pilot... he, he took her to holding. The Wraith will stay there," she answered. A note of uncertainty colored her words.

Fucking creature better stay there, I thought. "Are you really a doctor?"

She looked to the bed and slowly nodded. "Not a trauma specialist, but I can help."

The medical bots were good, but like all AI-based systems, they lacked the intuition of a human surgeon and were obviously devoid of any humanity.

"Save her!" I said, handing her a tube of the stolen Anadium. I tapped the medicine and nodded. She got the message.

"Hauk, this is Doctor Voss, she's going to help Deb."

Dami began scrubbing up at the nearby sink and donning the PPG. I gave a signal to Sumo, who had perched himself on the window to peer into the treatment room where his friend lay. "Come on, big guy. Let's go do what we do best."

~

Captain Packer led the quiet woman into the small brig and locked the door to the cell. He was vaguely aware something else was in the room with him, but the Wraith had calmed the man into forgetting that it was even there.

The place seemed deserted. Of course, no one had needed to be locked up, but the Korean sergeant had been basing his security detail from this wing. He didn't know if he was supposed to stay with the girl or not. "I'm a pilot, not a prison guard." The girl with Kovach instructions had been brief, but he'd gotten most of it. Checking in with the bridge crew, he let them know where he was, and he'd be up to relieve the helmsman shortly, but he had to finish securing the dropship first. He also wanted to make sure nothing else had hitched a ride up this time and take care of one more thing. He shook his head as he walked back toward the landing bay.

"We'll send a Marine to secure the brig, but that's all we can spare. Get your ass up here to the pilot's chair ASAP," Halo said. "You are acting Captain until and unless Prowler decides to stay."

Holy fuck, Packer thought. He acknowledged the order and went to secure his dropship first. He hadn't thought that far ahead. *Jesus,* things on this shit was changing too fast to keep up with. Truthfully, he had no interest in being in charge. He enjoyed flying, that was all he'd ever wanted to do, and now he had the most complicated airship in the world to drive around.

He glanced across the hangar bay at recovered fragment of wreckage the Marines had been trapped in, using it as a lifeboat. Beside it, a mirror twin of his dropship sat. It had some damage; some shielding was missing, and a starboard side hatch wouldn't make an airtight seal, but he'd been aboard and done a nominal systems check. She could be made ready to fly, and it would be nice to have a backup, but at some point, he had to train another pilot or two. They were too reliant on him, even he knew that.

The Space Force pilot did a quick walk around of his own TriCraft. He felt the sharp angles and the smooth black shielding. It always amazed him how it felt. It retained no residual heat, nor was it cold. It almost seemed to not be there. Although he'd flown the thing for years, it still felt odd to him. Odd and alien. He held his service weapon at low ready as he checked over every inch to make sure none of the critters from below had made the ride up this time. Nothing but the loading dock ever touched the ground, but just the sheer number of mutant monsters down there tonight had given him the willies, so had that weird girl, for that matter.

He paid close attention to the cargo holds, deep cavernous containers that lined much of the underbelly of the ship. The three repulser engines took up relatively little space for such a large craft. Satisfied he didn't have any external stow-aways, he made his way up the ramp. He needed to do the same thing in here, but first he had to deal with something.

"What in the fuck am I supposed to do with that?"

CHAPTER SIXTY-ONE

The cramped quarters were too small for all of them. Carol looked at the thing her son had built and laughed. He was so much like his father, just the good parts of the man, she hoped. The parts she'd fallen for so many years ago. Lux hadn't told her much about what went on down below, but she knew Xero had been there and the strange-looking drone had helped. Now the goofy little bot he was calling Rex was bumping into the walls and scaring Junie.

Carol understood the lockdown was related to whatever had gone on but got the distinct feeling that her son was trying to protect her. He didn't want his own mother to know he'd been in any danger. She knew she wasn't a great mom, but that didn't seem like the behavior of a child his age. Most boys loved telling their mom scary stories of all the dangerous stuff they had done. Again, she was struck by how much more mature he seemed since Last Day. She pulled him close and for just a second, he leaned into her and let her have her moment. Then he got busy chasing the puppy around the deck on hands and knees.

"I love you, Lux."

He looked up at her and smiled. "I know, Mom. Love you more."

That was what she lived for now. She could put up with the cramped quarters, bad food, and constant sense of mild motion sickness as long as they were safe. She'd felt what she thought was the dropship landing several times and wondered if Joe was back onboard. Her multiple calls to Lieutenant Riggs had routed directly to the woman's link address message box. Carol knew she was busy and had an entire ship to run. Even so, it wasn't her nature to not be in the loop, but she was trying to accept that she was a guest here.

Something heavy hit a wall farther down the corridor; the impact reverberated through the metal-composite walls. Fear flashed across Lux's face before he looked to his mother and forced a smile. He pulled the puppy close and keyed in a sequence on his controller. The bot he insisted on calling Rex floated forward and seemed to take on a more menacing posture. The sound came again, this time more like footsteps.

Carol's heart caught in her throat as she tried to think of a way to protect her son. Something she'd been totally unable to do up to now. She stood placing her body between Lux and the hatchway, which suddenly slid open.

"Hi, you!"

Sumo barked once as the captain walked in as far as he could in the bulky battle suit. Seeing him like this again made Carol recall all they had been through together. She rushed to him and threw her arms around his neck. They kissed briefly.

"I'm really damn glad to see you, Joe."

"Just checking in. You guys okay?"

Carol nodded, and Lux made eye contact with Joe and gave a single nod. There was a story to be told there, but both guys knew now was not the time. Kovach knelt down and stroked the little brown and black dog affectionately. Turning his head slightly and pointing at the heavily modified maintenance droid, he asked, "And who is this?"

"It's Rex," Lux said, pride obvious in his voice.

"Hello, Rex," Kovach said before stepping back.

"He can't talk yet. I couldn't find a voice modulation box."

"I can talk to him," Kovach said.

He allowed Ada to query the bot and then got a rapid-fire firsthand account of what the bot and Lux had been through.

Looking back up at the boy he shook his head. "Wow!"

"What, wow what?" Carol demanded. "Do you have any idea what's going on?"

"Something is loose on the ship," he said in a matter-of-fact tone. Kovach caught the look Lux was giving him and decided not to elaborate on her son's role in it to this point. "Deb was attacked and badly injured."

"Oh, God!"

"She's in med bay, and you should know Damiana is helping treat her."

"Oh, good, you brought her back. She didn't shoot you this time?"

He was glad there didn't seem to be any real resentment there. "Not yet, but the day isn't over." He moved back toward the door before going serious again. "Carol, have you ever fired a gun?"

She shook her head.

He then looked at the bot. "Lux, what software programs did you load?" Ada could have told him, but he was interested in what the kid had selected as opposed to what was already on the memory units.

Lux quickly went through the list. Kovach was surprised to see it included several newly created defensive command files as well as some that Xero had apparently uploaded to aid in defense.

"That's good. Really impressive, Lux." He wanted to ask him what had made him take on the project, but right now he was just glad the boy had. The drone looked more like a floating collection of obsolete parts, but it worked and had helped them fight back a Furie. That was saying something.

"We need to get it better quipped and also teach you a few things as well," Kovach said before looking at Carol. "If it's okay with your mom, of course."

Lux grinned and nodded enthusiastically.

"You guys stay here and seal the hatch. I'll be back when it's safe." With that, the man went back to warrior mode, quickly exiting.

"Prowler," Carol whispered, remembering his combat call sign as he disappeared again.

CHAPTER SIXTY-TWO

After several hours Xero had left the bridge and was finally resting in her quarters. The all too close encounter with the creature had shaken her placid demeanor to its core. Now, hearing that it critically injured the lieutenant just made her decision to shelter in place that much easier. Of course, for a tireless workaholic like she was, that didn't mean doing nothing. Deb had given her the quarters originally slated for the incoming ship's engineer. It was a two-room suite unlike nearly all the other quarters. One entire side was filled with actual books, books on everything from hydroponics to theoretical magnetic containment vessels.

She wasn't reading one of the books today. Instead, she was running an output test on the black data cube Kovach had given her. She'd slowly been working her way in, unlocking the thing's secrets layer by layer. It impressed her, which wasn't easy to do. The encryption method was so simple and yet so multilayered, like a digital Matryoshka doll, the Russian toy with smaller and smaller dolls all nested inside one another.

It had taken her a solid week to determine it was a type of storage device. She had used several more days in determining the programming involved, and now she was free to work on the encryption. Back home, she would have spent the time building a virtual sandbox and making a copy of the original. Here, that wasn't an option. For one thing, she didn't have the equipment, and secondly, every workstation was tied into the ship. All she had was her small personal terminal to use, and it lacked computational horsepower. As much as she wanted to move faster, she simply couldn't risk any other phantom code getting loose in the ship's AI.

Nothing about the data seemed malicious, but she was cautious to the point of paranoid by nature. You didn't use a storage medium like this for just anything. It was a puzzle, and like any good code-slasher, Xero loved the challenge. So far, what she knew was the cube transmitted data using an algorithm that rapidly alternated frequencies. Not traditional WiFi or Bluetooth, nothing as primitive as old radio-based signals No, this thing used an ultrafast connection that literally altered the resonant frequency of the air molecules to exchange information on a near quantum level. She'd played around with a very rudimentary version a few years back and been impressed but estimated it was at least a decade away from any real time applications. She'd been wrong.

She was two layers deep on the encryption but now facing a potentially more destructive key. If she input the incorrect information, it might lock her out completely, and she could see there was a data-burn executable behind that digital block. If triggered, all data in the crystalline lattice would be not just erased, but overwritten hundreds of thousands of times.

"Go big or go home. Right?" she said aloud.

She had run her own proprietary decryption application and felt good about the next step, but in reality, it was always just a guess. Nothing about this thing had been straightforward, why would she believe this would? Her finger was poised over the key, then suddenly, she stopped.

Sitting back in the chair, she stared at the object. Picking it up, she marveled at how it captured the light on its faceted surface. She'd mapped out every one of those facets and calculated all the dimensions of each. Something about this felt almost too easy, despite how challenging it had been up to now. This step felt less genuine. It was a trap, a dead-end, or even worse. No, this would require a different, much more nuanced approach. What until now had felt like a game, now seemed like something much more. Whatever was on this cube was important, that fact alone made it dangerous.

"Think, Xero, think."

~

She used the small food synthesizer in the cabin's galley. She felt sure it had been installed covertly at some point by an engineer who felt his time was too valuable to head to the mess hall. She programmed in the food she wanted, grilled tofu and wasabi over egg noodles, slid the compacted protein pack into the receiver, and sat back. The technology of these things intrigued her. She knew bio manufacturing had probably made more advances in the last half century than any other industry. Still, the ability for the coffeemaker-sized machine to build foods up from the molecular level just using a generic bit of organic matter and water was damned impressive.

She moved the data cube around in her other hand while she thought. This was impressive, too. It was miles ahead of anything she'd seen, and she'd seen it all. Or thought she had. She hated calling for help, but she was stuck. There was one person she could call. Xero knew that she probably shouldn't, it was not anything Riggs would have permitted, but getting the comms system working again had been her job, why not take advantage of it?

"Trans lunar comm charges may apply. Continue?" She tapped her comms unit.

The world goes to hell, and the damn telecom billing system still works. "Yes," she confirmed, keying in her access pin.

"Hi, you."

Xero smiled. She'd missed this guy.

"Hey, Valyn, how's life on Luna?"

"Better than Earth right now. Where are you calling me from? Not getting a source ID," he said.

She'd disabled all the identifiers on the comms array. Not that she didn't trust Valyn, but because he was inside the Gateway military compound, and those walls have ears.

"I'm in a bunker," she lied. She wanted to tell him the truth, but it was his boss that had ordered Riggs to surrender the ship. She couldn't put him in the middle of that fight. "Look, I need some help."

Valyn Orric's current role in the military was not why he was important to Xero. Their past started much earlier and under circumstances that most would never even guess. She trusted him...had trusted him with her very life. Trust was something that had to be earned with her. It never came easily.

"I'm probably not going to be much good. The admiral has me jumping through hoops trying to track down some of these rogue units. Military COC has gone to hell."

"COC?" she asked.

"Chain of command." She heard him yelling orders to someone, then his focus returned. "Sorry about that, what do you have?"

Xero described the physical dimensions of the data cube, crystal thing, then gave her friend the much more important digital specs.

"You sure? It's written in Virex-C? That language isn't even in the wild. High-level shit with built in multi-layered encryption."

"You've used it?"

"I can't discuss that."

She knew he had before, down at Lackland Air Base in Texas. Same place she'd been taken to when the shit went down.

"Virex-C has some very specific advantages," he said. "Advantages that also limit its applications."

This wasn't news to her but was more part of how Valyn thought. His mental process was linear, while hers was more chaotic. Both had their advantages.

"It's most often used for very high-end simulations. The code is very tight, efficient but flexible in adapting quickly to changes in input or new data. They did a lot with simulated lifeform testing. Near fully autonomous operation because it integrates so cleanly into the command pipeline between interface, processors, and hardware. You know, like on the terraforming probes they sent out to the outer systems' moons years ago. The things have to operate off the chain for years. The time lags on the comms would prevent them from efficiently being controlled back here or on Earth."

"So, it's a niche programming language?" she asked.

"Very," he answered. "Look, Xero, I must run but let's catch up. I need to know more about what's going on and how you're coping."

She knew he was being genuine. No way he would blow her off unless someone was breathing down his neck. The conversation was likely straying way too close for his NDA and security clearances.

"One other question," she said, not wanting to let the opportunity escape. "Any idea why a doctor would have this?"

Valyn was obviously busy with someone else again but soon asked her, "What kind of doctor?"

She hesitated before answering, "Biogeneticist"

"Like, the genetic mutants that are being reported all over the globe? What have you gotten yourself into, Xero?"

"I'm trying to find out, and this data cube might hold the answers."

She heard Valyn moving, sounds of other people nearby, then relative quiet. "Okay, listen, and you didn't hear this from me, but Virex-C is something different."

"Different how?"

"It's an artifact language," he answered.

She was aware of the term but wasn't sure of the context. "That means..."

"Right," he responded. "It has no origination point, no evolution. It sprang into the computer lexicon fully formed, and no one has ever taken ownership."

"Like bitcoin?"

"No... well, yeah, kinda," he admitted. "It's also never had one single bug patch or upgrade, nor any vulnerabilities discovered. It's an anomaly in the programming world mainly because it came out fully formed and nearly perfect. If your doctor was using this, it's because he was highly placed and doing some deep-cover shit."

Xero had run into other artifact bits of code. Most often it was found to have originated with various AI systems that had the ability to upgrade there own code. Over time they tended to develop programming languages that were distinctly inhuman.

Something clanked, maybe a hatch. Xero wasn't sure if it was on his end of the call or hers. "Look for a logarithmic extract, normally a long sequence before the holographic header. Programmers learned to write a backdoor in just because the language was so secure, they often forgot their keys and locked themselves out."

The call ended, and Xero sat back on the bed to eat her dinner. The cube held secrets, and she was one step closer to figuring them out. The clang came again, much closer this time. Definitely here on the ship... not on the moon.

CHAPTER SIXTY-THREE

"Halo is driving the ship. Whose bright idea was that?"

The Korean smiled; unlike his fellow team members, he didn't seem to enjoy putting the others down.

"Jenkins is a good man and an even better soldier," Gi said. "Besides, Halo has asked Captain Packer to take the helm as soon as he can. By the way, sir, I am very much happy to see you again, Kovach."

"Same, brother," I said, wondering if Packer did what I asked before heading to the bridge. The Space Force pilot had been integral to everything so far, but I had a hard time seeing him in a position of leadership. Even though he had the rank, the pilot admitted he was just a glorified bus driver. I didn't need officers who felt compelled to follow any order a superior officer might issue. Unless, of course, it was me issuing the order... then I wanted it followed without question, but then again, I'm no officer. Well, except on this ship for some damn reason. You know, it's damn hard being this crazy.

"So why is this lizard so hard to kill, Sergeant?"

"Something about this Furie feels different, sir... smarter, more..."

"Durable?" I offered.

Gi nodded and gave a slight laugh. "That's a very good way of phrasing it. Different from the ones we fought in the tunnels or in Texas, although that had to be the batch it came from."

I had been having much the same feeling. Not just about the Furies but everything we'd been fighting. It was like they were getting better, adapting to us as the enemy.

"So, any idea how Bayou injured it, and shouldn't that make it easier to locate?"

"Riggs is tough and obviously capable, but none of the injuries seem to have slowed this creature down so far. Xero was working on a way to track it, but now she's locked out of her primary lab until we locate it, so we're on our own."

"Copy that, Sergeant." They were both following Sumo as he followed the creature's scent. The husky's super-sensitive nose was naturally good, but like his handler, many of the dog's natural abilities had been enhanced.

Gi had already been through this section multiple times but remained silent. The Furie had bested him twice before, he would not be so arrogant as to think it couldn't happen again.

"Jesus Christ," I said rounding a corner and seeing the biggest fucking Marine I'd ever laid eyes on. "That's a good way to get dead, Corporal."

"Koog, sir. Sorry I was late to the party. Your man, Bishop, sent me this way."

I eyed the way the kid held the short-barreled tactical rifle. It was a standard Marine issue Silka LS8, the matte gray finish with the twin snouts where the barrels ended made it handy in close quarter fighting. "Not sure that toy is going to take one of these things down, Koog. They're bigger than you even and thickly armored."

"I read the brief, sir. The one from you and Captain Hauk. I got it covered." He flipped the receiver upside down so I could see that the standard issue magazine with 7.62 jacketed rounds had been replaced with Armorlite AX cutters. An ammo that had been exclusively designed for fighting against armored infantry, it had also been outlawed a decade earlier.

"Holy fuck, the Jarhead came to kick ass," I said to Gi. "How much of that do you have stashed away?"

"Probably not enough, sir, but a few cases were in the piece of the ship you saved."

I liked this kid. Not only was he big, but he also seemed smart, which in my encounters, was rare for a Jarhead. "Well, join the party then, Koog. Welcome to Banshee Team 1. I'm Prowler, and that's Sumo on point. Handle rear guard for us, Son."

"Yes, Captain," the oversized Marine said, falling in behind us as if he had done this a million times.

"Question, Gi, how do we know we're only looking for one?"

"We don't. Since none of us have any clue on how it got aboard, we can't definitively rule out more. Nor can we say there aren't other different creatures aboard."

Well, that was a scary as fuck thing to say.

Ten minutes later, Sumo was facing a solid wall looking as frustrated as I was. Between not finding this goddamn thing and worrying about my XO, Riggs, being under the care of Voss, who I still had no idea if I could trust, I wasn't having a great day… and then it got worse.

"When you coming to see me, Sport?"

"Pops, really, every fucking time I'm in the middle of something dangerous you call."

"Language, boy, your mom doesn't need to hear her baby talk like that."

"Mom died, Dad, remember?" I subvocalized. I pointed to a set of rooms we'd only given a cursory check to because it was just one big open space.

"Of course I remember, don't be an asshole, Joe. When are you coming to see me?"

I wondered briefly if 'Never' was an acceptable answer. "I'm off-world again, Pops." I knew he was aware of that. The former colonel had lo-jacked my damn brain. He always knew where I was, and if I was right, also knew what I was doing which, yeah… think about that. Your dad can literally see through your eyes and knows everything you are up to anytime he wants. I quickly determined I probably was hunting the wrong monster.

Sumo went rigid, then looked back at the three of us as if to say, 'What the fuck are you idiots waiting on, shoot something.'

Gi fanned us out in a narrow arc. We had overlapping fields of fire, but still had no target. "Ada, run spectral analysis full sweep." She knew to do this automatically, but I needed something to say.

"So, you know how the guys at work are always bragging about their kids?" My dad started ignoring the fact that I was in a combat situation. "You know, Tim says little Debbie made the all-star team. Or that asshole Shirer who acts like his boy will win the next X-prize for engineering when he can't even tie his goddamn shoes."

I muttered a mild acknowledgement knowing my dad hadn't worked in an actual office in years.

"So, what in the fuck am I supposed to say? Who can I brag on? I mean, let's face it, you were always a bit of an underachiever, but your mom always said, 'We must love him anyway.' "

"Contact, left," Koog said, laying into a darkened corner with a line of fire that stitched up the wall and produced a bright purple gout of blood.

Holy shit, the damn thing is nearly invisible. "Sumo, hunt!" I yelled. The blood trail was already thinning as I tracked it up the wall and across part of the ceiling bracing.

"Good shooting, Koog, how did you see it?"

"Lidar scan, sir. Standard issue on my HUD."

Well, shit, that made sense. Up here they would need to know exactly how far solid objects were. The lidar had the ability to peer through less dense materials revealing what was underneath.

"It's headed for the vent tubes!" Gi yelled before bringing his Mark-4 up and firing." Again, I saw specks of blood where the rounds hit home, but most of the creature was still hard to make out.

Back in the corridor, I tracked left with the dog, the other two went right.

"At the gun range? Hit anything yet?" Dad asked.

I eyed my counter and realized I hadn't even fired.

"Nope! Just here for show, Dad."

I tracked the conduit back to where it narrowed and branched out into pipes too small for the creature. No exit here. I turned to rejoin Gi and Koog. "Something on your mind today, Pops?"

"Hearing a rumor that Admiral Reese has declared you and Banshee squad to be traitors. Renegades who have illegally taken possession of an Alliance monolith-class carrier."

"Filthy gossip," I answered. "Reese is a doddering old fool from what I hear."

"Ha! Don't fall for it, kid. He's a snake, but don't count him out. He will make you pay for disobeying direct orders."

"You were on the call, Pops."

"Oh, yeah, the one where you told the acting War Commander to ummm... let me see if I can remember. Oh, yeah, you called him a 'washed-up Twat' and told him to "Go fuck himself!"

"Well, it sounds worse when you say it but yep. And we didn't steal anything. We happened to find a mothballed cruiser that no one was using and decided to turn it into a forward operating base. We needed the high ground. Total transparency. I wasn't even among the living at the time, so my participation was minimal."

"It's the largest surviving ship in the Space Fleet, kid, hell of an FOB."

"So, you think we should give it up? The one tactical advantage we've had since Last Day?"

I paused as up ahead, Gi and Koog split in opposite directions, both with guns up sweeping the ceiling. Despite my new ability to multitask perfectly, my dad's conversation was distracting me, and now was not the time for distractions.

"Hell, no, Son, tell the fat old bastard to go fuck himself again. Times have changed, I'm just saying watch your back."

"Got it, watch m..."

The impact from behind sent me flying into the far wall.

"Baaa.c.k," I wheezed out. My spine was again on fire, and my hands weren't working correctly.

"Hey, umm...yeah," I called trying to remember my teammates' names. I was seeing stars but sensed the Furie coming on me. Ada took over and used the suit's servos to raise an arm to block an incoming slash. My world came back into focus in fits and starts, and then I saw the damn thing.

"You're one... ugly motherfucker!" my dad said, obviously privy to my optical inputs or my suit's sensors. I didn't have time to ask which, but even more importantly, I agreed with his assessment. It was a freak of a monster. One arm raggedly torn off mid bicep and a line of wounds and old scars running across the torso. Even up close, the scaling and spikes gave it an eerie halo effect. Its edges were hard to pick out from its surroundings. I could easily see how it might have snuck onto or into the TriCraft with no one knowing. This one was somewhat different from the others we'd fought.

My blade was in my hand, always my preferred weapon in close quarter fighting. In this case, I knew the weak spots to hit. I went for the inner thigh, and somehow the one-armed thing managed to block me while also pushing me back against the bulkhead.

I heard incoming fire and realized Ada had signaled the two others. New wounds appeared on the scaly neck and chest, and I could see they were mostly glancing off doing no significant damage. I slashed out again and contacted a fleshy part of the beast's midsection. The vibrasonic blade cut deep, but the pressure from the thing didn't ease up. Suddenly, I was aware of a shape flying over me, and the Furie jerked backward.

My first thought was Sumo, but then I realized it was the crazy ass Marine who was now attempting to put the monster in a headlock. I gave him credit for audacity but bonus points for a takedown would not win the battle. Both of us together possibly could, though. I charged in and got between the creature's remaining arm and its body. Gi moved in, one of his swords raised high for a strike, when the Furie spun and snapped a kick into the Korean's chest. I heard the impact and knew he probably had broken ribs, maybe even worse.

Koog was pulling the head away and to the side but trying to keep that dangerous fucking mouth away from any of his edible body parts. Both my hands were busy pulling in the opposite direction. Sumo kept charging in for quick bites but fully understood the lethality of that claw if it got free.

"Pull, Prowler!" Koog yelled, straining with his own near superhuman effort.

I did and saw the thing's neck stretch to a point I could see actual flesh beneath the scales, pink flesh, human looking flesh. Some part of the thing began to tear, then I heard, more than saw Gi's sword slashing down through neck and across the thing's abdomen. The fight left the beast immediately, and I watched as the Korean sagged to the deck.

"Fuck, yeah!" the Marine yelled triumphantly, releasing the head which flopped sideways. I let go as well and let the body hit the deck with a thud.

"That's what you call 'Violence of Action!' " Koog yelled triumphantly.

I crawled over to check on Gi. "How did you manage that, dude? That was awesome." I was checking his suit's med readouts. He wasn't talking, and his eyes were unresponsive. I knew he'd taken a massive hit. The Furie's legs are pure muscle and hit like pile drivers. Every bit the same kinetic energy of getting hit by an autocar traveling at speed.

"Captain?"

I heard Koog but didn't want to stop my triage of G-Force to turn around. "What is it?" I asked as I signaled for a medic.

Turning, I saw Sumo sniffing something near the corpse.

"That," the Marine said, pointing with the toe of his boot to something in the pile of gore.

"Oh, holy mother of Jesus fucking Christ, what is that?"

CHAPTER SIXTY-FOUR

"Corporal Koog, we don't mention this shit to anyone."

"It...she was pregnant, sir."

The fetus lay on the floor unmoving from where it slipped out of its mother's severed womb. I wish I could say it looked like a miniature version of the hideous mother; it didn't. It looked like a baby... a human baby with a few obvious modifications. My assumptions were right, they had used humans or at least human DNA to help make these creatures.

Koog bent and separated a bloody mass of something from the child and checked for a pulse. I had already guessed it was dead from the ghastly gray color. He looked up and shook his head.

"You were a corpsman?" I asked, using the Marine terminology for a medic.

"Yes, sir."

"FMS or SARC?" I asked, beginning to guess what level the kid had reached.

"SARC."

I pointed for him to help Gi. Special Amphibious Recon Corpsman were highly skilled and highly trained. This guy was not only a good fighter, but he must also be smart. I looked at the corpse again as footsteps pounded down the corridor toward us. I quickly pulled an empty drybag from my suit and scooted the fetus into it.

This could explain why the damn thing fought so hard. Maybe even why it boarded the ship. She was looking for a safe place to deliver. Who in their right mind would have given these things the ability to reproduce? I had way too many questions, and answers just didn't seem to exist.

I helped them load Gi onto an air-gurney and watched as they rushed him away followed by another team who bagged the Furie and unceremoniously hauled it away. The SEs who had the gruesome task asked if I wanted to space it. Did I? That was a good question. We didn't really have any scientist on board who could study the thing, and I was sure no one else wanted to keep it on board. I flipped the corner of the body bag back and looked at the twisted face; at the same time, I covertly slid the bag I'd been holding beside her. "Place it in cold storage under priority-1 security lock-out."

Sumo came up and licked my hand; we were alone and safe for the moment. Assuming that Furie was the only one on board.

~

Koog came out of the showers and nearly ran right into her.

"Hi!"

She smiled; her long blonde hair falling loosely around her shoulders. Surprisingly, she was also wearing makeup. They'd talked a few times over the last week, or at least he'd talked, and she listened politely.

"How did it go out there?" she asked.

Wow! he thought. As far as he knew, those were the most words she'd said to nearly anyone. He was unaware the TDF mission, or his part, was public knowledge.

"It was fine." It wasn't, but he was under orders to not disclose the big problem they'd run into at the end. "We achieved the mission." Technically not a lie, and he should have shut up there, but he really wanted the Texas beauty to like him. "Also, got to help take down the beast down on Deck E."

"That was you?"

Damn, those eyes were hard to ignore. Of course, as long as it had been since he'd had a shore leave, any eyes might have had the same effect.

"Want to hear about it?"

"Yes. I would like that very much." She wrapped her arm through his and let him lead her.

"So, you ready to tell me your name?" he asked minutes later as they reached the hatch to his room. It seemed like the most basic of information, but the girl hadn't been willing to talk much until now. She still struggled to get it out.

"I'm Chelsea."

CHAPTER SIXTY-FIVE

Bayou was out of surgery and alive, that was all I knew. An exhausted Voss sat with her back against the med bay wall. When I walked in, her eyes barely registered me. I'd stopped by my quarters to shed my battle suit and get cleaned up.

"You slay the dragon?" she asked, her voice nearly as weary sounding as I felt.

"Nearly the other way around, but yeah. I do want your opinion on something related, but it can wait. How's she doing?" I nodded to the bed; Jordan Hauk was leaning over Deb and holding her hand.

"She's messed up pretty good, Joe. She's alive and the Anadium is helping, but she doesn't have your army of healing nanobots. Her injuries are horrific, she will take time, assuming they heal at all."

Jordan looked up from the other room, and our eyes briefly met. I could see the concern and the gratitude.

"I never fully knew they had been an item until right now."

Voss glanced over and smiled, "I don't think they ever stopped. I believe the job just always comes first for both of them." She reached for my hand to pull her up off the floor. "You know the type, right?"

Her body felt good against mine, and I held her a moment longer than was probably appropriate. "We should get you some food and a place to catch some shut-eye."

She patted my chest, "I can find my way, really, just need a hot shower and a change of clothes for now. You stay with Lieutenant Riggs, I'll find my way."

I'd never thought to ask her if she'd ever been in space, but she seemed to handle it like a veteran. "Ada, please see to it she gets assigned a bunk and can find the mess hall."

I slipped into the treatment room, around the end of the bed, lay a hand on the captain, and asked him the same question.

Hauk shrugged. "Doctor said she will survive, but we have to watch for infection. Who knows what germs or pathogens those things carry? I guess you got it?"

"Yeah. Me, Gi, and your boy Koog managed to take it down." I had stopped to check on Gi who was in the med bay a few doors up. He was sedated, but the readouts said he was in good condition.

Hauk chuckled. "Did Koog shoot it or just sit on it?"

I noticed that he kept stroking Deb's arm as he talked. "He put the damn thing in a headlock if you can believe it. Nearly decapitated it before Gi sliced its neck open."

"Must be from the Midwest," Hauk said. "They grow 'em big out there and teach them to wrestle in kindergarten."

"He's a hell of a Marine," I said.

"Copy that." Hauk stood and stretched. "Did he mention any of what went on out there?"

He was pointing in the general direction of the med unit's head, but I thought I knew what he meant. On the insane human bombing mission of the ghost ship. "No, we didn't have much time for anything except the monster hunt."

I looked over at Deb; that mission had sounded more like one of my hare-brained schemes than hers. "Why?"

Hauk looked down. "You're going to need to get that from her." He patted Deb's foot. "I need to go check on my men, but I'll be back after a while."

I followed him out to the prep room. "She can't tell me jack shit. What happened?" All I had heard was they achieved the mission. They destroyed what looked like an unmanned drone ship and regained control of the carrier.

"I'm under orders, Kovach. Her orders." He turned and started for the exit then turned. "I'm sorry Joe, but thank you again – you know for letting me know about Logan." He nodded once and abruptly left the room.

"Well, fuck." I went back and sat by my friend.

"Ada, see what you can find out about that mission. Let me know if our ship is still under threat."

She chimed in an acknowledgement. I knew she would have to interact with Belle, the ship's built-in AI to accomplish that. Something she often seemed reluctant to do for some reason.

"Joe, you may be interested in knowing Ms. Voss did not go to the showers or for food but is in the security wing. I believe she is going to interrogate the young woman being held."

"Goddamnit, Voss, why are you so fucking difficult?"

CHAPTER SIXTY-SIX

Alarms were going off all over the ship. Xero studied the screens intently. "I suggest battle stations, Captain."

Packer nervously swung the display over to take the ship's systems to its highest alert status. "Do we have a target solution?"

"Negative."

"Find me that bogie."

Packer chuckled at the sound of his own voice. Glancing up, Xero smiled as well.

"God-forbid we have to do this for real," he said, silencing the alarms and ending the training simulation. "I'm no combat officer."

"I'd have to challenge you on that, sir," Danny 'Halo' Jenkins said.

"How's that?"

"I've seen you enter combat zones several times now, and you've handled yourself and your ship like a pro."

"That's a dropship, Danny. No weapons. No offensive weapons, at least. I'm a glorified bus driver."

"You keep saying that, sir, but we know you're capable of this. You just like the TriCraft more, and I get that. They're fun to fly, top secret, and generally you only have to think about the small group of troops on board. Here, you have everything to worry about."

"These drills, though. I mean, look, I can keep this bird in orbit and all, but if you are counting on me to think tactically..."

Halo moved in close to the man and whispered, "Captain, don't ever talk like that on this bridge. Not when you occupy that chair. You copy me—sir?" Yes, technically, Packer outranked him, but that wasn't what was important. "These people need to trust you. Hell, you need to trust yourself. This ship will do the work for you... as soon as you and Xero figure it all out."

The acting commander nodded. He understood what his subordinate was saying; he even agreed with it in a strange, detached way. He just wished it was someone else wearing his uniform right now.

For her part, Xero also had questions. Why is there such a renewed interest in the ship's security now? They destroyed the stealth ship that had been annoying them, and Kovach had killed the beast. Bayou had left strict orders before she left the bridge the last time that combat drills were mandatory on every shift. It wasn't unreasonable; Xero was a civilian trying to learn military systems, and the 'military' personnel were mostly clueless about the ship's operations. It still didn't sit right with her. She felt she was only seeing part of what was going on, and that was a thread she couldn't help but pick at.

~

Kovach

My reduced need for sleep was a Godsend as I was wide awake and ready to rip a new asshole in whatever hapless Marine I found on duty. I'd decided to ignore Voss and the girl for now. I had other concerns I wanted answers for.

Sumo ran ahead of me as I stomped into the large workroom and up to the attendant behind the mesh grating.

"Just drop it over there, Captain," the older man said, barely acknowledging me. Also, on this ship I was in charge, a fucking officer even, but that was needless information right now.

"I am looking for CWO Akins."

"Looking at him, pal. What can I do you for?" the man said, dropping a tactical receiver on the work bench and using a rag to clean the cleaning solvent from his hands.

I knew this was the man. Ada had given me the checklist, duty roster, and the man's service picture, although he must not have updated that photo in twenty years. The balding, rough shaven guy looked a little like the pic. Then I recalled dragging him out of that piece of space wreckage a few weeks back.

"Chief Atkins, I have a problem."

"Call me Trip, sir. Everyone does and join the line. Seems like everyone has problems these days."

"My problem is with you—Trip!"

His easy-going nature and 'don't give a shit' attitude was commendable, normally someone I might consider a kindred soul, but this man had been the armory officer in charge of something that nearly got me killed.

I threw the upper plate of the battle suit through the opening at the man. Not something you normally ever do with your personal armor, and it's never recommended to piss off the armorer.

The move surprised him, but he reacted quickly, grabbing the torso. "Whoa, partner. What's the deal?"

"You outfitted my suit on my last drop. You did the check-out, and when it came time to pop the glide wings—guess what?"

The man pursed his lips together and rolled the back plate over to look at the underside. "I dunno, bud. Why don't you tell me?"

God Almighty, I am going to rip the fucker in two. "It—didn't—fucking—work!"

"Yeah, that's not possible," he said grinning. "You know how I know?"

I knew where the old man was going with this.

"Because you're standing here." He laughed, a deep, heartfelt, belly laugh. I may have bounced his head off the clear mesh partition.

"Ouch! Look, Captain, I worked the armory on the Denali for three rotations. I know the drill with your drop teams. Those glide wings are the one part we must get right, every fucking time. We don't... I don't take any chances there. If something is worn, it gets replaced. If anything is marginal, we update it."

His tone was more cooperative, but I still really wasn't getting any answers. "Who else was on duty?"

"Two SEs had been assigned here, but when I came too in the sick bay, they asked me to take over. No one else had any experience with ballistic drops gear."

"So, Tripp, if you were me, and my glider failed to open for the first time in my numerous fucking drops, what would you think the problem was?"

"The armorer," he said without hesitation. "Look," he said, expertly flipping a special suit key hanging from a lanyard and removed a panel the dislodged a piece I didn't even know came off. He then used the end of that strut to extend down into a cavity and popped out the entire empty grenade rack and what was left of the glider mechanism. He did all this while never breaking eye contact with me.

"You saved our lives, man. Hey, I get you need answers, but I am not your enemy. Shit, you're as close to a fucking hero as we have these days. Let me tear this all the way down, and I'll get you your answers."

I subvocalized to my AI, "Any sense of deception?"

"No, Joe, I do not believe he is aware of anything that could have been done to your suit. As you know, all battle suits are locked into the charging lockers after they are serviced, and only the registered user can unlock them at that point."

True, I thought. It had always been a pain in my ass to have to come to my station and key in my code and biometrics so the armorer could load and configure for whatever deployment we had scheduled. Still, we tended to get very attached to our gear. Our very lives depended on it. Shit, some ex-drop trooper had even released a love song to his battle suit a few years back. The fucking, catchy tune still popped into my head at times.

"Okay, Tripp, do that, but I want it all done on the check bench with the full vid-feeds." Every armorer had at least one station that recorded everything done on it. Usually this was for guaranteeing the right ordinance was being loaded, but it worked for this as well.

"Obviously, Captain."

The man's tone seemed mildly offended, which might be understandable, but he also knew the importance of my demands. If we couldn't trust our equipment, then we didn't need it. Honestly, I hoped the man was being truthful because I had something even bigger in mind for him to work on.

CHAPTER SIXTY-SEVEN

"I was simply checking to see if getting away from the creatures down there had reduced the girl's catatonic state." Voss said minutes later.

"And?" I asked.

"Nothing obvious, no change."

"Come-on, Voss." She and I were on our way to see Carol and Lux. She'd suggested it. I was a bit less enthusiastic being in the same small room with two women I'd recently been 'involved with.' Even though I am an asshole, I am an asshole who values his testicles.

Voss eyed me and grinned.

"What?" I asked.

"This." She waved her finger in a circle at me. "This whole thing. Absolutely precious."

I wasn't sure if she meant my guilt over sleeping with both of them or my fear of us all being together once again. Either way, I knew I was probably fucked.

"Glad you are amused."

The ladies' reunion was not at all what I had expected, or more accurately, feared.

They hugged and cried like long-lost sisters, despite a few of the things Carol had said to me in private. It was obvious they were still very close, and Voss fussed over Lux and his new dog even more. I hung around for a half hour before realizing that I was an unnecessary and possibly unwelcome part of this ensemble. Despite all, they were essentially family and had a bond that was more resilient than I'd imagined.

Excusing myself, I headed for the bridge. Strange that it was the one place I had yet to visit. As the oddly ridiculous circumstance that had me designated on-board captain and chief pirate on this ship, I should probably take a more active role in its mission. I knew that wasn't my strength, though, so felt better leaving it to others.

Bishop met me in the corridor leading to the bridge wing.

"Hey, Boss, ready to take over?" the man asked.

"Hardly, Priest. Were you down in med bay?" I knew he'd been; Ada tracked everyone and fed me updates on my team members.

"Yep, Gi is looking good, he should be released later today."

"Bayou?" I asked feeling bad that I'd left her there, but Hauk had come back and almost pushed me out of his spot by her bed.

He looked down and scratched his brow. "She looks bad, readouts say stable, but man... you know."

Yeah, I knew. "It's Deb, she always snaps back right away."

"Right! One of the toughest soldiers I know."

It registered with me he'd said soldier, not woman, and he was right. I had a reputation for being invincible, but Bayou was fucking bad-ass resilient as fuck.

"She'll be okay, man. Just keep thinking positive thoughts," I said, reaching the door.

"Oh, something else, Kovach."

I stopped and eyed the man. "Someone has been stirring up the crew. Says we've all been lying to them and shit."

"It's the military dude, nothing travels faster than rumors in the service."

"That's just it, it's not from within. From that damn civilian."

I had to quickly list the civilians aboard. "Xero, Carol, Voss?" Shit, there were dozens I didn't even know the names for.

"No, the blonde chick from the Texas drop. Came up with Red-7."

"No fucking way, I thought she wasn't speaking," I said.

He went for the handle to open the hatch for us. "Well, she is now, and you might want to handle it before it goes any further."

"I want to know what went on out there."

Xero and Packer sat across from me in the captain's ready room. Both looked at each other a bit dumbfounded.

Ada had briefed me on a conflicting set of reports on the oddly designated TDF mission. "I went out and picked them up," Packer said a bit too defensively. "That was my only role in the mission."

"Bayou and I did the planning. The timing and trajectories were complicated, so I had to run a number of simulations right up until the launch," Xero added.

"Then what?"

She eyed me for a second. "Me and the kid were running for our lives. That damn monster was after us. After that, they confined me to quarters until well after the mission was over and the threat eliminated."

That all jived with what Ada had pieced together, but that wasn't the story.

"Sir, can I ask why you don't just talk to Hauk and the big Marine? They were the ones out there."

"Bayou gave them orders to keep it quiet." I said. "Hauk won't disobey it, I haven't had time to ask Koog yet, but something else went down, and I want to know if we are still under threat."

The two of them made eye contact again.

"What?"

"Just..." Packer began, "Bayou left strict instruction that every shift we run battle drills. You know, training simulations in the ship's systems to better know how to use the vessel more effectively."

That seemed like Deb. Probably something she wanted to do from day one, but yeah, the timing seemed suspicious.

"Ada...sorry, Belle, I said talking to the ships own AI. Please pull up the duty roster for Lieutenant Riggs' last shift."

The large holodisplay showed the bridge crew. We'd been running a skeleton staff, so there were only eight names on the list, most of whom I didn't even know.

"Captain Packer—find these people and have them come see me now. Wake them up if you have to. I have the con."

He nodded and left.

"What's got you so on edge, Kovach?"

Leaning back, I eyed the unfamiliar space. "I don't know, Xero, trying to unravel all this shit. How to keep us alive, who was behind the Last Days attacks, what can we do to wipe out the monsters taking over the planet and is there any other way to save more survivors down there."

She pursed her lips and ran a hand through her close-cropped hair. I could see she was considering whether to say something or not.

"Spill it," I said. "Whatever it is, just put it out there."

She shook her head. "That's just it, Joe, I don't have much more of an idea than you. Just a hell of a lot of things that don't seem to add up correctly."

I considered everything I knew about this woman... person. She was exceedingly bright, genius level, and apparently one of the best hackers on the planet, but she enjoyed casting herself as a puzzle solver. This one, I knew, was probably already keeping her up nights.

"Tell me what you have... and your best guesses."

She nodded, "It will be esoteric, though."

"Go on," I urged gently.

"Joe, have you considered how far we have come as a species in the last 100 years?"

"No," I answered truthfully. The question was not something I'd expected. "I mean, I guess we have, but is that relevant to what's going on?"

"Maybe. I think it is, in fact."

She took the black data cube out of her pocket and set in on the table. It spun on its axis for a second before stopping, its many polished facets glittering in the room's light.

"You cracked it?"

She smiled and shook her head. "No...well, partially. I now can confirm that it is a data storage device."

"But it's related to what you were saying. That we've achieved too much too quickly or something?" I asked hopefully.

"Yes, well maybe. Let me just say what my thoughts are, and then we can discuss it. Right now, it is just a feeling, hell, just a guess would be more accurate, but it feels right. Like you, I trust my instincts, and particularly when I'm working on something like this, it helps."

I leaned back and nodded for her to go on.

"Humans have been good at making breakthroughs throughout history. Going from hunter-gatherers to farmers who domesticated livestock. Edison's first light bulb to unleashing an atomic bomb was only sixty years. Likewise, the Wright brothers' first flight to landing on the moon was sixty-six years. That was all before the information age at the turn of the century. Computers and the Internet revolutionized every industry from medicine, to design, to engineering. Then, almost overnight, we shifted much of our species focus to biology. First, improving our healthcare with a better understanding of nutrition and our food supplies by hybridizing more productive or beneficial crops, to gene therapies to treat chronic diseases. Then, bio-manufacturing took off and with it, gene editing to create virtually new forms of life. We can now assemble our food molecule by molecule. We are living in an almost self-sustaining spaceship in high orbit."

She could see that she was losing me. I was following what she was saying, I just couldn't see it leading anywhere useful.

"I know, it's a little difficult to lay it out just yet, but this is the gist of it. Humans are capable of some seriously profound leaps of logic and innovation. They seem to come at regular intervals in fact, but they are always evolutionary steps from where we were to where we are. Scientists build on the work of others. You don't get from Kitty Hawk to Tranquility Base without a lot of other flying vessels in between."

"But you are seeing something that doesn't fit this pattern," I guessed.

She nodded and tapped the cube. "What's on here may not be as significant as 'how' it is on here." She then explained to me the somewhat baffling Virex-C programming language. "It shouldn't exist. Neither should the repulser engines on the TriCraft, the Furies, or you."

"Me?"

"Yes, Joe, only a few of the enhancements Hammer Industries used on you have any actual scientific lineage. I could go on, several fairly common technologies as well, but mainly the things we are just finding out about."

"So, a few fully formed futuristic technologies leads to someone wanting to destroy the world?" I wasn't buying into large parts of her narrative.

She shook her head. "I don't think that's the case. Not the complete picture at least. Don't get me wrong, this group, or whomever you are chasing, pushed the buttons to make it happen, but I'm not convinced they knew what the hell they were doing."

I thought back to Carson's recorded conversation with the Van Gogh avatar. "How can you know that?"

"Because none of them seem suicidal. They all believed they had an endgame, probably money or power or both. If they had a specific containment protocol in mind to limit the destruction—it failed or is in the process of failing. From what the clues suggest, there will be no happy ending for this war. If we." She stopped suddenly to correct herself. "If you can't stop it, it's game-over for humans." She pocketed the cube again. "Joe, in my opinion, the Earth is being terraformed. All human life will be cleansed. The age of man is over."

I thought about the pregnant Furie, and a cold chill went up my back. *They didn't know what they were creating.*

"What?" she asked, obviously seeing my expression.

"There was a series of labs in the Ranier facility. They were even called terraforming labs. I assumed they were for technologies Hammer would use to transform other planets, like Mars."

She offered a grim smile. "They probably thought they were building something like that. Just like I am quite sure Doctor Reichert thought he was doing the world a favor in the augmentation he performed on you. Only a few probably ever knew that all this was going to be directed at our own planet."

"Assuming you're right, and even the masterminds behind this were nothing more than useful idiots, what are we dealing with? Are the gods just fucking with us for fun and games? Who is behind it?"

She stood as Packer came in with the first of the crewman I'd asked to see. "That is the real question, Kovach." She tossed the little black cube up and caught it. "I'll find us those answers. You just keep us in the fight."

CHAPTER SIXTY-EIGHT

The bridge crew interviews revealed little new information, if I am being honest, but the prior conversation with Xero was weighing on me. During the TDF mission, as it was tagged, I learned that Bayou launched and later recalled multiple ship-killer missiles. The GR-12 warhead was not a light duty weapon; the launch had been deliberate. What was baffling was, according to the weapons officer that day, the weapon was launched after Hauk and Koog had successfully detonated the I-8 Penetrator and presumably destroyed their target.

That was not a surprise to me. Ada had already informed the launch of the GR-12s, but the timing was new. Maybe she launched it just as a backup in case the other ship wasn't completely destroyed. I filed that one away to unpack later. The bigger revelation came from the comms officer. He said there was no radio traffic during or after the encounter. I knew from the logs Belle had pulled up that a call had come in, she just couldn't tell me from where. The logs had been tampered with.

The last crewman left, and I sat there staring at the door.

"They were lying," Ada said.

I knew that. I didn't need Ada's biometric analysis. My own bullshit detector was going off. "Yes, but why?"

"They are loyal to her, Kovach. Even though you are nominally in charge while aboard, Riggs has firmly established herself as their captain."

"So, where do we go from here? Bayou is still out. Hauk isn't talking."

"Corporal Coughlan," she offered.

"Hmm... Koog, yeah. He might not want to say what went on out there, but he knows something."

I returned bridge command back to Packer and left to go find the big Marine. He and I needed to come to terms on this issue today.

"Holy fuck!" I whispered. That was my initial thought, and ten minutes later, I decided it was still the perfectly appropriate response.

The mess hall was an angry beehive of conversations. Bishop and Jenkins were both there trying to look disinterested, but I knew my guys. They were ready for whatever came next. We'd made eye contact but nothing more. This was obviously one of those delicate situations that amassing a strategic hardpoint with a battletested group of RDTs might not offer the best optics.

The blonde woman had transformed from a traumatized victim to a fire-breathing asshole.

"The monster, the Furie was pregnant. The damn things are breeding. They don't want to tell us any of that do they? Who knows how many of those things are onboard with us?" She said.

My eyes were shooting lasers into Koog, who was meekly sitting beside the blonde woman standing in the center of the room. If the giant soldier could have made himself smaller, he would have done so. There was no other source that intel could have come from. Several of the others began yelling as well. Proving my Eighth Rule of Battle: 'No good deed goes unpunished.'

"Okay, who left the bag of idiots open?" I borrowed dad's line. Admittedly, it was not ne my best opening statements . I moved sideways through the increasingly hostile crowd toward the woman who seemed to be occupying the virtual high-ground of the mess hall.

"She is not the enemy," Ada whispered. I muted my AI.

"Do you deny it?" she yelled. "Tell us, it's not true. We are all still in danger, aren't we?" Spittle flew out of her mouth as she ranted.

"Karen, sit the fuck down."

She looked confused, "My name isn't..."

I forcibly cut her off by not so gently pushing her shoulder down toward the seat beside Koog.

"Don't give a fuck!" I answered sharply. "And yes, you are all in danger, we all are. Not sure if you peeked outside lately, but we're in a cold vacuum in a ship we barely know how to operate floating above a world where humans are quickly becoming extinct."

I moved my hand from the woman to the Marine's shoulder. I felt him tense at my touch. "This is a ship of war. Some of us are doing everything we can to keep you safe. Some, a lot more than others. Many have given their very lives so you can stand here and spout your fucking bullshit." I squeezed the hard muscle of Koog's neck before walking further down the row of men and woman. The kid had done a hell of a lot, and I wanted him to know that had bought him my thanks and my respect. But letting this bitch know the details and then not keeping her quiet, well, that was unforgivable... even for a Marine. I'd been back aboard less than a day, and I was ready to jump out an airlock. I began to wonder if Deb might have injured herself just to get away from the whining.

"This ship is a fucking lifeboat. We are trying to keep us all alive the best way we can. If you aren't helping us do that, then you are a liability." I turned and faced the 'Karen' again. "Am I making myself clear?"

"You brought a witch on board," the blonde said.

Fuck me! I quickly ran through the top ten most creative ways I could think of to end this bitch. The intel on the WitchWalker hadn't come from Koog, he didn't even know it. That means we had several security leaks.

"They know how to control the monsters. We think they helped create them," she bellowed.

"Koog, muzzle her before I do it."

The girl had spirit, had to give her that. Unfortunately, it was a negative spirit and had the potential to poison everyone on the ship.

The corporal tried to shush her, but she ignored him. I could tell she was spinning up for another round ov verbal abuse. Whatever she'd been saving her voice for was coming out next. And all at once, I was thinking how much I'd prefer it was my dad having this conversation with her as I was about to go off the rails. My hand clenched and unclenched. Even with Ada on silent I could feel her trying to tell me this was not the enemy. If so, My AI would have been wrong.

"Is that true?" she started up again. "Why would you do something so stupid?"

With my eyes, I motioned for my two men to spread out. Sumo had also entered and was guarding the door. If this thing went kinetic, I wanted my players in the right spot to wreak havoc.

"All civilians out, now."

The blonde girl was the only one I knew of, but two men stood up and headed for the door. The blonde didn't move.

"Get out on your own, or we will do so forcibly. This is a military vessel, do as I say."

"And you have no business being in charge of it, do you?" she yelled.

"Chelsea, please," Koog said, now physically dragging her toward the door.

So that was her name. Nope, she would forever be Karen to me.

"Halo, help the lady out and secure the room," I ordered.

To his credit, Halo was not rough with her but quickly separated the woman from the Marine and had her outside and down the corridor, although we could all hear her complaints trailing behind them. A minute later, he returned and resealed the hatch.

Shit, this is why I wasn't an officer... not a real one. I hated talking to large groups. At least sixty pairs of eyes were focused on me. The few murmured conversations died out as I turned to take in the entire room.

"We are soldiers."

I let the words hang there.

"Not Marines, not Space Force, not Army. Not officers, SpecOps, or Specialists. We are just soldiers now. One group of trained military professionals who have to work together if we have any chance of staying alive."

"We aren't soldiers," one of the SEs said from near the back. "I'm a procurement officer... a grocery clerk."

Most of the group laughed.

"You were a PO, but now you're a soldier," I said flatly. It was time to get these people's attention. "Listen, we don't even know what all we are up against. But we have to assume it's up to us to decide whether humanity survives...or not."

I moved to the edge of the table and sat down on the corner. "We all lost people down there, and I am sorry about that. We can't go unfuck ourselves from the last three months. All we can do is face what comes next." I hesitated a minute trying to determine how much of the rest to say.

"The civilian wasn't wrong. I did determine that the monster was pregnant. That may also be part of why it was so hard to fucking kill. Also...I did bring up a woman on the last trip who is now in our brig. She has taken no hostile action toward us, but like the corpse of the Furie, I want her examined. Anything we can learn about what we are up against can help us. Maybe...just maybe, in time, we can take back some of what was ours. Just keep in mind, we have to be united here. We are soldiers, we do what has to be done. If I am right, we will add more survivors, more civilians, so yeah... likely a few more Karens."

A nervous chuckle circled the room.

"Can we check on our folks?" one of Hauk's men asked.

I shook my head no.

"What about food and provisions, we don't have enough for a large group," another chimed in.

I hadn't really considered all the other lives on this boat. Every one of them had a story, family, love, and losses.

"What about my combat pay?" Halo asked, walking up and sitting beside me holding up one of his token rings. "My crypto account balance hasn't changed in months."

Even I smiled at that one. "I'll admit, we've had a bit too much going on to take everything into consideration. And no, we won't be able to now either... not all at once, but we can do better. As for checking on family, we can't go down, but let me go ahead and break it to you. If they are in the red zones, they are most likely gone. There's no surviving out in the wastes. As for your back pay, yeah, its waiting for you in hard currency, but you have to go to the banks in person to make a withdrawal."

More chuckles echoed around the room.

"We're going to try and concentrate efforts on the green zones, and we keep looking for areas down there we could use as a settlement because long-term up here isn't a workable option. These ships are designed for regular servicing and every five years a major retrofit. Space is not an easy environment to work in as most of you SEs know first-hand.

The hatch opened, and I was pleasantly surprised to see Sergeant Dae Him-Chan enter. G-Force looked pale but moved surprisingly well.

"Now, here is the other hero of the hour," I said, grateful for the interruption. "Gi and Koog took down that Furie, and I propose a toast, assuming we have something on this bucket other than water. Where is that procurement officer?"

CHAPTER SIXTY-NINE

Turned out, we had plenty of beer and nearly every other kind of alcohol you could think of. Apparently, the Space Fleet brass like the good stuff. Not like Pappy Van Winkles good, but plenty of Blantons 2055, which was very, very drinkable. We drank too much and had no right throwing a party like that, but I knew we needed to try to solidify as a unit. With all the external forces weighing in on us, and the internal struggles of cramming members from different branches altogether, plus Karen, a.k.a. Chelsea...well, we were ripe for a breakout, and I simply didn't have time to deal with a fucking mutiny. Plus, Bayou would never let me live it down if I lost her ship my first day back in command.

Still, I had work to do, and I'd already found that my body apparently metabolized alcohol nearly as fast as I drank it now. There was simply no way to get hammered anymore... that absolutely sucked balls.

"Corporal Koog, a word."

The mountainous slab of a man looked like he wanted to be anywhere but here. The beer he held was still half full, and I didn't think he'd gotten more than one.

"Sir?"

"You did damn fine work today, kid. Down on E-deck and out there in the vac." I'd heard the space engineers call the hard vacuum of space 'the vac,' and I just wanted to sound like one of the cool kids.

I could see him relax slightly, his shoulders no longer as rigid as iron. He'd been bracing for an ass chewing, and I would get to that but likely not for the reason he thought.

"I want to know exactly what happened out there after you set off the Penetrator."

"Umm, it's in my report, sir. Lieutenant Riggs signed off on it. Suit recording and everything."

"Yeah, I know. I want what's not in the report, and before you answer, let me remind you that fucking a civilian is your business, but revealing information I told you to keep quiet has put you and me on opposite sides of this fight for now. You copy me?"

He paled, and I knew I'd pushed the right lever.

"I didn't mean to say... she... Chelsea just..."

"Not the question I asked, Marine." I'd moved the kid to a small room off the mess hall, probably the galley manager's office. I was sitting on a metal desk mounted to the wall. He sat on a seat that was much too low for his frame. The overall effect made the giant of a man look small.

He hung his head. "I'm under orders."

I leaned over and tapped his skull, "Check the COC, chain of command. I am above Bayou. If she were able, she would be answering these questions. For expediency, you report to me now. We will not be having this discussion more than once, though—am I making myself clear?"

He nodded.

"Speak up, Koog."

"Sir, yes, sir!"

He fidgeted several more minutes before speaking.

"A second ship," he said finally.

"Excuse me, Corporal?"

"Yeah, a larger ship, looked Alliance but matte black , it had no markings."

My head was swimming, the data wasn't making sense.

"Tell me more."

He did. He told me how he and Hauk had taken refuge by the ship, and then a brief firefight broke out between it and the Stone Mountain.

The firing stopped, both ships backed off, and Packer came in with the TriCraft for a pickup.

"You don't know who it was?" I asked, still confused.

"No, sir, I guessed the original frame was frigate class, but it had some newer modifications on it. More like a luxury space yacht than a military ship."

"But it had weapons. What kind?"

"Point defense lasers and at least one missile battery. We could see the racks as the bay doors opened."

"They knew you were there?"

Koog shrugged, "I don't know, hard to imagine they didn't, we'd just blown up their drone."

Drone, the ghost ship that had been screwing with our systems had been unoccupied. "You sure it was theirs?"

"No, sir, I am not. But that seemed likely since they were only a few dozen kilometers away at most when the spy ship cooked off. I mean, they were there instantly."

"Who is your current CO?"

"You are, sir."

I laughed. Well, at least someone was listening to my little speech. "I mean before."

"Oh, Major Whitehorse. He didn't make it off the ship. I think he was with the command staff in the war room when the ship broke up."

"Koog, I like you, you're smart and capable but perhaps a bit too quick to act. I put you in as a probational add to Banshee. Team-1 is down a man with Gi on limited duty. But I have to level with you. I am really not convinced you are SpecOp material."

It was a harsh thing to say, but having studied the kid's service record, there was clearly a reason he'd not made it onto any of the MARSOC teams. Then, some genius had stuck him up here on a damn patrol boat.

"Yes, sir."

The man's expression told the story, he wanted this, and I was pulling it back out of his reach just when he thought he had a chance. He'd gone through MARSOC training, Marine Special Operations, as well as ASOW, Alliance Special Operations and Warfare training. Maybe not quite to the level of RDTs but damn close, and in some respects, he was likely even more qualified.

"You need to know why, Son. Why I am uncertain about you being part of my team. It is not your capabilities. It comes down to judgement and loyalties. Despite what I said out there, Banshee is who I am most loyal to, more than family, more than the fleet. Every member of Banshee feels the same way. If what you told that girl goes any farther, they will never accept you. Never! Do you copy that, Corporal?"

He nodded then added, "Yes, sir."

"Koog," my tone noticeably softening. "Look, Thunder-Junk, fuck who you want, it's not like we have that many options anymore. My... fatherly advice, though, is that girl is dangerous. You weren't there when we took her in. She's got some issues."

"Like what?" he asked, genuinely curious.

I thought about that night, about the fact that she seemed to be a mom but had no children. About how she was nearly delirious talking about the witch. I shook my head. "Not my place to say. Just be careful and think through your actions."

He was clearly expecting to get his balls busted, and instead, I gave him advice his father should have. As we went back to the party, I could see it had the desired effect. Now, I had to see if the rest of the team would accept him. One thing I was sure of was the farther we could keep him away from Karen, the better.

CHAPTER SEVENTY

"Where... where is that boy?"

"Captain Orric, the old man is looking for you."

Orric gave a grim smile. "Yes, Ensign, I heard his bellow."

"Admiral Reese," he said moments later. The great hall at Luna wasn't actually a hall, nor was it all that great. The admiral could have easily seen him if he even remembered who he was. Captain Valyn Orric was the last in a long line of aides to the Fleet admiral. Unfortunately for him, Valyn had been the one assigned the day everything went to shit.

"Yes... umm." The admiral seemed unsure of why he'd summoned him, but that was nothing new. He liked giving orders and having his thoughts transcribed into memos. Letters and notes that he wished to send to anyone who might have momentarily forgotten how far George Reese had risen in the ranks of the Space Force. One aide reportedly transcribed a letter from the admiral to a Mister George Jetson. The individual turned out to be a cartoon character that was old even when the admiral was a child. A framed photo of the cartoon now hung in the officers' ready room as an inside joke.

"The ship, is it still refusing to answer our hails?"

And just like that, the old man was back. His mind on point with that laser focus, which must have been the one positive attribute that had pushed his career forward.

"No longer responding, sir."

"And our emissary, did he... did it deliver the package?"

"Yes, sir, it did and then returned here, but they destroyed the stealth ship in the encounter." Valyn responded to the inquiry respectfully despite his misgivings about that mission. The admiral was now openly proclaiming himself War Commander. Hell, he might just be the highest-ranking flag officer left, but that was not a good enough reason to pretend to take charge of everything. This narcissistic fool was going to endanger even more lives—of that, Valyn was sure.

He ran through the rest of the update, and the admiral delivered his new edicts. Most of which were completely irrelevant or simply impossible to complete, such as ordering one of the new Echo Class long range cruisers from the Earth-side shipyard.

The captain walked away mentally shaking his head. He was not one to show disrespect in public. That he left to his oldest friend, Xero. He flashed back to where they'd first met. An underground code-slashers rave in East London. Xero was maybe twelve and living mostly in the public works buildings better known as the 'Brixx.'

He was a year younger and had it even worse. At that moment, his bed was in a broken-down caravan sitting beside a particularly rancid stretch of the river Thames. That was years after Gulf War Three. Like Xero, he'd been orphaned by the war. The difference was, his family was on the losing side; hers was part of the Alliance. Funny how none of that mattered then... or now. They'd connected first over computer coding and later over many things, including just surviving their childhood. Both developed a shared belief in doing whatever it took to find the truth or help make changes.

Captain Valyn Orric returned to his duty station monitoring the massive ship still in orbit around Earth. What he had been ordered to do next bothered him greatly. He'd never disobeyed an order, not even those he'd had reason to question, but the hubris of this action couldn't be ignored. The garrison here at Luna had no need for a Monolith class carrier. Everyone now knew the enemy was not the same one we'd been waging war on for decades. No... now it was the planet itself that was quickly turning against its parasitic human occupants.

Somewhere down there was Xero, probably holed up in a bunker trying to think her way out like she always did. This puzzle might be bigger than even she could conquer, though. Quickly selecting the view he wanted from the system, he then brought up the rendering. The data analyst and base AI created the constantly updating global map using all incoming sensor data. The green zones had decreased another 2.8% in the last week. They had dropped below the 50% mark the prior month. The infestation was taking over our home world, not like a cancer slowly metastasizing on an unwary victim, but fast, like a knife attack on a foe that once had been mighty. It was vicious, ruthless, and the end... inevitable. Earth was gone. Nothing left but to clean up the mess. "I'm sorry, Xero."

He punched in the long series of letters and symbols that were the ultra-secure encryption keys, then sent the message. "Proceed to rendezvous point Echo. Backstop is a go."

Sitting back, he placed both hands in his lap and did something he hadn't done since childhood. He prayed he was making the right choice. He thought the right choice would offer peace. What he'd just done offered none and somehow he knew he would need have to take more direct action.

"God help us all..."

High overhead, the message was received and decoded, then passed along to the man sitting casually on the edge of the console.

The guy had balls, had to give him that.

"There should have been a file packet attached."

"Sending it to you now, sir," the communications officer said.

The man rubbed at his arm absently as he read.

"Make way, best speed to these coordinates," the ship's commander said to the helmsman. "Prepare for anything—this one is going to be interesting."

CHAPTER SEVENTY-ONE

"Captain?"

I'm sure that I appeared to be resting, my head leaning against the wall, eyes closed. In truth, it was anything but that. The man's voice stirred me from my focus on trying to fit all of the players and pieces together in some sensible context. Two months ago, I wouldn't have cared. My job was a trigger-puller, a killer. But now, my mind wouldn't let me rest.

"How's she doing, Captain?" I asked, opening my eyes and straightening up in my chair.

Jordan Hauk looked bone tired, his face seemed etched out of pure stone.

"Deb is..." He seemed hesitant to say, maybe jinxing her recovery by voicing the words. "She is much better. Your Doctor Voss worked wonders." He gave a grim smile and nodded; I motioned for him to sit.

"So, she's going to be okay?"

I caught the man's look of uncertainty before he hid it. "Still chance for... you know, infection or..."

I knew what Hauk was talking about. A pathogen or transfer from the creature to its victim. Something toxic or maybe even worse. It seemed all these mutants had layered defense systems, which apparently multiplied if said mutant creature happened to be pregnant.

"She'll be okay, Jordan."

"May I?" he said pointing to an open bottle on the table.

I pushed the whisky and an empty tumbler toward him.

After several doublings of the amber liquid, he said what he came to say. "So, the AutoDocs have her in a forced coma for now. Doctor Voss seems to think that may take a few weeks for her to come out of. It's really up to her body how long it takes."

"She's strong, she'll be out sooner. But something is on your mind, and I have a feeling I know what it is," I said.

"Yes, thanks again, Joe, for telling me about Logan."

"You want to go get him?"

He nodded. "I know it's selfish and foolish, but he's all the family I have left."

I felt sure he'd gotten wind of my little speech down in the mess about family members likely being gone.

"Deb and I had kind of a deal."

"The mission, what did y'all call it, the TDF?"

He choked out a little laugh before answering. "Yeah, 'They Die First.' She was tired of letting someone else throw the first punch."

I liked it, Banshee had been needing a cool moniker, TDF sounded perfect.

"If you went on the space mission, she would get you down to where your brother is?" I said, taking a guess. It sounded like the kind of move Bayou would have made.

"Yes, me and a fire team from Red-7."

It was selfish, suicidal even, and well in keeping with the man's near legendary loyalty to his men and his brother.

"You know as soon as word gets out, all of Red-7 will volunteer to go. Most don't seem too crazy about staying on this space boat, anyway."

"Hell, Joe, half of them still can't keep solid food down. It's hard to get used to always feeling like you're falling each time your feet leave the decking. Still, I can't ask them to go. This is personal."

I leaned back in the chair and studied the man. He wasn't the only one wanting to get back to the surface. Not even the only one zeroing in on Paris.

"You did more than your part, Jordan. Put together a plan of what you need and get it to me by 1800 hours."

"Thank you, Kovach. You will let Deb know..."

I knew the man's loyalties were divided. He was obviously torn between staying with Riggs or going after his brother.

We stood together and headed toward the door. "We will keep a close eye on her. If comms stay up, you can get updates as often as you want."

He paused at the hatch. "You know, Kovach, you aren't half bad for a Space Monkey."

I burst out laughing. The dig was so out of character for the man. Space Force had been called Monkeys since the early days, referring to the original rocket test where countries sent primates into orbit.

"High praise from a space-walking ground-pounder."

~

I spent much of the afternoon with Bayou listening to the monitors beep and watching her IV fluids cycle in. She looked much better, but I needed her awake and in charge. I also wanted some answers. I needed to know who she was talking to that day. Seeing the ragged skin of her midsection being microscopically stitched back together, though, made me realize she wouldn't be giving me those answers... at least not in time to be useful.

"Kovach, it's Chief Atkins. That little thing you asked me about. Well, I may have an answer." I acknowledged the call and stood up to leave; the machines resumed their own lonely vigil of keeping Deb alive.

"Now it's a party," I heard walking up to the flight deck hatch.

"The Ghost—legend of Banshee," Priest said, smiling.

"Shut-up, Bishop."

"So, what's up, Boss?"

Banshee numbered only the four of us now, not counting Sumo, who turned the corner just as I keyed the code to unlatch the entry for the secured area.

"We have some decisions to make, and I have something to show you. Follow me."

The sound of footsteps echoed off the floors and walls. Compared to the rest of the Stone Mountain, this section was open and massive. It had to be to support the various craft that routinely landed or departed. Today it was quiet, or nearly so.

My men followed me around the edge of the fragment of wreckage that was still on the deck. Then, the sight of both TriCraft in their docking berths. Packer had said the second was close to being flight-ready, but we had only one pilot. That was something we were going to need to fix.

"What in the holy fuck!"

Halo said it, but every one of them had similar reactions. And despite the standing team orders of no personal weapons on board other than for security patrols, each one suddenly had something in their hands to fight with.

"Safety those firearms, gentlemen," I said, walking up to the other massive machine occupying the space.

"Tripp? What you got?"

The rear hatch was open, and the old armorer slid out of the cramped space with grease on his face and part of his shirt sleeve ripped away. A trickle of blood leaked down that arm.

"You brought a fucking Decimator on board, Captain?"

"Halo gets a promotion to Captain... Captain Obvious."

Sumo and I moved between the Warbot and the men. "Relax, it's housebroken." I looked at Chief Atkins' arm questioningly. "Well, mostly."

"Just a scratch, mere difference of opinion," the AWO said.

"I had the chief here run through some checks to see if there was any way that we could use this effectively. Chief Atkins, what did you find?"

The man rubbed his arm and spat a ribbon of brown, something, toward the floor. "Well, gents, this has to be the most complicated fighting machine I've ever come across. It also has more raw strength, weaponry, and sheer power and versatility than any self-contained fighting system in history. The damn thing doesn't even locomote like our other combat droids. No hydraulics or electro-mechanical servos. Instead, it uses a very flexible polymer with a tensile strength greater than carbon-fiber that contracts or expands based on an incoming micro electric signal."

"It has mechanical muscles," Halo said.

Tripp nodded. "Yes, that's why it is almost infinitely configurable. We can outfit it in a lot of versions. This is the sentry mode, which I assume is how Kovach found it, but I got deep enough into the maintenance menu to see even this one has about twenty different configurations available."

"Can we use it, Chief? Is it safe?"

"That's just it, Captain. I don't know. I mean, the main menus and stuff are standard military. I turned off the things that needed to be off like the EMP weapon!"

"Yeah, I had insisted on that one first. Kill it or jettison it out the space doors, I'd told him."

"I erased all security settings that could have possibly set it off down here, but you'd apparently already figured a lot of that out. This bastard has ordinance for days. I mean, it could stay in nearly any fight with the racks of ammo, as if the thing itself wasn't the single most deadly instrument of war I've personally ever seen. Only thing...the deeper I go, I keep running into some software that I just don't understand, never seen before."

I thought about what Xero had said and the Virex-C code.

"These things try to kill us, Boss. I do not want to fight alongside one," Gi said nervously.

"None of us do. This one nearly killed me down there, but we need help. Nothing we have can help us against the wave after wave of creatures down there."

"What about the witch?" Packer asked, looking at Gi.

As part of his security duties, the Korean had access to the holding area. Apparently, Koog wasn't the only one who couldn't keep secrets. Spreading secrets between team members didn't bother me nearly as much.

"Ultimately, yes, I think the WitchWalkers are the key. I've now seen firsthand what power they seem to wield over the wildlife dirt-side. We need to understand that, but for now we must fight. Humankind is being driven to extinction, and those survivors left down there will turn on each other before long. Many probably have already. Banshee must be prepared to fight men, beast, and machine."

I pulled my team away from the warrant officer before continuing. "Banshee needs another member. Bayou is out, and even when she recovers, I need her running this ship."

"Prowler, I haven't seen us recover an RDT puke yet. Nothing but Army and Marines."

"Halo is right, which is why I am suggesting we train one ourselves. Pick from the available soldiers on board. Ideally, I'd like more than one. Two more to stay with Bayou up here while we drop and can be a backup when needed."

"Who do you have in mind?" Gi asked.

"Corporal Koog is my first and only suggestion." I studied the men's faces; they didn't reveal much. "He's solid, a bit of a risk-taker, but also experienced deploying with Tier-1 teams. As a plus, he's a SARC. With Bayou out, the team needs a medic."

They all seemed good with asking the kid, so I shelved that for the moment. I just wanted to make sure I got to him before Hauk tried to volunteer him to join Red-7. We went back over to get all the details on what else the chief had found.

I called Xero to come down as well. I had a feeling we were going to need her help taming this beast.

CHAPTER SEVENTY-TWO

She snuck down another corridor, confident that no one would notice. The ship's systems were very comprehensive, and no one had taken the initiative to block the civilians out. Finding where they were holding the witch had been a piece of cake. Chelsea had no problem with most of the people aboard. In fact, she was quite fond of the Marine who'd been sharing her bed most nights. Still, the witch was one of those that filled her with a burning rage. It had been another one of those who'd cost her everything.

The amber, general alert light began flashing again. She knew that meant to return to her quarters or seek cover away from the outer hull. In fact, it happened so often, people were starting to just ignore them. Most said the crew was just going through training drills. Her being aboard a spaceship still made her laugh. She, of all people, was the last one anyone would have expected to be up here...or to even have survived so long. Her long fingers traced the outline of the pendant beneath her top. Ryan would have loved being up here, being an astronaut.

"Stop it!" she whispered. She didn't have time for that. Not now, maybe not ever.

As she neared another corridor, a sudden tremor shook the ship. She could feel something large moving in the decks beneath her. *Were they firing at something?* She thought that was the hangar deck, or maybe the other one where Koog and his team trained each day. She didn't care, she was focused on getting to the prisoner. She needed answers before putting the bitch out of her misery.

"All hands, this is the Captain. General Alert."

"Captain... ha!" He was another one of the assholes on her list. She knew he was just some kind of a sergeant. She hadn't forgotten the bastard embarrassing her in front of everyone down in the mess hall. She'd get him back somehow, but that would take more time.

The IAS Stone Mountain was normally crewed by thousands. Today, it was just a few hundred. Battle station assignments took precedent over everything. Corporal Isaac Randolph took his job seriously. His father had been a policeman and his grandfather a Marine drill instructor at Paris Island. He'd been honored when Captain Hauk had recommended him for the security detail. He missed the action dirt side but not the mud, cold, and monsters. He was glad for the change of pace, and the prisoner wasn't hard to look at either, although she had never said anything to him... or anyone else. He wondered if today's alert was just more drills or the real thing.

He checked on her, retrieved his service weapon from the brig's storage locker, and left the security wing heading to the armory where his alert station was. It took him a moment to get his bearings since he'd only been there once before. He consulted the flexible computer display wrapped around his lower arm just to make sure he was making the right turns. The blow hit him just below his eyebrow crushing the orbital socket and driving the small, zygomatic bone deep into his optical nerve just missing his brain. His body twitched slightly as Chelsea struggled to drag him into the empty bunkroom and removed his wrist computer. She dropped the piece of pipe she'd used to batter the man and took his weapons, slinging the rifle and holding the pistol. She grew up in Texas; she knew how to shoot even if she wasn't fond of it.

She told herself the man would be fine, but deep down she didn't care. It wouldn't bother her long. If he was dead, it was *not like he was her first.* The door marked 'Brig' slid aside with a wave of the man's wrist ID. It was even less secure than breaking into other areas of the ship. Chelsea Adams didn't like to be locked out; she had a need to know, to be informed. She thought it was one of her greatest strengths; her husband had mainly found it annoying.

It took her longer than expected to find the access controls for the hatch leading to the holding cells. Finally, on her third try, the metal door clicked open. As she moved into the narrow corridor lined by several small but comfortable-looking cells, her excitement grew. She was going to get some answers, maybe even find out all the secrets all these WitchWalkers knew.

The blonde woman stared at her through the armor glass wall. The prisoner was aware the thing was speaking, but like all the others who'd come, the words meant nothing. She was away from her...her, something. Her tribe? That didn't seem right, but it was close. She was disconnected from her pack, really from the circle of all living things. That made her uncomfortable but not anxious or worried. Those emotions simply no longer existed in her. She was made up of purpose now, a need to be part of something larger. Several times over the last few days, she'd had images of another life, maybe her own, but it all lacked context. A woman making a meal with others that looked like her. Sitting in a classroom listening to a man speak. Having sex with a young man with long dark hair. If the flash of thoughts was hers, did she have a name? Was she someone else before the entity she was now?

The disconnection was growing more pronounced. It felt like a lump of coldness in the core of her body. When she was with the plants and animals, it was that same spot within her that radiated warmth and fulfillment. It caused her to take actions that fed that warmth. Actions that apparently the thing in the window was angry about. If she focused hard, she could almost make out some words, even though she didn't think she spoke the same language.

"What happened to my children?" the woman screamed.

What are children? the prisoner wondered.

Visons of the myriad creatures that protected her flashed in her head. They were not the same as her, but they were all part of the same. Were they... her children? *That didn't seem right.* But perhaps not all that far off the mark. *I think I had a name,* she thought as the woman pounded on the thick cell door. The woman was pointing something at her and screaming. Normally, this was when one of her friends would race in and remove the threat. *Was it Liza, maybe Lesa?* she thought.

Chelsea was in a rage; the rifle wouldn't fire. 'Safety interlock active' its small display read, so she threw it down. The pistol was a good old-fashioned mechanical version, though, it would fire. The witch still hadn't moved, had barely even acknowledged her. She beat on the control panel to open the cell door.

She hadn't fully thought this out; she needed Koog. He could access everything here. She needed his access credentials. She ran from the room to the team's ready room. One more place she wasn't allowed, but she knew where it was. They had even hooked up down there one night as he was getting off shift. She had to get her hands on that bitch; she wanted the truth. Then, she wanted everyone on board to understand what a threat the witch was and what a fraud that damn captain was.

She felt more than saw the ripple on a nearby wall, then was overcome with a sense of fear and dread. She immediately wanted to be anywhere other than here. She knew this had to be more tricks of the WitchWalker, but there was no way she could stay one second longer. She ran out of the security office in a blind panic.

CHAPTER SEVENTY-THREE

The calmness in the man's voice nearly sent Nevis Carson over the edge. "How in the hell could you not realize who you had captured? Kovach was supposed to be one of ours. The last act of rebellion by that fucking doctor. Now he may be the biggest threat we have."

"I was told they had killed him," Acevedo said.

Nevis thought on that. He'd received the same intel. Video confirmation of it, in fact. The damn spy from the Sisterhood had put a bullet into the man even as he was lying on the ground near death. How had the drop trooper gotten back together with the woman? And more importantly, why were they suddenly allies against him?

Like any good lawyer, he only enjoyed asking questions that he already knew the answers to. Today, he was in the unaccustomed spot of having none. "Where are you now?"

Bertrand told him, and Nevis quickly rattled off a safe-house in an adjacent green zone. "Get your injuries taken care of, then report back to me on your progress in forty-eight hours. The clock is ticking on this one, Bertrand."

The tall man had never failed him before, but up against the Sisterhood and the SpecOps soldier, the odds were against him still... this Kovach fellow bothered him. He would have to be put down. There was no room in the plans for a glitch like him. No one in the Order could allow a potential hero to emerge, not this late in the game. The Sisterhood had been his to deal with and by extension, now the soldier as well. If Acevedo wasn't the right tool to use, he had others.

Reluctantly, Nevis tapped his comms unit to initiate another connection. Thank God the telecom satellites would be reliable for a few more years. They knew the orbits would degrade overtime, power supplies would fail, but there were always backups and redundancies. He was lost in considering the eventuality that calling someone might actually take effort once again when the voice answered.

"We aren't scheduled to speak, Carlson. That means you've fucked something up." The woman's icy tone was cold to the point of being Arctic.

"You are, of course, correct," he said, feigning subservience to the woman. "There may be a situation developing that I felt the directors should be aware of."

"Tell me."

Her tone was all business, the words offering no judgement nor any place to hide. Nevis Carlson told her of the success in Paris and the failure in Maine.

"You are certain it was Master Sergeant Kovach?"

"I've uploaded the holovids and the bioscans my man took before he broke free. They should be in the secure folders under my section."

"You realize this means Magnus' treachery went deeper than we knew."

Magnus Reichert hadn't been part of Carlson's mission, and therefore, he bore none of the responsibilities for what the man had done. Still, he'd been roped into cleaning up more than one of the man's messes. He'd heard even more troubling rumors concerning some of the assets from the facilities. *The good doctor was full of surprises, it seemed,* he thought.

"Should we activate the Wildfire protocol?" Nevis asked.

"For one man? Hardly. Don't be an idiot, Carlson. Once we cross Line-X, it will no longer matter. If you can't handle it..."

He knew what she meant; she didn't need to finish the thought.

"I'll review the files, and if it's warranted, I'll present them to the committee. If they need you, well..."

The line went dead; the woman had ended the call. Were they still on track to cross Line-X? That was the tipping point when the momentum of change couldn't be altered by anything other than nature running its course.

Nevis considered his options. He was no one's lackey, at least not in his mind, but admittedly, the committee would only see his failings. He sipped the outrageously expensive Domaine de la Romanee-Conti La Tache Grand Cru. It wasn't as full-bodied as the 2017 he'd once had, but the 2048 vintage was still superb. Some losses from the old world would be harder to take than others. The stereo played a version of the lovely aria, Che Gelida Manina. The music, wine, and sunset view of the Mediterranean carried him away for a moment, but he knew there were decisions to be made, work to be done. After the cleansing was complete, he would have plenty of time to savor the pleasures once more. Then, he would deal with all those who had stood in his way, just like he had Magnus. He deserved to have a seat at that table, and one way or the other, he would make it so.

CHAPTER SEVENTY-FOUR

"I don't think you're supposed to be here."

Chelsea jerked as she looked up in surprise. "I... I was just waiting on my boyfriend."

"The big Marine. Yeah... don't think so. They're still down on the training deck." His eyes roamed down her body, stopping on the ID card she held in her right hand. He smiled.

"This area is off limits to everyone other than the drop troops. But... I suppose you knew that already, didn't you?"

Chelsea's heart raced, her mind tried to offer an excuse, anything that might keep her from being thrown into the brig herself. That would make that witch's day, to have her locked up beside her. "I needed to get something from Koog's locker."

"He gave you his access code?"

No, she'd guessed it was the same as the entry code he used for his living quarters. "Yes."

The uniformed man shook his head. "I don't think so. You're in big trouble... I mean really deep shit." He rubbed at his crotch ominously, then offered a crooked grin. "But maybe we can work something out."

He walked away, motioning for her to follow. Her whole body trembled, but she followed.

"What's your name?" she asked, managing to hide her nervousness better now. *Just keep him talking.*

"I'm Corporal Howell, ma'am," he said without turning. "My friends call me Rob."

"Can I call you Rob?" she asked with only a trace of seductiveness in her voice. She knew men, she knew soldiers. They all ran on hormones, and that was something she could use.

He leaned against a sturdy-looking hatch and held out his hand. "That depends, honey. That all depends on you." His words had taken on a sing-song tone now.

She looked questioningly at the outstretched hand, unsure of what he wanted. Then he pointed to the ID card she still clutched in her fist. She passed it over reluctantly, sighing in frustration. He swiped that card, then asked her for the access code. She told him the six numbers. The door slid inward noiselessly, and he pocketed the card.

"Follow me, honey."

She trailed him into the darkened space. Blood raced through her veins, and she felt her heart beating out of her chest. Then her eyes adjusted to the darkness. They were in a large space, one of the hangars. Howell was much closer now, suddenly his lips were on hers. She pulled back a little in surprise, and the man stiffened. "Sorry, Rob," she whispered as she pulled him close. Their lips met again.

The sex was rough, lacking passion, tenderness, or anything other than the physical act itself. He'd slammed her up against a metal bulkhead when he first took her. The cold metal of the hull biting into her bare flesh. Then they'd made it to a stack of plastic pallets where he continued his sexual assault. She allowed herself to go through the motions as long as it served her needs. Yes, it was rape, but she filed that away to the corner of her soul where the dark things lived.

The man climaxed, then soon began again. *Shit*, he was obviously using some of the newer performance enhancers. She knew he would be able to go several times, which he did. Why on earth would a soldier be taking those things up here with so few women aboard? She knew...guys were all alike, soldiers were all alike. Her eyes were filled with tears, her muscles ached, and her vagina was sore as he came the last time and finally rolled off her and almost instantly fell asleep.

Chelsea listened to him breathing, he was snoring deeply within minutes. She stood and pulled her clothes back on, retrieving the ID card from the man's uniform before moving deeper into the darkness.

Her first instinct was to leave. Now, her thought was to find a weapon to club Howell to death with, but she'd dealt with him. No way would he be a problem for her now. Besides, she was curious as to what other secrets the military was hiding here. She stumbled through a crowded storage room, then through an open hatch and into a hangar bay. She'd been here before. This was where the odd-looking ship had landed after picking them up in Texas.

Something was different, though. The standby lighting in the hangar deck was much better than the darkened storage room. She walked around two of the black triangle-shaped ships. They were so alien. That thought faded as she saw what they had placed against the far wall.

She cocked her head trying to take it in. It was too large to be a loading machine. No, they built this thing for war. She could see the weapon attachments. The whole thing just looked menacing and evil. She ran her hands over the smooth, black surface in a gesture that the man back there might have enjoyed more. The sheer power of this thing thrilled her on a level she could hardly express. This was a Warbot. She'd heard about them, mainly from the soldiers around her hometown and the ones that found her at the coast. Those guys seemed to fear them and also desire the machines. She now understood that kind of emotional turmoil.

This was a weapon. Was it one she could find a way to use? Thoughts of the WitchWalker faded as greater possibilities took hold of her fractured mind. She searched every inch of the mechanical marvel; she wanted to see it powered up. She wanted to know it's potential.

Her fingers traced a seam along a joint, running vertically along the inner thigh. Nothing physically happened, but her thoughts became muddied as if she'd walked into an area of low oxygen. The sensation was alarming, but she pushed the fear aside. She ran her fingers back several millimeters until the pulse of nothingness took her again. Through trial and error, she discovered the zone was incredibly small, maybe less than a half inch on a machine the size of a dump truck.

She decided to see if that was the only one. Undoubtedly, the soldiers and code-slashers had already gone over the thing looking at its programming and capabilities, but her way was more pragmatic. She wanted to know what they might have missed. It took her nearly fifteen minutes to find a second spot, a neutral zone where the same feeling of emptiness filled her. This one was up on the main chassis, just beneath the left upper appendage. The thing looked less like an arm and more like something for cutting down fields of grain or something.

She searched another half hour but got worried the soldier might wake up soon, and she suspected he wouldn't be pleased with her wanderings. Finding none other of the neutral spots, she began trying to press both spots at the same time, but the distance was too great by several feet. Then, she touched the lower, then the upper. Something happened, but she couldn't describe what it was. A connection of sorts. She then touched the lower spot once more and clearly heard a comms signal inside her own head.

Chelsea had a nonfunctional internal comms device. It was a cheap knock-off that had quit a few years after she and her husband, Carson both splurged on a pair. She had never been able to upgrade or have it removed. Those things were far beyond the modest income she and her husband had. Now, though, it seemed to be working once more. Then she heard it. Not the war machine, but a man's voice. She turned, looking back into the darkness, although she knew it wasn't Rob.

"Hello," she whispered.

She heard a chuckle, "Hello, my dear."

CHAPTER SEVENTY-FIVE

The calls from my dad were getting more frequent, and I swear he was angrier every time we talked.

"Build a fortress. That's your plan?" he asked.

"Maybe."

"It's not a plan, it's the problem. It's what got you here in the first place, dumbass."

"How's that?" I asked, totally confused.

"Your generation insulated yourselves from the real world. You drove cars that are so engineered, so refined, they do all the hard work for you. You live in ivory towers, cut off from the dirt and grime and harshness. You've engineered the joy of living out of life."

"So, we made things too comfortable? That's why humans are going extinct? I don't think so, Pops."

"Your life was never comfortable, Joe. I made damn sure it wasn't, not because I'm an asshole... well, not totally because I am one, but because being human, being a man is about overcoming, learning from the mistakes you made, adapting to the unpredictable. There was nothing unpredictable in the world before Last Day, was there? Maybe what streaming channel to watch or who had the better sales on Black Friday for more shit you really didn't need."

Okay, I have to admit. I couldn't really argue with that. The world of 2075 was beautiful but had an inherit sameness, something was missing, even if we didn't exactly know what it was.

"Life was never meant to be boring, Son. Civilization beat the big threats back a century ago. They conquered starvation, predation, and most other obvious dangers, then moved onto the more banal like making soap that you couldn't slip on in the shower. We bred generations of kids that don't know how to do shit and spend half their lives whining about it and the other half trying to figure out what other boring piece of shit they should be angry about."

"It sounds like you are a fan of the apocalypse, Pops."

"A fan? No. But was it needed, was it inevitable… oh, hell yes."

"So, building a fortress isn't the way to keep the survivors alive, then what is?"

"Shit, Joe, that one is easy. In fact, you must know it already. Teach them how to fucking fight back. No…teach them how to win. Don't adapt to the world as it is, make it the world you want to be in."

What the old guy was saying made a lot of sense. Way more than I wanted to admit.

"Won't that just put us right back where we were?"

"Yeah, maybe in a few thousand years. It's a cycle, Joe, get on—enjoy the ride. Somewhere in the middle, if mankind makes it, there will be a bit of happy equilibrium. Plenty to eat, houseplants that aren't trying to kill them. Medical advances to keep us from killing ourselves off too fast. Life should be dangerous. Every kid should have a fucking diving board to jump into a pool that's too fucking deep to stand up in and still breathe air."

"Not everyone will survive," I said.

"I think that's the point, kid, and I believe that ship has sailed. Not everyone needs to survive for mankind to win. We get better, we get farther down the road, if we get lucky, a few will make a goddamn difference. That only matters if we make it to tomorrow. You're a fucking war machine, Joe. Share what you know, share what you are. Fight back but make goddamn sure the rest of humanity is fighting beside you. Ideals are peaceful, our history is violent."

I heard him sigh; something was different about this call. "Make it count, Son."

Dad actually said goodbye for once. His words were having an effect on me, even if I didn't want to admit it. Something inside of Joseph Kovach had also changed, and I'm not just talking about the obvious stuff. I was starting to care; I was feeling the need to be better, to be more than just a soldier. I didn't think I was ready for that, but I had a feeling I was going to find out soon.

The big Marine was being run through his paces by Gi, who seemed none the worse for wear after battling the pregnant monster.

Bishop leaned against the Wulf transport watching the sergeant run the kid through the drills. "How in the hell are we going to turn him into a drop trooper?"

It had been three days since we'd agreed to give Koog a shot. The team was down too many men to use effectively. As I'd expected, Hauk did make a play for him as well, but Koog had already said yes to me by then. Now, I was pretty sure he was regretting it. The onboard training was supplemented by a ruthless VR training sim. It was the same system we used to stay sharp and train for new missions. He would get a hell of a workout and a boatload of new techniques in a very short amount of time.

"He successfully completed the Combo two years ago," I offered in response. The Combo, or Alliance Combined Special Forces Skills and Ability Assessment, was legendary and brutal. None of us had ever been through it, other than the few elite teams of Alliance regulars. You had to be invited to try out, and Banshee... well, we hadn't been. The Combo was like SEAL team hell week times ten. They pulled instructors and training techniques from the toughest military programs in the Allied nations. Then, molded it into a ten-month gut-spewing torture that had a ninety-two percent failure rate. Legend was that more soldiers committed suicide in most rotations than completed the grueling trial. If you took just the U.S. SEAL, Delta Force, Ranger, and dropped in the Marine Raiders and Force Recon training programs, you would have about forty percent of the hell they included in the COMBO.

"That's some boss-level shit there, man," Bishop said, his respect for the kid climbing noticeably. "What about actual drop training, though?"

"Yeah, that's going to be a problem," I admitted. New RDT recruits typically did training drops in a special tandem pod from high altitude, then eventually low orbit. Supposedly, you should have a minimum of thirty training drops before your first actual combat drop.

"OJT," I said, walking away. *On-the-job training.*

Jordan Hauk caught me on the way to the bridge. "You have a moment?"

I knew what he wanted. He'd presented his mission plan several days earlier. I'd given a provisional okay, and he'd used the time to assemble and outfit his rescue and recovery team. Ada had given him complete access to the intel on the site. It was going to be a meat grinder, no way I could justify risking more lives to save one. Still, the captain was determined to go, and I had no right to keep him here, or the men of his fire team. I assumed his decision to go had been made. "Yes, Captain, follow me." I subvocalized Ada to have Damiana join us.

After checking that the ship's status was nominal, I ushered Jordan into the ready room. Voss joined us minutes later.

Jordan was clearly confused. "I don't think I need a doctor. Not just yet anyway."

Voss had been working on new intel from the Sisters of Light that some of the acolytes, or whatever the junior Sisters were called, had been taken by the same group holding Jordan's brother.

"Damiana isn't just a doctor, she has other skills," I offered lamely, then blushed looking over at her and realized what I had said.

"It seems we may have a common enemy and a mutual need to avenge those we care about," Voss said.

"No offense, Doc, but this is going to be challenging as hell. Our intel is spotty, we... I really have no idea what I'm going to be up against," Hauk said.

"Jordan, trust me on this. She can help."

"I can help you already, show me what you have on the holding camp."

Hauk looked at me in confusion. I was pretty sure I knew what he was thinking.

"Just like that, you want me using second-hand intel from a civilian."

If Voss was offended, she didn't show it, but then again, she never showed much of anything personal. "Take it, leave it, Captain. What you do is up to you. My friends are planning an attack. If you aren't going to join us, I suggest you stay out of the way."

"Your friends? Care to let me in on who we would be fighting with?"

"No."

One of the bridge crew rapped lightly on the hatch, then opened it hurriedly. "We need you, sir. We have a situation developing."

I smiled at the other two and moved for the entryway.

"I think you two have it well in hand. Let me see what other species I might be able to piss off today."

CHAPTER SEVENTY-SIX

"What we got, Ensign?

"A ship, sir, coming in fast on convergent vector."

I calculated the likelihood of it being friendly at less than twenty percent. Basically, everybody hated us and our presence aboard this ship.

"Ready weapons, point defense systems online."

That was about all I knew about ship-to-ship fighting, but we did have an outstanding weapons officer. Another Marine from the recovered fragment. Like Bayou, I had full faith in the woman's ability to keep us in the fight.

"Helm, bring us about for maximum firing solutions."

It wasn't like we would be firing canon broadsides at each other. With orbital velocity, you shot for where something would be seconds or microseconds later, and for us that might be several hundred miles ahead. Slight variations in our orbit might cause an enemy to miss us by miles. I was more concerned with presenting as small a radar target as possible to the approaching craft.

"We are being lit up by side scanning radar, sir. They want to make sure we know they are here."

"Intentions?"

"Unknown, no communications on any channel."

I paged the ready room. "Hauk, you and Voss work your shit out on the way. I want you off this boat now."

I heard an undertone of mumbled complaints, but they both seemed to grasp the situation.

"Hard copy, Kovach."

I gave the order for Packer to ready the dropship. Hauk's team couldn't drop like Banshee, they needed the bus.

Minutes later, I saw the unknown craft enter our proximity field; alerts began going off all over the bridge.

"Jesus Christ, she's nearly as big as us."

"IFF?" I asked, wanting to know if the ship identified as friend or foe.

Specialist Otero was working the tactical station. "Neither, sir, signal is present but shows a neutral party."

Neutral party? I had to think about that one. It's a civilian ship? My mind and Ada's began running through the possibilities but quickly came down to only one likely candidate. A civilian ship that large...

"It's the Sao Paulo," I said out loud.

The tactical officer nodded in agreement. "I can confirm, configuration is a match."

What would an unarmed passenger ship want with us? Last I heard it was in a lunar parking orbit being outfitted for a Mars settlement run.

"We're being hailed."

"Put it through to the ready room." I wondered if this was a repeat of what Bayou had gone through.

Hauk and Voss were rushing out as I went in. Hauk shook my hand, and I wished him luck. He asked me to watch after the rest of his men while he was away. Voss hung back momentarily, then gave me a quick hug, then a much longer kiss.

"You got this?" she whispered.

I nodded. "Maybe. Go take care of business." We both knew we might not be meeting again. I found myself in an unusual, conflicted place. I had no time for feeling anything like this at this moment.

"The ship?" she pointed to the proximity alert screen.

"The Sao Paulo."

She looked as confused by my answer as I was. "You...you need to..."

"I will. The captain has to gather his people and gear. I tend to travel light." She flexed her wrist, and the tiny handgun was in her hand, then vanished back into her reflex holster again. Once again, I'd forgotten about that. So much for no guns on the ship... seemed like no one had listened to that order. "Thank you for... this. A moment of peace in the midst of the storm. I do have dragons to slay now, though."

I kissed her again and moved past. "Good hunting, Voss. And remember to take your pet."

Only I knew the truth of what had happened with her Sisters at the Chateau. Nevis hadn't just taken out a stronghold for the Sisterhood but also a field hospital and orphanage for hundreds of children injured and homeless since Last Day.

Settling in behind the holodisplay, I watched through the clear armor glass bulkhead as Voss walked away. "Ada, are we tied into ship's defenses?" I asked before accepting the call.

"Yes, Prowler. Belle and I can remotely override anything needed if your weapons officer needs help."

"Let's hope it doesn't come to that."

"This is Commander Kovach with the IAS Stone Mountain."

Technically not a lie. Somehow, I'd gotten a posthumous field promotion. I just hadn't tried it on myself until now. The face that stared back at me was too handsome and too young and...he was smiling. That bothered me on several levels.

"Commander Kovach, I'm Captain Orric from Fleet Command, and we need to talk."

~

The dropship slid noiselessly out of its cradle and out the starboard launch door just minutes before the Space Fleet envoy's ship entered the same landing bay from the opposite side. Banshee team in full battle gear was strategically placed along the walls. It was silly, it was overkill, but I liked a good old-fashioned show of force. I signaled to close the space doors and heard the crackle of the stasis field generator shutting down as the bay doors sealed.

The small shuttle's rear bay opened, so that anyone could see the cargo bay was empty. That was a good move if he was looking to build trust. The same man from the earlier call unlatched himself from the pilot's seat and began moving aft. Remote cameras fed every move the man made into my HUD. Yes, I was now in full battle armor as well.

Captain Valyn Orric, the assistant to the self-proclaimed War Commander Reese, walked down the ramp and directly up to me. He was in a simple, red flight jumpsuit, one of the very plain garments favored by personnel on Luna.

"Master Sergeant," he said, smiling and sticking out a hand. "Or is it, Captain?"

I snapped a crisp salute then shook the outstretched hand. "That depends on who you ask."

He eyed the digital name tape on my chest plate. I knew my normal chevrons and rockers had been replaced with captain's bars.

It seemed to take him back slightly to realize he didn't outrank me. Since he was the adjunct to a senior flag officer with Fleet Command, maybe the last senior officer in the fleet, he did, in fact, still outrank me. I was certainly much further down the food chain. Honestly, at the moment, what mattered was my armor more than the rank insignia on my chest.

"Permission to come aboard," he said with a wry smile that seemed totally out of place.

I held up my hand. "That depends. What is your business on the Stone Mountain?"

"Straight to the point, Kovach. I like that. I've been ordered to take possession of the vessel by any means necessary."

The man's response was as direct as my own and not unexpected but still surprising. "And yet, you show up in that." I pointed out the thick polyglass portals in the space gate toward the Sao Paulo, now just an orange dot several dozen kilometers away.

He smiled, "There is a method to my madness, and we are a bit thin on transports."

"So, you have armed assaulters waiting to board us if I don't hand over the keys?"

He didn't seem to get the ancient reference; the kid was too damn young.

"I felt like diplomacy might be a better... um, first step. I wanted to speak with you and see if I can grasp what your plan is for the ship. Do you have a mission objective that perhaps would benefit everyone?"

Well, that was damn polite of the little asshole. "Well, shit, friend. Permission granted. Let's talk."

It seemed that Fleet Command was trying something new. "I don't trust this guy, Ada," I said mentally. "Find out everything on him and keep scanning that damn ship out there."

I motioned to Banshee to stand down and walked the man up the main corridor toward the large and totally useless war room. The massive space was designated for Fleet officials and dignitaries; the oak paneling and overstuffed chairs were not intended for the rank and file, so it had remained unused until now.

Ada pinged me with a bit of initial data which helped. I followed up on one interesting fact with her before pouring the man a drink from the bar.

"Scotch, neat," I said, handing it to him before completely removing my suit's helmet and placing it beside my bourbon.

He sipped and smiled. "I see my briefing on you was correct. You have an embedded AI, don't you?"

"He wouldn't know that Joe. His clearance level is not high enough," Ada said internally.

"No games, Valyn, why are you really here?"

"Two things, Joe, and yes, they are related. First, I truly want to hear from you about what is going on down there. Second, how does keeping this Space Force carrier and you at the helm help the situation down there?"

Damn, I was really hoping for a less reasonable question. I wanted to hate this guy, but well, fuck. I took twenty minutes and filled him in on almost everything we'd encountered on the planet. Every horror, every machine, every vacant town and destroyed city.

"So, people aren't sheltering in place? We were informed that survivors were being held in massive bunkers and others were told to shelter in place. It didn't seem too bad because a lot of the bunkers said only a trickle of people were even showing up."

"Captain Orric, they aren't showing up because they are dead." I rattled my glass as I stared out the porthole on the opposite wall. "We aren't fighting a war, Orric. We are fighting extinction."

He seemed to think about what I said for a minute before asking me about the second part. Why should I get to use this ship?

"Because I can," I stated flatly. "Look, Valyn, I have been a mostly good soldier, but there is no one calling the shots right now. Not anyone on the side of humanity at least. Not anyone I trust to be in charge, especially your admiral."

"That is a dereliction of duty and failure to follow orders of a superior officer."

"So, court-martial me, but even then... good luck getting your ship back."

He took another sip, then lifted his glass and touched mine. "I think you just crossed your Rubicon, sir."

I stared at him long enough for it to get awkward, then he gave me a crooked grin that disarmed me despite my armor. The kid was good looking, dark wavy hair, neatly trimmed beard. Middle Eastern if I was right, although Ada's intel showed he was a Brit.

"So, tell me, who do you think created these weapons?" he asked.

"The hybrids, the monster?" I asked, caught off-guard by the sudden shift in the conversation. "We did, I think." Correcting myself, "I know Hammer Industries was at least partially behind it, but I'm not sure the plan isn't much bigger than that." I filled him in on the intel concerning Nevis Carlson and the so-called 'Liberty Strike.'

He stood.

"So, now what, you summon your boarding party?" I asked.

"Nothing like that I'm afraid, Joe. I have to make a tactical decision. If I don't think we can take the Stone Mountain back mostly intact, I have orders to destroy you."

He didn't move to leave, instead he walked over and refilled his scotch. "You?"

I shook my head.

"So, you are using this ship as an FOB? How does that work?"

"It's the ultimate high ground."

"If you have a drop team," he said.

"Or orbital bombardment weapons," I added.

"Touché, and you do have both. But I see a problem."

"Just one?" I asked.

"You can't be in command of both this ship and your drop team. As soon as you are off this ship, anyone could assume command."

"Like you?" I'd already seen in his file he was qualified to command a destroyer class starship; he could manage one this size, too.

"I do have my orders, Kovach."

"She's coming in now," Ada said.

"Just know, we are all survivors up here. We fought our way here, many of us died getting here. We won't give it up easily." I finished talking as the hatch swung open, and Xero glided in.

The captain's eyes went wide, as Xero threw herself into his arms.

"How did you get here?" he asked.

"I'll give you both some time," I said, leaving them and walking past the two security sentries guarding the door.

"Joe, I didn't tell Xero anything. Should I have asked them to help?" Ada was brilliant, and even I caught her use of the gender-neutral pronoun, but she still struggled to comprehend human behavior. Then again, so did I.

"There's nothing you could say that will change anything. The man had his orders, and I trust Xero to do the right thing. She's a very smart girl, guy...person. Discreetly monitor the conversation and let me know when they're done. Meanwhile, I'm going to see how we might fend off a boarding party. Arggghh! I love being a pirate!"

CHAPTER SEVENTY-SEVEN

"What are you doing down here, kiddo?"

Junie was licking at my boots, and Sumo was off to the side pretending to ignore her.

"I… I was helping Xero with something, but she got called away," Lux said.

"Oh," I nodded, knowing I was the one who made that call.

"She had you helping with the Warbot?"

"Yes, but Mister Tripp said it was perfectly safe. She helped me with Rex, so I owed her."

The kid was also on a first name basis with our Chief Armory Officer, why wasn't that a surprise? I then noticed the little service droid he called Rex back against a charging port in the nearby wall. I'd first mistaken if for a piece of scrap from the battered ship fragment.

"Your mom okay with you doing this?"

Lux grinned in a way that let me know Carol was unaware of his current activities. "She was taking food to the WitchWalker. Sergeant Gi asked her to help. Is she really a witch? That was what Aunt Dami said."

Gi had mentioned one of his guards had been injured in the last drill and was still in the medbay. I guessed he was running shorthanded. "I dunno, kid, maybe."

My guys had Koog going through another round of training sims in the far corner of the bay. I motioned them over.

"So, what did Xero have you doing?" I asked Lux.

"Trying to find out why the remote operator function isn't working. There is a space for an operator inside, but it's really cramped, too tight even for her."

"She had you inside—that?"

The kid nodded.

My comms chimed, Ada's signal that she had something. "Joe, two things. First, Deb seems to be regaining consciousness."

"Thank God," I whispered.

"Also," she continued, "I have been monitoring the very private conversation you asked me to."

From her tone I could tell she found it distasteful. Hell, so did I, but I wanted Xero brought in for a reason. And now, I needed to know if it was working or not.

"Captain Orric told Xero he isn't supposed to be here. He arranged the ride on the Sao Paulo under the guise of it being a resupply run."

"He's off the rez?"

"Not the reservation exactly, but essentially, yes. This trip seems to be all his idea."

Now, I really was confused. Valyn seemed like the perfect officer for Fleet Command. A rigid, by- the-books leader. Why would he be calling an audible on something as critical as this?

"Okay, keep me posted."

Halo, Gi, and Priest were still in battle armor. Koog was back in the training version. It gave him simulated damage without too much of the real thing, although he would be bruised and sore afterward. Danny rubbed Lux's hair. I had to smile. If Halo liked the kid, he was something special.

"What's up, Boss? The Fleet guy okay, or do we need to deep space a body?"

"He's okay, for now. Still not sure what his game is, but I think we need to be ready for anything. Koog, get back into the full battle rattle. Training is over for today."

"Copy that, Captain." The Marine departed for the team's ready room.

I eyed the group and smiled; we'd been through hell together but somehow kept managing to pull off the impossible. "I've got an itch."

All of them except Gi started groaning.

"Last time that happened the world ended," Priest growled.

"Did not, I wasn't even on a mission that day."

"What is this itch?" Gi asked in confusion.

"Ummm... my intuition, Sergeant. I have a feeling that something is up, and I want us locked and loaded for whatever the hell it is."

"Me, too?"

I looked down at the source of the tiny voice.

"You too, what?" I asked.

"Should we be locked and loaded?" Lux pointed at the Decimator.

"No!" I turned back to the men, then had second thoughts. Turning back, I saw... disappointment. The kid wanted to be part of this. But he was a child. Man, what a shit childhood for the dude. Still, my dad's words were haunting me. I pointed at the Warbot, "It's not loaded now?"

Lux's face brightened. "Some things are, but we returned normal ordinance to storage."

"Ordinance?" I looked at my team. "Okay, he has to stop hanging around you guys."

"Mister Tripp set it up so I can back the Warbot into the loader slot. We practiced it and everything."

I glanced up at the loader slots; nine of them lined the closest bulkhead. Our own suits used them for hot swap reloads, and if the carrier held fighters, that's how their ammo would be brought up from the armory as well.

"What else did Mister Tripp show you?"

Lux gave a small snicker, "Nothing, really."

"Okay, Lux, show me what you got."

Lux tapped a control on the datapad, and part of the massive bot spread out and up revealing the cockpit. The kid landed in the undersized seat and had the access doors closing in seconds.

"Joe, you sure this is a good idea?"

"Probably not, Halo, but we may need that rust bucket if the shit goes sideways." We all watched as Lux spun the iron giant on its axis and backed it rapidly up against the loading hatch. Clamps automatically slid down and latched to the back, and the query panel showed on my HUD.

"What you want loaded?" Lux asked.

Xero must have hacked the thing's comms system to work with our own. Any live ordinance would need command authorization from me or... the chief armorer. The kid had called my bluff, now I needed to decide how far I wanted to play this hand.

"Lux, can anyone else operate this thing as it is right now?"

"Not unless they can fit in here. Like I said, Xero is working on the remote teleprez thing."

Telepresence, yeah that would be helpful. I recalled the brief melee session I'd enjoyed down below. "What about its sentry mode, could we rely on it to not attack us or damage the ship?"

"Kovach, you know you are having a tactical discussion with an eight-year-old kid," Priest whispered.

"I'm nine."

"He's nine, and the thing has excellent sound sensors, dumbass. Also, this kid survived down there on his own longer than nearly any of us have so far."

"Full load-out," I said and keyed in the authorization at the same time. "I want to see how fast this thing can be ready for action from a cold start."

I heard the whirring of the automated weapons chute and felt a rumble as ordinance was cycled into empty racks and holders inside the giant machine.

"Battle ready status is green," Lux said just a few seconds later.

Shit, that was faster than even I could have a weapon detached from its maglock up and firing. I could see on my own display that the loadout was only at about forty percent, but it was increasing fast. "Full load in under two minutes."

Lux wanted to undock and move back into the formation with the men, but I was able to lock him out of moving the fully loaded machine.

"Impressive, Lux, but cool your jets for now."

"I can assist the boy if it comes to that," Ada said. "My access to the machine is excellent, and even without the telepresence, I believe I can operate it in the standard sentry mode."

"Let's add this into our plans along with the Marines who are combat effective and any of the remaining Red-7 guys. Divide them up into fire teams."

"Issuing them weapons?" Gi asked, the concern evident. He had a right to be on guard, some were near mutiny just a few days earlier.

"Not yet, but have it staged close. We may have to be weapons hot in a hurry."

"Captain, you are needed on the bridge. We are picking up another ship. The Sao Paulo is backing away from its parking orbit fast."

I turned and started for the door. "It may be happening. Move, gentlemen. Lux, you can exit but stay close to the team."

CHAPTER SEVENTY-EIGHT

Xero watched her friend closely. Ada had transmitted the info directly to her comms implant before the ship-wide alert sounded.

"Valyn, you need to tell me what you know about this. I can't protect you if the shit is about to go sideways."

Her friend's face was ashen, the man certainly didn't seem to be a part of whatever action was headed their way. "It's not us, Zee."

"Not us as in not the Space Force?"

"Maybe, I don't know. I just know you are in extreme danger. There are elements at play that even I don't understand."

"Why don't you call your ship back? You're going to need a ride. In fact, keep her close, she would be useful as another lifeboat for whatever survivors we can bring up from the surface." She rose from the table, "I have to go, they'll need me on the bridge." Her even tone belied the anger and betrayal she was feeling.

He rose as well and lightly placed a hand on her arm. "Xero, use me. You know I can help."

"Help?" she asked incredulously. "For all I know you are behind it. You will stay here until the Marine guards escort you off this ship or kill you, which they will do if you are here to cause us harm."

"I'm not, but I may be the only chance you have of holding onto the ship."

She knew Valyn was qualified to command a monolith class warship, but he'd been at Fleet Command for too long, and things were anything but ordinary.

"Guards!"

The two uniformed sentries appeared in the door. "Please escort my guest to the bridge level holding cell."

"You're making a mistake," he said in protest before leaning in and embracing Xero.

"Maybe so. I don't make many, but it won't be my first."

The guards held position as Xero turned to face her friend.

"Zee, you know more than you are letting on. I can see it. That means you know whoever is behind this is not the military."

"Who do you think it is, then?" She needed to go help on the bridge, but this might be the only time to get honest answers from Valyn.

His eyes fell to the floor. "I don't know. Honestly, the military doesn't have the power most people think. If it did, War Commander Reese would be the one coming up in an attack ship instead of whomever that is."

"Don't call him that." She spat the words out.

He nodded. "Fair enough. What I am saying is the military is just a part of this puzzle, has been since the Cold War. We are the result, not the cause."

"Not following, Val."

"Who makes money from war? The contractors, politicians, consultants. The Alliance didn't form to protect its nations. They formed to share the profits—profits from making war on anybody or everybody."

She moved closer toward the hatch. "No one is profiting now. Did someone overplay their hand?"

He shook his head. "No, I think this was always the plan. Someone was playing the long-game while everyone else was just set-pieces trying to get rich."

He did have her attention now, although she wasn't totally sure why. "If not profit, then what?"

Valyn shrugged. "Hubris, fear of losing out to some bigger fish.

Maybe because they thought they had found the keys to rebuilding the world. Hell, who knows?"

~

"Prowler, it's heating up."

I was racing through the corridors, my brain processing information that my conscious mind hadn't even come to terms with yet. Ada's words registered, but I'd already guessed the next move.

"Incoming missiles," the weapons officer said, her crisp voice showing shakiness around the edge.

"Countermeasures active," I said unnecessarily, the ship's own defensive system would do that automatically.

"Identify hostile. Is it Valyn's people?"

"Joe, Deb is regaining consciousness," Ada said again.

"Shit!" I yelled as I passed the passageway leading to the med bay. I wanted to see her, needed to see her, but priorities. Sadly, she was so much more familiar with the ship's capabilities than I was, I considered going back. This time, I had to rely on her team and Ada to get us through whatever happened next.

"Ship had no IFF," Otero called in response to my last question. "No beacon of any kind, nor does the radar profile match any known vessel."

So, not Space Force. Not an official force at least.

"Prowler, our Space Gate is lowering," Ada said calmly.

The outer hangar door, or 'Space Gate,' lowers automatically only for other Space Force assets. Normally, they required a verifiable IFF transponder, but suddenly someone seemed to be able to do it without that. I had Belle and my AI working to regain control.

"Stasis field still in place?" That was what really kept our people safe inside the hangar. Ships could enter through the field, but the atmosphere couldn't escape. It was a truly ingenious system. Probably another advance that Xero would question as being too advanced for our level of knowledge. "Affirmative," the AI said.

I felt the primary batteries open up with what I assumed were the countermeasures. All my years aboard ships like these, and I had never once heard any weaponry being used.

My comms unit came alive with random voices, "One got through."

The ship shook violently. I would have been gone crashing into the side bulkhead, but Ada had increased the magnetic force in my deck boots.

Moving through the last hatch to the bridge, I barely noticed the Marines standing guard outside the adjacent hatch. "What have we got, people, critical damages first."

They filled me in at the same time Ada was re-prioritizing for me based on her own understanding of risks and needs. In less than a minute, I learned a lot of what the crew knew. Unknown ship, first salvo appeared to be ship-killer missiles. Impacts have done minimal damage so far.

"Incoming energy weapon."

"Point defense systems going hot," the weapons officer said as she keyed in the targeting for the high-energy lasers.

"Prowler, distance to target is over fifty kilometers, beyond the effective range for our energy beam weapons," Ada said.

I nodded, already coming to the same conclusion. "We have to do something. We are in the mightiest surviving warship in the sky. Give me some options."

"Xero," I said, noticing her at the workstation for the first time.

She looked up and nodded.

"Our guest," I bobbed my head to the corridor, now understanding what I had ignored earlier.

"Yes, he wanted to help, but obviously I couldn't bring him into the bridge without your okay."

Valyn Orric's flight and command credentials flashed past in my ocular overlay, and I thought I understood.

"Bring him in," I yelled to the Master of Arms, who'd been a recent addition to thc bridgc staff.

"Our sensors are being jammed."

"Which ones?" I said as calmly as possible to the young ensign.

"All of them, sir," he responded.

"Belle, what's going on?" I yelled for the ship's AI.

"Ada, I need help!" I whispered.

She made no comment but nearly immediately, I felt the ship accelerate hard and rotate into a steep banking maneuver. The man at the helm began fighting to regain control before I told him to stand aside.

"Captain, I mean, Master Sergeant," Orric said, walking confidently into the Command Center. The two guards flanking him looked much less calm.

"You have nothing to do with this attack?"

"No, sir! But I had anticipated it."

That stuck with me. He was more than what he appeared.

"Xero said you can help. I trust her, even if I don't trust you... yet."

The younger man went to speak, but I cut him off, "Give him what we have." I looked the man in the eye and made one of the toughest decisions of my life. "He has battle command. Ada has the con... for now."

Valyn nodded. "You will soon need to decide if you are ready to be a pirate. There is no going back from that choice."

"I'm a patriot, Sir. That you can rely on," Valyn said, turning to the main display.

He went right to work and seemed up to speed issuing new orders in under a minute. "If this was a traditional force, I would expect railgun darts next, but looking at their Delta-V, I think we have other things in store."

The Delta-V was the enemy ship's approach in relation to us. I could see there was an intersect at some point in the future.

"Boarding?" I asked, already knowing the answer.

He nodded.

"Banshee, battle ready, prepare to repel boarders."

I fought the instinct to rush down to the landing bays and join them. Right now, I have more to risk right here.

"What about the kid, sir?" Halo asked. "Should we get him out of the Warbot, or you know... don't we like need a note from his mother or something?"

I shook my head. I'd totally forgotten about Lux, but he was probably in the safest spot on the ship. I told Halo to leave the kid where he was and use the Warbot if he needed. The boy was growing up fast, and this was a lesson he likely wouldn't forget. Now, I had a big decision to make. Leave the bridge in the hands of a Fleet officer with questionable alliances and go fight or...

My thought was cut off by an unexpected voice in my ear.

"Joe."

"Riggs?" Her voice was weak and gravelly, but she was indeed conscious again and apparently needed to talk. I just couldn't spare the time.

CHAPTER SEVENTY-NINE

Chelsea knew this was the moment to act. Even without hearing from her new ally. This was certainly his doing. In the initial conversation he'd laid out steps she could take to make her plan come true. To make that happen, though, she would have to do something for him. She didn't like it but felt like an outsider on this ship, anyway. *Fuck 'em all.*

She moved the access hatch to one side and retrieved the small pistol she'd taken off the security guard. If knocking the man out raised any suspicions, they hadn't been directed at her. To most of the crew, she was invisible. Peering around a corner, she spotted the bump of the security camera on the ceiling. She was not invisible to those. Luckily, the deck she was heading to was not well surveilled, that had been one of Rob's contributions to her plan. The little weasel seemed to know all the blind spots in the ship's systems. She tucked the gun into her pocket and headed off.

The corporal was waiting for her right where he said he would be. He still repulsed her, but she gave him a quick kiss. Sure, she'd had to fuck him a few more times, but the man was scared to death of Koog and Banshee. He didn't want to risk getting caught with her, so he only showed up when it was absolutely safe to do so. *A useful idiot,* she smiled. That was basically what all guys were.

"You sure this will work?" she asked.

"Oh, yeah, Tripp has me going through all these things, all the time. I have to clean and service the battle suits, loaders... all kinds of stuff."

She didn't know who Tripp was, but it didn't matter.

"I even screwed with the captain's drop suit. I would have loved to have seen his face when his wings wouldn't deploy."

Why would he have done that? she wondered. Hadn't the man saved his life when he pulled his unit off the ground? "But he's still alive."

"I know, right? The man's impossible to kill. You should hear some of the nicknames the other guys have for him. There's even a rumor that he was dead and came back to life."

Yeah, she'd even heard that one.

"So, look, honey, after this you going to, you know...let me get to know you again?"

Ugh, the man's euphemisms were nearly as bad as his breath. "Maybe, depends on how good you are."

"Oh, don't you worry, Babe, I'll be really damn good. Still don't know how doing this will get you in with that prisoner, though," Howell said.

"This is mainly a distraction," she cooed while watching him unscrew the composite panel with a portable driver.

"This system is just a piece of shit...I don't even really know. It's not even part of the main network systems, just backup safety and maintenance logs; nothing vital. How do you even know about it?"

She hadn't mentioned the odd conversations with the man via the Warbot. That was not anything Corporal Howell needed to know. Despite his stupidity, the man still was a soldier and might have some issues with what was going to happen next. He moved out of the way, and she began entering a long series of command codes from the scrap of paper she'd used to write them down.

"You must be some kind of hacker genius," Rob said. "Like that hot, Asian chick."

Chelsea ignored him and waited for the prompt to say the patch had been accepted. She felt the gun digging into her abdomen as she leaned into the awkward space. She wondered if she could just kill Rob here, or if she would need him again. Either way, he wasn't touching her body again.

Honestly, she didn't know what the code she just entered would do. The man first wanted her to establish control of the Warbot for him. He kept calling it a Decimator. Nothing she had done had worked, and the man had finally given up.

"What do I call you?" she had asked the next time they talked. It was hard because she had to be relatively close to the Warbot for the connection to work. It was too far away from her for a signal to be relayed. Those calls being discovered by the ship's sensors scared her, but the man kept reassuring her it wasn't possible.

"Call me Ahdeen, Nomar Ahdeen," he had said, the deep, baritone voice echoing just a hint of an accent.

"This will get me access to the witch?"

"Indeed, my dear Chelsea, and it will eliminate the RDT soldier. The one who embarrassed you. Both of our problems will be gone forever."

CHAPTER EIGHTY

I had no time for a visit, so I called the medbay instead. The erratic and brief conversation with Deb rattled me to my core. Surely it was the result of the trauma she'd been through, not based on actual fact.

"I did my best to bring her up to speed, but she was talking crazy. My adrenaline levels were spiking, and Ada was doing her best to keep my systems from overloading with the anticipation of battle.

"He...he's dead Deb. There is no way it was him. You were there." I hated visualizing what it must have been like for her seeing the face on that call. Computer generated or something, hell I saw Van Gogh on a call a few days ago.

Carol caught up to me on my way to the hangar deck. In my battle suit and helmet, she could probably just make out I was talking to someone. I stopped and stared at her.

Carol could see something had shaken me. Something more than just the battle alert.

"Is everything okay?"I ended the call and raised my visor.

"Yes... no...shit, I don't know. You just need to get to the shelters."

Carol touched my arm. "Joe, what's wrong?"

"We're being attacked." It wasn't a lie, but that wasn't the main reason I was so conflicted.

"Look, wait." I knew I was wrestling my own internal demon, but quickly I came to a decision. "Can you get to the med bay and check on Deb? She's regaining consciousness. It's in a protected section of the ship, you'll both be safe there."

"I need to find Lux," was her anxious response.

The thought of the kid buttoned up inside an enemy Warbot flashed in my mind, but I kept that to myself. "I know where he is, I'll get the guys to keep him safe."

She touched my arm again and then pulled me close. "Joe, I need you to keep him safe. You...okay? I trust you."

She leaned in and kissed me, not a great kiss but maybe just what I needed to calm down. I leaned into her, I wanted to say much more but this wasn't the time.

I nodded mutely as I turned, resuming my lumbering gait toward the hangar. The heavy armored boots made a resounding thud with each footfall.

"Hey, Junior, they locked you up yet?"

My dad's timing was always impeccable, always at the worst possible time. "Not yet, Pops, but the day's still young."

Honestly, it seemed like the enemy was more intent on killing me than placing me under arrest. "Dad, I don't even understand who we are fighting. The coalition is gone, Space Force is being bossed around by a pretender, and my XO just begged me to stand down. Surrender the ship before any more lives are lost."

A felt a shudder as something hit the ship. The lights blinked off and on a few times, then stabilized. A massive whirring began filling the corridor. It was a sound I had heard only in simulations.

"That's the rail guns warming up?"

"Yeah, Pop, I think so."

"Joe, forget what Deb said. You have to win this. You need to end them today if you can in fact... whatever the threat is. The war for humanity isn't going to be decided up there, but down here. I'm hearing strange reports that the creatures are massing together."

"Why?" I asked, opening a hatch just as the ship lurched sideways from the rail gun's recoil. Say what you will, but Valyn seemed to be fighting back. "Are they preparing to move on the survivors?"

"No... not yet at least. No, Joe, I think they may be...building something."

My team waited for me, waited... for battle. The outer space doors were open, the stasis field the only thing keeping atmo inside the bay. My men all stood in rigid formation on the far end of the bay, skylined against the black field of stars. "Gotta go, Dad."

"Banshee!" I screamed out. "Time to earn our keep, guys!"

"Sumo, on me."

I eyed my team display for Lux. Anticipating what I was looking for, I saw the kid's icon on my far right. We had to keep him safe, but that Warbot was too valuable a weapon not to use.

"You can handle that remotely?" I asked Ada. She assured me she could handle most of it, and Lux was more than capable of the rest.

"Shield what he sees, Ada... he's just a kid."

I turned back to where the team was already taking up defensive positions. "Koog, get us eyes out there."

"Out there where someone is firing lasers and missiles at us?"

"Yeah, what... you want to live forever?" Halo said with a nervous chuckle.

"No," the big kid said, lumbering out past the safety markings. "I wouldn't mind making it through the rest of the day, though."

I briefly considered telling the men some of what Deb had said but knew this wasn't the time. We needed to be together and focused on the mission.

"Ada, get me Captain Orric."

Sounds from the bridge echoed into my helmet. "Situation, Captain."

Valyn sounded calm as he smoothly laid out the most relevant points. "Unknown ship, unknown capabilities. The initial attack caught us off-guard as the missiles seem to be using some type of stealth field. Only saw them the last few kilometers when their targeting radar went active. Profile and blast signatures do not match any known enemy or allied weaponry."

"So, is the enemy ship in range? What about the rail guns?" I asked.

"Kovach, we have this handled. Just be ready." He paused, and I sensed he was issuing orders. "Probably like you, I think this is merely a distraction. They must want the ship intact."

I felt a stab of icy fear as I realized I'd just handed the ship over to a possible enemy. Still, it felt like the right decision. Also, he knew how to use this massive weapon; I was just playing Captain. Back here was where I belonged.

"Orric, one thing."

"Yes, Prowler."

"No time to go into it, but do not give up control of this ship, not to anyone. Including Lieutenant Debra Riggs."

"Not sure I understand, she is the listed commander of the bridge wing."

"I know, and she is a gifted soldier and a friend, but I don't think her goals and ours are the same right now. She's regained consciousness, so it's something we're going to have to deal with. Let's just choose a better time and place for that—deal?"

"Deal, sir. Good hunting."

I changed the switch for team comms, then selected the one I wanted.

"Hey, Lux, how you doing?"

"I'm great! This thing is awesome."

"You know what you are supposed to do?"

"Yes, sir," he said with a tone that closely mimicked the crisp communication style of the other team members. "Keep anyone from out there from getting in here?"

Simple and accurate, I thought.

"No heroics, kid, okay? Your mom will skin me if you get hurt. You're our backup, alright?"

"Yes...sir." His voice had a somewhat more subdued tone now. I didn't bother to inform him that his mom was going to have my hide in either case once she found out what I'd had him do.

"Contact, starboard side, four o'clock low," Koog said.

"Ada, make sure his suit is in active camo. I want him blending into the ship's hull." I then gave the orders to make ready. In seconds, two targets popped into the open hangar door. They were heavily armored, and we let them get well inside the bay before Halo and Priest both made coordinated head shots. Both invaders went down.

"They aren't Alliance or Coalition. No insignia at all," Halo said, echoing my own thoughts as I zoomed in on the enemies' battle suits.

I heard Koog, but the limited battle space was heating up too quickly to focus on the man's words. I had barely enough time to radio up that we had boarders, when the entire hangar seemed to erupt into a massive firefight. There were dozens of things I should have considered. Risk to the ship, having a kid on the fire team, how much could Gi handle after his recent injuries, but my focus, my entire reason for being, was tunneling down to a very specific point. Bayou had it right, not today, but weeks ago when she said it, "They die first." That was the way to run this mission and... win this war. My Rattler was placing precise and regular shots down range. Enemy soldiers were falling, but not enough. For every one of them who fell, it seemed two more took their place. No matter how good or how fast Banshee was, there were limits. The math just wasn't in our favor.

Sumo wanted off his virtual leash, but there was little he could do to men in space-rated battle armor. The hangar deck was now occupied by dozens of combatants. I had Ada call up the Marines and Hauk's troops. I'd held them behind the blast doors just in case I was wrong about how and where the attack would come from. Now, we needed them. Hell, we needed all the trigger-pullers we could find. Banshee's elite status didn't help when it became a numbers game.

Priest dropped to one knee as a violent blast caved in the decking where he was standing. Gi dashed over, blasting a combatant into pieces as he grabbed an arm and hoisted his fellow soldier out and over to a position of cover.

I could tell that Priest wasn't the only one injured although he was getting back to his feet already. We were being overrun, and the help from the Marines holding our rear guard was ineffective against the overwhelming frontal assault.

"Who are we fighting, Ada?" I asked, as multiple rounds seemed to impact the same spot on my helmet. These guys were fucking good.

"Unknown, Prowler."

"Take a fucking guess, then."

"Based on various tactics, armor, and weaponry, I would guess they are Tier-1 PMCs... hired guns!"

Mercenaries, yeah that fit, but the best of the best. If our enemy had recruited globally, that could be a huge number of operators. We had to reshape the battle space quickly.

"Lux, you're up, buddy," I said, then had Koog join the fight. I slapped fresh mags into my rifle. Odd thing about armor. If both sides have it, then the advantages are neutralized. It comes down to precision and tactics or who wants it more. Halo's sniper shots were still taking a toll, but most of the shots each side was throwing had little actual effect.

"Going kinetic, guys," I charged.

CHAPTER EIGHTY-ONE

Carol leaned in closer. Debra's voice was weak and gravelly, but her eyes were as sharp as ever. They could both feel the missile launchers firing two decks below. She could barely hear the woman's words.

"You have to make him st...top."

"Joe? You want me to stop him from what? Fighting back?" Carol gave a nervous giggle. "You have met him, right?"

Deb offered a false smile, she was fading again, the cocktail of drugs in her system forcing her back into unconsciousness. "He can't win this, Carol. And..." The lieutenants' eyes closed sleepily. "He's going to get us all killed," she said faintly.

"How Deb? How is fighting off the enemy going to do that?" What she first assumed was the ramblings of someone delirious was ratcheting up to full-blown panic.

"How?" she repeated. She knew he wouldn't stop without more specifics than a vague warning. She doubted he would stop at this point no matter what. Joe was a warrior, a protector. It wasn't what he did—it was who he was.

Deb's hand reached out and clutched Carol's shirt with surprising strength and pulled her close.

"Tell him this," she rasped out in a whisper. Her next words shot ice into Carol's veins.

"He can blow our reactors if he doesn't get the ship. He has the codes."

Carol stood quickly and raced from the room. Now she was desperate to get to Kovach.

She took the stairs at the mid-deck access, turned, and started sprinting for the aft hangars. That had to be where Joe had gone. Rounding the corner, she ran headlong into a soldier who tossed her aside in a protective move.

Carol lay there dazed, looking up into the cold eyes of the blonde girl. It took a second for her name to register. "Chelsea?"

Chelsea just stared at the woman. She had a mission, and this busybody loved getting into her business. What was she doing here now of all times? Chelsea shifted the food container to the other hand. If anyone asked, she was bringing lunch to the prisoner... just doing her part.

The uniformed man reluctantly offered her a hand up. Carol reached up and felt the egg size knot forming on her head where she'd clipped the bulkhead.

"What's the hurry?" the man asked.

"Have to, have to get to Kovach," Carol said, still dazed.

"Good luck with that, I hear reports they are fighting off a boarding party from that ship."

Carol was having trouble putting together anything sensible but nodded. She turned to leave.

Chelsea decided to toss a verbal hand-grenade as Howell had informed her of a small detail that she felt sure Carol was unaware of.

"Your son is in there fighting with them?"

Carol froze and turned back to the woman. "What?"

"Yeah, the corporal here even helped them fabricate a kid-sized suit of armor for him just like his hero."

The man smiled and nodded. "Yep, smallest set the fabricators could print."

"Lux is in there with them?"

Chelsea shrugged uncertainly. "Guess so."

Carol turned and fled down the corridor in a blind panic. Chelsea smiled. "Bitch."

Turning back, they headed up the short hall to the security wing. No one else would be around to bother her now. Rob had told her that every soldier had been called to the hangar bay to prevent enemy incursion.

"That woman will never get into that bay," he said laughing. "They will have a gauntlet of Marines and Red-7 troops between her and her kid."

"I know, but it's fun to screw with the simpletons."

Another round of missiles shook the deck plating. It seemed the battle was ramping up out there as well. Chelsea fingered the small ID card hopefully, then felt the gun in her pocket. She would like to be there to see what happened to that bastard Kovach, but getting answers from the witch was her priority. She just had to hope she could control her fear better this time.

"Hey, you there!" a voice called out. "Corporal Howell."

"Oh, fuck," Rob said, turning slowly.

Lance Corporal Hadroop stood a dozen yards away, his assault rifle hanging loosely. "Come with me, we must haul more magpacks to the hangar deck. The lads are running low."

Rob glanced at Chelsea before nodding and following his superior. Chelsea shrugged it off, she was deep enough now that she didn't think an escort was necessary. Too many other things happening for anyone to worry about someone taking food to the prisoner.

They had found the guard she'd hit. He remembered nothing, and everyone assumed he hit a bulkhead in the earlier attack. The good thing for her was they hadn't changed his access code—she hoped. Chelsea waved the ID card and the hatch clicked open. She checked to make sure everyone else was gone, then tossed the boxed lunch in the trash. She then used again used the ID to open the door to the brig and moved in to see the WitchWalker looking exactly the same as before, except they had her dressed in one of the standard gray shipboard jumpsuits now.

Chelsea grinned maniacally as she opened the thick, clear door to the cell. This was what she had been waiting for. Five minutes alone with this thing. She would get her answers. There was no fear, no sense of impending dread this time. Chelsea smiled; she'd conquered those internal demons as well.

If the other woman took any notice of her, it was impossible to tell. Chelsea was tired of the act and backhanded the woman across the face. Blood spewed from a cut opening on her lip, but otherwise the blow seemed not to register.

She hit the witch several more times in quick succession. Chelsea was winded by the third blow, the witch's face was beginning to swell, and her nose was also bleeding. Still, she showed no sign of registering the attack.

"What happened to my children?" Chelsea yelled. "What in the fuck are you?"

The woman sat in mute testament to whatever drove her. The attacks meant little to her, the pain—nonexistent. What she did have, like all of her Sisters, was the gift of foreshadowing. Not always the secret sight of things not yet happened, but glimpses of possibilities. In this case, she had seen all that was unfolding. None of it was a surprise.

Chelsea gathered herself up for another assault bringing up a knee into the seated woman's face. Her strike found nothing but open air. Moving faster than Chelsea thought humanly possible, the witch was behind her driving a powerful punch into her lower back. That was followed by two powerful slaps to her ears bursting both eardrums simultaneously. Pain shot through her skull like a knife.

A back kick connected with her mouth, loosening several teeth. Chelsea spat out the blood, turning to see her attacker raising the stool for a strike. Chelsea braced, but the woman turned away in a 360-degree arc and caught her under the chin, snapping the jaw bone and fracturing her neck.

In horror, Chelsea realized she couldn't move. Her one eye that seemed to be working saw the woman's bare feet move close. If she stomped down, Chelsea knew she would be dead. Instead, the witch knelt and spoke in a voice that sounded like wind on a dark night.

"They are in a better place, Chelsea Adams. Anywhere would be better than with you."

Chelsea watched as the feet retreated out of the cell. Tears filled her eyes, but her broken body wouldn't even let her mourn.

CHAPTER EIGHTY-TWO

I unleashed everything my suit had to push back the front line of assaulters. My Rattler carved a path through the enemy, and I saw Gi moving up along my left side doing the same. Maybe I could keep going, but my magazine charge was racing toward zero. "Koog, get some," I yelled. I felt a plasma round reach skin beneath my hip joints. Other enemy troops began targeting me and pushed me back the several hard-earned yards.

A fireteam from Red-7 had set up some of the K8 Disruptors, not real effective in space, but I welcomed them just the same. The massive rounds took out several of the invaders at once. "Give 'em hell, boys!"

"Priest is down again," I heard Halo say.

I ordered Koog to fill in the line on that side. "Push them!" The tactic would have worked with a less well-trained or more lightly armored enemy. These guys were a much more even match for us, and they had the numbers. I hated to do it, but I gave the silent order.

The Decimator unlatched, and Lux all but pirouetted the giant war machine into the heart of the battle. The twin plasma cannons began spitting out rounds that were an order of magnitude stronger than anything either side had. The shots chewed through the enemy armor and meat like they were paper mâché.

"Clear shooting vectors," I ordered as we began crab walking to each side, staying under the kid's assaulting fire. I hoped Ada was controlling the weapons, but seeing the movement and target selection, I was less than certain. The Decimator was a fucking killing machine, and I had no idea how I'd ever battled the things. It took less than half a minute to clear the hangar of enemy troops.

"Koog, see what else we have coming in. Lux, reload that thing," I yelled, my voice already breaking from the fatigue. "Banshee, reload in turn."

I didn't think it was over, but Orric's warning that the other attack might be a distraction kept ringing in my ears. The pile of dead bodies ahead of us was a pretty high price to pay for a distraction, though.

"Corpsman!" I yelled, seeing Priest pulling himself across the floor toward us. A damaged leg left a trail of blood back to where he'd fallen.

The Marine medics and I got there at the same time. "Good shooting, Priest. You good?"

He nodded. "I will be, sir." They pulled him onto the power litter and raced toward the rear hatch.

Lux was coming out of the Warbot, and I realized he was in a full battle kit. The armorer must have decided he needed to really be part of the team. I fist bumped the little guy. I could see through his visor that his eyes were big as saucers. Then I realized he was seeing the casualties and the blood. Ada had undoubtedly shielded him from most of that down in the cockpit, but out here....

"It's not like a video game, is it?"

"No, Lux, it isn't. In fact, it's the ugliest thing in the world," I said sadly.

I pulled the team patch off of my own armor and handed it to him. "I think you more than earned this today."

He raked his helmet back into its receiver, looked down, and slapped it on his shoulder, the magnetic patch adhering instantly.

"Uh, oh!"

I heard it at the same time. "Oh, shit!"

Both of us had the same look as my blood ran cold and pretty sure Lux wanted desperately to become invisible.

"Mom," he said in a dry whisper.

Turning around, I could just see Carol's arms frantically waving over the head of the soldiers guarding the hatch. She was yelling frantically for Lux. "Too late to hide, isn't it?" He asked.

I laughed, signaling for them to let Carol approach. I was going to catch hell, but I deserved it.

Monitoring the attack up on the bridge, Xero briefly noticed a light blink on in an auxiliary service sub-routine. She thought nothing of it, but it was one more reason she was determined to get the entire operating system of the Stone Mountain overhauled as soon as she could. Ada had even allowed her to copy her code into a type of sub-mind that she could mold into the ship's neural network. She trusted machines to keep an eye on the complex systems much better than humans.

What Chelseas' code did was mostly harmless; it bypassed one set of safety systems that required the hangar bay stasis generators to be active anytime the massive airlock doors were open. Otherwise, anytime an incoming ship landed, everything in the bay would get sucked out along with the air.

Carol rushed to her son, pausing briefly when she realized he really was in a battle suit. She pulled him into her arms before glaring at Joe with a pure hatred only a wronged mother could manage.

"I trusted you, Joe."

Kovach looked back at the pile of mutilated bodies, the blood, pieces of soldiers that coated nearly every inch of the rear deck. He'd fucked up, he knew that.

Just as he turned back, his helmet snapped closed, and his boots magnetically locked themselves to the decking. He saw Lux's had as well.

'Hangar depressurization imminent,' appeared in his HUD.

Carol had no suit, no protection from the vacuum of space. He reached for her just as he saw the cold of absolute zero hit her skin. Her face froze inches from her son, and her body was sucked out of the open airlock along with scores of enemy corpses and several of the Marines who'd been working to clear the deck.

Lux freed his boots and raced for the opening determined to save his mom. I knew that was impossible, but the kid launched himself fearlessly into the void of space.

The hangar resealed itself just as fast. The stasis field shimmered back into place, leaving nothing but blood stains where the brutal fight had taken place.

"No!!!" I screamed as I raced toward the black wall of stars. Suddenly, I felt the emotional side of my brain shutting down. I knew it was my battle augmentation cutting in. The trauma of what was going on was being shunted aside for the purely logical. I hated it, and...I welcomed it at the same time.

"Ada, I need a plan. What can I do to save the kid?"

My suit had a built-in air supply, and I could track him, but how long would that last?

"The other TriCraft," she responded. It was all we had on this deck, but no one was even sure it would fly. Packer was still dirt-side dropping Voss and Hauk.

"Who can fly it?"

"You can, Joe, give me a minute to synch with your cerebral cortex."

I raced to the machine, pushing various people out of my way to get there. It seemed all the Marines and Army personnel had flowed into the bay after the shield wall went up. "Koog, with me!" He knew space better than any of the others, and I thought that might be handy. The hangar bay was in bedlam. If the enemy wanted a distraction, they damn sure had one now.

Sumo raced up the ramp ahead of me eager to help any way he could.

"Keep the track on the kid," I told my AI. I knew his mom was gone, I couldn't lose him, too. Shit, this was all my fault.

I punched the controls as if I had done it a hundred times. The launch sequence was simple, but as I keyed the undocking command, it came up red. "Fuck!" *Why hadn't I tested this thing?*

"The unlocking mechanism in the docking cradle is jammed," Ada said. "We cannot launch."

There is a difference between an AI and a human brain. We care, we make shit work, we improvise. My mind locked onto a plan. A batshit crazy plan, but it was better than nothing. I told Ada what to do.

Via the external displays, I watched as the Decimator undocked and had Ada remotely guide it to the docking cradle. The thing grasped two of the hard points on the ship as well as the cradle and began pushing the entire assembly through the open bay doors. I felt things being torn away as the point of the craft cleared the bay, then suddenly, we were free of the ship. The repulser engines all went green.

We pushed as hard as possible to get the ship following Lux's beacon. Panic filled me, Sumo kept barking, and Koog was readying a recovery line.

"Enemy ship closing fast." The comms broadcast surprised me. I'd all but forgotten we were still in a space battle.

"Prowler, do you require assistance?"

That was Captain Orric's voice. God, I hoped I could trust him.

"Keep these bastards off of us, we are on a recovery mission for one of our own."

I said the words but didn't actually hear them. My entire focus was on the blinking green dot. The speed, angle, spin, everything centered on getting that kid on board this ship.

"Hard copy on that, Prowler. We are moving away from you at speed, though. Our guns will only be in range for seven minutes. God speed, we will pick you up on the next pass."

I saw a flash on the display up to our left and knew the Stone Mountain had scored a hit. Seconds later, several missiles flared and headed back along that same line.

"Closing on target, three kilometers, begin slowing."

I'd already done the calculations and started the braking maneuver. Packer was right, these things handled like crap laterally. Still, it felt like I'd been piloting one for years. Just as that thought occurred to me, the ship lurched to one side. I saw the reason. One of the repulser was out of alignment, and its field was interfering with the other two. It likely sustained damage when the original ship broke up around it. I worked to counter the effect but needed Ada's help to keep us moving in the right direction.

"Closing, 800 meters," Ada said.

I couldn't see anything but black on the displays but trusted her to guide us in. "Koog, are we ready?"

"Maybe—I think so."

"What the fuck does that mean?"

"No airlock on these ships, Boss. Remember?"

"Oh, right, so what's the plan?"

"Main hatch, it'll blow all the atmo, but we all have suits and can regenerate once we are buttoned up."

I glanced down at Sumo to make sure his was sealed. Looking around the deck, I saw something that made my blood run cold. A pair of bare legs hung below a tarp on a side bench.

"Venting now!" the Marine yelled.

"Belay that!" I jerked the tarp off and stared open mouthed at the WitchWalker sitting calmly. Blood covered her face and mouth. She wouldn't survive the venting. Still, it was her or Lux, I had no options.

Looking up, I saw Koog staring in disbelief at the girl. How had she gotten here? She'd obviously used the confusion in the bay to slip in unnoticed, but how?

"There—use that." Koog was pointing at a storage compartment beneath the bench. "Is it airtight?"

"No idea, but it's something. I'll get an emergency air bottle." I wrapped the woman in the tarp, going around her body numerous times as tightly as possible.

"We're here, Joe," Ada said. "Lux is just outside."

"Hurry, Koog!"

He strapped the oxygen mask on her face. The only part of her not covered by the tarp. She seemed to watch everything we did but didn't help or fight us. I closed the lid, and Koog produced a roll of sealing tape from somewhere and ran a line around the lid. It wasn't much, but fuck it, she'd been nothing but trouble so far.

"Lock us down, Ada."

I kept a hand on Sumo as the hatch opened. The air in the ship turned instantly to fog, then ice, as it raced out the open hatch. This had to be a first in the operation of the top-secret TriCraft. As Koog clipped me in, I saw the fear. I felt it, too. I relied on Ada to give me a path to the kid. A green arrow appeared in my HUD, and I leapt softly in that direction. He was tumbling about thirty meters off our port side. My suit lights picked up his own suit in seconds.

Reaching him, I saw he was conscious. In fact, he appeared fine other than the tears streaming down his face. I clipped into his suit and pulled him close. "I'm sorry, Lux." I heard and felt the racking sobs, and as Koog began pulling us back in, I realized we weren't alone. The stiff form of a body was following us. Lux had reached his mom and tied her off with his own suit cord. I, too, couldn't stop the tears.

We were back inside the ship in under a minute, but I felt sure that was too much for the prisoner. Ada repressurized the ship, and I lay Carol's body as gently as possible down on the rear bench. She looked beautiful, almost like a Greek statue. Her skin had frozen solid, but her eyes hadn't ruptured. They looked like they could come back to life. Despite our onboard medical capabilities, there was no coming back from this, though.

Lux unsealed his suit, then dropped it to the floor. He rushed to his mom and lay his head on her chest. I moved away and gave them the space they deserved. He was an orphan now, and it was my fault. It was all my fault.

I dried my own tears and turned to see Koog pulling the limp body of the girl from the locker. She wasn't dead. I saw her legs taking steps on her own, but she wasn't fully conscious either. Koog walked her over to the opposite seats and strapped her in.

"We have multiple problems, Joe," Ada said as I sat back down in the pilot's seat.

Scanning the displays, I understood at once. This ship was in worse shape than I thought. "We aren't going to stay in orbit long enough for the Stone Mountain to reach us, are we?"

"No, at the rate our orbit is degrading, we will enter upper atmosphere twelve minutes before they arrive. Also, the Stone Mountain has suffered a massive explosion. I am not sure of their status."

"Shit." *One thing at a time.* "Everyone strap in, it's going to get bumpy. Koog, the girl okay?"

"Seems to be, Prowler, but hell, how would we know?"

She's still breathing, that in itself was a miracle. My mind and my heart kept going to the loss of Carol, but I had to compartmentalize that I was in a busted-ass ship, no supplies, heading down to a planet that was intent on killing us, with a kid, a dog, and WitchWalker. Even with the big Marine, I didn't like our odds of survival down there. That's the trouble with this game, fate doesn't give a shit about the hand you are dealt. Play it or fold, those are your only choices.

A controlled descent is better than an uncontrolled one. I pushed the cyclic forward; the craft immediately nosed down and canted to the left side. The pain, which all of us usually felt inside a TriCraft, was always worse on the drop. It hit us instantly, but not just the usual low-level joint pain; it was magnified many fold. It was agonizing, and I could hear Lux cry out. My head felt like it was going to collapse. Even blocking out most of the pain, I was still barely hanging on to consciousness. The misaligned repulser engines were having trouble compensating. Since no one seemed to understand how the damn things worked, who knew if this was going to be fatal or not. Either way, gravity would get a vote, and seeing our altitude numbers plummeting, I felt like it would win the argument of who gets to end our lives.

"Ada," I struggled to get the thought out. "Notify the Stone Mountain we are going down."

She paused longer than was necessary to make the call. "I'm sorry, Joe. They are no longer in contact with us."

The ground was rushing up at us, and I could feel the strange sensations begin to decrease slightly. One of the others, Koog I guessed cried out in pain and then the sound of retching. I hope they removed their helmet. The map on the holodisplay was flashing red, and I had no lateral control. We were headed for the biggest red zone in North America. The wastelands.

CHAPTER EIGHTY-THREE

Acrid smoke began filling the cockpit, and alarms blared. I tried desperately to regain control, but it was no use. The craft was trapped by the gravitational pull of the planet. Displays blinked on and off; I heard one of the others give a cry of pain. This ship hadn't been ready to fly, I should have left it with the rest of the space junk.

My hands worked methodically resetting the engines, changing nav points. The augmented part of my brain knew what to do. The meat part just accepted that I was a failure and was about to die...again. I hadn't asked for this, but still, much of it was my fault. I deserved to pay the price, but these others didn't, especially the boy. The ground was rushing up at us now, only seconds remained.

The ship shook violently as it plummeted toward the ground. I tried to steer it away from the mountains in the distance, but it was no use. We were going down way too fast, and there was nothing I could do about it. Something was burning, more smoke poured into the main cabin

Impact was abrupt and violent. I had just yelled, "Brace" when we hit. The sensation of full gravity returned, and the realization that movement had ceased came on in a rush. The ship crashed into the rocky terrain with a deafening roar. The impact sent me flying forward, slamming into my restraints. The ship groaned and creaked as it skidded across the uneven ground, kicking up dust and debris.

It was obvious the TriCraft was never meant to actually land. No part of the craft could be considered structurally sound. Now, I felt cold air and knew the hull had been breached, but the air was clearing and, hey…I wasn't dead.

The readout in my HUD was black. I was in one piece, I think, but checking on my passengers revealed the first of many problems. Lux was unconscious; I removed his helmet but could see no apparent injuries. Koog appeared to be in the same shape, and I knew the reason. While the how of the dropship's operation was mostly a mystery, some things about it were obvious. One was the intense pain we usually got on the ascent or descent. One pilot had told me it was because of the way the repulsers interact with the fabric of space. The repulser engines on this craft were out of alignment, so the squishy, meatsack humans bore the full brunt of all the forces at play.

All but two, myself and the witch. Even though she had escaped a prison cell, somehow managed to sneak through an ongoing battle, only to then be partially exposed to the vacuum of space, and now aboard a crashed dropship. She seemed fine. Her eyes watched me, with a bored expression.

"Can you help?" Her look never changed.

"Ada, are you up?"

There was no sound from my internal AI. I could almost feel the disconnect with her. Ada had been implanted into my own neural pathways last year, and as strange as that seemed, she had become a constant presence in my life. Now…I felt nothing. Just a void, an emptiness in my skull where she should have been. I felt, more than saw, my dog curled beneath my feet. I worried he was injured as well but felt his rhythmic breathing. Like the rest of us, he wasn't well, but the loyal husky was still with us. I moved his battle suit back on his neck and stroked his fur, thankful for small blessings.

The dropship was canted up at an angle, part of the left point was crumpled in. We'd landed badly, that was obvious. I scrambled across the slanted deck to check the kid again. Lux was unconscious but breathing.

He had a nasty bruise across his forehead, and one eye was partially open and looked blood red. I paired my suit's computer to his and reviewed his condition. I had his suit administer the recommended treatment and moved over to the big Marine whose condition seemed much worse. His pulse was shallow; the suit had done multiple sessions of CPR in the last ten minutes and even done a defibrillator charge when his heart stopped. I removed my gloves, unlatched his helmet, and raked it back into its receiver.

Checking his armor, I saw a huge dent in his right side just above the waist. That could mean internal injuries as well. He'd hit something, or maybe he picked that up in the battle. I had no idea, and honestly, I needed Ada to guide me on what to do. TriCraft only have the basics, no real medical bay. His suit already had him sedated. I leaned back, and my hand brushed against something cold and hard. I knew what it was before I even looked.

Carol's body lay there cold, dead, but still beautiful. Her son's gloved hand still rested atop hers. He'd been determined to save her, not realizing she was gone as soon as she hit the vacuum of space. A wave of incredible sadness washed over me. The guilt, regret, and shame of my decisions where she was involved. It was inexcusable, and I had to face the fact that I had caused her death just as much as anything. Tears flooded my eyes, and nothing I could do would hold them back.

I sat there next to the woman I'd cared more for than anyone else in my life, and next to her was her son. One was gone, and the other was suddenly my responsibility. I pushed his helmet up and rubbed his hair out of his eyes. Such a bright kid, a survivor, and he would need to be because I had brought us down in the worst place imaginable.

The ship's lights flickered and went out. The dim blue emergency lighting kicked on and gave the interior a surreal glow. Sumo crawled up the slanted floor and laid his head in my lap. The WitchWalker still just stared blankly. The cold emptiness in those eyes chilled me. It was reflective of the planet now. Apathy, no hatred, no love...just nothing. Almost like I didn't matter, humans...didn't matter.

A fragment of memory flashed though my bruised brain. Hinge and me sitting in on a debriefing on advanced AIs. The expert told us that the worst would not be AIs upgrading their own code and eventually taking over and wanting to wipe us out. It would be that we simply no longer mattered to them. We would be as inconsequential as ants are to humans. Bayou's strange warning also bubbled up to the surface. That one I had to bury; I just was in no position to unpack it right now.

Turning back toward the boy, I heard his mom's voice telling me to protect him. It was something I hadn't managed to do for her.

"We have to take care of him, Sumo."

The dog turned to look at Lux and seemed to agree; he lowered his head, resting it lightly on the child's chest.

My dad's words from our last call came back to me. *Teach them how to fucking fight back. Teach them how to win. Don't adapt to the world as it is, make it the world you want to be in.* That's what it was going to take to survive out there. I didn't think we would get back into our fortress high above anytime soon. If what Deb had told me was true, that might be for the best. In either case, that was not the most pressing issue. We were going to have to go out there in the waste, find a way to survive and get back in the fight.

Something large hit the outside hull. Off in the distance, I heard a bloodcurdling howl. The WitchWalker's eyes darted up at the sound. One thing was certain, this might be the wastelands, but we would not be alone down here.

EPILOGUE

Valyn studied the charts and frowned. "Where are they?" he whispered to himself.

No debris field, no transponder, but if what the bridge crew was saying was true, the TriCraft wasn't even on the manifest for this ship.

"They're gone, sir."

He nodded, "And the enemy ship?" They'd exchanged several more volleys with the mystery craft but still were having trouble detecting it clearly on sensors.

"Who are you?"

The voice surprised him, and looking up, his shock only increased. The woman looked like death. She was wearing a hospital gown, and blood stained one edge of a large bandage. He did recognize the face, though. "Riggs?"

"I'm Riggs, who are you?"

The tone evoked no safe passage. Despite his rank, this woman was in command. Thankfully, Xero came to his aid. "Deb, this is my friend, Valyn. Joe put him in command while he fought off a boarding attempt."

"He's Fleet. Joe wouldn't have done that," Deb said, grabbing for the back of a chair and dropping into it heavily.

She tapped the side of her cheek, "Prowler, come in – Sitrep."

"We can't raise them either, Deb. He's no longer on the ship."

"Did those bastards pick him up?" She pointed to the threat screen. It was clear, but they all knew what she meant.

"No, we don't think so."

"Captain Valyn, you need to surrender the ship."

"Not an option, Lieutenant."

"It's our only option, sir. I've been trying to explain that to everyone – even Joe."

"Riggs, this ship is the last battle-worthy vessel of our entire fleet, maybe the last best hope for humanity's survival, and you want me to hand it over to an unknown enemy? An aggressor who may have had a hand in starting this...eradication of our planet."

Her head sunk. "If you don't, we are already dead...sir."

"Incoming missiles, multiple bogies, sir."

ABOUT THE AUTHOR

JK Franks is the popular author of numerous post-apocalyptic and near-future techno-thriller novels. He is an admitted tech geek, science nerd, cyclist, and storyteller. JK Franks' world was formed by a childhood growing up during the Space Age when he developed a love for books. He became an avid student of history and science and a regular reader of everything from reference books to dusty, old biographies. Once he discovered science fiction, he never looked back.

His work is mostly near-future thrillers, characterized by meticulous research, hard science, and a gritty, seldom-matched realism. "I hate stupid characters," states Franks. "Or even worse, smart characters, acting stupid." All of his work combines his passion for hard science fiction, well-crafted characters, and superb storytelling.

No matter where he is or what's going on, Franks tries his best to set aside time every day to answer emails and messages from readers. You can visit him on the web at www.jkfranks.com. Please subscribe to his newsletter for updates, promotions, and giveaways. You can also find the author on Facebook or email him directly at media@jkfranks.com.

OTHER BOOKS BY JK FRANKS

The Catalyst Series

Book 1: Downward Cycle

Life in a remote, oceanfront town spirals downward after a massive solar flare causes a global blackout. But the loss of electrical power is just the first of the problems facing the survivors in the chaos that follows. Is this how the world ends?

Book 2: Kingdoms of Sorrow

With civilization in ruins, individuals band together to survive and build a new society. The threats are both grave and numerous—surely too many for a small group to weather. This is a harrowing story of survival following the collapse of the planet's electrical grids.

Book 3: American Exodus

This companion story to the Catalyst series follows one man's struggle to get back home after the collapse. No supplies, no idea of the hardships to come; how can he possibly survive the journey? Even if he survives, can he adapt to this new reality?

Book 4: Ghost Country

Since the solar superstorm and CME almost two years before, the Gulf Coast town of Harris Springs, Mississippi, has suffered from gang attacks, famine, and hurricanes and has battled a crusading army of religious zealots. Now, they face their greatest challenge: outsmarting a tyrannical president and escaping an approaching pandemic.

Cade Rearden Thrillers

Book 1: State of Chaos

He's exhausted and brutally traumatized. Now, Spec-Ops Captain Cade

Rearden must finally listen to the voices in his head...or everyone on Earth may die. If you like near-future technology, complex heroes, and high-octane action, then you'll love JK Franks' explosive new adventure.

Book 2: Midnight Zone

Nightmares are real in the cold, dark waters of the deep. National Security Agent Cade Rearden is used to secrets. Assigned to protect the ultra-dark-ops organization known as The Cove Project, he grapples with his role of defending a country still in crisis after a deadly super AI has devastated much of the U.S.

But when part of his team mysteriously disappears beneath the idyllic waters of the Caribbean, Cade finds himself thrust into a web of lies and mystery, at the heart of which lies an eons-old secret that somebody will kill to protect. Grappling with his inner demons and struggling to locate his friends, Cade stumbles upon a government cover-up...and terrifying creatures, hidden miles beneath the surface of the ocean.

The Fade Novels

The Night Gate

Since losing his daughter seven years ago, Pike Shepard has struggled to maintain a normal life for himself in the coastal community of Blackwater. It's a quiet life, until a beautiful scientist shows up on his doorstep with a desperate plea for help. Dr. Kate Cassidy has uncovered a new aspect to quantum entanglement: the ability to not just see the multiverse but a way to travel through it. Her device allows them to SideSlip between parallel dimensions that are at once familiar and quite bizarre, wondrous, and terrifying. Pike learns they aren't the only ones with this ability, and the others want them gone.

Savage Earth Series

Book 1: Nightmare Factory

In the not-too-distant future, a devastating global attack takes place and planet Earth is on the brink of extinction. In this sci-fi thriller, Master Sargent Joe Kovach has been through a personal hell as he struggles to adapt to his new enhancements. As battles escalates, so does his determination to uncover the group who triggered this brutal extinction event that has left the planet overrun by mechanical and genetic horrors.

Book 2: Eradication

In a world ravaged by a devastating attack, the remnants of humanity are barely clinging to existence. Months have passed since the enemy unleashed hordes of murderous creations that now engulf the planet. Amidst the chaos, One renegade group takes refuge on Earth's last remaining space vessels, orbiting above the desolate wastelands. They are Banshee Team, and they are alone beacon of hope in the face of annihilation. They are committed to uncover the truth behind the brutal attacks and lend their expertise to turn the tide of this merciless battle.

Connect with the Author Online:

** For a sneak peek at new novels, free stories, and more, join the email list at jkfranksbooks.com.

Facebook: facebook.com/groups/JKFranks/

Amazon Author Page: amazon.com/-/e/B01HIZIYH0

Goodreads: goodreads.com/author/show/15395251.J_K_Franks

Other Sellers https://books2read.com/catalyst1

Websites: JKFranks.com or JKFranksbooks.coim

Twitter: @jkfranks

Instagram: @jkfranks1

Printed in Great Britain
by Amazon

33118022R00225